This edition, issued in 1955, is for members of The Companion Book Club, 8 Long Acre, London, W.C.2, from which address particulars of membership may be obtained. The book is published by arrangement with the original publishers, William Heinemann Ltd.

THE SOJOURNER

"A blessed companion is a book"—JERROLD

THE
SOJOURNER

★

MARJORIE KINNAN
RAWLINGS

THE COMPANION BOOK CLUB
LONDON

*Made and printed in Great Britain
for The Companion Book Club (Odhams Press Ltd.)
by Odhams (Watford) Limited
Watford, Herts
955.ZT*

For we are strangers before thee, and sojourners, as were all our fathers: our days on the earth are as a shadow, and there is none abiding.

I CHRONICLES XXiX. 15.

THREE crows flew low over the fresh mound in the Linden burying-ground, dark as the thoughts of the three unmourning mourners. These were the widow, Amelia Linden, and the two tall sons, Benjamin and Asahel. The funeral assembly had gone. The clomp of horses' feet and the rattle of wheels were faint down the frozen lane. There was a pure instant of silence. Then a wind keened far off in the west, nosed across the hills and leaped into the clearing, snapping its fangs at the limbs of the oak trees. The last leaves shivered to earth and scurried like thin brown rats across the grave.

Amelia turned the black veil back from her face, and walked to the carriage. She settled herself in the front seat.

"Benjamin, take the reins."

Asahel moved to the heads of the span of horses to unhitch them from the cedar post. He stroked the velvet muzzles and the horses nickered. He slid off the blankets, and, placing them in the rear of the carriage, found his elder brother sitting stiffly with folded arms in the back seat. His mother's face was grey. He waited for her to move into the driver's seat. The untethered horses sidled restlessly. When young Dan lunged and Amelia did not stir, Asahel jumped clumsily into the carriage and jerked the reins. The team broke into an unseemly trot for home.

The bereavement of life rather than grief for death chilled Asahel's bones. There was no sorrow among the three in the carriage for the harsh, snarling man left behind under the wings of crows, except the sorrow all men feel face to face with death, even that of a stranger dead on the turnpike, which is an unassuageable anguish for themselves, the evidence of their own destinies. Yet this was a moment, surely, when mother and sons should draw close together, pile high the barricade, build up the fire, against the outer darkness. Instead, his mother and Benjamin were still separated by the violent quarrel he had heard last night from his bedroom. He had not heard the words, he could not guess what they might quarrel about, but it was the first time his mother had not found her elder pleasing in her sight. Asahel had hovered for his twenty years outside her adoration, like a shy and hungry dog that skirts a lighted house, longing to be called in for a plate of food and a few caresses. Because he loved Benjamin too, he had no sense of loss for himself, was warmed when his mother's eyes lighted for his brother, and asked only to be present. Now with his father's death something had come between these two, life was hurt more cruelly. There were no longer Benjamin's bright sun with its two satellites, Amelia powerful and near, he far and futile, but three cold stones pendulous in space.

The November gale caught them full at the turn into the Linden place. The time was late afternoon, but sky and landscape were as grey as though there had never been a sun and so there was no sun for setting. The house loomed large and bleak on its rise above the road. Its windowed eyes were blank. The low scudding clouds seemed to catch and tatter on the two tall brick chimneys. Asahel drove the carriage up the drive to the side and stopped. Amelia waited for Benjamin to help her down. He did not move. She stepped out then and took the gravelled path to the door, her billowing black skirts flattened against her thighs.

Asahel turned the horses around and drove across the road to the lower-lying barns. Here Benjamin got out and rolled open a wide sliding door. Asahel drove up the earth ramp and over the rattling board floor into the dusk. The brothers took down overalls from nails on a wall and pulled them over their good clothes. They unharnessed the horses together. Asahel led young Dan to the stock stalls on a lower level and the mare followed. Benjamin pitched down hay while Asahel measured out oats. Only one cow was fresh at the moment and Asahel milked her, stripping her carefully. Benjamin scattered fodder in the lot of the assorted cows and calves. The sheep had not yet been brought in from the hill pasture for the winter.

Nothing remained to be fed but the hogs and poultry. The chickens, guinea-hens, geese, ducks and turkeys, always ravenous, assumed from the colour of the sky that it was evening and made a raucous crying. Benjamin brought them grain while Asahel took the foaming bucket of milk to the house and returned with skimmed milk and slops for the hogs. The brothers worked together smoothly, Benjamin quickly and impatiently, Asahel with deliberation. Benjamin was finished first. He leaned on the rail of the pig pen, waiting, Asahel hoped, to speak with him, to tell him of the quarrel. Benjamin had nothing to offer. He was perhaps avoiding facing his mother alone, or there might be nothing, after all, to say.

The two young men shared as few similar genes as was possible, still to be blood brothers. The differences in physique made folk say: "Ben favours the Lindens," and "Ase isn't like any of the family, either side." Benjamin was hard-muscled, six feet tall, quick fighting, quick dancing, moving lightly like fighter or dancer, rocking on the balls of his feet, with panther-coloured hair and green eyes, so that all his effect was of one of the great cats. Asahel, twenty years to his twenty-three, reared, six feet four, like a gaunt sapling, over his brother, and as though in apology for his assumption of the greater height, carried himself stooped and gangling. His hair was black, with an Indian straightness, his face was high-cheek-boned, his deep-set eyes were grey with black striations. He was all slowness and awkwardness, his big feet a nuisance rather than a help. His hands, of terrific strength, hung like gnarled pine stumps at the ends of long bony arms.

The disparities of the brothers' minds and spirits were profound.

Benjamin had had four years at the Academy, while Asahel, after the simple schooling of the one-room stone school-house two miles down the road, had been kept at home to work. Yet it was Benjamin who remembered nothing from his text-books, scarcely read the weekly county paper, and Asahel who knew those books secretly by heart, and read, as laboriously as he did everything else, any scrap of paper with printing on it, poring hungrily over the magic of words. It seemed to him, who was all but inarticulate, that if he could read enough of them he would know the answers

11

to the questions that tormented him. He had no way of knowing that wiser men had asked those questions, which never had been, perhaps never would be, answered. It was Benjamin who was wild, who ran away periodically, who returned with empty pockets and not even a tale to tell. It was Asahel, who had been no more than twenty miles from home, who travelled in his mind so far that those who thought they knew him would have been terrified by his consorting with the stars.

Benjamin hesitated at the kitchen door.

He turned abruptly to his younger brother.

"Listen, Ase. You've got to back me up. I'm leaving for good."

This, then, had been the quarrel.

Asahel's first sickness was for his mother. In the barren ground of her life, of her own character, Benjamin had been the bright tropical bloom that satisfied and startled, making the desert not impossible. Only Benjamin had brightened those hard black eyes, only Benjamin had brought music to that low, cold voice. He had seen his mother stiffen in her chair on a winter night, thinking she heard the loved one's step on the icy road, sit back trembling because it was not he. He had seen her lift her arms, like a bird taking happy wing, when at last he came, Benjamin, he came. Then he was sick for himself. His heart, too, had beat so fast that he was dizzy, when Benjamin came home. And this was not for any meagreness of life and thought without his brother, but because of his own gift for love and for devotion. It did not seem to him this bond could be one-sided.

He washed out the empty swill-buckets at the rear pump. Now was the moment to call on words, to find the proper ones to hold his brother home. The place would be desolate without him. He could not let him go, to roam the world in trouble. He turned the buckets upside-down to dry. He followed Benjamin, wordless, into the kitchen.

Part of the ample funeral foods brought by relatives and neighbours sat on the white-clothed table in the dining-room beyond. Coffee simmered on the back of the kitchen range. A pitcher of buttermilk was cool and fresh from the stone cellar. The brothers washed their hands at the cistern pump and dried them on the roller towel. Their mother poured coffee and led the way to the table. Benjamin picked and chose from his favourite dishes, but ate little, his mind and body restless. Asahel heaped his plate at random and plodded away, as at a job of haying. One food was almost the same to him as another. He was seldom conscious of hunger, and he ate prodigiously, filling his stomach slowly, steadily, like an ox, until the moment came when he realized, with a mild surprise, that he could literally hold no more. He was the delight of fine cooks, who took his absent-minded capacity for appreciation.

Amelia said: "Asahel, if you can bring yourself to finish eating, I need your help. Benjamin has something stupid to say."

"I've told him, Mother. Ase understands. He agrees. Don't take it out on him, when it's settled."

"Oh. Settled. He's perfectly contented, I suppose, to farm it alone. There isn't enough money, you know, to hire a man to replace you. This is a three-man farm, at the least. Now it's to be down to one boy. Or am I expected to work in the fields?"

The last mouthful of pie stuck in Asahel's throat. His mother shocked him. How could she bring herself to put Benjamin's leaving on such a basis, when he knew her heart, as his, was crying: "Son and brother, we cannot face life without you, because of love, never because of living!"

She said: "Asahel, do you care to speak for yourself, or will you have another piece of pie?"

They were both looking at him, each asking in their ways, one bitter, the other eager, for his support.

Benjamin said: "Ase, you know I've always hated farming. I wouldn't even be any help to you. I'd be leaving when you needed me most. I can't change it. I'll admit it now, I was afraid of Father. I kept coming back because I was more afraid of him away than here. Ase, you're a man to plough and sow and reap. You'll manage without me. I'll give you my share in the farm. Just let me go."

Amelia smoothed the black funereal satin over her thin breast.

"You forget that the place is mine. Neither of you can give away a share he doesn't own. Your father was a difficult man, but he saw his duty, and the farm is mine, all mine, until I say otherwise. I shall not release you, Benjamin, from your share. It will be yours as long as I live. You can't run away from that. Well, Asahel?"

Still he could not speak. Benjamin pushed away from the table and went up to his room. He returned to the silence with his valise, his coat over his arm.

He said: "How much money do we have?"

Amelia went to her downstairs bedroom and came again to the table with a tin box, and opened it. She counted out the paper notes and the silver. She set aside a portion.

"This should cover the funeral expenses and a tombstone."

The remainder amounted to little over six hundred dollars. Benjamin pocketed a third of it. On a scrap of paper he scrawled:

"Rec. of Amelia and Asahel Linden payment in full for share in Linden farm. Signed, Benjamin Linden."

Amelia stared at the paper, then threw it in the door of the red pot-bellied stove.

She turned away into her room and closed the door behind her. Benjamin shrugged his shoulders.

"She thinks I'll be coming back again. Maybe some day, Ase, when I'm rich."

He took from his pocket their father's gold hunter's watch, given him by Amelia before the funeral.

"Keep this. No, take it."

He turned to go.

"Don't hitch up. I'd rather walk. I'll catch the night train west from the village. I'm a dog to leave you, Ase."

Asahel followed him out of the front door, across the porch, down the steps, over the lawn, to the road. The road ran level for a way, rose a little, dipped down to the valley where the stream ran under a wooden bridge, wound its way four miles to the village of Peytonville, to the train, to the West, to the unknown and far away.

He wanted to say: "Don't leave me. Take me with you."

Benjamin said: "Don't come any farther."

He held out his strong arms and drew him tight. Asahel trembled.

"Better marry Nellie Wilson in the spring, boy. Then you won't miss me so much."

Asahel said at last: "I'll never be done missing you."

Sunset had come, yet there was still no sun, only livid and evil streaks in the west, where Benjamin was going. The bond was a stout cord that tore him and would not release him, and he was drawn by it to the little rise. Benjamin was a small figure on the wooden bridge far below. Asahel lifted his arm and waved, but his brother did not look back. He turned back towards home. There was now no colour in the sky. The world was fast darkening. Everything was retreating, going away into distant places, and he was left behind, to plough, to sow, to reap.

★ 2 ★

ON a cold December morning Ase Linden paced slowly, studying them, the acres whose crops must soon be planned for. A dusting of granular snow whirled across the frozen ground ahead of a biting wind. His father's old buffalo greatcoat hung long and loose on his gaunt frame. His hands were paws in fur-backed leather mittens. A musk-rat cap with earmuffs sat low on his head. His deep-set eyes searched the landscape, his long nose sniffed the scent of coming snow, his shaggy-furred shoulders were stooped. He looked a winter-poor bear come wandering from his den. He crossed the road to the south and took shelter for a moment in the lee of the log cabin.

The Linden land was fertile for the most part. Its three hundred acres divided themselves naturally into woods, pastures, and fields suitable for varying crops. A country road bisected the farm. The house sat back from it to the north, the barns to the south. The richest soil lay south and west of the barns. Here the money crops were grown, the beans, the wheat, the potatoes. The land dipped to a willow-bordered stream that ran from east to west, and the cow

15

pasture began beyond the stream. The hill that lifted again, still to the south, was stony and was given over to the sheep. The high extreme south-eastern corner of the land consisted of forty acres of wood-lot, from which trees were cut selectively for fuel and for building. The woods ended suddenly and blackly with a hemlock-rimmed bog, from which springs seeped down to join the brook, and so dangerous that a cow breaking loose and wandering there would perish within a few minutes if unnoticed and un-rescued. A crystal lake, believed to be bottomless, fed the stream from the east, and the western border became marsh, infested with small rattlers.

The land on the house side of the road ended to the north-west with a smaller wood-lot and with a sugar-bush adequate to supply a family with maple syrup and sugar. Wheat was grown west of the house as well, alternating in years with the southerly field. Rye, oats, and barley, corn and buckwheat, were staple crops for home consumption. A small fruit and vegetable garden was near the house to the east, where it received full sun all day. The house itself was large and square, white-painted, eared with red chimneys, with a fine fan-lighted doorway carved in a Greek design. It was distinguished, but bleak, uncompromising, needing, Ase recognized, the softening of trees and shrubbery. Across from the house, a few hundred yards west down the road, still stood the original Linden home, a log cabin chinked with white marl, and beside it an icy spring, stone-enclosed.

The wind veered and caught Asahel full and the cabin no longer sheltered him. He moved on slowly, across the level field. There was no living thing in sight. The stock was snug in barn and cote. No sheep nibbled among the granite, no cows drifted across pasture, no horses rolled in clover, no poultry pecked and clattered. The farm was only bare land, frozen clay and loam waiting for new moulding at his hands.

He halted to the south where the field dipped gently to the stream. He heard the muffled rushing of the current under the ice. The willows along the borders tossed scraggled branches like the sparse, whipping hair of hags who had once been beautiful and by miracle would again be young and

16

garlanded and fair. He turned and looked back toward the cabin, small and huddled at that distance. This level field, he estimated, would run close to twenty acres. In the six weeks since Benjamin's leaving he had given it special thought. Knowing that Ben was done with the farm, it had seemed to him important that some sections of the Linden land be given over to crops which, once established, would be both profitable and requiring little care. Sizeable fruit orchards were plainly the answer. He visualized here an apple orchard. In spring a pink and white cloud would draw the bees to hum among the blossoms. Birds would nest and sing in the summer greenery. The waxen globes would shine like lamps in autumn, yellow and green and red, windfalls would thud to earth, to lie deep in buckwheat sown broadcast between the rows, to be crushed, wine-scented, in dripping jowls of swine and cattle, to be stung by wasps. The black boughs of apple trees in winter made, he thought, patterns like no other tree.

His father had never planned an orchard. No growing thing was graceless, but that scowling, snarling man, Hiram Linden, had seemed purposely to avoid all crops that flowered in beauty. All were utilitarian, sown with surliness and harvested with oaths. Ase was the first Linden of three generations to consider the earth and its bounty with reverence and affection, to long to adorn it as best he might during his tenure. To the Linden men ahead of him, it had been only a means of subsistence. His father, his brother, had been not even grateful that the rich loam made the tilling so little arduous, the lush harvests so rewarding.

The apples here, then, he decided, if his mother would allow it. He moved down the slope to the brook, crossed carefully on the icy stepping-stones, trudged up the farther slope to the sheep pasture and halted again. Because of the granite out-croppings, no other use could be made of the high expanse. Sheep were profitable in any case and the flock might well be enlarged. In that case, his mother would have to permit him a dog, a sheep dog. He had never had one, where every farm lad had his own. Amelia, through distaste an indifferent housekeeper, had always forbidden it on the excuse that she would have no dirty animal following to the kitchen door and tracking up the woodshed. He had accepted the verdict, as he must, puzzled and unsatisfied. The truth unguessed, or unacknowledgeable, was that she would admit no living thing save one to her affection, her tolerance or compassion. The fire within her was a hoarded thing, nurtured jealously, an iron box of hot embers for the warming of the hands of one. That one was Benjamin. Ase had gone his boy's way in loneliness, tagging hopefully after his brother, longing to be tagged in turn by some soft-eyed mongrel, equally faithful and adoring.

He opened a gate into the stock lane. Well, he thought, perhaps soon he would have his dog. It was not so important, now he was a man. The wind whipped under the buffalo coat and chilled his long scant-fleshed legs. There was no need to go to the end of the lane to the hemlocks and the bog. He had known for a year or more that it was time to begin cutting from the wood-lot adjoining the hemlocks, to give a rest of growth to the lot to the north-west of the house. There was no need, either, to pace the south-east acres above Pip Lake. They would be required for some time for wheat and corn. Eventually, he would like to try there a small peach orchard, increasing it from year to year if it thrived. The rounded summit was probably too exposed to the cold, but it seemed to him that the slope rolling towards the brook and the barns, and the eastern, dipping to the lake, offered protection for such delicate fruit and trees. This soil was pebbly, with a high admixture of clay.

He turned down the lane to the barns. He would have a look at the stock in passing. The wind at his back ruffled the curls of the buffalo pelt, it pushed him downhill, so that his big feet stumbled over rocks, his gait more awkward even than usual. Opening the gate to the sheep-shed he heard familiar horse's hoofs on the road, the scrape of the runners of the light cutter on the inadequate snow. His mother had returned sooner than he expected from her drive to the post office at Peytonville. She had insisted on making the trip with a superstition, he felt, that if she went alone a letter from Benjamin would be waiting for her. He joined her at the side driveway beside the house. She handed him the reins. He looked at the newspapers in her gloved hands.

18

"No," she said. "Nothing from him. Nothing at all."

He put the cutter in the light carriage shed by the driveway, unhitched the mare, led her to the barn, stalled, fed, watered, and curried her. Because of his slowness, he was occupied more than half an hour. He went to the house and hung his coat and cap in the woodshed attached to the kitchen. He found his mother warming her hands by the living room stove, still dressed in her velvet pelisse, bonnet and fur capelet. She was a slight woman past fifty, long of neck, with smooth black hair, small black eyes and a tight, thin mouth. She carried herself stiffly erect in well-made clothes of good material. She was not unattractive until she focused her eyes on a human being, when their unblinking coldness gave the effect of the stare of an adder.

She lifted her head and turned the jet-like glitter on her younger son.

She said: "I have been expecting Benjamin to return every day. This is most unusual. He has never been away so long without writing me. I begin to feel something different about this absence. He went with a reason and for a purpose. It comes clear now to my mind. He is ambitious, if you can understand that. He wishes to make a much-needed backlog of money to bring home. It will take him a little time. He naturally prefers to have good news before writing me. It will come. Meantime——"

She studied him, frowning.

"Are you listening to me? Your expression is completely blank."

Behind the mask of his face Ase was suffering. It seemed to him that he must awaken her to the truth, as one shakes a sleeper in a nightmare. Yet for her it was not nightmare, but a sweet dream from which she would be cruelly aroused. It was necessary, he thought. How else might life begin again for her?

He said desperately: "Mother, Ben is gone."

"That's exactly what I am talking about. It may be as late as summer before he comes home. Meantime, you must make plans for the spring planting. I have come to a decision. I am putting everything here in your hands. Get advice if you need, but not from me. I know nothing of these things. And care less. It is a hateful life. But the farm is all we have and I expect you to make the most of it. Everything is up to you until Benjamin's return."

He did not speak.

She said sharply: "Do you understand? Are you prepared to take this responsibility?"

He nodded. She went to her room and closed the door.

He was ready. He had been ready a long time. He was old in farm lore. He had learned it with fascination from childhood, as the child of a musician absorbs the patterns of sound, and may astonish its elders by climbing to the piano-stool and playing accurately a little tune at the age of five. Benjamin had vanished for three months the summer when Ase was sixteen, their father had been out of his mind with fever, and the stripling, with the help of a stupid ox of a hired hand, had brought through the crops to a prosperous harvesting. Because he loved the earth, its ways, its seasons, its flowering and its fruiting, he accepted the charge of these acres not as a burden, but as though an unrequited passion had been suddenly returned. His heavy spirits lifted. Whether his mother's gift of authority came of her necessity or of her acknowledgement at last of his manhood, he could not tell, nor did it matter.

He was surprised that she had given him complete free-dom of decision. He was somehow not surprised at her refusal to admit that Benjamin was gone perhaps for ever. He had best leave her unmolested in her dream.

The fire in the round-bellied stove had died down. He built it up until the mica front glowed red. He sat close, leaning forward in his mother's Boston rocker, and was still cold. A bleakness lay over the room, over the house, that was of an icier substance than the winter temperature. The large sitting-room was well proportioned, with bay windows on two sides to let in the sun and the sight of trees and flying birds, the barns, the rolling contour of the farm. Its cherry, pine and walnut furnishings were solid and good, as were the furnishings of all the other rooms, yet none had sat here in content or ease. The warmth and vitality of the land were strong past harming. The dwelling-house was chill with human misery and always had been.

He wondered how far back the Lindens went in time, as Lindens, and which was the first to start the strange, interlocked, unhappy and often violent chain. He knew nothing of them past the first one in America, a Hollander, whose name of Lindh'oeven, or something of the sort (there was an old deed in the attic with such a name), had become simplified with pioneer usage and spelling to 'Linden'. This was in the middle 1600s, and the Hollander had married a Frenchwoman. An English strain came in somewhere later. Amelia was second generation Scotch-Irish, with all the Scot dourness and none of the Irish lilt. He had heard that the Irish were supposed to be a light-hearted people, but the only signs of it, certainly, had been in Benjamin.

Perhaps the trouble had begun with his immediate grandfather, Arent Linden. He had moved inland from the Hudson River valley, had taken up a large tract of land, and had two sons, Joshua the elder and Ase's own father, Hiram. It seemed to him that it was a repetition of the Biblical story of Jacob and Esau, one son beloved, the other despised, for Arent Linden and his Joshua had made a pact with Hiram, that if he would help them clear six hundred acres of land in this virgin place, would help them build two houses, they in turn would help him clear three hundred for himself, would build him a house, too, and a prosperous family would establish itself in the wilderness. The betrayal had been complete.

Hiram had worked for his father and brother, unpaid, merely fed and clothed and sheltered, until he was in his early thirties. The time came at last to turn to his land, to the building of his home, and they had laughed at him. That could make a man snarl at life. That could make Amelia, a bride no longer young, in a log cabin, nurse her spite, like some half-mad woman watering a poisonous weed in a flower-pot. Yet it seemed to young Ase that the greater the injustice that came to one, the deeper would be the desire to give justice and warmth to one's children.

His father had fought through, after all, had cleared his land, which proved richer than that of the other two, had sold his timber on a high market, had built at last his house, larger if not so fine of line and contour as the earlier, more gracious ones, and now was dead and unlamented. And Benjamin, who had provided, carelessly, all this house knew of light and laughter, was gone, taking the brightness with him. Ase considered the spell cast by his brother on all who knew him, for spell it was. It was conceivable that Ben would conquer the world, for he moved like a whirlwind, catching up men and women breathless in the brief gusts of his enthusiasm. It was also unlikely. Ase knew and acknowledged his brother's instability. Ben's restless impatience took always the apparently easy way, he raced light-footed and light-hearted, his tawny hair, his cloak of charm, streaming in the wind he created, until the swift feet met the smallest rock, the shallowest ravine, the slightest thickening of the forest, when he stopped confused in his tracks, then was off again in search of a smoother path through a more open glade.

For this, Ase felt no criticism, but only concern. His love was so vast a thing that he longed to clear away the rock, to bridge the ravine, to fell the forest, ahead of Benjamin. If he had received in return only the most casual affection, all the more room was left in him for the longing, some day, to be truly as one with his brother and so end his aching loneliness. He could not take offence at his mother's blindness nor surely at her own adoration of her elder. He had a timid hope that in her loss she might turn a little towards him. He loved her, too, with tenderness, and wished he might be other than he was, to please her. He supposed he was difficult to care for, inarticulate and brooding, unbeautiful and awkward.

Amelia had not come from her room. It was nearly noon. For all her bravado, he knew that she was in torment. He went to the kitchen and made a fire in the range. He prepared a meal as best he was able. He went to the cellar for a bottle of elderberry wine. He poured a glass of it and took it to her room.

She sipped the wine and nodded her thanks.

"Come, Mother. Dinner's ready."

His cooking was no worse than her own. She had done no baking for a week and the bread was hard and stale. She was especially fond of sweets and took a great deal of jelly

22

with her bread and tea. The wine and strong tea set her to talking with animation. She told anecdotes of early hardships. Suddenly she frowned.

"Asahel, I want you to tear down the log cabin. It reminds me of too many dreadful things. Anyway, it's an eyesore."

To him the cabin was significant and beautiful. When the apple trees were grown sheltering around it, the stone chimney, the brown walls with white marl chinking, would seem those of a little house in a fairy tale. For an instant he pictured himself living there with Nellie Wilson, of whom Ben had said: "Better marry Nellie in the spring." But Nellie was Ben's girl. She could not be taken over as he had inherited Ben's discarded clothing; could not be given away as Ben had given him their father's watch. He set the thought aside and wondered how he might dissuade his mother from the cabin's destruction. He had neither power nor words to influence her. She had many irrational impulses, and if he paid no attention to this one perhaps she would forget it. Ben of course could have had her decking the cabin with banners if the notion struck him.

His mind groped towards a question that had lain dormant and festering in him all his life. There was something more in his mother's passion for Ben and her coldness for him than was called for by Ben's grace and charm and his lack of it. He had been a toddler when she had struck him smartly because he made mild protest that his older brother had run off with his new birthday toy. Blinking through tears he refused to let fall, he cried out "Why?", and even then the question had held the larger implication. From his mother's expansive mood he might now draw his answer. His throat tightened, the words were hopeless captives.

Amelia said: "At first I was happy in the cabin."

Her face was one he had never seen. Her eyes were half-closed, the thin mouth was relaxed and soft, lifted at the corners in a smile. The sallow skin glowed luminous, like an apricot in sunlight.

"Very happy. I had waited so long. I was past thirty. Still handsome, I believe."

She closed her eyes entirely.

She went on dreamily: "I could hear the spring bubbling in the night. There was a red rambler rose outside the window and once he reached his hand out in the moonlight and broke a spray and laid it on my pillow. The thorns scratched my cheek and we laughed together."

She opened her eyes and leaned towards him.

"I have had two husbands, you know," she said.

He stared at her.

"Oh, they were both named Hiram Linden."

She touched her handkerchief to her lips.

"Everything else was different. The minds, the bodies— two different men. I loved the first one, oh yes, I loved him. I lived with him a year. He died. He was killed, of course. Your grandfather and your uncle killed him. For a year he thought they meant to keep their promise. Oh, the fine house, the cleared acres, when they came to pay back his years of servitude! When he knew the truth, it killed him. And why? Because he was a coward. He died because he was a coward, and I told him so."

She wiped her wet forehead.

"The first man gave me my only truly begotten son, my Benjamin, conceived in love. The second gave me you."

She looked at Ase and the adder's eyes did not flicker. He was cold to his marrow. The answer was coming, it was sharp and fanged, he would now avoid it if he could.

"I never lived with the second Hiram Linden as a wife. I loathed the sight of him, I loathed his touch. He didn't give me you, he forced me. He forced you on me. Not in love, not even lust. No, in anger. I hated him to the last inch of his guts. And I hated you."

She sat back in her chair. Her voice broke.

She said: "I can't help it. I'm sorry."

His first impulse was to take himself from the house of horror at once, free her from the very sight of him, free himself from her eyes and the ice of her voice. He went to the log cabin and built a fire on the hearth and crouched before it. He thought desperately of fetching his friend Tim McCarthy for comfort and for counsel, then knew the matter was private and shameful and he must look it in the face alone. He was stricken, a tangible knife in his heart would be less painful, a kinder thing, than this sharp-bladed knowledge. The fire died to embers and he sweated in the cold cabin, then felt the chill and brought in broken boughs to feed the fire again. The sun dropped towards its setting and the pale gold filtered through the dusty windows. Well, then, what had happened, after all? Only that where he had lived under lowering clouds the storm had broken over him. What had been a puzzling uncertainty, without meaning, was become a fact. He had guessed and wondered, and now he knew.

He watched the fire until it was safely ashes. He stood up and stretched his cramped legs. He drew a long breath in what seemed a clearer air. The truth was a liberation. He could go on. The earth was still solid under him. He felt a surge of pity for his mother. Even as she rejected him, she needed him. Trapped in the ruins of her life, he thought, she was also brave. He returned to the house to find her staring from a front window at the empty road. He stoked automatically the sitting-room stove. He could find no words of comfort, but he laid his big hand on her shoulder.

She said, not turning: "Why do you waste the wood?"

★ 3 ★

ASE LINDEN had three friends and a flute. The oldest friend was an Indian, Mink Fisher. Their natures, their gravity, had spoken each to each when Ase had been four years old. The Indian had come to trade. He had stood in the wood-shed doorway tall and straight, blanket-wrapped, black braids of hair over his shoulders, an eagle feather in the band across his bronze forehead. The little boy had thought: 'It is the king of the hawks'. They had studied each other and then Mink had held out his hand and Ase had walked to him and laid his hand in his with a child's deep sigh of content. They had become as father and son. From Mink he had learned all he knew of the lore of nature. Through his boyhood and early adolescence the Indian had come to him several times a year, often from many miles out of his way. Now Mink had not come in five years. Ase grieved and longed for him.

His second oldest friend was the gypsies. He thought of them collectively, as he did not single out one grape from a cluster or one marsh marigold from a field of marigolds. The gypsies had been coming since he was six. They came every summer, camping by the willow stream or near the cold flowing spring by the log cabin. For the few days of their camp he was one of them. He came then as close as was possible, for him, to neglecting his chores. As a boy, he ran with the gypsy boys. As a young man, he sat with the elders, danced and sang and ate and drank at their summer nights' festivities. Of late he had been closest to the matriarch of the tribe, the Old One, the queen; to her husband and to their daughter Elissa. Elissa stirred his blood so that when he touched her in the dance he trembled like a colt. She was an unlit bonfire ready for the spurt of his match. The Old One looked on with approval, and he did not understand why or how he had abruptly turned back with Elissa from the hemlock shadows towards which he had been leading her on a soft June evening. The gypsies had not appeared the summer before. Ase was fearful that he had offended the pride of the girl; even more, perhaps, that of her mother, the queen.

His third friend was Tim McCarthy. No king had sired McCarthy, no queen had borne him. He was a drunken little old Irishman from the bogs of Aran, a hired farm hand by necessity, a fiddler by the grace of God and to the glory of man. Ten years ago he had drifted into the neighbourhood with his fiddle under his arm, a bottle in his pocket, a dirty white she-dog at his heels. He had hired out first with Hiram Linden. He had lasted until his first spree, when he reeled into the house, singing and fiddling the bawdiest of Irish ballads. Amelia had had him off the premises before the sun went down. Meantime, he and the lad of eleven had become fast cronies. The little man, full of fables, his music and his dog fascinated the boy in equal measure. The Wilsons, the Lindens' nearest neighbours, two miles to the east, had taken Tim on for a while. He was now reasonably settled yet another mile east, to be near his young friend Ase, with a farm family who put up with his instability in satisfaction over the lower wages he was willing to work for. The little dog was dead, replaced by a male of her progeny as white and dirty and devoted. When sober, there was no better hired hand than Tim McCarthy. At all times he was kind and gentle, and wise, save for the drink, which had him. He had the Gaelic gaiety and melancholy, like the streaks of fat and lean in Irish bacon.

McCarthy had given Ase the flute, which he counted also as a friend. Tim's fiddle had stirred the hearts of many a man and woman in two lands and on the sea between them, but he had never induced so rapt an absorption as in the thin, solemn boy who had such trouble speaking. It seemed to McCarthy that Ase found the music another and a richer language, one that spoke familiarly and in which he might find tongue. He tried to teach him the violin, but the boy's hands, already huge, were fatally clumsy, and while he managed the bow well enough his already gnarled fingers could not touch one of the delicate strings without impinging on another.

McCarthy said finally: "Me boy-o, 'tis hopeless. 'Tis like a pair of drunken woodchucks stompin' on me fiddle."

Watching Ase piping one day on a willow whistle, McCarthy lifted a finger and said: "Whoosh now. I've an idea born to me."

He prowled the marsh for the proper hollow reed, and carefully, his blue eyes intent, his cheeks rosy with excitement, ruffling his white hair now and then in exasperation, he made with his pocket knife a serviceable flute with half a dozen stops. The day was Sunday and he worked from noon to sunset.

"There now," he said. "If it works, I'll be fitting a better mouthpiece and trying to call back where the other stops should go. Give it a blast."

The boy had learned the crude, sweet instrument as though a young bird learned to sing. McCarthy deprived himself of his drink for several months, disappeared for five days, and having walked the twenty miles each way to and from the city of Trent, appeared again still sober and triumphant, with the gift for Ase of as fine a flute, ebony and silver, as money could buy. On his next month's wages he became magnificently drunk. Before he collapsed, to be driven by Ase to his place of employment and put to bed in the loft, the old man and the boy had played fiddle and flute together in the hemlock woods until the birds flew close to listen, and they looked up to see the Linden sheep flocked in a semicircle before them. Tim had been so taken by laughter that it made an end to the playing and he gave himself to finishing his jug. Now Ase was twenty-one and McCarthy was in his late sixties, and Ase was master of his flute. The pair were called on for their music at all the country gatherings and dances. It was Tim who did the trotting back and forth between the two farms, to visit. Two evenings seldom passed without Ase's finding the little man and his dog waiting for him at the barns when chores and supper were done with.

From the coldness of the Linden house Ase had walked with these friends into strange worlds, warm and golden. The world of Mink Fisher had most nearly fed and satisfied him. It was primal, enriched by Indian myth and legend of bird and beast, of cloud and wind and spaceless sky. It was an amplification of the earth he knew and there was nourishment in the stars.

The Romany world dazzled him with its freedom and its brightness. It was spangled and embroidered. Oriental, exotic, the open road its lamp and its god. Its songs around the camp fire came from far away and long ago, songs of feuds and castles, of roving minstrels, of dark deaths and gypsy passions. McCarthy's Celtic world was fey, peopled with leprechauns and fairies, with red-bearded kings and gold-haired queens who never had been and never could be. There were fierce battles here, and a deal of bitter injustice and the righting of it, and from behind the mist that shrouded the green and silver landscape there came the sound of a mysterious laughter.

These glimpses into distance, these few steps into magic places, left Ase still the onlooker, still hungering to share more deeply, to become a part of even farther realms and stranger people. He had no friends of his own age. His longing for closeness to his brother absorbed him. It did

28

not occur to him to seek a brother among his school-mates or the neighbour lads. Benjamin was the spring from which he must quench his thirst if it was to be assuaged at all. He was stirred and touched by the generosity of his three friends, taking their affection as a gift past his deserving. He did not guess that they recognized in him imagination and spirit like their own, a bigness of mind, a rare understanding and tenderness that warmed them too, made them feel valued, as they valued him. He knew only that he was a stranger and they took him in. They spoke to him and he was a little able to speak with them. He found voice fully in his flute alone.

Of the friends and the flute Amelia disapproved with all the sting of her acid tongue. Mink Fisher was a stinking savage, likely to murder them in their beds. The gypsies were roisterers and thieves. McCarthy was a common Irish drunk. It was further proof of the stupidity of her younger son, his unfitness, that he made bosom companions of the scum of the earth, foreigners to boot. She succeeded in imposing on him a certain sense of guilt when he slipped away, as he must, to meet them. Otherwise he was unshaken. He cleaved to his friends with quiet stubbornness. They were of a noble goodness, he knew, and the core of his integrity was impregnable to his mother's malice.

Her outright forbiddal of the flute puzzled him. She was not a religious woman, save in a hard, perfunctory fashion. It seemed only that in the dark place in which she chose to live she was determined no colour, no warmth, no rhythm should ever enter. It was impossible to yield to her on this, either, for the release of music was too great. To spare her, he took care to play with McCarthy out of her hearing, in winter in the barn, warmed by the body heat of the stock, in summer under the hemlocks by the wintergreen bog. When the need came on him alone, he rambled over the hills, piping as he went. He kept the flute hidden in a linen handkerchief on a shelf in the hay-mow.

THE Wilsons were plain people. There was a large houseful of them, good-natured, hard-working, earthy. From much of the country stock the sons went on to become lawyers, physicians, business men, teachers, but the Wilson boys and men were unthinkable as anything but farmers, and the girls would always marry men of the soil. They were a solid, continuing breed. Their red barns were impressive, the house nondescript, but bright with white paint and masses of old-fashioned flower-beds. The interior was divided into many small rooms, inartistically and comfortably furnished, cluttered with Wilsons and the paraphernalia of the men's boots and mackinaws, the women's sewing and canning and preserving. Their table was famous even in a land of plenty, laden three times a day with half a dozen meats, fruits, vegetables swimming in cream and butter, pickles and jellies and preserves, endless pastries, heaped together for handy self-helping like a medieval hunting feast. For all the food they stowed away with such cheer and relish, the Wilsons were runty. Pa and Ma Wilson were a pair of wrinkled hickory nuts, the boys were small and wiry, only the girls profited by the family physique. They were merry little things with dozens of beaux, fresh and appealing until age and child-bearing should turn them gaunt and withered as locust shells. Nellie at twenty was the prettiest of the lot. She was diminutive and dainty, with plump little breasts, apple-round, apple-firm, an impudent short nose firm, pointed chin and dimpled mouth, eyes the blue of wild chicory, and gold-chestnut hair that rippled to her shoulders in round finger-curls. She was an incorrigible minx and a mischief.

Amelia Linden condescended to the Wilsons. They were decent enough, she admitted, if too much given to hilarity, undeniably prosperous, but the men were not 'gentlemen', the women were not 'ladies'. She called them 'common', and so they were. Nellie had been Benjamin's girl since she was sixteen. It had approached not quite a scandal that they had not married. Amelia had handled the situation with a rare caution. Her early sarcasm failing to keep Benjamin away from the girl, she had looked uneasily to the future. She would detest any woman who claimed him, yet she was terrified lest by her disapproval she alienate him. She encouraged him in his prowlings elsewhere, slipping him money for trips to Peytonville and Trent, yet when he returned, he would be smoothing his hair with a wet brush like a pleased tom-cat washing his fur, and always off down the road two miles again to Nellie. She had decided shrewdly that if it was Nellie he must bring home as bride, she was safer with such a little snippet than with a wife more worthy of him. His infatuation with the pretty face and tiny round figure would pass, and she herself, offering no criticism save an occasional significant lifted eyebrow, would be entrenched and waiting, a constant contrast, so that he should inevitably turn more and more to the superior woman, in appreciation and relief.

Ase found himself increasingly haunted by thoughts of Nellie. He had not seen her since his father's funeral two months ago. He drove his mother to Peytonville to church on Sundays, but the Wilsons attended church in another direction. There had been no meeting of the Grange, and the Wilsons and Lindens, as families, had never exchanged casual visits. Tim McCarthy had reported that the sweet Nellie had been moping, but the lads were crowding in again, like yearlings trying the fence, he said, now the big bull was gone to other pastures.

Ase had tried to put out of his mind Ben's words: "Better marry Nellie in the spring." He was uncertain how to take them. Ben had often teased him about his mute admiration of Nellie. The words might have been only another jest. Again, they might have been intended as a seal on the finality of his leaving. Since Ben was without subtlety, Ase came slowly over the weeks to the belief that his brother had meant them literally, meant as well that the miracle was possible.

The thought of Nellie Wilson began to creep in on him as irresistibly as the sun reaching into dark crannies. If he might have Nellie for his wife, he would be cold no longer, no more alone. He dreamed of her by night and awakened with his heart pounding. He acknowledged now what he had ignored through loyalty to Ben, that Nellie was his true love and always had been. Because of Nellie, hidden away, smothered, in his heart, he had turned back from the hemlocks with the gypsy girl.

The time was February. Something was supposed to happen then—what was it? He remembered. Ben was to have taken Nellie to the mid-winter dance of the Grange. He frowned at his stupidity. He should have asked weeks ago if he might replace his brother as her escort. She would have accepted another by now. He could not picture Nellie as waiting. Not even waiting for Ben. If she refused his invitation face to face, laughed at him, he knew that he would stumble away from her, damned and lost. After his mother had gone to bed he wrote laboriously by lamp-light, and sent the formal note by Tim McCarthy.

"Asahel Linden requests the pleasure of the company of Miss Nellie Wilson at the Grange dance, if not too late in asking."

McCarthy brought the answer in her round childish writing.

"Miss Nellie Wilson thinks it's high time Mr. Asahel Linden was asking."

★ 5 ★

AMELIA said: "It is most disrespectful to your father to attend a dance so soon after his death."

Ase finished tying his black tie before the kitchen mirror. She had always had some unreasonable reason against his occasional excursions into the country festivities. Having had no respect at all for her husband, fiercely satisfied to be rid of him, and having no interest in the opinions of others, her attempt now to deter him on such grounds struck him as ridiculous. In his new understanding of her he decided that denying herself warmth and communion and gaiety, she wished even more to deny it to him. Any excuse served her, and he thought it would be simpler if she made none, since she could not or would not speak the truth about it.

She persisted: "You must cut a pretty figure at a dance, even without the bad taste of dancing on your father's fresh grave. You've outgrown that suit. Look at your wrists and ankles, sticking out from the cuffs and trousers."

He had looked at them in his bedroom. The good black broadcloth suit was three years old, and between eighteen and twenty-one he had finished the last few inches of his gangling growth. He supposed he must look like a scarecrow. Yet no one had laughed at him, no one indeed had seemed even to notice. He carried a dignity past harming by the chance of ill-fitting clothes. He had always gone to the social gatherings, as he went to Mink Fisher and the gypsies, under a slight cloud of depression imposed by his mother. Now his deep-set grey eyes were without embarrassment or guilt. He was as he was, he and his flute would be welcome. His mother's whip flicked over him without the old pain.

She said: "You must feel out of it when you go to these affairs. You don't even have a girl."

He would prefer not to speak, for something would be resolved this evening, but he said: "I'm taking Nellie tonight."

She studied him, drawing her heavy black eyebrows together. He was prepared for a storm of rage, or one of her familiar stalking withdrawals to her room, as violent in their way as her words. She surprised him by nodding after a moment.

"Very good. Very proper. You are a better brother than I thought. You must keep the others away from her until Benjamin returns."

He was not prepared for this. The Seth Thomas clock on the lamp-shelf whirred and struck the hour. He was due at the Wilson farm this moment. Nellie would be sputtering. He had hitched Dan to the light cutter before bathing and dressing. He wrapped in carpeting the brick heated red-hot on the range. He said "Good-night, Mother", and went to the carriage barn, placing the brick under the straw for Nellie's feet. He untethered Dan, and on the road touched the whip to him lightly. The young stallion's shod hoofs struck fire on the glazed snow. He was only fifteen minutes late, but all the Wilsons save Nellie had gone on. The front door flew open. He had a glimpse of her against the low-turned lamplight, bundled in a red cape and red fur-trimmed bonnet, her curls escaping, her party bag swinging from her mittened hand. The door slammed and she ran across the snow and was in the seat before he could move to help her. He drew the buffalo robe around her and her small gaitered feet found the hot brick.

She said: "I almost went on with the folks. Be just like you to forget to come for me at all."

He wanted to say that he was as likely to forget to breathe, but although he cleared his throat to speak, no words came. He was dizzy at having her close beside him, her shoulder against his arm. He could not see her face in the dark night, but he was conscious of the round little shape of her, her warmth, a vitality so electric that it seemed to him sparks would fly as from Dan's shoes if he should touch her. The sleigh bells jingled sweetly. Nellie chattered lightly, of neighbours, of other dances, her voice, he thought, as silver as the bells. There was no opening for graver matters. He was content in any case to absorb her nearness.

At the door of the lighted Grange, she said: "I suppose you brought your flute. Will you have to leave me much tonight to play?"

He read her tone as wistful and he felt light-headed.

"They expect me to play, but I won't have to. I'd rather——"

"You'll have to play some. I just wanted to know how often. I promised Sam Turner the dances when you're busy."

He helped her out of the sleigh and to the door, then turned Dan into the stables, to tie his halter to a hay-filled stall, to cover him with a blanket. He returned soberly to the hall. He was on a fool's errand tonight. Or any other night. He had allowed himself to be tangled in a web-like dream of his own making. He had presumed on a meaningless remark of Ben's to build a cloud castle where he did not belong and could never enter.

He saw Nellie at the far end of the long room, laughing with half a dozen young people. She had a gift for women as well as for men. The girls of her age accepted her with little envy, were faithful friends. Older women respected her matter-of-factness, her common sense in spite of her pranks, beyond all, her known domestic talents. Ase watched her, yearning. She wore a flounced dress of silk organza, the blue of her eyes, with a satin ribbon the same colour tied around her curls. The pert bow at the top was a butterfly on golden wheat.

Tim McCarthy joined him, brushed and combed and in his Sunday best.

He said: "You do be looking as forlorn as a rooster in the rain. Pay no attention tonight to the Nellie's flirting. I'll not call on you yet for the flute. Do you be dancing."

Ase made his way to Nellie. She gave no greeting, but, still laughing, tucked her arm in his by way of acknowledgement and claim.

He said: "I'm not playing for the first dance, Nellie."

McCarthy went to the raised platform. He had kept away from the liquor, so that he might be at the disposal of the company. He was ready to play as long as they cared to dance. The little man seemed a full head taller. He came into his own as head fiddler and caller. He tuned his violin with authority. There were a second fiddle, a guitar, a harmonica and an accordion. Tim sensed that the dancers were eager and yet shy.

He called out: "A good evening to all. Now we'll be having a bit of a warm-up."

He gestured to his orchestra, and set off on an Irish jig. The Mahoneys and the Shehys tittered, looking at one another, and the two middle-aged couples took the floor for the jig. The wild dance shook the solid new boards. Everyone clapped in tune, other feet thumped and shuffled to the irresistible lilt. The ice was broken. When the Irish couples ended, red-faced and sweating, bowing to the applause, all were ready for the square dance.

Old, half-forgotten men and women took their places, standing straight as possible. Children who knew the figures paired off without self-consciousness, practised swinging and sashaying earnestly. Ase bowed before Nellie and led her out. He was proud of her, his heart was too big for his chest. She was almost as pretty as he thought her. Aunt Jess the

35

midwife swam on to the floor like a ship in full sail, leading Grandpa Wilson, twice her age and half her size.

McCarthy lifted his bow, called: "Face your partners!", the music of 'Turkey in the Straw' burst out, and the square dance was on. Tim was as fine a caller as a fiddler. He had imagination, so that he varied the figures between the simple and the intricate, the restful and the exhausting. The old folks thought they felt young again, but found themselves saving their strength, those of courting age injected a subtle lure and passion into the formal figures, the children danced frowning and with concentration. Aunt Jess had been at the hard cider and was dancing with abandon, a mistake for a woman of her bulk. Yet Grandpa Wilson was plainly having quite as good a time. The big woman and the little man were sashaying with the best of them. Nellie was a blue-and-gold feather, and Ase came as close to grace as he would ever come, his long legs moving like pistons, huge gnarled hands lifting Nellie clear from the floor when he swung her. The rhythm of the dance was joy, its community was release.

The ancient ones swore they had never been less tired, the lovers wandered away to corners, the children slid and swooped and jostled one another. The music was insistent, the dance almost too intense, and it ended sharply. All the dancers were relieved to collapse on the chairs and benches around the walls of the hall. McCarthy mopped his forehead.

"Come now, Asahel my friend," he called. "Let us play only a little quiet song while the dancers rest."

Ase went to him and picked up his flute.

"That gypsy love song," Tim whispered. "While not truly restful, 'twill give the folks back their breath."

In the beginning there was a clatter of talk, the children scrambling, and then the gypsy song took over, and spoke to each man, each woman. The tremulous violin made the young uneasy. Was love to prove so sad as this? The flute cried to the elders. One wrinkled hand groped to find another. Had love been after all so sweet? So sad, so sweet, the ancient song assured them. The last note faded away, to be a ghost again. The hall was hushed. In the silence a child wailed loud and suddenly, being frightened by the magic. McCarthy laid down his fiddle and Ase his flute.

McCarthy whispered: "Maybe we've done too good a job of it. 'Twill take us a mort of thumpety music to liven them up again."

When he judged the dancers ready and rested, he gave the lead in 'Little Brown Jug' to the guitar and encouraged the squeaking second fiddle and the harmonica.

"Do be twanging it up, boys," he called out, "fast and lively. Some of the gentlemen need to be working off the hard cider."

The laughter overlay the brisk tune, small boys whooped, the dance resumed.

There was a pause at midnight. A light supper was served. The drinking men were sobered by the food. The full, sleepy children were deposited on benches, on quilts on the floor, the older women volunteering to watch over them. The younger women changed their dresses, as was the custom, for the strenuous dancing had them perspiring and dishevelled. The prettiest dresses were saved for the last hours of the dance. The atmosphere of courting was as positive as lightning. Girls arranged their flounces, tightened their corset strings, pulled their bodices lower, slapped their cheeks and bit their lips to redden them, used a trace of rice powder surreptitiously, a drop of scent at their breasts. The dancing was less boisterous. Waltzes and the Virginia reel replaced the square dances.

McMarthy led off in 'Good-night, Ladies', and called out: "'Twas a fine evening and I'm hoping you are appreciating my sacrifice, staying sober. Another time I'll not be finding meself so noble."

The girls changed their slippers, bundled into warm cloaks and bonnets and mittens, the mothers gathered the sleeping children, the men went to the stable to hitch the sleighs. The pre-dawn was clear and cold. The snowy road was a silver carpet-runner under the stars. Nellie snuggled under the buffalo robe close against Ase.

She said: "You'd be warmer if you weren't all bones."

They drove in silence. It was unlike her not to chatter. This was the moment, if he was to speak at all. He had taken too much for granted, he was certain. Surely Nellie would be waiting, like his mother, for Ben's return. If not, if the field was open, how could she consider having him? And if the impossible were possible, what of Amelia? He had not been prepared to have her consider him a watchdog for Nellie, a eunuch guarding the gate against the prince's coming.

Nellie said: "Ase——"

He turned his head. Her face was graver than he had ever seen it.

"Ase, Ben's not coming back."

She pushed back a curl from her forehead.

He said: "I didn't think you knew."

"He told me. Ben played fair, in his way. Did he tell you, too?"

"Yes."

The horse was pacing and the sleigh bells were noisy. Ase drew on the reins. Dan snorted and slowed to a walk.

Ase said: "I thought you might be waiting for him."

She shook her head. "I was a fool to wait as long as I did."

The way was clear for his question and he could not phrase it. She put her arm through his.

"Well, Ase? Ben say anything about you and me?"

His heart thumped painfully. Ben's words seemed unfeeling, unsuitable.

"Did he?"

He nodded.

"Tell me."

"He said to marry you in the spring, Nellie."

"Now, Ase, you don't have to ask just because Ben said so."

Her eyes twinkled in the starlight. He had had no words of his own, he had used his brother's and he was trapped in them. Surely she must know how he had adored her, Ben's girl, from a distance. The cords were tight in his throat.

"I want you——"

"Oh. That's different."

He wanted to cry out: "I want you with my spirit and my loins, with every bone and nerve of me, I want you for warmth in my house, in my heart and my bed."

His love was suddenly stronger than his awkwardness. He dropped the slack reins and took her in his long arms. His lips found the warm hollow under her firm chin. He felt her stir against him. She took his face in her mittened hands and pressed her mouth to his. Her kiss was long and hungry. She pushed him away, breathing pantingly, like a cat. His blood raced like the water over the mill-dam, so that he thought it must spill from him as violently.

Nellie said primly: "I haven't said I'd have you."

His pulse slowed. How could she have him? He wanted to say: "I am a poor stumbling thing after the glory of my brother, my feet bound to the earth, my head lost in the clouds, but I have my love and my faithfulness to offer."

He said: "I know. How can you?"

She was grave again. She laid her hand on his arm.

"You're a good man, Ase Linden. That's how. Ben and I —never mind—that's over and done with. Ben wasn't for any one woman. I always liked you next best. I shouldn't have teased you. I knew how you felt about me."

The east was streaked with red and gold. Light glinted on the sleigh bells, on Nellie's curls. Ase seemed to see her for the first time, fair as the mythical woman all men dream of. Her eyes were honest, somehow anxious, somehow sad.

She said: "I'll make you a good wife, Ase."

The road turned into the Wilson farm. Lamps were lit in house and barn, for the men would do their chores before breakfast and then have a few hours of sleeping. Ase held her again, but tenderly, with humility and gratitude.

"Nice to get it settled," she said.

★ 6 ★

THE sun rose behind Ase as he drove home. The faint warmth touched the nape of his neck, reminding him of the feeling there of Nellie's mittens. The snow-piled roofs of the red barns were rosy. The large white Linden house was snow-capped, too; the drifts were piled to the windows. It would be not much longer aloof and bare, unwelcoming.

He changed his clothes to do the morning chores. He moved quietly, not to disturb his mother. Since Benjamin had gone, she slept late, making no pretence at preparing breakfast. He built a fire in the kitchen range and put on the coffee-pot and the double boiler of oatmeal. The handling of the milk and cream and butter had devolved on him.

He went to the dusky cellar and lit a lamp there. The Jersey cream was nearly an inch thick in the wide shallow milk-pans. He skimmed most of it into an earthen crock, saving out a pint pitcherful for table use. He poured the skimmed milk into a bucket for the hogs. In the kitchen he rinsed the pans in the zinc sink fed by a rain-water cistern pump. He pushed the bubbling coffee-pot to the back of the range. He took the pig slops in one hand and the clean milk-bucket in the other and went to the barn for the milking. He fed the stock and returned to the house, to strain the foaming milk into yesterday's clean pans, and carried them carefully down to the cellar shelves. The hanging shelves were planned for family quantities of canned fruits and pickles and jellies, but they were almost empty. A jar of preserved quinces would have been palatable for a winter morning's breakfast.

The sun poured through the east window between range and sink. He laid a red-and-white checkered cloth on the kitchen table and set two places. He hoped Nellie would continue to have breakfast in the kitchen in cold weather. The warmth of the range, the crackling of the burning wood, were pleasant. Amelia was still sleeping. He ate a dish of oatmeal with crumbled maple sugar and spoonfuls of the thick yellow cream while the bacon fried in an iron skillet. He set one plate of bacon in the warmer for his mother. To his own he added eggs poached in the fat. He made himself toast. The butter-dish in the pantry was empty and he went down-cellar again for a fresh crock. Something was the matter with his coffee. Even the golden cream failed to turn it to a pleasing colour, it was grey and unsavoury.

He washed his dishes and the morning's milk-pans and bucket, scalding them with boiling water from the kettle, and set the milk things on a shelf in the woodshed. He brushed his crumbs from the table and left the wire toast grill handy for his mother, with eggs ready for soft-boiling in a small saucepan. The barn needed cleaning, the sheep were nearly out of fodder, but these chores could be done later. He went upstairs to his icy bedroom, undressed to his underwear, and got into his cold bed. His head was thick, but he could not sleep after all. There was too much joy to be savoured and, with it, too many plans to be made, the problem of Amelia to be mulled over. He had hoped she would join him for breakfast, so that in leisure over their coffee he might give her his news and try to answer whatever might be her inevitable objections. She had disparaged Nellie to him and to his father, well out of Ben's hearing, but she had accepted her for Ben's sake. If Nellie would do for Ben, she would be not only suitable for him, but likely to be considered too good for him, as was his own opinion. Yet Amelia had approved his taking Nellie to the dance as a means of keeping her safe for his brother. He decided there was nothing for it but to convince his mother that Ben would not be claiming Nellie, ever, because he would not be coming home at all. He drowsed, imagining Nellie close beside him, and went sound asleep at last.

When he awakened it was two o'clock in the afternoon. He pulled on his clothing and went downstairs. He found a note on the kitchen table from Amelia. It was her sewing circle day and one of the members had dropped in, driving by, fortunately, as her son had failed to appear to hitch the horse and sleigh for her. He wondered at her faithfulness to the circle, which sewed for foreign missions, for she was neither sociable nor friendly with neighbours or fellow church-goers, nor a good seamstress, nor interested in the heathen poor. Actually, she had joined a group composed of the simplest of farm women, for to them she was both queen and oracle. She returned from the luncheon meetings richly fed of belly and of ego.

Ase made himself a light meal and ate absently. He washed up and swept the kitchen floor. He brought the accumulated cream from the cellar and turned it into the wooden butter-churn. The faint sourness had a clean, fresh smell. He set the churn a few feet from the range to warm a little. The clock struck three. He was restless. The barn work was not too pressing. There would be time to walk the two miles east to see Nellie before the evening chores. He wanted to set a wedding date, he wanted to prepare her for his mother. He hesitated. Half at least of the large Wilson family would be sitting about the house on a cold winter afternoon. There would be jesting and no privacy at all.

He heard footsteps on the gravel path, lighter than his mother's, and then Nellie's voice, calling to her dog. It seemed for a moment that he heard these sounds only in his day-dream. If not, perhaps she was not coming here, but was passing on her way to some other place and person.

She called: "Ase! Wake up!" and beat with her little fists on the panelled door.

Shep was barking with excitement, as though his mistress were calling to a man in danger in a house on fire. Ase was too slow to open the door to her. She was in the room, the dog delighted behind her. She wore her red hooded cape and had a basket on her arm. It occurred to him that she was Little Red Riding Hood, with the wolf transposed, because of her, into this amiable sheep-dog.

He said: "Nellie, I've been thinking about you."

She took off her cape and shook imaginary dust or snow from it and laid it over a chair in a curiously domestic manner, as though the chair, the room, the house, were already hers.

"You always just sit and think."

She lifted the lid from her basket and handed him a plate covered with a napkin.

"I saw your mother go by with Mrs. Barnes so I made you this pie."

He was deeply touched. He took the plate, staring at it.

"Well, open it up, Ase. Maybe you don't like pumpkin."

He removed the napkin. The plate held only a mound of flour.

"Oh, Ase, look what I've done. Brought you the wrong plate. Now I remember, I just sat and thought about making you a pie and then forgot all about it. Well. But I guess your mother has all kinds of good pies and you wouldn't want mine, anyway."

This was surely malice, for Amelia Linden was famous

42

for her distaste for cooking, for the execrable products that resulted when she did finally turn to stove and oven. Nellie laughed. She swooped into her basket and brought out the true pie, golden-brown and redolent.

"You should see your face, Ase. Oh, my——"

Her laughter was that of a child, high-keyed and delirious.

He smiled sheepishly. He should have known this was another of her jokes. Yet he wanted to turn her over his knee and spank her. She had raised his spirits so high, then dropped them down again. But after all, she had indeed brought him a pie. He could not tell which was honest, the jest or the gift. Since she was Nellie, perhaps both.

He said: "I'll eat it for supper."

She looked critically around the room. She had not been in the house since the home funeral service for Ase's father. A small couch stood near the bay window. She sat down and patted the seat beside her, for him to join her. He put his arms around her. She gave him a quick cool kiss and pushed him away.

"Never mind that now. I saw a chance to be alone with you to make our plans."

He said: "I'd have come to you, but your family——"

She laughed.

"I know. Well, don't you think the sooner the better?"

He was stirred that she was as anxious as he.

"Oh, Nellie, I do."

"I can be ready in a couple of weeks. I'd like to be married at home and then come straight here. All right with you?"

He reached for her in answer, but she stood up impatiently and walked around the room, studying it. She frowned.

"I've got to do something with this awful house. I'd like to get it fixed up and feel settled by April. I want to spend most of my time outdoors at planting-time. I want a big garden. That little thing you've had is a disgrace, not enough stuff for the table, let alone canning for winter. I want to start flower-beds and get things growing at the front of the house, anyway. It looks like a barn without any plants or shrubbery."

She sat beside him again and chuckled.

"Think I'm going to have to fight your mother to do things my way?"

He took her small capable hands in his big ones.

He said gravely: "She won't mind anything about the house or garden. But, Nellie——"

She looked at him sharply.

"What's the matter? You don't think she'll make a fuss about our marrying, do you?"

He nodded in misery.

"Because of Ben, I suppose." She was thoughtful. "Why? Ben walked out on me."

"She won't believe he isn't coming back."

"Oh. I'm supposed to turn into an old woman waiting for him, just in case her precious takes the notion to show up and claim his property. Well, he won't, and I won't. She can go to the devil."

She was adorable, he thought, in her flushed anger. It was part of her vitality, a warm, sputtering, healthy explosion unlike the cold venom of his mother's rages. He stroked her hands.

He longed to tell her of his mother, to enlist her understanding and her pity, yet would not betray one woman to the other. He thought again with pain of the hurt they must inflict on her, if she were to accept their union.

He said: "You'd better tell her what Ben told you about his going."

"I'll tell her, all right. He said one reason he was clearing out was to get away from her. Said she drove him crazy."

"Nellie, no."

"It wouldn't kill her. The old dame's tough as hickory."

"Please, Nellie."

She laughed suddenly and patted his arm.

"Don't worry. I'll behave. She won't raise half the hell as if it had been Ben. I'm getting a good farm and a good husband and I'm going to make a good job of it."

Her matter-of-factness made love-making impossible. She relaxed against him with the bland ease of a kitten that has had its supper and is ready for a warm lap, but chooses not to be caressed. She allowed him to hold her, but slapped away his hand when his fingers strayed to the fascination of her curls. She had enough of snuggling shortly, and left the couch to prowl through the dining-room to the kitchen. He followed at her heels, and Shep the dog followed, both of them watching her in anxious adoration. She gave her verdict on the kitchen. A good scrubbing, fresh varnish, ruffled red and white gingham curtains at the window, some bright braided rag rugs on the bare floor, would make it passable. She touched the churn.

"Your mother's let the cream get too warm. Her butter'll be soft."

"I did it."

She looked at him, moved the churn in front of a chair and began plunging the wooden dasher up and down. The butter came, too quickly, she said, and soft, as she had predicted. She asked for cold well water from the outside pump, worked the butter in a bowl, asked for a mould, but there was none. She packed the butter in a crock and sent him down-cellar with it. She washed and scalded the churn, speaking with disapproval of the kitchen furnishings. She poured glasses of fresh butter-flecked buttermilk and lifted her eyebrows when no doughnuts or cookies were to be found to serve with it.

"No wonder you're all bones. You don't get enough to eat."

He was enchanted with her bustling domesticity, her air of kitchen command. She belonged here already. She glanced at the clock.

"I ought to be going, but I want to have it out with your mother and get it over with."

Amelia came near sunset. She walked through the front rooms, removing bonnet and gloves, and stopped short in the kitchen doorway. Ase rose to greet her.

Nellie said: "Good evening, Mother Linden."

Amelia stared.

"What are you doing here?"

"Visiting."

"So I see. Since when does a young woman call on a young man?"

"When they're engaged."

Amelia said: "Asahel, suppose you give me a reasonable

45

explanation of all this. I'm not in a mood for this girl's flippancy."

His throat was dry. He swallowed. He looked imploringly at his mother and then at Nellie. The most gracious and soothing of words, even if he could find them, would not be adequate.

Nellie said: "Speak up, Ase."

He said: "Nellie and I are going to be married, Mother."

He saw the storm move in on her. She would kill him with a shaft of lightning if she could. He braced himself against her eyes, her voice.

"You traitor. You miserable, skulking oaf. You trip over your own feet and then plot to fill your brother's shoes. Behind his back, you wait until his back is turned, you sneak in and steal what's his, like a weasel."

Nellie said mildly: "I'm hardly a chicken on a roost, Mother Linden."

Amelia turned. Ase wished Nellie had not spoken. He had long borne the fury, could bear it now; he had hoped to spare her.

"Perhaps this treachery was your idea, Miss?"

"Actually, it was Ben's."

"What are you talking about? He'll expect you to be waiting for him when he comes home. Don't think I want you for him, you aren't fit to wash his feet, but he chose you, I was ready to accept you because it's what he wanted."

Nellie's eyes were blue fire. She walked close to the dark woman. A small, fierce hawk faced a coiled snake in deadly battle.

"Now listen to me. I'm going to marry Ase and you're going to accept that, too. Ben's gone for good. He told me so. He told Ase so. The last thing he said to each of us was for us to marry. Ben didn't want me for keeps. Ase does. I'm Ben's nice little present to Ase. It just happens it suits me. It suits me fine. Ben won't be back. Do you understand?"

Amelia gripped the back of a chair. Her knuckles were white. Her hands went limp and she sat down slowly.

"No," she said.

Nellie reached for her red cape and threw it around her shoulders. She snatched her empty basket. The dog Shep

46

came from behind the range, where he had slunk uneasily.

She said to Amelia: "I don't intend to quarrel with you, either. We're going to live pleasantly. I'm going to have things comfortable and nice."

Amelia said hoarsely: "You can't come here."

"Oh yes, I can."

"You can't live in my house. If you do this thing, this betrayal of my Benjamin, you can't live in my house. You'll have to go to the cabin."

"I will not."

Nellie set down the basket and spoke more patiently.

"Look here, Mother Linden, I know you're upset, but you've got to face facts. Now you hate to keep house and I like it. You like good food and you don't lift a finger to cook. I'm going to set the best table in the township. It makes sense for me to take over and run things."

Amelia dabbed with her handkerchief at dry lips.

"I'll move to the cabin myself."

"All right, move there. A good idea. You can eat with us and not have any responsibility at all. You'll find you'll like it."

She laid her hand on Shep's head.

"Come on, boy. Be dark before we get home."

Ase said: "Wait, Nellie, I'll hitch up."

"No, thanks. I'll walk off the rest of my mad."

She stood on tiptoe and kissed him lightly on the cheek. She touched Amelia's cold hand.

"It won't be so bad, Mother Linden, once you get used to it."

"When is this happy event to take place?"

"I told Ase, the sooner the better. Two weeks. Goodnight."

She was out of the house in a swirl of cape and curls. He heard her swift feet over the crunched snow and the joyful bark of her dog. He wanted to hurry after her. He started for the door.

Amelia said: "Asahel!"

Her voice was hysterical.

"She said the sooner the better. Don't you see? She's carrying Benjamin's child."

47

He felt a sick numbing. He was mired in a nightmare and could not move or escape. She twisted her hands together. Her words came in a rush.

"She tried to trap him. He doesn't know, of course. He wouldn't have gone if he'd known. She disgusted him and he went away. She found she'd sprung the trap, but then he was gone. So now she's trapped you."

He shook his head like a tortured bear.

He recognized in anguish that it was possible.

"It isn't true, Mother. But if it was—I'd want her."

More than ever, he thought, more than ever, to protect her, to protect his brother, even, the child.

"You'd take his left-overs? You'd take up where he left off?"

"Yes, Mother."

The clock ticked in the silence. The range had not been lit, nor the sitting-room stove, and the house was chill. He waited.

Amelia said in a low voice: "If I ever needed proof you were born a fool, this is it. Very well. I wash my hands of it. You may make your accounting to Benjamin. He would prefer to give his own name to his child, even by that hussy. You'll have a pretty time explaining your presumption when he returns."

She gathered her wraps and went to her room.

He sat thinking. The picture was clear and without offence. Nellie and Benjamin, volatile alike of nature, had struck a spontaneous fire, and Ben had certainly possessed her. She was not with child, Ase knew. She was honest enough to have told him. He knew, too, with horror, that his mother had committed herself, almost insanely, to the conviction of her eldest's return, and would twist facts ruthlessly to fit that conviction. He wished he might have had Nellie to wife free of the dark sucking bog through which his slow feet must move, across which his wordless thoughts must find their way.

He was late getting to his chores. He milked and fed the stock by lantern-light. He strained the milk in the kitchen and put it away. He washed his hands and face, and then his hands again, as though something more unclean than the good animal smell might be washed away. He was not hungry, but he looked about for materials for a supper. In his absence at the barn, Amelia had been in the kitchen. She had made herself a pot of tea and had eaten a large wedge of Nellie's pumpkin-pie.

<h1 style="text-align:center">★ 7 ★</h1>

THE Linden house on their wedding day was as ready for Nellie as Ase could make it. It was at least immaculately clean. He had engaged a girl, Hulda Svenson, of a new-come Swedish family, for the past two weeks. She had given the first week to cleaning and preparing the log cabin. Amelia, trapped in her own angry decision, had moved there, taking the best pieces of furniture from the house. She had settled down in self-imposed martyrdom, slyly pleased with what she considered her new weapon. Her treacherous younger son and his scheming bride had put her out of her own home. Benjamin would be outraged by their treatment of her when he returned.

Ase brushed his black felt hat and looked about. The wood-boxes were freshly filled. Hulda had cooked and baked generously, had laid the dining-room table with a white linen cloth and the best china and silver, for two. She had brought a table bouquet of fern and geraniums from her mother's house plants. The windows shone, the cleanliness emphasized the bleakness. The sitting-room was bare without the cherry secretary and walnut centre table. He dared not leave strong fires, but the dampered stove and range would hold considerable heat for an hour or two. He put on the broadcloth greatcoat that had once been Ben's and was too short of sleeve for him. The March day was raw and he would be more comfortable in the old buffalo coat, but its shabbiness seemed unsuitable. He walked to the cabin and knocked on the door. Amelia opened it a crack.

She said: "You're wasting your time. I haven't changed my mind. I'm not going. I want everyone to know exactly where I stand. Go on."

She closed the door. He turned away. He drove in the light buggy against a blustering wind towards his marriage. There were no more than half a dozen carriages hitched at the Wilson place. The guests were Nellie's relatives and closest friends. Tim McCarthy waited for him at the door. His presence was comforting. Ase was unable to shake off the feeling that he was an outsider. The Wilsons wore an unwonted solemnity. Nellie was their treasure and the wrong bridegroom had come for her. He had an instant of panic when it seemed that he was indeed taking what did not belong to him. Ben should be here in his place. He should have been the one to go and Ben to stay.

He saw Nellie with her father by the fireplace banked with house plants. He had expected to see her in bridal gown and veil. She wore a dove-grey silk suit, the only bridal touch her flowered toque with a wisp of veiling. She was matronly and collected. The costume, he supposed, was tactful. The preacher motioned. The ritual drew him into its formal pattern.

"Do you, Asahel, take this woman——"

His blood hummed in his ears. Her hand was warm in his.

"I do."

With all his heart, oh, with all his heart. McCarthy handed him the ring.

"With this ring I thee wed."

It was a gift from Tim. It had been his mother's and generations before her had shone on the hand of an Irish chieftain's bride. It was wide, of hand-beaten reddish gold, massive with some mystic, forgotten design. Nellie eyed it with delight. She gave him a quick look of surprise and pleasure. She lifted her face for the nuptial kiss. In the rear of the room Tim broke into a soft tune on his fiddle. The Wilsons crowded around.

The noon wedding breakfast was hearty. There was hard cider for the men and elderberry-blossom wine for the ladies. The house was like a bee-hive with chatter, metallic with the clatter of silver and dishes. Nellie moved here and there, exhibiting her ring, accepting the guarded congratulations. The marriage had astonished them all. Ase ate and drank patiently, shook hands, watching for a sign from Nellie to be away from the confusion. She left the room to give instructions to her brothers for her vast pile of belongings. They would bring these to her the following morning by wagon. There were chests of china and linen, trunks of clothing, trays of ferns and flowering winter plants, boxes of preserves and jellies and vegetables and fruits of her own canning. The family had given her a cherry highboy and table to replace those Amelia had taken to the cabin. Her dog Shep was to be brought, and her mother cat with the last litter of kittens. Shep leaped against her, aware of the impending change. She beckoned to Ase.

"This crazy dog will just follow me anyway, Ase. We might as well take him with us."

He nodded.

She said: "Come on, let's get away."

They ran from the shower of rice and old shoes. McCarthy stood with the buggy at the door, holding the stallion's head. Ase handed Nellie in and turned to shake hands with his friend.

"You can come to the house now, Tim."

"Praise be. The barn's no place for fiddling. I'll wait a decent time of days before rapping on your door."

He leaned close and drew Ase down to whisper in his ear.

"I'd not be telling Nellie about the ring. 'Twould spoil it for her to know it came from the McCarthys."

He winked and waved them off. Dan reared and set out at a fast trot for his home stable, threatening to bolt for it. Ase needed both hands to control him. The March slush flew from the wheels. Bare tree limbs lashed against a grey sky. Nellie was silent. He lifted her down at the Linden door. He was obliged to let her enter the house alone, for Dan was plunging. When he came through the woodshed into the kitchen, carrying her valise, she was putting wood in the range. Shep had found a proper dog's corner behind the wood-box. He beat his feathered tail on the floor in contented acceptance. Wherever Nellie was, Ase thought, was home for both of them. He took the wood from her, filled the range and opened the damper. He put his arms around her and laid his cheek against hers. The moment was too profound for passion. She patted his arm and drew away.

"Let me change my clothes, Ase. I've already got some smut on this silk."

He and Hulda had prepared Amelia's front downstairs bedroom, but Nellie would have none of it.

"I can play her game, too. We keep her room just as it is, all ready for her, for everybody to see. She'll draw in her claws after a while."

She chose the large bedroom above it that had been Ase's father's. It had a matching open fireplace and was well furnished with hand-made black walnut and cherry pieces, including a large four-poster bed with a hard horsehair mattress. Her own feather bed would supplement. She would need another dresser for her own belongings. She sent him downstairs. He built up the fire in the sitting-room stove. Nellie appeared shortly, pert and pretty in fresh blue and white ruffled gingham. Her hair was still pinned on top of her head in the matronly fashion that had so dismayed him. He felt for the pins with clumsy fingers and loosened curls fell around her face to her shoulders. She laughed.

"I was trying my best to be Mrs. Linden and you've spoiled it."

He wanted to explain that she was little Nellie Wilson still to him, and ever would be. He could only stand and drink in the sight of her. The clock struck five of the afternoon.

She said: "You'll have to change your clothes to do the chores."

He was unwilling to sit at their bridal supper in common shirt and jeans. He kept a pair of overalls at the barn and he would be careful. It was dangerous to leave her for a moment, he might well only have dreamed her presence, might return to find her gone.

He said: "Wait for me."

He took the milk-bucket and went to the barn.

Nellie had the milk-pans ready for his return. She had set a few of Hulda's foods on the dining-room table. She was frowning.

"Who set the table, Ase? It's laid for two. What do we do about your mother? Take a tray to her?"

"Hulda took her everything this morning."

"Good for Hulda. Ready in a minute then."

She held her finger to the light, the red-gold of her ring showing burnished.

She said: "Never thought you'd have anything so handsome for me. Where'd you find it?"

He spoke the truth proudly.

"It was a gift from Tim McCarthy. It belonged to his mother."

"Oh."

As he watched, the gold seemed to turn to brass.

Nellie said: "A pity. I thought maybe it was valuable."

She took warmed foods from the oven. The hanging lamp shed soft light and shadow over the white napery. He kissed her gravely before they sat down. He said a silent grace of thanks for her, presiding over their table. The wind blew in gusts down the chimney, a pleasant intruder, like the dog, who waited politely from the kitchen threshold for his own plate. Ase helped Nellie with the supper dishes and put them away in the cupboard. She would need a day or so, she said, to find where things belonged, not that she was likely to keep them as they were. She went upstairs ahead of him. He turned Shep out of doors for a few minutes, brought a piece of old carpet from the woodshed for a bed for him by the range, filled the wood-box, wound the clock, and went with a lighted candle to the bedroom. Nellie had put a match to the fire laid on the hearth. It was blazing and when he had undressed he blew out the candle.

She drew back the bed covers for him. There were lace and blue ribbons at the throat of her night-dress. Her eyes were bright in the firelight. Her breathing was fast. He was trembling but there was no uncertainty in his strong arms and limbs. She met him avidly. The miracle mounted on pulsing wings, soared over spaceless peaks and throbbed away into the distance with silver feathers fluttering. A hard beating recalled him, like a drum. It was his heart. She was limp, her heart pounding, too, and he held her tight, never to let her go, Nellie, his love, his own.

She said: "Well!"

The word had an odd note, as though she were agreeably

surprised. He stroked her soft hair. Her skin was silky as her wedding-suit. Her throat under his lips was like the down of milk-weed. His power surged again, he drew the night-dress from her shoulder and kissed its roundness. She did not respond. The firelight flickered high and he saw that her eyes were closed. She was sound asleep. For an instant he felt abandoned in a lonely valley. But she was such a little thing—— she looked more child than woman, her cheeks flushed, her curls tousled on the pillow. She was tired, he thought, as a child is tired. He held her carefully, his arms cramping under her.

She roused towards midnight and came to him again. The great wings bore him higher than before. Her response was that of some famished creature finding food. When he released her, she was panting.

He said: "Oh Nellie——"

Her breathing slowed. He reached for her, to draw her close. She moved his hand from her breast.

"I can't sleep that way."

She turned on her side, away from him. She reached behind her and touched his hand in reassurance.

"'Night, now."

He lay stiffly. She was not asleep. She gave a little sigh that was neither of repletion nor of drowsiness. It struck ice to him, as though a window had blown wide in a bitter gale. He had fed her hunger. He would always be able to feed it. He knew with a sense of desolation that the bread he offered, though it nourish her, was without salt or leavening.

<h1 style="text-align:center">★ 8 ★</h1>

THE early morning mist filled the valley. The willow trees along the stream lifted through it like cloaked and long-armed travellers rising from a night of sleep beside the water. The mist was milky, holding a subtle nourishment for the young leaves of maples and the pale timid buds of wild apples. Oak and beech and elm still brooded, leafless. The earth in late April was expectant. The winter wheat pushed up green spears anxiously, long confined by snow. A lone phoebe spoke from the woods, not quite singing.

The team of horses snorted the damp air from their nostrils. Ase's feet behind the plough sank deep into the moist loam. He was reverent before the first spring ploughing. It was better than anything except the harvest. The growing period was too disturbing, with its threats of undue rains or untimely drought, of unseasonable frost, sometimes of summer hail. No, it was the sowing time was best. Who knew then, scattering the seed, what fabulous crops, what strange magnificent ear or head of grain, might not follow? He felt so, too, about his unborn children.

The sun brushed the last of the mist from the willows. The thin pendulous arms showed a pale green covering. A flight of red-winged blackbirds circled over the marsh, late this year, Ase thought, in their homecoming. Turning at the end of a furrow, he looked up at the house. He saw Nellie come into the side-yard and begin hanging out the washing. At this distance, she was a little girl pinning up doll clothes. He saw Shep race around the corner and make off with a blue shirt from the basket, the wet arms trailing. He reined in the horses to watch Nellie give chase, around and around, her curls flying, until Shep allowed her to catch him. Then she was bending over him, and when she released him, the dog was wearing the blue shirt, his front legs through the sleeves, the collar buttoned around his shaggy neck. He heard Shep's barking and Nellie's impish laugh.

He clucked reluctantly to the team. His grave young face was as softened with its smile as the square house with the morning brightness. The shirt would need to be washed over again anyway, and Nellie must have her fun. She was a constant and incredible delight. She had plunged into her homemaking with gaiety and zest. She was a lamp in a dark house, a fire on a cold hearth, food on a bare table, and she had brought him in from the outerness to light, to warm, to nourish him. Ase was a little eased of his fears for her content. Yet his knowledge of their shared loss kept his brother always in his mind. He ploughed abstractedly all the morning until he heard the ringing of the great bell calling him to dinner. The massive iron bell was hung above the loft of the carriage

barn beside the house, and he smiled again, thinking how
Nellie made a game, too, of ringing it, falling clownishly flat
as she pulled each time on the heavy rope.

The noon meal was on the table when he had finished
his slow stabling, watering and feeding of the team and
had washed up at the outside pump. Nellie was pouring
coffee. He took the pot from her and set it back on the
wood range. He tousled her curls with his big hands. He
kissed the back of her plump moist neck. She was not for the
moment amorous and she squirmed away. She pushed the
two big cups of coffee into his hands and he took them to the
dining-room. She followed with hot biscuits. She would
indeed seem a little girl playing house, except for her
efficiency and talent. She moved with the quickness of a wren
and had the house immaculate within an hour each morning, except on the strenuous weekly cleaning day. Even his
abstraction about food recognized her genius as a cook. The
winter supplies were going fast, but she worked miracles
with ham and bacon and poultry, with puddings and pies
and tarts from her wild berry jams. The windows had come
to life with her curtains, with ferns and potted geraniums
and fuchsias. She pointed to the table bouquet of wilting
spring violets.

"Bring me back something fresh this evening. Trillium's
nice, the red ones."

He had smelled arbutus under the leaf-mould in the
hemlock wood by the bog, but by the time he had finished
the slow chewing of his mouthful of food, to tell her, she
was chatting about her garden plans.

She said: "Listen!"

It was seconds before he heard the wheels on the road, the
'Whoa!' and a wagon stopping. Nellie looked the table over
quickly, estimating the amount of food, and was at the back
door at the moment of the unmistakable peddler's rap. It
was to be hoped it was the familiar tinker, for the Linden
house pots and pans were too meagre for her needs; but it
was a stranger. He was a little man with red cheeks and nut-
brown eyes. Shep greeted him amiably, recognizing the good
earth smell of clothes and body. The peddler cradled a
bundle of twigs in his arms.

Ase, behind Nellie, said: "Good-day, sir."

The little man bobbed his head politely. Nellie poked his bundle. He lifted one finger, warning of a mystery and a revelation.

"Guess! You'll never!"

She said: "Fiddle. It's kindling. I want pie-pans."

"They just look like kindling, child. Oh, but the life's in them. They're full of sap."

He nodded and pulled the sacking aside, as though he showed the face of an infant.

"Apple trees! And peach in the wagon, and pear and plum and cherry. Imagine!"

His zest was contagious. He was as full of sap as he claimed for his twigs. Ase felt an excitement. He had been inquiring where he might buy fruit trees, and now they arrived at his door, an orchard come to him of its own accord. The clock struck half after noon. Nellie bustled to china cupboard and kitchen, laid a place for the visitor, brought coffee and poured buttermilk and water.

"Sit down and have your dinner, and talk your business with Mr. Linden. I've an errand." And she busied herself with a wicker basket and was gone.

The peddler heaped his plate and sighed. He bowed his head an instant, more in gratitude to Nellie than to God. Few tables this time of year were so bountiful.

"You are kind to a traveller, Mr. Linden."

Ase cleared his throat.

"The name is——?"

"McCarthy, sir. McCarthy."

He held a chicken leg sideways, like a fiddle-bow, and Ase knew now what the man would say as he was saying it.

"I have a brother in these parts somewhere. What delicious chicken, juicy inside as my saplings. Heard in Ohio he was around here."

He lifted the drumstick. "And who do you think told me? If I'm not mistaken, your brother, Ben Linden. Unless there's other Lindens, 'twas your brother. But no mention of the little lady—your sister, your wife? This gentleman said his brother might be interested in fruit trees—excuse me," and he reached for a wing—"and my own brother Tim resided in this township."

He dispatched the wing and buttered a biscuit.

"If Tim can be said to reside."

Ase said: "Tim McCarthy works at the farm east of my wife's people, the Wilsons. He comes here often, when his chores are done."

"Well, now. I thirst for the sight of him. So my brother's here and yours is out there. Ohio. Where I raise my beautiful fruit trees. They call me 'Apple McCarthy'."

The strawberry preserves drew one hand, the biscuits the other.

"Your brother Ben, now, he was planning to leave Ohio soon. My, these are wild strawberries, ain't they? Nothing like the wild small fruits for flavour. But my trees are cultivated, grafted, no runts amongst 'em. Biggest apples you ever see, and the peaches, my!"

Ase struggled to ask the impossible question.

"Ben—— My brother."

"Oh yes, Ben Linden. Didn't do as good as he expected, he said. Had him something lined up farther out. Heading on west, he said. Years too late for the California gold, he said, but silver was promising. Fine young man. Make his pile some day, sure. Couldn't decide should he take his Ohio girl with him. Don't do that, I said, they get prettier farther on you go. How he laughed at that! Right you are, he said. Would that be gooseberry jam? Thank you. Now, the fruit trees. How many can you use? Don't let me hurry you."

Not as well in Ohio as he expected——

What had Ben expected? The Ohio farm lands were said to be so rich that by the time a man finished dropping the seed corn, the first kernel had sprouted. But Ben would never look to land to make his fortune, unless to buy and sell it. That too would seem dull to him. He was forced on, to the west, towards gold and silver, towards some fabulous cave of diamonds. Ase wondered if the Pacific Ocean would halt his brother. Perhaps when he reached that far watery line he would turn and retrace his steps. But years from now. Years from now. Ben would make the continent last him a long time.

McCarthy said: "I specially recommend my Albemarle pippins."

Ase said: "I've been wanting a sizeable apple orchard across the road. I want mixed fruit trees for the house. But isn't autumn a better time for setting?"

Speech was not so difficult when he talked of things he knew, of crops and trees and stock.

"I see you know your business, young man. Autumn's much better. But if we get plenty of rain, you'll have a year's start. And a young fellow with as strong a back as yours wouldn't kill himself if he had to water a few acres of saplings. Come on out to the wagon."

Ase realized that he had forgotten his mother's dinner and that Nellie had taken it to her at the cabin.

He said: "I'd like my mother and my wife to have a say. I'll get them."

He turned back.

"When you give my mother news of Ben——"

The little man nodded.

"Oh, you can trust me. I carry messages for families clear across the country. Every mother's son is half Midas and half saint."

He winked. "Helps business to bring good news. But you, now, you're a man that draws the truth."

Because Amelia was not ready to let him go, for fear that he would carry away with him some undelivered word of Benjamin, or from him, Mr. McCarthy was persuaded to stay the night. The evening was the first pleasant one with his mother since Ben had gone. Nellie had been bland in the face of her animus, but the air was constantly tense. Amelia drew from the peddler long and loving messages direct from her son, along with Ohio incidents in which he played a splendid part. She swallowed them whole in her hunger. Amelia turned once sharply, to catch the girl unaware at the talk of Benjamin. Nellie's pretty face seemed as unconcerned as that of a puss meeting last year's tom. When the supper table was cleared, Nellie covered it with a red baize cloth and washed the dishes while the men began their figuring.

Amelia said: "Mr. McCarthy, this farm is mine, but I

consider that my elder son holds a third interest. With my third, I must agree with my younger son."

McCarthy asked politely: "Would the land where the orchard's to go be representing any special third?"

"No, the farm has not been actually divided."

"Then would you be taking the word of a man wise in orchards, if nothing else in the world? This assortment I have written down here will give the finest fruit for family uses and a large market crop besides, to put money in the bank for all of you."

Amelia nodded. The list was Ase's own. Nellie smiled, putting away the extra raspberry tarts in the cupboard. She lifted a finger and McCarthy half-lifted one in return. The little lady would have her snow-apple tree, and the old termagant none the wiser. The list would include Grimes Goldens, Greenings, pippins, russets, Maiden Blush and Northern Spies. A crab-apple tree would go either side of the smoke-house, and along one line of the enlarged fruit and vegetable garden a row of pear trees, Bartlett and Seckel, two peaches, a freestone and a cling, a sweet cherry and a sour, a Greengage plum and a Damson. McCarthy had six grape vines left, Concord, Niagara and Delaware, and an arbour was planned north of the wicket gate. He had a dozen poplar saplings. The Linden house had long needed tall trees before it, for softening. Nellie's heart was set on maples, but the poplars were almost providentially at hand. The poplar was a sad tree, but it grew sturdily and fast. Ase had always liked the tapering spire, the rustling together, like restless hands, of the leaves. Nellie agreed to the purchase and planting.

McCarthy said: "'Tis strange now, this place has been waiting all these years for McCarthy to bring you the fruits of the earth. What a sight 'twill be, all the colours in harvest time of a patchwork quilt. There's the total figure——"

Ase studied the column gravely. It would take almost all his reserve cash. He had hoped to hire an extra hand this summer. That would have to wait, and he would have to put in longer hours of his own. But all his seed was paid for, he would soon have lambs and calves to sell. He could spare the coming colt. Nellie had already brought the hens into higher egg production and had half a dozen brood hens setting early.

McCarthy said: "Ten per cent replacement for any dead in the autumn. Ten per cent off for cash. 'Tis a good deal for me, for you'll be taking all my stock before it dries on me."

Ase brought out the tin cash-box. Apple McCarthy looked away tactfully while he counted out the money. Amelia leaned forward and swept it into three rough piles.

"There. We'll say the orchard's owned three ways. You can put the three names on your receipt, Mr. McCarthy."

Ase stared at the divided cash. The slips of engraved paper, the discs of metal, had been last year's wheat and corn, to be exchanged in turn for other rich and living things, if only the willing labour of a strong man's back and hands. The money seemed now not the gift of fruiting vines, but an unclean medium for human division.

Nellie said: "That's right, Mother Linden."

She winked at McCarthy. Their quick little minds met like the juncture of two bright brooks. He picked it up.

"Right indeed. You'll be marking off the unborn orchard, so's if it has to be watered in a dryness, it's every man for himself, and God, I suppose, to take care of the watering of Benjamin's portion."

Amelia's spite retreated, like a snake crawling away.

She said: "Why—I didn't mean it that way. Only to make things clear."

"And clear they are, to McCarthy surely. The receipts, Ma'am, here you be."

She said: "I'll go back to the cabin, Asahel. No, don't come with me. Just light my lantern. Good-night."

McCarthy sighed after her.

"Ah, but families do be a mixed-up business. 'Tis that has kept me a bachelor man. There's more peace amongst the apples."

The soft spring night was suddenly violated by a dog fight, a mild one, only the token bravery of Nellie's Shep against an intruder. The intruder proved after all a friend, for it was Tim came through the door, the two dogs wagging themselves behind him. He looked around timidly.

61

"I've been lurking about till the old lady should be leaving," he said. "Pray God 'twas not some other lanthern flickering down the road."

He was struck by the stillness, and then he knew his brother.

"Ah—— 'Tis you—— These many years now!"

The two small men, as like as bird's eggs in a nest, wrapped short arms around each other, thumped each other's backs, and wiped away an Irish tear or two.

Ase thought: 'This is why I trusted the stranger's dry twigs instantly. I knew him for the same as Tim.'

An almost physical pain struck him. He longed to have himself and Benjamin enwrapped as closely as these two other brothers.

Tim said: "To the glory of God, I brought me fiddle with me, and Ase here would be having his flute handy, and, Brother, did you not bring along your harmonica, I'll swear I never knew you."

The music seemed to Ase the best he had ever known. Tim's fiddle outdid itself, the harmonica filled in all the empty spaces, and his own flute was almost as sweet as he had ever hoped for. It was Nellie, he thought, who made the difference, even more than the new added instrument and the delight of the McCarthys in their meeting. She patted her foot and laughed and tossed her curls at the lively tunes, and when Tim twanged the first notes for a gypsy song she stood on tiptoe and lifted her arms like a butterfly's wings, and danced and spun deliriously in the Linden parlour that had so long been gloomy.

She brought cool sweet milk from the cellar, and doughnuts, and they ate with a sleepy satisfaction. The McCarthys separated, Tim to call his white dog to follow him down the road, his brother to the Lindens' downstairs company bedroom.

Nellie said: "Ase, I don't like what your mother said about owning the farm. Is it true?"

"Yes."

"Ben told me he was giving you his share. I thought your father left the property to you two boys."

"No."

"Oh. Then she can—— Has she made a will?"

"I don't know. Nellie, it doesn't matter."

"It certainly does matter. I tell you, I don't like it at all."

She cleared away the plates and went ahead of him to bed. The house was still. Ase went to the cupboard and brought out Ben's geography left from the Academy. He turned the pages slowly. The United States of America. Here they were now. Here beyond and south was Ohio. On the broad splayed map it seemed quite clear. Here was the West. He pictured its spread and desolation. The West went farther. Here was the end, the continent ended. This, now, was the Pacific Ocean.

Oh, Benjamin, my brother, he begged, stop there. I shall tend the orchard.

★ 9 ★

APPLE McCARTHY seemed to be made unhappy by Nellie's breakfast. He eyed sorrowfully the pile of griddle cakes on his plate. He poured maple syrup over them until his plate ran with gold. He took a tentative forkful, laid down his fork, swallowed a mouthful of the strong coffee lightened with heavy spooned cream, and reached for the platter of savoury sausages. He chewed, staring at nothing, then pushed his plate aside.

"'Tis punishment," he said, "nothing but punishment."

Nellie lifted her eyebrows.

"What's the complaint about my cooking, Mr. McCarthy?"

The little man beat his chest with his fists.

" 'Complaint!' says she! 'Complaint!' 'Tis the cruelty of life I complain of, to be in heaven and then kicked out again. Lucifer, that's me, Lucifer McCarthy. If I could leave me stummick here behind me, mayhap I could bear the road."

Nellie laughed.

"That's one way of asking for more hot cakes," she said, and went to the smoking griddle on the range.

McCarthy said: "Look now, Asahel Linden. Would this be fair or would it not be fair? I to stay a bit to help you

plant the fine young trees, whilst Mistress Linden sets a
place for me at your table. No charge on either side."

Ase said: "The work is worth good wages, but I'm short
on ready money."

"'Tis a deal, then."

He buttered his fresh six-inch stack of griddle cakes.

"Now I can eat me fill with a clear conscience."

He sighed.

"Where on the blessed earth would I be getting better
board and company? After all, I but part with the little trees
to pass the time and make me simple living."

It was agreed that haste must be made on the planting.
The saplings had been long on the road. McCarthy had kept
them moist in their burlap wrappings. They were instinct
with life, the tight buds were aware of April, and if the
stirring roots did not soon find foothold and nourishment,
an orchard would die a-borning. With time to spare, it would
have been best first to plough the entire acreage, but the
loamy soil was soft with spring, grass and weeds yet tender,
and Ase began the digging of holes to receive the beginnings
of trees. Apple McCarthy followed behind him, expert with
the setting, the tamping down of the earth. Working back
towards the log cabin at the end of the second row, Ase
looked up to see his mother staring from the window. She
appeared at the house for the noon dinner, but Apple had
given out of inventions concerning her Benjamin. She
queried him closely as to whether Benjamin was certain
already to have left Ohio. She had been thinking, she said,
that she might ride there in the apple-wagon. Something
had prevented her son's return, an illness that he was hiding,
or a temporary lack of funds. Or if he was on the way to
making his fortune, he would rejoice to have her join him, at
least for a while.

"I promise, Ma'am, he was leaving for westward close
behind me, and where you'd be finding him now, no man
can tell you."

She did not appear in the house again.

The planting went fast and well. The completed field
had a strange appearance.

Apple said to Nellie in private: "At the moment, 'tis as

though the old harridan in the cabin had raised a crop of witches' brooms."

The geometric pattern of stark black twigs was more of graveyard than of nursery. Fire might have swept an orchard, leaving this stricken residue. But the fire was in the mounting sun, the sun unwrapped the sheathed buds with hot fingers, showers came daily, the roots clutched and swelled, and one morning Ase saw under the early mist a drift of palest green. The young orchard was in leaf, it had come through, it was alive.

Apple McCarthy was reluctant to move on. Nellie complained of the delay to her own kitchen garden and took him for helper there. He used his horse and Ase's Brinly plough to turn the ground. She was ambitious, and after the past Linden leanness the fenced plot she planted seemed enormous. There were carrots and beets, cabbages and turnips and rutabagas, Irish potatoes and sweet, peas, tomatoes and lettuces, onions and sweet corn, pole beans and simlins and patty-pan squash and cucumbers. Ase's commercial planting would provide her with string beans, and pumpkins and Hubbard squash were to be planted with his field corn. She drove over the countryside in the light buggy collecting seeds and slips of herbs from her friends, mint and thyme, sage and dill, rose geranium, sweet lavender and rosemary.

Ase ploughed the apple orchard and sowed buckwheat broadcast. Nellie turned from the kitchen garden to flowers, and Apple McCarthy said it must be his last bit of helping, for the pot-belly her table had given him was in the way of his stooping. She was up with the morning star, cooking breakfast by lamplight, and by the time the birds were twittering sleepy fragments of song and the pale early sun washed the polished floor and bright braided rugs with silver, breakfast was over, Ase sent to Amelia with a special tray, and Nellie was out of doors, digging as busily as the robins pulling earthworms near her. Ase lingered in his coming and going, to watch her, round and plump, her curls damp over her intense, flushed face.

Tim McCarthy came every evening. The twilights lengthened. The yard grass grew thickly and Ase herded the sheep across the road to crop it smooth. Ase and Nellie and the brothers sat on the sweet grass to play and sing. Shep beat his plumed tail beside Nellie, and her mother cat, bulging again, came from the barn to sit heavily in her lap and purr. A lamp burned late in the cabin on the brightest nights, and if Amelia heard and hated the sound of music and of laughter, she gave no sign. Ase went several times to say good-night to her, but as his footsteps approached her door, the light went out and there was no answer to his rap.

June came in, the buckwheat made a tapestry for the embroidery of the full-leaved apple saplings, Nellie's garden was up, with satisfaction she picked the first greens and the first early flower. Apple McCarthy hitched his well-fattened horse to his wagon and was at last on his way, woeful in parting. The summer passed in hard work, for Ase was single-handed at heavy crops that needed at least another hand. Nellie was in a frenzy of canning and preserving. The mother cat littered behind the woodbox in the kitchen and Nellie moved in a welter of kittens until the most ambitious climbed to the table and upset the cream, when the whole batch was relegated again to the barn.

In August Nellie informed Ase that she was with child. She had suspected it a month ago, but was only now certain. The birth would come some time the following April. He was profoundly stirred, but she was as casual as though she announced a pleasant morning. A woman was wed, she tended her household, she bore her children. She laughed at his gravity and tweaked his long nose.

"If you'd worked a little harder," she said, "it would have started earlier. I'd rather have my babies come in the winter and have it out of the way by spring."

He supposed that the large size of the Wilson family made birth to her more commonplace. He asked her permission to give his mother the good news. She nodded.

"Sooner or later something will bring her around," she said. "Maybe this will do it."

He found Amelia dipping water from the spring by the cabin. He laid his hand on her shoulder. He could say only the few necessary words.

66

"Mother, Nellie's going to have a baby."

She lifted the dipper to her thin lips, then poured the remainder of the clear icy water over her hands.

"Of course. I told you myself. Very soon now, too."

She leaned over the pool and in its mirror carefully arranged her crow-black hair.

★ IO ★

NOTHING was real to him except the scent of lilacs. He had slept a little towards morning. Wakening, his thoughts were as nebulous as the April dawn. He was suspended in a grey void, and it seemed that he and Benjamin were dead together, and some other with them, whom he could not place for the moment. He had not meant to sleep. And had he slept, and was he now awake? When a man closed his eyes at night he did not know whether he would open them in the morning. And was he then dead or living? He did not, himself, know. Only another, observing his breathing, could say: "The man is not dead, but sleeping."

A breath of April wind stirred the curtains and the fragrance of the lilacs came stronger and with it that sense of danger. He started up from the couch and staggered a little. Nellie's lilacs, that was it. Nellie had brought the lilac bushes from her father's home—when was it?—a year ago, and they were in bloom, sickening of odour, and Nellie was in labour with his child. Now he heard her cry. He went to the pump to splash cold water on his face and hands, for it seemed only decent to be clean as he went to her.

Aunt Jess the midwife met him at the door of the downstairs bedroom.

She whispered: "The pains are coming faster. I think she'll make it soon. Come in and speak to her."

He groped to the side of the great white-sheeted bed. Nellie was as white, but veins stood out as blue as her eyes. Her curls were wet on the pillow. She turned her head towards him.

An agony seized her and her face twisted. She moved her

head from side to side and moaned. The midwife gripped her hands.

"Bear down harder, Nellie dear, bear down. Aunt Jess is holding on to you. Ase, you'd better get out. Call the girl. Get my hot water going, lots of it."

He stumbled to the kitchen. He had kept a low fire all night in the range, and in minutes he had it roaring, and pots and kettles filled with pure spring water, and boiling. The Swedish girl, Hulda, hired for the time being, came down the back stairs rubbing the sleep from her eyes, then seemed to shake herself, and went into brisk action. She trotted back and forth with hot water and cloths warmed in the open oven. She took a moment out to start a pot of coffee.

"Don't leave it boil over, Mr. Linden."

He should be doing his chores, he thought, but he could not bring himself to leave the house. The first ray of sun reached the garden and pointed like a finger to a few early green sprouts. Nellie had worked in the garden for an hour after her first pains, her chubby little fingers scarcely reaching past her great belly to press a plant here, scatter a row of home-saved seeds there. It seemed to him that all planting of seed was a man's work, but she had driven him out when he had finished cultivating, fertilizing and laying off the rows. Green stuff made good milk for the cow, she had said, and winked, and she knew the way she wanted it. The hired girl scurried in for another kettle of water, sweating.

She panted: "Coming fine, Mr. Linden. Don't look so mournful."

The words were like a bone thrown to a good dog by the fire. He felt lost, almost an outsider. The world had turned completely female. He seemed to have had nothing to do with the child, nothing with the woman. He was only tolerated in his own house. The she-rites of fertility possessed it. He heard then the wail, the strange, anguished, angry protest against human birth. He stood up, shivering. Where had the creature of his making come from, that it was so disturbed to leave? What would be his share in making its life not quite as intolerable as the scream said it feared? When the midwife at long last called him, her voice was

68

triumphant, that of an Amazon blowing a trumpet made for a woman's mouth.

He walked past her to the bed. He had a moment's dread that Nellie would turn her head away from him. How could a woman forgive a man for so much pain. He had forgotten her own cat-like pleasure. He looked down at her. Aunt Jess had bathed her with sweet-smelling soap, and dressed her in her bridal night-gown with lace ruching at the throat, had brushed her shining curls and tied them with a blue satin ribbon. Nellie's eyes were twinkling.

"'Twasn't much fun," she said.

She arranged mysterious folds of cloth at her side, drew one away to show the child, red, wrinkled, apparently blind, and wretched. She puckered her own face in imitation.

"If 'twasn't a boy," she said, "I'd say, drown it. Guess being ugly don't matter."

He stared. He had helped with the birthing of countless lambs and calves and colts. He had come on baby squirrels and foxes in the nests. This was his first sight of a new-born human. All the other animal young arrived complete, contented. It was as though they were born knowing—or not knowing—some fearful secret.

He said: "I suppose he'll change. Nellie—how are you?"

She patted her stomach under the covers.

"Empty, thanks be. Empty of everything. I'm hungry."

The great bulk of Aunt Jess filled the doorway. Her face shone like a harvest moon.

"Fine boy there, Ase. Never brought a better. You'll have help on the farm before you know it."

He looked with a vast surge of pity at the miserable little bundle of flesh. It was blood of his blood, flesh of his flesh, bone of his bone. It would be a fine thing to have a tall son to plough and harvest with him, to plant seeds and crops and fruiting trees perhaps as yet unknown of. It was also shocking to imagine this unhappy thing, now making sobbing sounds in its throat, as already precipitated into the world, toiling with hard hands, its back bent under more weight of hoe or axe or pitchfork. He yearned over his son and over his beloved who had borne him.

Nellie said: "Now maybe he won't want to farm. His

69

Uncle Ben didn't. Aunt Jess, go tell Hulda to fix me a big breakfast."

He reached out for her hand and knelt and held it against his cheek. It was so small and warm, so strong and certain. His fear for her fragility left him and he put his arms around her.

She said: "Better send Hulda down the road soon to call Ma. You have your breakfast, then go bring your mother."

He had been astonished from the beginning by her patience with Amelia. The venomous barbs had fallen away from her soft skin as though it were underlaid with rawhide. He was touched now, and grateful. Nellie had refused to have her mother in the house during her labour. He believed that she had forbidden it to save embarrassment at the exclusion of his own. Actually, her animal instinct had insisted on the presence only of the capable midwife.

Ase brought Amelia to the room before Nellie's mother had time to arrive. Amelia might surprise them all, he thought, by behaving well, but he felt safer to take no chances. She began by speaking courteously enough.

"A boy, Ase says. That's good. Men are needed around here. You don't look as if you'd suffered."

Nellie patted the blue satin bow. The glitter in her eyes was surely a sign of well-being.

"Take a look at him. Pretty as his Pa."

Amelia eyed the infant.

"What will you name him?"

Nellie said: "We sort of thought you'd like to have another Benjamin."

Ase was puzzled. They had agreed on the name of Nathaniel, if the baby was a boy. Amelia stepped back from the bed.

"Haven't you any decency at all?"

Nellie's bright eyes widened.

"Why, Mother Linden, what do you mean?"

Amelia was trembling.

"After you and Benjamin—oh, you are a shameless thing."

"You mean it would look as if it was Ben's baby. Guess you've forgotten Ben's been gone a year and a half. They don't make babies out of old women's nasty ideas."

It seemed to Ase that he must reach out to pull his mother from this trap Nellie had laid for her. Yet perhaps Nellie had been right, to force Amelia into the open, and so lay a ghost. He laid a hand on his mother's arm. She shook it off.

"Forgotten how long he's been gone? Every hour's been a drop of blood gone out of me."

She put her handkerchief to her lips.

"I'm sorry, Nellie, for what I suggested. I was—mistaken. But I must forbid the name of Benjamin. He will want it for a son of his own."

"Well, then, how about 'Nathaniel,' Ase? Call him 'Nat' for short. You can stop a dog or a boy better with a short name, when they're getting into mischief."

Amelia gathered her torn dignity about her and nodded.

"A very good name. It's been in the family. I, of course, shall always call the child by the full name."

She turned to leave.

"But don't get the idea that the boy makes any difference about the land."

The battle, then, was a draw, but with blood let on both sides. Somehow the air was clearer. He opened a window, and past the white ruffled curtains blowing came the scent again of the lilacs, not now quite so sickening.

★ II ★

McCARTHY was playing his fiddle from the wintergreen beside the bog. The last of the hayers had gone home in creaking wagons, whistling to be done so early of an August day. Ase stood alone in the high south opening of the hay-mow. The new-mown timothy and clover smelled as sweet as honey. The late afternoon sun reached into it, as though long fingers fondled golden hair. Ase liked the colour and texture of hay at any time, even towards the end of its life, when brown and dry as an old woman. It was most pleasant at this moment of its fresh cutting, piled thick and yellow in the big shadowy loft. Soon the mice would breed there and squeak and scurry, the barn cats would climb the ladder

71

to hunt them, the hens would leave their own house with its trim rows of troughs to steal their nests in the fragrant softness, having at last to be helped down ignominiously with their broods of downy biddies, to more conventional quarters.

McCarthy's fiddle grew harsher, the sound like robins chirping. Ase smiled. Tim was signalling him to join him with his flute. A week of good work was over. His winter wheat had ripened early, the thrashers had come, a score of them, the days had been filled with the rich noise and confusion of the threshing machine, the talk and roars of laughter of the neighbour men come to help, and since other wheat was not yet ready, they had stayed on to help Ase with his haying. He would join his help to the other, on other farms, a little later. Single-handed he had raised a huge stand of heavy-headed wheat and could afford next year a hired hand of his own. Wheat was bringing more than two dollars a bushel, and after saving out next year's seed and enough to take to the mill for the grinding of his own flour, with middlings and good bran left over for his stock, and paying the miller his tithe of the grain, he would have several hundred bushels to sell for cash.

He took his flute from a broad beam in the hay-mow. He played a few notes on it. They fluttered like the cry of turtle-doves, joining the robins. He walked slowly up the sheep-lane, up through the high south pasture, towards the bog.

The scent of the wintergreen, crushed by Tim's sitting, met him along with Tim's dog. He stooped under the low-hanging hemlock boughs and dropped down on the dark redolent carpet beside his friend. The spot, so close to the menacing bog, was secret and satisfying. From the high, shaded place he could see the entire farm, with the great square house looking white in the sunlight, and far away. An odour stronger than the wintergreen came to him. McCarthy was drinking again.

Tim said plaintively: "Fancy now, the first time we've been to play together since the past sweet spring-time."

Ase put his flute to his lips.

"No, boy, now I have you alone for the instant, I'd be

talking a bit instead of making the music. I'm somewhat on the drink, and feeling bold. I'll be reading your mind and heart, a thing part happy and a thing part sad."

Ase stroked the head of the white dog and waited. It came to him that he could only be at ease with those who read his mind and heart and spoke aloud for him, where he was unable to speak for himself. Benjamin had sometimes done this for him. This little Irishman, twice his age, often did so, too. Nellie read his heart, for all his wordlessness, but he realized with discomfort that the trackless chaos of his mind had for her no meaning. He corrected himself. It had had no meaning for Benjamin, nor for McCarthy, either, nor the gypsies. The Old One, yes, and Mink the Indian. Crushing a leaf of wintergreen between his strong fingers, listening for what McCarthy, drunken but yet wise, might have to say, he was swept by a wave of loneliness.

Tim said: "You're after being so young, for the things that have come to you. You have the grand pretty wife, the right one for you, and the baby son. You're by way of being prosperous, and you'll be needing the prosperity, for one reason and another, the new babes that will be coming, and the brother. Aye, the brother."

He reached behind him and took a long pull from his jug.

"The brother. And the mother——Now well I know, to cast a slur on a lad's mother is to have him at the throat. I'd not be doing that. 'Tis plain you love the woman, for all the harm she's doing to you, and 'tis this harm of which I'd be speaking. Say nothing, me boy-o, but let me tell it as I see it."

McCarthy had never before gone so far. The hostility between him and Amelia had been quiet and tacit. It seemed to Ase that he must stop his friend at once, for loyalty to his mother, but, as always, he could not answer.

"So, my Ase-one, you have the mother grieving for the other son, and she will be making trouble for you and the sweet Nellie until the end of her life. And what frets me, she'll be having you feeling yourself the hired man on your own property."

Ase knew instantly and unhappily that Nellie had talked with Tim.

Tim continued: "Your mother tells it up and down, not

open, but sly-like, how you're doing the fine job for Benjamin, and it's pleased and astonished he'll be on his return to take over, at the richness building, the new orchard and all. Now I'd not see your heart be broken along with your back. I'm full of ideas, and one is to have it out with the old harridan—excuse me, 'twas me brother's word. Make her sign papers if needs be, not to find your wife and babies by the side of the road one fine day."

McCarthy took another swig.

"You'd not spend the best of your life, would you, working as you work, on land you held but temporary?"

Tim had opened a door to the small dark room he had been avoiding. Ase entered it with relief. He had only half asked himself too many questions. For all his joy in Nellie and the child, in the crops like miracles, the orchard taking hold of the earth with strong roots and young exultant branches, he had suffered from his mother's hints and secret smilings. The first unfaced question had been actually of her sanity. To deny facts, to insist on fancies, was this what made for madness? It seemed to him that every man and woman must do this to some degree, must refuse in the privacy of the mind the unacceptable, taking for truth in the heart the longed-for and desirable. No, he decided, his mother was not truly mad .She had an obsessive love for her absent elder son, but why not? Benjamin drew such love, as he knew for himself. And it was not for him, the younger, quite accidentally unloved, to condemn her vagaries.

He pulled a leaf of wintergreen and crushed and tasted it. McCarthy and the white dog sat quiet. Ase dismissed the next question as he asked it. Ben would not be ever coming home. Here was perhaps the greatest anguish, for in his deepest love and yearning for his brother he feared Benjamin was a lost soul, would always wander, strong and beautiful and admired, incompetent, reckless and futile.

But suppose he was mistaken, that Ben did return, either prosperous as he had boasted, or broken by life. Why, then, the way was clear. Nothing would give him greater content than to share all he had made, had built, with his brother. Powerful or crushed, Ben was so intimate a part of him that it made no difference, Ben could receive all the enriched land or share it, it was all one, when a man so loved his brother.

The land. Ase stroked the little dog. The land. Why, any man had only temporary rights on the earth. His mother's talk of control, of ownership, Tim's talk of legal rights and papers, these were nonsense. No man owned the land. He wondered again how long the earth had existed before the creation, emergence, evolution or what-not, of humans. He had hoped to find the answer in his copy of *Smith's Illustrated Astronomy and Poetical Geography*, but while he still pored of nights over the volume, he was left unsatisfied. He asked himself now what he expected of the land. A thought brushed him briefly as to what he expected of life itself and he dismissed it. But the land. It was not what he expected of it, but what it required of him. He felt himself on firm ground. The land asked to be worked, to be taken care of properly, and in return it would nourish all men, as long as they were indeed its brothers.

McCarthy said: "You are the most wordless man ever, but do be saying in words, would you waste yourself working temporary?"

Ase said: "Why, yes. I would."

He could not understand his mother, nor even his wife, but he had such pity for his mother, such adoration for Nellie, that he would give his best to everything, land, mother, wife, child and vanished brother, to go on steadily. His way was clear. He put his flute to his lips.

McCarthy said: "Then the saints preserve you. I've no more to say."

He tuned his fiddle and lifted his bow. He led off in an Irish lilt. By tacit consent the friends played the gayest of tunes. There was no need today of the sad sweet songs that often eased their shared melancholy. When the sun dropped low west of the bog, Ase went to his belated chores. McCarthy clutched his jug in one arm, his fiddle in the other, and staggered home behind the little white dog. The dog watched over his shoulder, for there were times when his master did not make it.

75

12

NELLIE was cutting dahlias at the far end of the garden. Ase stood motionless by the swinging gate to watch her, as though not to disturb a humming-bird at its darting. She moved quickly from one flower to another, laying the blossoms in a basket on her arm. Beyond the cultivated flowers inside the white picket fence, wild asters were autumn-blue and he saw that Nellie's dress was the same colour. The honey bees were working feverishly and wasps spun drunkenly over fallen and rotting fruits. The smell of harvest was everywhere. Nellie turned and came down the garden path with her skimming trot that was like a plover on the ground. His heart turned over inside him. Her simplest and most habitual movement enchanted him. She saw him standing, tall and dark and gaunt, his lean young face soft with his yearning. His moments of obvious adoration brought out the most mischievous of the constant imp in her. He opened the gate and took the basket from her.

She reached up to put her arms around his neck and said: "Close your eyes if you want something sweet."

He leaned low and self-blinded for the expected kiss. In an instant she slipped a ripe Seckel pear from the basket and crammed it against his mouth. She rescued the basket as he jerked away, startled.

He sputtered: "Nellie!"

She said demurely: "I was going to kiss you, but look at your dirty mouth."

He wiped away the crushed fruit furiously and glared at her. She used her handkerchief solicitously to dab at his lips. Then she laughed. He had never learned, wondered if he ever would, not to fall into her traps. Each time that she tricked and upset him, he was first angry, as she intended, then foolish and fatuous, and she intended that, too. It did not matter. She was Nellie. It was not so much that his discomfort gave her pleasure, he supposed, as that his slowness, the very clumsiness of his devotion, challenged her swift spirit. He sensed that he should, this instant, spank her as she spanked the child Nat, and then carry her upstairs

76

and make some pretence at assault. She was always most fevered after one of her pranks. Yet violence appalled him, seemed both animal and stupid. He could not be otherwise than himself. He took the basket from her and followed her into the house.

He was aroused, too, his senses were acute. Fragrance overwhelmed him at the kitchen door. They were mingled, as notes in music mingled, as bird songs wove themselves together in the spring. They were part of the richness of harvest-time and of life itself. Of life, he corrected himself, with Nellie. The house, until her coming, six years ago, had had a musty, sterile odour. He separated now one scent from another. Apple rings were drying in pans at the back of the slow-burning range. There was the smell of molasses cookies, of raspberry-tarts, of clover and buckwheat honey, of butternuts, hickory and black walnut nuts, the spice of rose geranium Nellie had brought inside in fear of sudden frost. Under the Brussels carpet in the dining-room and the two front rooms fresh oat-straw had been laid down during Nellie's whirlwind autumn house-cleaning, both for winter warmth and softness underfoot, and he was aware of the scent of that too, a usable and comforting part of the harvest. He smelled the freshness of the clean starched white curtains at all the windows. He smelled the acidity of the dahlias and marigolds in Nellie's basket, and under the flowers the pears, the heavy panicles of grapes, purple, white and red, cloying in their sweetness. It was almost too rich a time.

He was obliged to admit to himself that his mother's absence was an important part of his pleasure. Apple McCarthy had written that Ben had been reported somewhere in Indiana, having gone West and planning to return there. Amelia had a cousin in the state and had gone to her at once. Her plan, under the cloak of the unquestioned relatives' long visits, was to search for her son, hither and yon, in Indiana. With her going, a dark storm had passed over, the doors had swung wide, the lavishness of autumn had come inside. There seemed more room in the house, more room in the world. He checked his thoughts in pity. He would give his own contentment if he might so better furnish the cold empty place in which his mother dwelt.

Empty of all but Benjamin. There seemed no question now but that her obsession had taken her a step or two inside that palace of black ice where men are shadows and shadows become men. She had called tentatively down the labyrinthine corridors for her lost son, thinking she heard his voice. A few steps farther, and surely she would find him.

The house was comfortably warm, the sunlight streamed through the polished windows, but Ase felt chilled. He went to the sitting-room stove and touched a match to the pine kindling under maple logs. He pulled a stool close to the blaze and held out his hands to it, palms suppliant. He heard Nellie's quick small feet upstairs, and small sounds that were Nat and the younger boy Arent rousing from their afternoon nap. They seemed far away, another man's wife and children. A gust of wind shook the poplars beyond the house and cast a handful of yellow leaves against the window, then dropped them to the ground. He had planted them, but they were not his poplars. This was not his ground. This was not his house. He was a stranger.

He passed one hand over his eyes and shook his head to clear it. He was impatient with himself, ashamed. He had everything a man could ask for. He wondered in horror if his adoration of Nellie was not love at all, but only the panic of a drowning man clinging to his rescuer. For she was rescue, truly. She was the bridge between his isolation and the warmth and safety of life itself. But his life was good. What was it then he wanted so and needed? He had lost a father to death and a mother to a mania, yet it was not a loss, for he had never possessed them. He had lost his brother. He knew this for a positive pain. And he had not possessed him, either. He asked himself if he wanted Benjamin here with him, working the land against his will. He could not ask this. Did a man's love consist only of the elements that brought him comfort? And why one human being rather than another, or was the love a thing nameless and faceless, given out of a lonely need, as a child clutched a china doll or a rag wrapped round a husk of straw, murmuring endearments? Should he have gone with Benjamin, did he want only to be with him wherever he should go? Or was it his destiny to be always unfilled and lonely? He felt himself coming closer to a truth, and as his heart beat faster, the truth evaded him.

Nellie said: "Ase, for goodness' sake. Brooding again. I called you twice. Here, watch the boys. And don't forget, the red heifer's due to calve. Better keep her in the barn tonight."

He lifted his bowed head. She deposited Arent in his lap and pushed young Nat towards him. He looked at his five-year-old son and Nat stared back at him. From the beginning, the child had eyed him with a certain coldness. He had made clumsy advances, but from his cradle the boy had rejected them.

He longed to draw Nat close against him, to say: "We have both arrived strangely on earth and shall depart strangely, and we are related for the moment, so let us try to speak together, alien as we may appear one to the other."

The little boy said: "You're ugly."

Ase said gently: "I know."

He realized that his sadness offended the child. Yet some children were touched by adult grief, ran with small warm arms outstretched, as though with prescience that one day they too would be grown and even more sorrowful than sometimes happened to them, as though by giving comfort now, they would store it safely away for their own later need and use. Ase was conscious of an unchildlike hardness in Nat. Astonishingly, Amelia had accepted him. When her mind wandered, she called him 'Benjamin's boy'. Nat spent long hours with her at the cabin. Ase wondered if Amelia's tense resistance, her distaste for himself had been passed on to the boy. In his own youth she had often said: "You know, Asahel, you are extremely homely." There was something he should tell Nat this instant, but he could not think what it might be. By way of a lesson in consideration for others, perhaps he might say: "You remember when you cut your finger? When you tell me I am ugly, you hurt me inside, just as the knife hurt you." As he hesitated, Nat ran from the room to the cookie jar, and then to find his mother. Arent whimpered and Ase moved to a rocker and rocked back and forth until Nellie came again. This child was not quite three.

He had not forgotten the red heifer. He had a stall ready

79

for her, thick-bedded with clean straw. He joined the hired man Joe at the barns, Shep at his heels. Nellie's ageing Shep had finally decided that following Ase was on the whole more rewarding than following his mistress. She spent most of the time in the house, and while he was a dog fond of his rug near the kitchen range, beside the wood-box, and returned two or three times a day for a snooze, and to make certain she was there, and safe, the fields and hills and woods with Ase were irresistible. He wagged his feathery tail, for they were a little late in driving in the cows.

Ase said: "I know, Shep. Come on."

The dog bounded ahead and met the cows, already gathered at the pasture gate. The grass was short and dry, the nights were growing cold, and they were anxious for the extra feeding and the protection of the barn. Ase indicated the red heifer in the lane and Shep cut her out, so that she might be driven to her special stall. Ase saw the calf change position in her belly, her bag and teats were swollen, and he prepared the things he would need if she had difficulty with her first birthing. He gave her a wet mash along with her hay.

Joe finished the milking. The hired man was not as clean as he wished. A bit of trash floating on the foam of one bucket told its tale of improperly washed teats. Ase deliberately poured the cats' milk into their dishes from the cleaner bucket. When Nellie saw the trace of dirt as she strained the other, Joe would get the lecture he deserved, but which Ase always found it too embarrassing to give. Unless one of his helps was harsh with animals, he offered no criticism. Every decently raised farm man and boy in the section knew how work should be done, and it seemed to Ase offensive to remind them. In the end, the example of his own slow, steady perfection of labour was likely to convert or shame them when they were remiss. Joe was leaving soon, to work through the winter in a wagon-works. Tim McCarthy had asked for the job, but Nellie with surprising tartness had not allowed Ase to consider it. He leaned over to stroke the gentler of the barn cats, washing their milky whiskers, and sighed. Tim was indeed the most unreliable hand for miles around, too old for much of the heavy work, besides, but he was his friend. Ase felt uneasily that the time was coming when Tim would need actual shelter, and he would like to have slipped him into his household while he was not yet quite impossible. The red heifer mooed anxiously. He studied her and rubbed her nose.

"Not yet, girl. Maybe tonight."

At the door of the kitchen he stopped and smiled to himself. Joe was getting more than his sins warranted. Ase shared Nellie's immaculateness, but her passion for it went to unreasonable bounds. An outsider hearing her now would believe that Joe lived in a pig-sty and had added half its contents to the milk-bucket. Joe came out shaking his head.

He said: "Guess I'll go to town tonight if I can have the wagon. She may start in again."

Ase nodded. He knew Joe was courting.

He said: "Take the buggy."

Joe's grin thanked him. He started to say: "Don't drive Dan too hard," but then could not dampen the man's pleasure. Joe washed up hastily at the pump and tiptoed up the back stairs to his room to change his clothes. Joe should have hitched up before he washed and dressed, Ase thought. Horse-and-leather was a good clean smell, but a woman didn't want it all over a man's hands when he touched her. He decided to take another look at the heifer before supper, and while he was at it, he could have Dan in the shafts by the time Joe reached the stable.

The sun went to bed under a patchwork quilt of the colours of the autumn leaves. He was glad to be delayed outside, to stand and watch it. Nellie was impatient with the autumn of the year, for it means a reduced activity when all the harvest was in, too great a confinement in the winter house for her liveliness. The season stirred him deeply. A man could see what he had accomplished. There was time to sit and think, when his slowness and his thought went unnoticed. Perhaps his mother would return this winter with news of Benjamin after all. Perhaps her Indiana visit would restore her balance.

He waved Joe down the road, acceptably unodorous, and stopped beside the poplars to look back to the south across the barns, the fields, the softly rolling hills. The poplars had

81

grown fast and tall. The corn was in shock, and in the last of the sunset he saw it glinting golden, and the piled heaps of pumpkins as orange as the late October sky. A blue haze hung over the orchard. The orchard, he thought of it tenderly as Ben's orchard, had produced its first large marketable crop. There were still late apples to be picked that needed the touch of frost, the Northern Spies and the russets. These would be the tangiest of all, and would keep all winter long in the stone cellar. The easy summer apples had been sweet but insipid. He wondered if strength and goodness needed a touch of hardship to come to true maturity. No, he decided, this was not necessarily so. His mother had been subjected to the frosts and they had only made her acid.

He washed with special care.

Nellie said: "Did you let that dirty Joe take the buggy again? The wagon's good enough for him. I don't care if he is courting. You're too easy on the help. I'll tell you what you can do, Ase Linden. Keep the buggy for your nasty hired hands. You can buy a new one, just for me. I want one with red wheels and rubber tyres."

He could certainly afford a light rubber-tyred buggy, just for Nellie. He would break the three-year-old colt to it, and she would have her own rig. He wished he had thought of it himself, to have surprised her with the gift, perhaps drive it up to the side door on Christmas morning.

He said: "Why, I'll order it this week."

Nat, staring wide-eyed, began to hop up and down.

He shrilled. "Dirty Joe! Dirty old Joe! Joe can't ride in my mama's new buggy."

He clutched his mother's skirts and wailed: "Can I ride in it, Ma? I can ride in the new buggy, can't I, Ma?"

She tousled the child's tawny hair.

"If you keep clean, the way Mama likes."

Ase's face twitched.

He said meekly: "Can I ride in it, too, if I keep clean?"

She recognized one of his rare, frail attempts at humour and laughed. Nat stamped his foot.

"No, you can't! It's just for Mama and me!"

Nellie snapped: "Behave yourself, Nat. Papa can ride in

it because he's paying for it. It'll be his buggy and then he'll give it to me."

Nat shrieked: "Give it to me, give it to me!"

"Now Mama will slap you in a minute. You grow up to be a big man and make lots of money. Then you can buy all the buggies you want, just for yourself."

"I won't have to let anybody ride in them?"

"Not if you don't want to, if you buy them yourself. They'll be your very own."

"Oh, good!"

Ase was disturbed. A buggy, a wagon, such things were meant to be shared with anyone who needed them. He had once loaned a horse and wagon to a sick tramp, and it had been months before they were returned to him, battered and worn, but the vagrant had reached his home before he died. Ase did not want his child to come to look on property as so personal, to consider it good to exult in an exclusive ownership when another was in need. At the same time, it did not seem suitable to correct the mother in the presence of the boy. In any case, Nat was too young to understand. He had noticed that children seemed innately selfish. Nat would get over it. The farm was only recently prosperous, he and Nellie had worked unspeakable hours, and she was undoubtedly trying to impress it on Nat while young, that money represented hours of human toil. There was time enough, he decided, for his son to learn the other things.

Nellie gave the two children their meal in the kitchen and put them to bed. She and Ase sat leisurely over their supper in the dining-room. The table was laid as always with a fresh white linen cloth, a bowl of late yellow roses was a central core of fragrance, the food was savoury. The intimacy, without Amelia, without Joe, without the youngsters, was overwhelming. He laid his big gnarled hand over Nellie's soft small one. For once, she did not bustle about, clearing the table, washing the dishes, sweeping the kitchen floor. He slipped away to lay a fire on their bedroom hearth. She joined him almost instantly. He held her in what seemed a sweeter closeness than ever before. Perhaps his deepest satisfaction was that he found himself, for her, a great and true lover.

Nellie was asleep, her back turned to him afterwards, as always, when he remembered the red heifer. He left the bed cautiously, not to awaken her, drew on coat and trousers, lit a lantern and went to the barn. The heifer was indeed in trouble. The calf was large and the heifer young. He was obliged to help, to pull the wet thing into the world. The heifer went at once to the devouring of the after-birth. He was familiar with this apparent monstrosity and it had always puzzled him. Yet somehow it made all of life an endless cycle. There was first of all the love, and he was certain the animals felt love as well as humans, for no female of horse or dog or kine could be forced to accept a male unwillingly. So the male element permeated the female, the seed lay deep, as the seeds in the earth, there was the long gestation, the release then, and the triumph of birth and of harvest. Perhaps the bovine swallowing of the after-birth was only another step in the eternal nourishment, beginning the great round once again.

He stepped out into the starlit autumn night. He longed to know the relationship of the planets, the stars, the earth, one to another. His book on astronomy was surely inadequate. There must be another book somewhere that would tell him all he must know of the revolving of these various strange masses. He read the Bible constantly, for its profound study of men in trouble and in joy, for the relation of human living to other living, for the possibility of a man's reaching into the outer space for a comfort the earth did not provide. He was still dissatisfied.

He went quietly to his bed. He lay dozing until the morning, when it was time to visit the red heifer again, to give her, now nursing her calf, an extra feeding, to take care of the rest of the stock, for Joe had not appeared after his own night of pleasure.

* 13 *

THE earth was thirsty for the snow. The winter wheat, in peril of its life, shrank in need to be covered with the soft white blanket. The snow began falling at dusk from a still and milky sky. The flakes at first were large and loose. They slapped against walls, against the boughs and trunks of trees, with the wet impact of a child's kiss. They clung, slipped, melted, and the earth for an hour or more drank them in like rain. With the sudden dark, the air turned cold, the ground stiffened, the snow gathered itself together in compact crystals and fell hard and fast, as though the elements had had enough of softness. The sharp particles hissed against the window-panes, then settled down to a steady pelting.

Ase sensed the coming of the snow in mid-afternoon. He never failed in his planning, but because he worked so thoroughly and so slowly he was often somewhat behind. He had begun but had not finished the laying of straw in the sheep-shed, the placing of salt-pans and the cleaning of feeding-troughs. The hired man Joe had moved on early to his winter factory work, probably to be nearer to his sweet-heart. Ase needed him now and knew he should have insisted that Joe help complete these preparations before leaving. He could not hold any man against his will. Hurry was impossible for him, but he made a more concentrated effort, tense against the tenseness of the sky, and finished the furnishing of the shed for its woolly winter guests. He filled the watering-trough and set out for the high pasture. The dog Shep was anxious, understanding that some routine was about to change. He hesitated when his master did not go in the direction of the cows, followed at his heels uncertainly, then knew in an instant it was the sheep to be brought in, and bounded ahead up the brown hill. The sheep too had felt the impending snow and had taken refuge in the hemlock woods, dangerously near the bog. They were not in sight and Ase was disturbed.

He called: "Sheep, sheep, sheep!"

The sweet tinkle of the wether's bell answered him. Shep heard it, scented the flock, and was far ahead of Ase, to turn them gently, to drive them from the dark woods, over the hill, down the lane and into the shed, snug and welcoming. The bleats were excited, but, hungry after the late poor feeding, the sheep began a contented nibbling on the bean-pods waiting for them. They ate daintily, their velvet noses twitching. Ase heard the first snowflakes plashing against the safe walls, and while there was much work still to be done, stood watching and listening. It gave a man almost more satisfaction to care for, feed, animals than human beings. He wondered if there was at once something fine and hateful in dispensing comfort to animals, so that a man felt himself quite a fellow in being so generous and so kind, and never mind the return the creatures gave him in one way or another. He left the sheep-shed and with the dog drove in the cows, the heifers, the calves. As usual, he had stood stock-still too long, and night had come, and he was obliged to light a lantern to finish the feeding and milking.

The snow was thick underfoot and on his shoulders. He put out the barn lantern, hung it on its hook, and went bowed towards the house with the two buckets of milk. The house was lighted. Nellie had lamps lit in the sitting-room and the dining-room. He knew that she hated the dark. He set down the milkpails to rest and stared at the bright house. This was a man's great joy, to come at nightfall after his day's work to a lighted house. The light was orange, and where it fell on the snow outside it was yellow, and his beloved was waiting for him with food and warmth and comfort.

Nellie said: "What on earth's taken you so long?"

"The sheep."

The snow scratched on the window-panes like the feet of squirrels on a shingled roof.

He said: "The snow came in time to save the winter wheat."

"I suppose so. Nasty winter. Come on, supper's ready."

He ate abstractedly. After supper Nellie fussed with her house plants, moving them away from the cold windows. She put a shawl over her curls and made a dash out of doors to cut from under the bay windows the last of her zinnias, frost-bitten but still bright and gay.

Ase was awake early the next morning. The snow was still falling. He was certain that all the stock was comfortable, but he wanted to feed them early, to speak to them, to assure them that they could be cared for during the cold time ahead. He dressed and went down quietly to the kitchen by

86

the back stairs. A rich, pungent smell came to him. He stood inside the kitchen, astonished. Mink Fisher, the Indian friend of his childhood, lay curled up under his blanket beside the still warm kitchen range.

It was because of this dark man's teachings that Ase had moved so silently that he had not awakened him, Mink, who was seldom surprised by approach of bird or beast. How long was it now since Mink had been here, usually discovered so at daybreak, by the fire? Ten years or more, yes, more. Ase associated him with the log house, with the open hearth fire whose embers flickered all night long. Mink grunted in his sleep, as though he sensed the bystander. His face was as Ase remembered it, thinner perhaps, the nose more hawk-like, the cheek-bones sharper. The straight black hair was grizzled. There was none of the collapse of age, only a finer mark of long facing of the elements, alone and unafraid.

A wave of memory came over Ase, he was a boy again, who had been a boy so brief a time. The Indian had been more of a father than his own. He was the last of his tribe, the Fishers, in that territory. No one knew where they had gone, or what had wiped them out, or why Mink did not find and follow other Indians, but came and went, solitary, trapping and trading for a living. He was famous for his mink pelts and so they called him "Mink". The Linden place was the only one where he had stopped overnight, and this was because of the silent, grave-eyed little boy who trotted after him so trustingly, a boy who, everyone said, looked and acted himself half Indian.

Here asleep lay the source of his knowledge, his voiceless love, of wood and field and stream, of where the ginseng grew. They had speared fish at night on the deep Linden lake, Pip Lake, Mink called it. They had released from the traps, if not too badly maimed, the female fox and mink and 'coon and otter, for the game was getting scarcer, Mink said, and these were the seedbeds for the precious fur. They had cut hemlock boughs for couches, and roasted grouse and fish and partridge and venison over ash and hickory coals, or buried corn in the husk, potatoes in the skins, under hot stones to bake to tender sweetness. Amelia's food had tasted particularly insipid after these things. And it was Mink who

87

had traced the stars for him, who had taken him by the hand and led him barefoot across the Milky Way, at home among the meteors and planets.

Ase turned back up the stairs and made a small noise, not to arouse his friend too near at hand, too suddenly. Mink was on his feet when he came down again. The Indian's eyes filled with wonder and with light. He spoke a greeting in his own tongue. Ase had known much of it once, but now it was strange to him. He came close and Mink laid his hands on his shoulders and looked long at him. The Indian nodded.

"Man now," he said. "Boy gone."

Ase built up a fresh fire in the range. He put on a pot of coffee to boil and brought out cold meats and breads and pastries. They ate together without words.

Mink asked: "Father?"

Ase motioned to the ground.

"Mother?"

He gestured to the south, and made a sign of three moons passed.

"Brother?"

Ase waved towards the west. Mink frowned. The west was the way the spirits went. Ase understood, and struggled to bring back a few of the ancient words to tell the story of his brother's journeying. Using the pantomime of his boyhood, he began to walk slowly the length of the room, bent and plodding, then lifted his hand to shield his eyes against the imagined western brightness, and turned his head from side to side in puzzling. Mink nodded. The brother, then, the wild one, had gone west on foot, in search of something. Mink had never made friends with this older one. He eyed Ase keenly. He recognized the difference in the restlessness of the two boys he had known. The other's was of feet and body, of something of the white man's greed, no doubt it was gold for which he hunted. This one like his son, this one's uneasiness was of the mind and spirit. He caught sight of a child's garment hung to dry behind the range. He touched it.

"Squaw?" he asked. "Papoose?"

Ase nodded, held up one finger, then two. Mink made motions, indicating the curves of a woman's body, held up

88

two fingers, cradled his arms and held up one finger, asking, with his old eyes crinkling, whether there were two squaws and one papoose. Ase grinned and made reverse gestures, no, no, knowing Mink was jesting, one wife and two young children. They laughed together without sound, Mink shaking his lean belly.

The sun had risen without their noticing. It streamed through the east window beside the ruddy range, the sky-fire stronger than the man-fire. Nellie would be coming to the kitchen soon, the chores were not done, but it did not matter. Ase wondered how she would feel about Mink, for he recalled that his mother had kept apart in his childhood when the Indian came. Nellie had got along famously with his other friends, the gypsies. Yet she had shared with them, and with him, at those times, their blitheness, the singing and playing and the dancing. That was the world of the heart, and she lived there with his always. He recognized that the world where he met with Mink, and it did not seem now that the Indian had been gone any time at all, was the secret world she had never entered. On the instant, he dreaded their coming together. Nellie had a devastating gift for mockery, and he could see her imitating the gestures of his friend, and his own in answer. Mink was watching him closely.

"I bring gift. I trade. I go," he said.

He turned to the large bundle beside his blanket. He unrolled it swiftly. There were mink pelts and otter, but the bulk was a wolfskin rug, mingled grey and tawny, warm and thick, faced with dearskin, the skins sewed beautifully together with deerhide lacings. Mink pushed the rug towards Ase.

"You," he said.

This was the gift. It was too lavish. Ase shook his head. Mink pushed it closer.

"You. For boy."

The gift was to the little boy Mink had taught and loved. Ase could not refuse. He made a sign of gratitude and acceptance. The trading began. Ase visualized a cape for Nellie of the mink. Its warm chestnut colour was only a few shades darker than her hair. He did not see how he might

89

use the otter, then he saw strips of it, soft as kitten fur, to trim the children's winter coats. Somehow he was sure the new baby would be a girl, and next year Nellie could make a little cap and muff and mittens for their daughter. The trading was business. He made a generous offer and Mink hesitated. He wanted to make up for the gift of the rug, and he could only wonder what it was Mink wanted. In the old days, he remembered, trade was in goods only, furs in exchange for knives, for guns, for cooking-pots, for dress goods. Mink indicated coins between the hands. It was cash money, then, was called for. Ase went to his tin box, brought it to the kitchen, opened it and made a sweeping motion. Mink was to take from it what he thought proper for the furs.

The Indian brushed aside the paper money and took out silver dollars and half-dollars. He looked up questioningly. It was still not nearly enough, Ase decided, and he put as much silver again in Mink's hand. The Indian accepted it and rose with dignity.

"Too much," he said. "But I need." He added bitterly: "White man's life."

It was inconceivable to Ase that Mink should be so desperate. The Indian had stood to him for all freedom, all natural happiness. Now he needed these stupid bits of metal, dug from the mother-earth, to subsist. It came to him with a shock how living had changed, if not in his own lifetime, within what might be called his memory, for the tales of a man's father and his grandfather surely made up part of his own intimate recollection. Mink's people had possessed these lands when the first Linden arrived here a hundred years ago with his wagon-load of household goods, an axe by his left hand, a muzzle-loader by his right, instruments both of destruction. He thought how few generations it required to make up a century. A hundred years were no time at all. True, the land now produced more bountifully, there was food for many thousands of people in place of the dark virgin forest, the axe had only made for a substitution. And the Lindens had never turned their guns on the Indians. The first one had a gift for healing, of men and animals, a talent as a blacksmith, and Mink's people had come to him from the beginning in amity and friendship. When the bloody arguments were settled, between pioneers and Indians, the Indians were gone, all the Fisher tribe was gone but old Mink, and the Lindens were here, and Ase was increasing their tribe. And now Mink had no squaw, no tepee, no camp-fire to return to, as orange-glowing and welcoming as Nellie's lamplight. The honest exchange of goods was done for, he must have pieces of the white man's metal to live by. Ase felt himself a usurper, part of a breed of men who had brought a plague upon the country.

He touched Mink's hand.

"You stay," he said.

Mink shook his head.

"Too late," he answered. "I go west."

His mouth twisted whimsically.

"You come."

Mink had not asked him to go away with him when he was a boy. He knew he would have gone then. For a moment a longing swept him to go with Mink into the sun, to sleep on hemlock boughs under the stars for ever.

"Too late," he echoed.

He made a parcel of meat and bread for Mink to carry with him. He touched the wolfskin rug in thanks. There had not been wolves here for many years.

"Where?" he asked, and Mink pointed again to the west, and indicated that the rug had been traded from man to man from the far plains until it ended here, a gift for a vanished little boy.

Well, and if this bulky thing had come so far, and Mink was going back over the trail, a message might come and go as well.

"My brother," he said, and described Benjamin as best he could, now he was a grown man, too, and asked of Mink that he have the western Indians inquire of his going-by, and asked that word be sent back of Benjamin's health, even of his existence, some token from his own hand, or, best of all, because of the grieving mother, some white man's words written down on a piece of paper.

He thought that Mink might trace Ben where others had failed. It was part of a pattern. Mink's return was scarcely

91

surprising, a natural thing. It seemed to him that friends were part of the indestructible tapestry of one's life, that no matter if a thread disappeared there, it would eventually reappear here, or in some other place in the design, as long as it was a thread that mattered.

He said: "You come again?"

Mink shook his head. He touched his forehead and that of Ase, he touched his breast and that of the other. They would be always together in those inviolable secret places, and if they could not again speak face to face, it would not too much matter. Ase watched his friend as far as the western rise of land. Mink would go cross-country, never on the travelled roads, he would go up hill and down dale until he reached his destination and his death. Ase watched after him as he had watched after Benjamin. He saw the old Indian wrap his blanket more tightly around him and stride away with a long loping, his head bowed a little under the falling snow.

Ase cleaned up the kitchen. He looked for a place to hide the wolfskin rug and the mink and otter pelts, for now he could surprise Nellie at Christmas after all. He concealed them at last on the upper floor of the carriage-shed beside the house, under the pile of winter popcorn, not yet strung up under the rafters. When he returned to the kitchen, Nellie was there. She had at once discovered the amount of food missing.

She said: "You must not have had enough supper last night. You can hold more than any man I know. You didn't need to wash your dishes."

He hesitated. It would be nothing to tell her of the visit, she would ask few questions, would never grumble about the food, for she was generous with tramps. Perhaps that was it, his friend, his almost-father, would seem to her a tramp. He was obliged to let Mink get safely away from her. She stood still and wrinkled her sensitive nose.

"Now what on earth? I smell something rank as a bear."

He smiled.

"Probably some wild creature's just passed by," he said. "Some wild friendly thing."

14

THE sky at noon was metallic. The brass sun hurt the eyes but there was no heat in it. The icicles hanging from pump and eaves held their own against it. The thick crust of the snow was smooth and nacreous, blue shadowed like the inside of an oyster shell. Pip Lake was already frozen three feet deep. The day was as cold a one as Ase could remember. He turned the big two-seated sleigh from the barn into the drive at the side of the house. Nellie and the children were almost certain to be ready, but since the horses were still warm from the snug stalls, he put their blankets over them. Even a five-minute wait might chill them. He heard Nat howling and decided he must be getting a last-second face-washing. Out of the sun, the cold bit like ivory fangs. He went upstairs in the carriage-house and took out the wolf-skin rug from under the piled popcorn. It would spoil Nellie's surprise, but after all, it was only two days before Christmas, and she would never need the warmth more acutely. If his mother's train was late, it would be night before they returned from Peytonville.

The horses stamped against the cold, their breath congealed, the harness bells jangled. Nellie came out of the house alone.

"I know," she said. "You expected to take the boys. They'd only get tired and fretful. Hulda'll put them to bed early."

He said: "Nat's old enough."

"He'll never know the difference."

"I heard him——"

"Oh, he yells about everything. He doesn't like Hulda. Tell you, Ase, we don't know how we'll find your mother's mind. Better to meet her alone."

He nodded. This was true. He helped her into the sleigh and lifted the rug. He laid it across her lap.

"Merry Christmas," he said.

"You're a little early, I must say."

She stroked it and examined curiously the deerskin lining, the intricate stitching.

"Nice. Where'd you get it? Where's it been?"

He stowed the blankets in the back of the sleigh and turned the horses down the road towards the town. Nellie sniffed at the rug.

She said: "It's got something to do with that smell in the kitchen not long ago."

It seemed discreet enough now to tell the truth. He explained briefly.

She said: "I don't think I'd like Indians. They stink."

Yes, he thought, they stank, and it was the rich stink of earth, of leaves, of burning wood, of the musky cleanness of animals. She snuggled down under the rug. She was wearing the little red-riding-hood cape and bonnet, with her curls escaping around her face. She looked as young as on the afternoon when she had burst in on him with her dog and her pie and her jest about the pie, and her making the way clear for them after Benjamin had gone away. He put an arm around her and she nestled against him. He had wanted to thank her for insisting that he write his mother to come home for Christmas.

She had been so matter-of-fact about it, saying: "Tell your Ma Nat would like his Grandma to see his Christmas tree."

Nat had expressed no such desire, and it seemed to him even more delicate of Nellie to phrase it so.

She had added: "Tell her we're having a roast goose and I want to know about the stuffing."

He was dimly aware of the female flattery involved.

The sleigh passed the Linden one-room school-house, turned into the main road to Peytonville, passed an increasing number of houses, and then they were in the village itself. The little town was decked out at its best. From side to side of the main street hung garlands of ground pine dressed with red paper bells. Folk from miles around had their horses hitched there, all the stores were bright with Christmas wares. Ase found a hitching post, blanketed the horses, and helped Nellie down from the sleigh, to do their most important shopping at Mr. Peyton's General Store.

It was the first time in several months they had been to town together. There was a stir in the store, Will Peyton came from behind a counter to pump their hands. Hank

94

Golightly and Sam Banks rose from their draughts game by the stove to greet the young couple. Ase felt warmed by the friendliness. Nellie recognized shrewdly the respect given to a rising citizen of property. She could remember when no one would have noticed the entrance of the Linden boy, the quiet one. Ben, of course, had always attracted attention, as had she. She preened herself a little and took advantage of Peyton to bargain sharply.

The Linden farm produced most staples except for such items as tea, coffee, lemons, refined sugar, store cheese and biscuits. Nellie was well-stocked on these, her Christmas baking was already done, but for fresh layer-cakes to be baked tomorrow. She set herself at the choosing of holiday luxuries. She bought gifts of dress goods for the women of her own family, mufflers for the men, and for Amelia decided on a pair of fine black kid gloves and a bottle of toilet water. It came to Ase that she had no conception of the value of the wolf- and deer-skin rug, had accepted it casually as scarcely a gift, only a warm useful covering that smelled like Indians. The choice mink and otter pelts would seem equally trivial to her. He made an excuse and went down the street towards Miss Minnie's millinery and notion shop. He was stopped along the way by village acquaintances and by farm neighbours met ordinarily only at harvesting or at meetings of the Grange. He was glad to turn into the warmth of Miss Minnie's shop.

The pot-bellied stove was rosy-red, the window-panes were steamy, the dry female scent of ribbons and laces, of artificial flowers and feathers, met him. Miss Minnie looked over her steel-rimmed spectacles and wiped her perpetually dripping nose on the back of her hand, which she then offered him. On a second thought, she worked her handkerchief from her apron pocket and blew her nose clamorously. Ase looked around him helplessly.

She said: "You expecting to meet your wife here, Mr. Linden?"

"No. I want a present for her."

"Well, aren't you the clever one. Not many husbands'd think of coming to me for Christmas for their wives. And nothing, I say, tickles a lady like a new hat or bonnet or what

95

we call in the trade a frou-frou. Now it's funny, two-three
the drummers stops at the Peyton House, they come to me
to buy, my! the laces and frills, but don't tell me it's for
wives. I may be an old maid, lived in Peytonville all my
life—oh, trips to the city, you know, to buy—but I say,
I know human nature. A body'd almost think you wasn't
married to Nellie. Now that's a thought, folks say you're
daft about her yet, and two young ones and another started,
they say, and you can't bear her out of your sight. Let's see
now, that's nonsense, I remember when you was married,
and Preacher told it he never did see a groom look so solemn
—what am I talking about, of course you're married, but it's
a sweet sad thought, the other. And her so crazy about your
brother once."

She caught her breath and snuffled. Ase had a desperate
impulse to walk out of the shop. Then he was suddenly
amused. The sweet sad thought would tickle Nellie as much
as a new hat. He wondered if he could manage to tell it so
that she could see Miss Minnie as he saw her now, manless,
ferret-like and sniffly, realized it was beyond him.

Miss Minnie said: "Now maybe, being for a wife, you'd
like one of my own hand-painted cake plates. I wouldn't
boast, but I'm famous for my hand-painted roses."

He said hastily: "No, no thank you. Something personal."

His eyes lit on something blue, the colour of Nellie's eyes.
He pointed, but the milliner was holding out to him a
monstrous thing, presumably a hat, wide-brimmed and a
mass of cotton-cloth pansies.

"Now, Mr. Linden, in the trade we call this a confection."

He wanted to say: 'Save it for the drummers,' but he could
not offend her, and he pointed again to the blue thing that
he now recognized as a sort of bonnet. It was made of satin,
smooth as Nellie's skin. It seemed to be, what was it, quilted,
it had a pert pink rose at one side, and wide blue satin
ribbons that he could picture tied in a bow under Nellie's
firm little chin.

He asked: "Can you put that in a fancy box?"

"Why yes, Mr. Linden, why yes, you have such good taste,
of course it's expensive, but I see you don't mind that."
She hesitated.

96

"Twelve dollars?"

He took out his leather wallet and counted out the notes. The price shocked him, but he could not wait to see Nellie's face adorably surrounded by this bit of blue.

Miss Minnie said: "Now something else, perhaps? A little tippet? Some lace for the throat? Another little, let's say extravagance?"

He thought of his mother, and bought lace for her, and a fine shawl. He slipped his purchases in the back seat of the sleigh and met Nellie at the Penny Store. They bought there toys for Nat and Arent and Nellie's nieces and nephews, and gum drops, peppermint and liquorice-sticks, barley-sugar candy, and bright ornaments for the Christmas tree.

The afternoon had turned dark and even colder. Amelia's train was not due until six o'clock. Ase had saved another surprise for Nellie, supper at the Peyton House. He began to worry about the horses. He took Nellie to the hotel, left her in the red-carpeted lobby, and returned to drive his team to the livery stable, ordering oats and a warm mash. It had proved an expensive day, but he was satisfied. When he returned to the hotel, he found Nellie in conversation with what must be one of Miss Minnie's feather-buying drummers. He invited the man to join them for supper, but the stranger refused.

The supper was a disappointment, compared with Nellie's cooking, but there were delicacies on the menu, such as oysters. Nellie was animated and he felt a surge of pride, seeing that the other diners, men for the most part, watched her. The Peyton House clock showed ten minutes to six and he and Nellie walked the short distance to the railway station to meet Amelia's train. It was only a little late. Ase rejoiced when Nellie ran to embrace his mother as she stepped down. He seemed to remember that since the planting of the apple orchard Nellie had changed her attitude, had given Amelia every attention. Perhaps after all the two women would become friends. He brought the sleigh, tucked them into the front seat beside him, drew the rug over them and set out for home. The sleigh bells rang sweetly.

Amelia was cheerful as Ase had never known her.

She said: "I was really in despair not to find my Benjamin. I advertised for information of him, you know, in all the Indiana papers. But I got the best of news. A young lady answered me from near Indianapolis and I went to see her. Benjamin had left for the West again, a month before. A wonderful opportunity was waiting for him, some sort of mining partnership. She was hoping that I knew the exact location, as he had forgotten to give her the address."

She coughed delicately.

"Yes, they are engaged. I must say, I was charmed with her. Very pretty, and the only child of an invalid and wealthy widower. Ben's prospects are bright indeed. He will return for her in the spring. She was delighted with my suggestion that they come here at once. She was certain he would agree. He had spoken of me tenderly, most tenderly. He has been waiting to write me, to come to me, as I knew, until he could come in happiness and prosperity."

She touched Nellie's mittened hand.

"I hope this doesn't come as a shock to you, my dear. It was to be expected."

Nellie said dryly: "The whole thing's exactly what I'd expect."

"Good. You have only yourself to blame for losing him."

Ase felt Nellie stiffen beside him. She started to speak and did not. She nudged him in the ribs and gave her little chuckle.

She said demurely: "Ase and I are very pleased for Ben."

The understanding came clearly to him from her that Ben had only moved on into the void from another of his familiar conquests. Well then, his mother would be contented until the spring, and into the summer, drawing sustenance from this chimera.

He decided not to mention the possibility of getting a message to Ben through Mink, it was too remote. He would wait until she began to brood again and needed some fresh hope to cling to. She chattered of details of her visit. She had an extra box with her, gifts, she said, for the children, and how was her little Nat?

Nellie said: "There'll be another this summer, Mother

98

Linden. Time for a girl. We thought she'd be little Amelia."

They had not discussed a name, but Ase was touched.

His mother said: "That might be a handicap, if her life proves as sad as mine," yet she seemed gratified.

The sky over their shoulders had a ruddy afterglow. A wind had risen, and for a hundred yards before they took the turn by the school-house Ase thought the sound he heard was its howling through the naked tree-tops. Only the brilliance of the snow made it possible to see the figure at the foot of the school-house steps. He halted the team. He knew at once this was Tim McCarthy, in trouble again, and the howling had come from his little white dog, invisible against the greater whiteness. Tim had evidently used the last of his strength to try to enter the school-house. The dog barked now shrilly and ran in excited circles. Ase lifted the huddled frail body in his arms. Tim was unconscious, breathing in deep rasps. Ase laid him on the straw of the floor of the back seat and tucked the horse blankets around him. Tim had on the lightest of clothing. It was impossible to know how long he had lain there in the bitter cold. Ase motioned to the dog to jump in. The animal was shivering and pressed close against his master.

Amelia said: "Tim always manages to fall drunk where you'll find him."

Nellie said wryly: "It's a habit he can't get out of, along with the liquor."

The two disparate women at least had this consolidarity. Nellie had lost her tolerance of Tim, he could not tell how or when.

Ase was stepping into the sleigh when he recollected. It was seldom that Tim went out celebrating without his fiddle. Ase went back and searched near the steps and found it. He laid it on the back seat and set off. Hulda's lamp in her bedroom was the only light in the house. He must remind her —no, Nellie would be sure to—that the Lindens did not spare the oil, and always wanted lamps lit to welcome them. He hoped she had kept the fires going. Hulda was a good girl, she had helped Nellie off and on since the birth of Nat. He drew up at the side of the house.

Nellie said: "Not a light. Probably not a fire in the house.

99

I'll get things going, Ase, you can bring in the stuff after you take Tim home."

Nellie knew as well as he that Tim's employers were away for the holidays and had left behind a young hired boy to take care of the stock, against the certain eventuality of Tim's Christmas drunk. She had probably forgotten.

He said: "I must bring him in."

He went ahead to light the kitchen lamp. He heard the women murmuring together.

Nellie said: "Now Mother Linden agrees with me, Ase, you've got to take that nasty old man right on to his own home."

They stood united against him, against his friend.

He said: "He doesn't have a home."

Amelia said: "The people he works for are responsible for him. Not you."

Ase said: "But he's sick."

Nellie snapped: "You bet he's sick. He'll be puking all over any minute."

It seemed to him that he could hear Tim's agonized breathing through the very walls. How long had Tim lain helpless in the snow?

He said: "He's getting old. I'll take care of him, he won't be any trouble."

Nellie said: "Spoil Christmas for your old drunk, then. I won't go near him. Mother Linden, you sleep here tonight. I don't see why you don't move into your old downstairs bedroom here, to stay. I hate thinking of you alone in the log house."

Amelia said: "My dear, how thoughtful of you. I shall."

He lifted Tim from the sleigh and went with his burden into the house. He carried his friend upstairs to a bedroom over the kitchen which always kept a certain amount of warmth. He pulled off Tim's heavy brogan shoes but left on his clothing for the moment and piled quilts and a goose-down comforter over him. Tim's breathing was stertorous.

Ase drove the sleigh to the barn, unhitched the horses and made them comfortable. He still had the milking to do, the feeding of the stock, the watering. The animals greeted him in their various tongues and he responded with a touch here, a word there. When he returned to the house he saw that his wife and his mother had had a cosy bite of food and tea together. Both had retired to their bedrooms.

The fire in the range had died to ashes. He built it up, made scalding tea, took it by the back stairs to Tim's room, lit a lamp, and forced two cups down him. Tim muttered. Ase undressed him, stole another comforter from the near-by bedroom and spread it over his friend, waited until Tim broke into promising sweat. He dried the old man with his own shirt, tucked the bedclothes close around his neck, and went downstairs again. He had forgotten Tim's dog. He went out into the icy night and called. The little dog was crouched by the wood-shed door. Ase brought him in, fed him generously, then led him up the back stairs. With a moan of joy, the dog leaped to Tim's bed. Ase drew back the top coverlet to let him snuggle inside.

Ase remembered that he had not unloaded the sleigh. But none of the Christmas contents would be harmed by the night's cold. Only Tim was in danger. He went to his friend three times during the night, to cover him again against his feverish tossing.

★ 15 ★

THE kitchen on Christmas Eve morning was apparently chaos. Ase stood baffled in the doorway, with no place to set down the milk-buckets. His hands were numb with cold, his nose felt frost-bitten. The centre work-table seemed to have had a vast cornucopia spilled at random across it. The big grey goose lay ready for plucking, apples, onions, Hubbard squash raisins were piled around it, a pan of crumbled bread would become stuffing, a bowl of cracked hickory-nuts needed to have the meats extracted, cranberries would make a ruby sauce, ears of popcorn wanted hulling, a basket of eggs awaited a broken sacrifice. The kitchen sink was piled with used bowls, the table between sink and stove was covered with buttered cake-tins, Nellie was spooning batter into a row of them with machine precision. The coffee-pot simmered at the back of the range, buckwheat batter gave out its sharp yeasty winter smell, a skillet of sausages was frying slowly.

Amelia looked in from the dining-room door.

"I'd thought I'd keep out of the way until you're ready for me. You might just bring me a little tray of breakfast to my room. I have my fire going."

The back-stair door opened and Nat reached for the last steps precariously, little Arent clutched dangling from his front, like a huge puppy. Nellie turned in time to thump down her bowl and gather up the younger child as Nat stumbled. She dropped Arent in his high-chair, opened the oven door and slid in six layer tins of cake batter, pulled the soapstone griddle to the front of the range, pushed more wood in the fire-box, led Nat to the wash-stand and mopped and dried his face and hands.

"Milk-pans in the woodshed, Ase," she said. "Strainer on the shelf. Strain for me, then wash up for breakfast. Go make yourself comfortable, Mother Linden, have you a nice tray in a jiffy. Nat, find Arent something to play with. Here, give him his spoon to bang."

She dipped buckwheat batter on to the griddle, turned the sausages, stirred the oatmeal, Arent beat his silver spoon on his wooden tray, Nat dragged the cat from under the stove by its tail, was scratched for his pains and howled. Nellie was the whirlwind and she was also its calm and cheerful centre. When Ase came from the wash-stand, she had breakfast on the dining-table and had begun to help Arent eat his oatmeal. She handed him the spoon and he finished feeding the child. Nat was helping himself busily to one cooky after another, making a ring around his porridge-plate. Nellie whisked past to the company bed-room with a steaming tray for Amelia. She took a look at her cakes in the oven, sat down at the table, brushed the curls away from her moist forehead, poured a cup of coffee, and, it seemed to Ase, breathed for the first time. She was plainly as happy as a cat in a wool-skein.

He said: "This going to keep up all day?"

She nodded.

"There'll be nothing much to do tomorrow but roast the goose and the turkey, cook the vegetables. You can hull the popcorn or pick out nut meats this morning if I don't find time."

"I can pluck the goose for you."

"No, thanks. I want to keep the down separate. You'd get absent-minded and have it half-full of feathers. I'll keep you busy, don't fret."

He watched his chance to mix a bowl of oatmeal with cream and sugar, to pour a cup of coffee and to slip up the back stairs to Tim. He hesitated at the door of the bedroom, set down the dishes, and went to his cupboard for the bottle of medicinal whisky. Tim was awake. The old man had escaped pneumonia, but his exposure had settled into a deep bronchial cough, and he was wretched in general.

He said weakly: "Ase, the trouble I am to you."

Ase fed him several spoonfuls of whisky. They grinned at each other, for it was not his usual way of taking it. He managed the coffee and half the oatmeal. He closed his eyes. Asc pulled the window blinds against the bright morning light, tucked in the bedclothes and tiptoed away. Sleep and warmth would take over the healing. He was more relieved than he could have believed. The old man had evidently not lain too long in the cold, or he was tough as a hickory knot, or both.

Amelia decided to be company, at least for the time being. She spent the day arranging her personal belongings in the pleasant downstairs front bedroom. Nellie took her two of her prettiest house plants for decoration. Ase worked steadily at whatever small jobs Nellie assigned him. His great slow hands hulled the popcorn and picked out nut meats. Nellie forgot him, until she noticed the bowl of shelled nuts overflowing, when she stopped him. Nat sat on a stool and worked the wooden churn dasher faithfully up and down until the butter came. The family had glasses of fresh buttermilk and doughnuts in mid-morning. Nat built a set of barns in a corner with the corn cobs. Arent fell asleep in his high-chair. Cakes came and went from the oven, were turned out to cool, were filled and frosted and sugared. Pound cakes had been made a few days ago, fruit cakes weeks before. Mince-pies filled a long shelf in the stone cellar. In the afternoon Nellie made pies of pumpkin and squash, brown and fragrant with spice, set bread dough to rise, and in a sudden panic that there might not be enough to eat on Christmas Day made up fresh batches of molasses and sugar cookies and a dishpanful of doughnuts. Amelia proved vague about the stuffing for the goose, and Nellie went quietly ahead with her usual recipe.

Supper was early and light, so far as Nellie could possibly set a simple table. Amelia joined them. Nat whined for some of the fresh coconut cake. Nellie had foreseen the danger and produced a tiny one for his own, baked in a small tin lid, and frosted as thickly as the big company one. He was delighted and made it last a long time. When Nellie made griddle cakes she always made special ones for him, the size of a half-dollar. Ase looked over the table uneasily, to choose something helpful for Tim.

Nellie said: "You don't have to sneak the old bother's food to him. I'll fix something, if you think he's slept off his drunk."

"He caught cold," Ase said.

"Anybody else would have caught his death."

"He has a bad cough, Nellie."

She sighed and looked tired for the first time.

"All right. I'll make him a hot onion poultice when we go to bed. Anything to get him on out of here in a hurry."

She sent him upstairs with an invalid's supper of poached eggs and hot milk and buttered toast. The old man's eyes filled.

"The dear Nellie, now," he said, "taking thought for an old bastard doesn't deserve it. I'll be making it up to her somehow."

He seemed to relish the delicate food. He sat up straight.

"Mother of God, me fiddle!"

"It's safe in the woodshed."

"Praise be. No matter how the drink takes me, I do usually keep a good grip of it." He eyed Ase sharply. "This time I did not, eh? Praise to you, then, Asahel Linden my friend."

Ase said: "I wanted some Christmas music tomorrow."

"Tomorrow? Eh, now. Me sick on your hands for the Lord's birthday, and no gifts in mine."

Ase ached to comfort him, to assure him that his presence was gift enough, his very life a precious thing. He hoped that in the hubbub of a big family Christmas Day, Nellie and Amelia would greet the old fellow at least not too unkindly.

He said: "Nellie'll make you a poultice tonight," and returned downstairs.

Arent had been put to bed, but Nat was allowed to stay up to watch the popping of corn, its stringing, and the stringing of the reddest cranberries, into long festoons. Ase had a small spruce concealed in the woodshed for a Christmas tree. Amelia helped with the popcorn as though she made the major contribution to the holiday preparations, but she was cheerful and talkative.

She took Nat on her lap and said: "Now Grandmother will tell you about Santa Claus."

Her telling of the fable was drab and unconvincing. Nat squirmed. He was most interested in the idea that St. Nick meant presents for him. By what mystic, reindeer-driven means they arrived was not important.

"So tonight," Amelia finished, "while you're asleep, Santa will bring things for a good boy, and tomorrow you can have them, and it's called 'Christmas', and we'll have roast goose and great big cakes and plum pudding."

She retired to her room and Nellie put the boy to bed. Ase brought the little spruce and set it up in a corner of the living-room. He handed Nellie the strings of popcorn and cranberries, the bright ornaments from the Penny Store. She dusted tinsel over the boughs. The little tree was gay and sparkling. They arranged the gifts under it. Nellie made a hot onion poultice for McCarthy's chest, turned it over to Ase to apply, and went to bed.

Tim protested the ungodly stink of the poultice, but resigned himself.

"'Tis me punishment," he said.

Ase brought the dog in to him for the night. He went down alone to the kitchen, still redolent, still warm. He fetched his Bible and by the light of the kitchen lamp turned the pages until he found what he was seeking. "The Lord's birthday," Tim had said.

"For unto you is born this day in the city of David a Saviour, which is Christ the Lord."

He had been troubled as his mother told Nat of Santa Claus. He had wanted then to tell his first-born son this older and more stirring story. Presents, why, they were things to give, not to receive, the Wise Men had brought gifts, not waited avidly for them. He was disturbed over Nat's young greediness, and Amelia—yes, Nellie too—seemed to encourage him in this.

He turned a page back and read: "And there were in the same country shepherds abiding in the field, keeping watch over their flock by night. And lo, the angel of the Lord came upon them, and the glory of the Lord shone round about them: and they were sore afraid."

As always, the majestic language moved him; the talk of shepherds, abiding in the field. It seemed to him that a man might meet God, if ever, in the fields, for so much of creation was there. McCarthy was a religious man, for all his sins, and an articulate. He would ask Tim tomorrow to tell Nat of Christmas.

He closed the book and put it away. A log of charred wood collapsed and crashed against the quiet of the house. The clock on the mantel ticked noisily. It was nearly twelve o'clock. Nellie's family would be arriving early the next day and there would be confusion. Although it was so late, he decided it would be best to give the sick ewe her drenching tonight. One of the Wilson men would be glad to give him a hand tomorrow, yet a stranger would disturb all the sheep, and the ewe would be more difficult to handle. He mixed the draughts, lit a lantern, put on his greatcoat, tied a muffler over his fur cap and went out into the still night to the sheep-shed.

The sheep looked up in curiosity from their beds in the deep oat straw. Their smell was rankly sweet in the sheltered close. The sick ewe was drowsing. Ase opened her mouth gently and had the draught down her throat before she could become alarmed. The sheep took the lantern-light for morning and began nibbling at their straw. The ram looked benevolently over his flock, then nibbled, too. Passing the stable, Ase stepped inside and held his light high, more by way of greeting than for anxiety, for all the other stock was in good health. The red heifer who had had trouble with her first calf rose from her knees in her stall, recognized him, lowed softly and started at once to chew her cud. The cows, the horses, breathed heavily. One of the barn cats peered from a manger, its eyes wild and red in the lantern-light. It ducked away and there was the squeaking of a caught mouse. Ase left the creatures to their sleep.

He thought he had never seen so many twinkling stars. They were not moving, he thought, but were bound to cosmic stakes, from which they struggled to be free. The earth must look so to a night-watcher on another planet, tugging at its tethers. He wondered what force held each one in its appointed place. He had read in the astronomy book that the earth revolved around the sun, the moon around the earth, and that these three were part of a larger stellar system. And how far did that system extend, and how many other such systems were there, and was there any end to them and any end to man? He had read in fascination in Ben's Academy books of what was called the force of gravity, which pinned men down to earth so that they did not fly off into space, kept each one dancing up and down on one spot. If a larger eye, God, for instance, watched them, men too might appear to be struggling against invisible deep-set stakes.

And was God there among the stars, Himself the gravity, Himself the great inter-revolving, or was He, as the preachers said, only an omnipotent human, white-bearded, stern and harsh as Asahel's own father, with an odd capacity for watching critically every man's thoughts and actions, disapproving particularly of fornication and of the theft of property? The still night was so bright that Ase blew out his lantern. He stared upwards. Whatever the truth, he found himself drawn to those outer spaces. It seemed to him that he must perish if he could not make some sort of communication, back and forth, just as he was desolate because he had lost touch with his brother. He found himself denying this so-called force of gravity. It could not be what tied men to earth. It was a heavy weight, an unendurable pressure from the outer-land, and if a man could once break through it, soar high like a bird, he would be free, would meet, would join, something greater than he, and be complete at last.

Walking slowly to the house, he scented the strong odour of a fox.

'Help yourself to the mice,' he thought, 'leave the chickens alone.'

A sound of distant chimes came sweetly to him. The church bells of Peytonville were ringing. It was midnight of Christmas Eve.

★ 16 ★

CHRISTMAS DAY was clear and sparkling. The sun gathered its strength. The icicles were struck to the heart, wept long crystal tears, lost their grip on their week-long home under the eaves, fell tinkling and broken to the ground. Nellie had slipped early and quiet from bed. Ase, over-sleeping, was late with his chores. It was the first time the morning sun had met him returning with the milk-buckets. He had given all the stock an extra measure of grain, scattered more hand-fuls than usual of barley and wheat and corn on the snow for the winter birds. The sick ewe was better. He found Nellie deep in the paring of vegetables and the good smell of breakfast waiting. He strained the milk, took the wide shallow pans to the cellar shelves, and on his way up the back stairs to Tim McCarthy met the old man coming down. Tim was shaky and unshaven.

"The merriest of Christmases to you, my friend," he said. "Now I've found me health, isn't it best I be taking my own road?"

The wistfulness was naked under his bravado. As he spoke, he staggered and clutched at the wooden railing beside the steep narrow stairs. Ase steadied him. His heart ached for the lonely man.

"You're family, Tim," he said. "We want you here."

"Ah then, bless you. I'll eat at table, not to be a burden to the darling Nellie. And I'll fiddle for you, come evening, if it's the last fiddling I do this side of heaven."

The white dog came behind him, yawning, asked to be

108

let out, to make an admirably large puddle in the snow. Nellie did not look up. Ase cleared his throat.

"Tim's better," he said.

"Then maybe he can give me a hand," she said tartly. "There's still a lot to do, with Hulda gone for the holidays."

Tim said: "I'm good as any woman in the kitchen, Nellie dear."

She dropped an onion in its pot of water and stood up.

"Breakfast's ready. Ase, get the boys out of your mother's room and wash their faces. Tell her to come sit down. I can't bother with a tray."

It seemed to Ase that she had a delayed irritation, quite understandable, from her hard work the day before. He was unwilling to admit that she could be annoyed over Tim's spending Christmas with them. Breakfast was not out of the ordinary, but the quantity was a menace to the coming Christmas dinner. Tim insisted on washing the breakfast dishes. Amelia retired to her room. The mid-morning sun blazed on the snow and ice. Ase wrapped Nat warmly over his yells to have his Christmas gifts at once, and took him out of doors, along with a lump of suet to hang from a poplar tree for the birds. Nat found the fallen icicles and ate the fragments like candy.

The sleigh bells of the Wilson family came ringing down the road. Ase and Nat met them, the women went into the house, the men put away the horses and lingered in the barns to talk of farm affairs. The sun was high. Amelia came from her room dressed in her best. She was condescending to Nellie's people. Nellie changed her percale dress for a silk one and replaced the gingham apron with one of frilled organdie. The families gathered in the living-room, where the Wilsons had added their gifts to the others under the Christmas tree. Ase looked at his mother. She took charge.

"Now when I give the word, everyone looks for his own presents. Ready? Go."

The adults and the Wilson children went modestly to the piles of packages to search for their own names. Ase was pained to see Nat plunge wildly, scrambling under the tree, and to hear him howl as he could not identify what was to be his alone. Tim appeared in the doorway.

He called out: "Nat, me boy, wait a bit. Uncle Tim'll be helping you."

He put an arm around the child, bent with him under the tree, and brought out Nat's gifts.

"Look now," he said soothingly, "here's all of this, come, we'll open them. And who's loved the little Nat so much to have all this for him?"

The child grabbed avidly at his presents, was shown by Tim how to spin the beautiful shining top. Tim drew from his pocket a silver dollar and handed it to the boy. Nat dropped the top.

"Money!" he screamed.

He ran to his mother.

"Look, Ma! Is this enough to buy me a horse and buggy?"

The Wilson clan laughed.

Nellie winked and said: "With a pair of bays."

Amelia said: "Tell the child the truth. Nathaniel dear, you'd need a pile of silver dollars so-o-o high to buy a horse and buggy. You can save this one, and when you grow up, you must find a way to get lots more of them, and then you can buy anything you want."

He scowled.

"What way?"

"Why, almost any way. Except stealing, of course. Lawyers and bankers make money."

Bert Wilson offered: "Buy land cheap and sell it high's a right good way."

Harry Wilson said: "Any business a man can build up for himself. Long as it's his own."

Nellie's father said: "Anything but farming," and the prosperous Wilsons laughed again. Amelia listened with approval. Her black eyes were bright. Nat began to wail. He held out the dollar with distaste.

"It isn't enough. It won't buy anything."

McCarthy said: "Uncle Tim's sorry, boy. 'Twas all I had."

His shining gift had become a shabby thing, to be apologized for. Ase wanted to explain that it stood for hours of a man's hard labour, for an old man's life running fast through the hour-glass.

Amelia said severely: "Nathaniel, money always buys

things. This will buy a hundred sticks of penny candy. Think of that. It's your first dollar, too, all your very own."

The child looked at the piece of metal with fresh respect. The moment's awkwardness was eased. The families compared their gifts, thanked one another. Nellie clapped her satin bonnet over her curls and danced around the room for admiration. She left it on when she went to the kitchen to baste the goose. The men settled down to talk of crops and stock and prices. The women bustled about to help Nellie put dinner on the table.

The table was extended almost the length of the dining-room and a smaller table was laid in a corner for the over-flow of children. The platters and tureens of food scarcely left room for the plates and silver. The sweets were a full pastry shop, arranged on the sideboard, as reminder to leave a little room for them in the stomach. The Oriental spices of the plum pudding steaming in its linen jacket lay sharply over the pungency of the table.

Ase motioned Tim, hanging back timidly, to a seat beside him. The women began heaping plates to pass to the children. Nellie's father announced that Ase should carve the goose under his own roof, but he was so almighty slow, and the goose happened to be in front of his own place, and he'd have it sliced—there now, one breast clean already—before Ase could get a hold with the carving-fork. The Wilsons roared. Ase sliced the turkey carefully, remembering each one's preference. Tim touched him on the knee.

He whispered: "May the Lord bless this fabulous bounty to the good of body and soul."

Ase closed his eyes an instant. He thought of Mink Fisher and prayed that somewhere he had found a deep warm cave and sat by a fire with venison roasting over it and was not walking through the snow with a hard bit of meat or white man's dry crust of bread in his gnarled cold hand. He prayed that Benjamin might be sitting with friends before another generous board.

With dinner eaten and praised, the tiered cakes and pies wrecked and ruined, the plum pudding turned out of its cloth and set ablaze with applejack, two bowls of sauce to pass, one hot and yellow-foaming, the other a hard sauce creamed to a feather, the company disintegrated like the mounds of food. The men, drunk with over-eating, staggered out of the house that suddenly confined them. They drifted to barns and sheds and scuffled their feet and leaned against stalls and picked their teeth with golden straws. The women sat lethargically at table a few minutes, then set Nellie at putting away the devastated remnants while they washed and dried the dishes, laid a fresh damask cloth and set the table for the evening supper. The small children fell asleep in chairs and corners, the older nibbled on Christmas candy, knowing they should have been allowed to eat it before dinner, when it would have tasted better, and here and there a boy found greed or courage for a bite or two of firm-fleshed winter apple.

It was too early for the evening chores. Tim and Ase sat by the fire without speaking. The kitchen clattered with the rattle of plate on plate, the multiplied crash of women's voices. Nat and a young Wilson cousin had a brief quarrel over a toy. The little girls hugged new dolls dreamily. The boys lost heart for barley-sugar candy and peppermint and liquorice-sticks, for tops and drums and pocket-knives. They collapsed flat and quiet on the Brussels carpet.

Ase looked to see if Tim were over-tiring. The old man's chin was on his chest. He was sleeping soundly. The return of the men for supper roused him. He played a tune on his fiddle, supper was called, was eaten, and in a drugged group-understanding the Wilsons hitched up their teams to the sleighs, the women gathered up children like armfuls of rags, dropped them deep among rugs and straw. The sleighs slid smoothly away under the early starlight, the bells jangling, only the horses fresh, high-stepping. Amelia graciously offered to put Nat and Arent to bed.

Nellie said sleepily: "The pudding was good, if I do say so."

Ase said: "Where's Tim?"

"Oh, he went on with some of the folks. Said the walk the rest of the way'd do him good. Said tell you, thanks— what was it now?—anyway, thanks."

The moment had never come to ask McCarthy for the telling of the Christmas story.

Ase stopped the plough-horse at the fence corner, for rest in the shade of a maple. The June morning was fresh, but the direct sun brought out the sweat. Old Shep threw himself to the cool earth, his red tongue dripping. He was inclined to be a foolish old dog, and followed Ase behind the plough for hours, when he would stop, seem to question himself, and answer that they were evidently going nowhere and that he was wasting his time. Ase cooled quickly in the shade. He stepped into the bean-field and looked to the south. On the far slopes the cattle moved in pools of white foam that were daisies. The sheep beyond, clean in their new wool, were visible only when they fed on into patches of buttercup or clover. Nellie had complained of a trace of wild garlic in the milk and butter. He must have missed a few clumps in last year's hunt for it. He himself did not mind the faint flavour, it gave a certain richness to the June gold of the colour. Nellie had so much butter to sell, he had best trace and uproot the garlic in the pasture.

He walked between the bean rows. The young plants were healthy, but it was clear he would not have the crop of the year before, raised south-west beyond the apple orchard. This high field west of the house was not fertile enough for such a rank feeder. Wheat, rye or barley, buckwheat, these the land would raise, hay, of course. Corn was the proper crop for these acres. He had not had corn here since his father's death. He examined the plants for signs of damaging insects. Only the bees were buried head-on in the first of the bean blossoms, scanty, he feared. The bushes ploughed under after the last crop was gathered would enrich the soil at least.

Next spring he must plant corn. It would grow taller than he and fill the sky with the sabres of its leaves, plume-topped and rustling. He straightened instantly and looked across the field, almost in panic, then eased. The road that wound into the west was visible. It dipped, narrowed to cross the wooden bridge over the willow-bordered stream, turned up the next hill and curved in plain sight until far away. He had been unable to plant here any crop that would block his vision. Back along that road would come Benjamin or news of him, if either came at all.

He went back slowly to take again the plough handles. He supposed June was a fine month everywhere. Roads all over the country would be lined with flowering thorn and hazel. Birds would be nesting clear to California. The roads would be stony in places, or made of clay, or churn into a fine powder like flour, but they would all feel good under a man's feet. They would feel good to the hoofs of a horse. A shadow passed across the field. An eagle was flying westward. Ase thought he did not want to walk west, or ride, but to mount an eagle. From that height he could recognize Ben wherever he passed him far below. He felt desperate and earth-bound. He lifted the reins and the horse turned to the field. The ageing Dan felt the reins slack and only ambled between the rows. By noon, when the dinner-bell rang, Ase had not finished the cultivating as he had expected.

The family was at table as he came in from the wash-bench. Nellie and Amelia were giving conflicting orders to the children. The relations of the two women were reasonably amiable. Nat was demanding plum preserves before he would accept more substantial foods. Amelia, so strangely a glutton, especially for sweets, was backing him up. The younger boy Arent waited patiently to be served when the argument should be ended. The baby girl 'Melie beat on the tray of her high-chair. Ase had hoped she would resemble Nellie, but she was a tiny copy of his mother, after whom she had been named. Perhaps the next baby would be a girl, too, and another Nellie. The children ate heartily and rapidly, then broke into a clatter of talk. Nellie was chatty as always. Amelia was in a mood for talk as well, and the dining-table sounded to him like chirping sparrows finding a ripe grain-field. Nellie passed dishes to him and he ate automatically without consciousness of meat or bread or fruit.

His silence at table had been troublesome when he was a boy, especially on the days when Benjamin was missing. Now it went unnoticed under the cheery confusion. He seemed also to have less and less to say. The baby was cooing like a turtle-dove. With a happy wing-like motion she swept her mug of milk to the floor. Nellie sighed.

"Hoped I was through cleaning today."

She brushed back her curls with the gesture Ase loved. The children were ordinarily her entire affair, but Ase rose and went to the kitchen for a cloth. Nellie watched his awkward mopping in amusement and took the cloth away from him to finish. She had the strength and stamina of a cat, but she seemed tired today. The new baby was no more than on the way; Nellie was having spells of sickness, which she had never had in pregnancy before. He would drive to the Svensons' tonight to see if Hulda could be spared again this summer. It was no time to be thinking of an out-going road, of eagles flying westward.

He returned to his cultivating. The bees droned. Ase decided he would rob part of one hive in a week or so. He enjoyed taking each new variety of honey to Nellie. The combs of apple-blossom honey would be recognizable, pale as April sunlight. The bean-blossom honey would be nearly the colour of Amelia's amber beads. Clover honey, later, would be the colour of the brook water beneath the willows, the golden-rod again would darken, and last would come the buckwheat honey, red-black, strong and pungent, and his favourite. He thought now of the various honeys in glass jars, joined to the sparkling jellies on the cellar shelves, and choosing one was like choosing a jewel. He had a colour plate of gems that had come with his encyclopaedia. Holding his bony forefinger under each one, memorizing the names, he had recognized not only the amber, but the clear ruby of the currant, the amethyst of the plum, the jade of gooseberry, the sardonyx of the buckwheat. He had bought the encyclopaedia this spring off a road drummer and was vaguely disappointed. Most of the information was strange, and he read with absorption of the people and animals of other lands, of alien fruits and vegetation. But when he turned eagerly to learn about the stars, the planets, the cosmos, he did not find the things he was seeking. He had thought a book so large and thick would have some answers.

Old Shep lay under the maple tree with no attempt to follow the ploughing. Ase turned down the final row. The mid-afternoon sun was in his eyes, but he thought he saw movement on the western horizon. He stopped Dan and shaded his eyes. A small rounded white cloud seemed to be rolling slowly along the road. Then another and another. A familiar joy filled his chest. The gypsies had come back again with summer. He finished his row and hurried Dan to the barn, to be ahead of his friends to greet them.

The white-topped wagons turned off the road and lurched to a stop beyond the flowing spring at the edge of the apple orchard. The drivers jumped down and stretched their arms and legs luxuriously. The back doors of the wagons flew open and wooden steps dropped to earth. Children spilled out like apples from an open sack. They were the first to see the tall gangling young man coming towards them. They shrieked and pointed. The men lifted their hands high and shouted.

"Asah!" they called. "Asah!"

They poured around him like the swirling waters of the brook in flood. It was necessary to touch him. The women came more quietly, their eyes bright as their gold loop earrings. The slanting sun flashed on the gold, on the shining dark eyes, on the white teeth. There were three new babies to show him. The queen, the Old One, took his hand and pressed it against her vast breast. Her voice was deep and tender.

"Asah, the bes' friend," she said.

The leader suddenly shouted at the men.

"Horses die for drink while you play! Plenty time talk to our Asah."

The men unhitched the horses and led them to the mossy watering-trough below the spring. They scooped water in their hands and drank, the drops crystal in the sun. The children remembered the dipper and would drink only from that, crowding for their turns. The horses were hobbled and turned loose to graze. A narrow strip of grass grew between the road and the beginning of the buckwheat planted in the orchard. The buckwheat shoots were young and tender. Ase saw the horses munching instinctively towards them. He would not hurt his friends by halting the horses now.

The women brought out their great black iron cooking-kettles and smaller copper pots and pans. Boys were sent for twigs and branches to start the camp-fire. Young men brought the whole carcasses of two lambs from the wagons and set about dressing them. A calf was tethered to graze. Ase smiled. The lambs had certainly come from a flock near Peytonville and just as certainly had not been paid for. He did not recognize the calf. He himself was perhaps the only farmer in these parts from whom the gypsies did not steal. But then, they had no need to. The women took over the meat for cutting. The kettles were half filled with water from the spring, pieces of meat and fragrant herbs were added. Girls sat about peeling onions and potatoes. Spits were set up for roasting haunches and special titbits. More wood was needed, to make beds of coals, to keep the fires burning for the cooking and for the night's lighting.

Ase said: "Send the boys up the lane past the barn. There's hickory wood cut there."

Speech came easily with these people.

He said now to the leader: "The feed's not too good here. We'll take the horses for oats and hay. You can put them in the pasture with mine, or in the stalls."

The leader flashed his teeth. His name was unpronounceable and Ase called him "Pav."

"Horse like us. No stalls. Everything best under sky. Food, sleep, love," Pav said.

Ase smiled and nodded. The horses were led to the barns and given oats, then led out to the fenced pasture and turned free without hobbles. Dan and Moll and Prince snorted, ran circling, remembered the small, pied, sturdy visitors from last summer, halted to touch noses. The Romany animals broke into joyful racing over the pasture hill. Ase and Pav leaned on the pasture gate and watched them.

Ase said: "The roan is new. Why, isn't he Grimstedt's four-year-old?"

"Is so. I trade my old Betsy for him."

"What did you give to boot?"

"Little brass ring, is all."

Ase stared at him.

He said: "'The roan's worth four of Betsy."

117

Pav poked his friend in the ribs and chuckled.

"I tell only you. Secret. I buy eggs old Grim, pay two times too much, say nothing. I say: 'I need money so bad. I sell you my fine Betsy ten dollar.' Old Grim lick lips. He know Betsy worth twenty-five, thirty. He make trade quick like a wasp. I take little brass ring off Betsy's collar, put with kiss in pocket.

"Grim ask: 'What that?' I say: 'Reason I can sell Betsy ten dollar. I take money now.' Grim go crazy."

Pav looked around as though the birds were spying and said close to Ase's ear: "I tell him sometimes one mare, not all, sometimes special mare, with gypsy brass ring on collar, she find gold and treasure. Just stop short over gold and treasure and switch tail. I show him gold ring, old gold pieces. 'Oh yes,' I say, 'Betsy just stop short and switch tail. I dig a little. Rings, gold, always there, sometimes not much, sometimes big much, always something. Oh yes.' Betsy not so young, I say, I never cheat him. I got young mare can do same thing with brass ring on collar, so I not lose. Grim shake like leaf. So, I get fine young roan for Betsy, just give little brass ring to boot."

Ase smiled. It was common knowledge that Grimstedt, mean and miserly, was convinced there was buried treasure on his land. Pav began to shake with mirth. He poked Ase in the ribs again.

"Now, best of joke. Betsy terrible balker. Old Grim gonna have holes dug all over three hundred acres."

Pav let loose the full peals of his laughter and Ase was obliged to laugh silently with him. Pav sobered.

"Greedy man biggest fool in world," he said.

Ase longed to pass on the story to Nellie. Her humour ran to practical joking, and certainly no joke could be more practical than this one. Yet he was bound to respect Pav's confidence and should do so. The two men turned back to the barns. Pav watched idly and talked of other deals during the past year, rather more honourable but equally shrewd. Ase did his chores and started to the house for the milk-buckets.

He said: "When I'm done, I'll bring you a few things for supper."

Pav said: "You eat with us tonight. We go tomorrow. So long till next year to talk, play."

Ase nodded.

Pav said: "Bring the flute. We got new song."

Ase turned at the front path to the house.

He asked: "Think it'll be safe for you around here next year? Old Grimstedt'll be ready to trade Betsy back with a charge of buckshot to boot."

Pav's dark eyes twinkled.

"No worry, my friend. Betsy so old she be dead next year, way old Grim gonna keep her hunt treasure. So I say old Grim: 'Too bad, too bad.' I let him cheat me then. Maybe one dollar."

Gathering the milk-buckets and the skimmed milk for the hogs, Ase wondered why he was not more shocked by the Rom's dishonesty, himself with a passion for the truth. It must be from the very fact that each deal had been based on some man's avarice, of which Pav had only taken advantage. No man honest in his heart would have been taken in. The stealing of stock was a more serious matter. Yet even here, the gypsies only stole from those who drove them off with oaths, or refused to sell them the needed foodstuffs, such as milk and bread for the children and hay and grain for their horses. Where they received fair treatment, they repaid in double measure.

Tonight he had four brimming buckets of milk. He had to make two trips between barn and house. Nellie was busy in the kitchen and he strained three of the buckets. He approached her with some uncertainty, to ask for the other bucketful, for the egg and butter money was her own and gave her many small luxuries dear to her, a pretty shawl, a new piece of china, or something special for the children. He cleared his throat. She looked over her shoulder from her work at the stove.

"I know. You've come begging for the gypsies. I saw them. Heard them. Save your breath."

She laughed at sight of his doleful face.

"Now what do you want for them? You know I've never refused you. Just get it out quick before your Ma comes complaining."

He put his arms around her little plump body and nuzzled her warm neck. It was true, she had never refused him. She was as open-handed as he. Only in the case of Tim McCarthy something seemed to harden in her.

"Sweet Nellie," he said.

She kissed the tip of his nose.

"You don't need to make up to me, either," she said, "to get things extra."

She pushed a pot to the back of the stove. She brought a large wicker hamper and began heaping it with fresh salt-rising bread, pats of butter, cottage cheese, jars of apple butter and preserves, doughnuts and cookies, and, balanced carefully on top, three pies. He watched her with adoration.

She said: "See you've saved a bucket of milk. Suppose those wild young ones don't get it very often, but, Lord knows, they look as healthy as ours. Hurry up now, Ase. Don't stand there gawking at me. You've seen me before. Remember? I'm Nellie Linden. Better come back for the milk."

She gave him a shove.

The hamper was heavy. He carried it in front of him with both hands, feeling the terrain under his feet slowly, so as not to stumble and spill off the precariously perched pies. The hamper stood for days of Nellie's work. Yet that work seemed always to sit lightly.

"You've seen me before. I'm Nellie Linden,"

Indeed, she was his Nellie Linden, his love and his delight.

The gypsy children shrieked over the hamper and were hushed by their mothers. Generosity was too rare a thing to permit a greedy peeking and grabbing.

Ase said: "From my wife——"

He glowed with pride in her. The queen, the Old One herself, unpacked the hamper. The sweet foods were laid to themselves on a white cloth on the grass. A great bowl of cottage cheese made a focal-point and the other dishes were grouped around it. The Old One's daughter Elissa smiled at Ase and wandered away. She returned with hand-fuls of daisies and scattered them among the foods to make a banquet table of the earth. The odours from the stewing-kettles and the spits were rich and heavy on the evening air. The meats would not be done before nightfall. The Old One gravely gave each now silent child one doughnut and one cooky.

She said to Ase: "We wish all your house to eat with ours."

He inclined his head in thanks. He returned to the house for the milk. Nellie had evidently given away her full supply of bread, for she was stirring up a bowl of muffin batter.

He said: "I'd like to eat with the Roms tonight. The Old One wants all of us."

In the earliest years of their marriage Nellie had often joined the gypsies with him for a night of singing and dancing. His heart had thumped to see her twirling light-footed to their tunes. Once a black rage had filled him when she danced alone with Pav's handsome, intense son. For the last three years Nellie had no more than made a morning call at the camp.

She said: "I'm not in the notion, Ase. What I want under my bottom tonight is my bed, not the hard ground."

She looked at him innocently.

"I knew we'd be asked, so I spoke to your Ma. She'll go along with you."

He stared incredulously. His spirits sank. His mother withdrew at the time of the gypsies as she had once done from Mink Fisher's visits. Her dislike of them had always a little chilled his pleasure. She must have got wind of the big hamper, had perhaps seen him carrying it down the road, and wished only to see for herself the amount, in order to protest the giving. Her presence would fall across the gaiety like a rain of sleet. Nellie's round little breasts began to shake.

"Ase, Ase! Your Mother doesn't even know yet they're here."

He felt the usual mingling of irritation and relief. This time the relief was the greater. His face of course had given him away, where he would never have expressed in words his horror at the thought of his mother among the gypsies. He picked up the bucket of milk.

Nellie said: "Now get home some time tonight."

He hesitated.

"Where's Nat? He might like to go."

She looked at him shrewdly, so that he wondered how much she knew.

"Pa stopped by when you were milking. Nat asked to take Arent and go on home with him to spend the night."

Ase nodded.

"I won't stay too late," he said. "The Roms have to move on tomorrow."

When Nat was four, he had introduced him happily to the gypsies. He remembered his tremulous joy when they had first begun coming in his own boyhood. His first evening of music and play with them had been like a new star in his sky. They had accepted him at once, as had Mink Fisher. On summer days he had watched long hours from the westerly slope for the first glimpse of the rolling wagons. He had run to the bridge to meet them, to have room made for him on the lead driver's seat, only to be overcome with shyness, until their warmth and affection eased him.

He had watched Nat's face in anticipation of the growing light of boy-wonder. Nat had stared big-eyed, had circled around the gypsy children as though they were strange animals. The dawn-glory had never appeared, the young imagination had never leaped with fire. Ase had thought that Amelia must have passed on in advance her contempt to the child. Yet her displeasure had been for himself no more than a chill wind on a bright spring day. Nat had since played an occasional desultory game with the gypsy boys, always one of his own planning, and he the leader. He had once eaten with them and had made rude faces over the rabbit stew.

Last summer Nat had led the boys to the bog in a game of Indians. If the gypsy adults knew what happened, they kept it to themselves. What Ase saw for himself was the group of boys, without Nat, coming in silence to the camp-fires, half carrying one of their smallest, pale and shivering and covered from head to foot with the evil muck of the bog. The other boys had wiped it from his face and eyes as best they could. The boy's mother took him over, to wash and dress and comfort, scolding him at the same time for going near the bog.

122

Ase asked the group of silent boys: "Why did you go to the bog?"

They shrugged their shoulders.

One said: "To play. We didn't know it was near."

He was obliged to ask: "Did Nat take you? He knows better."

There was no answer.

He persisted: "I must whip him if he did."

The boys looked at one another and began to giggle.

One said: "We were just running. Nobody takes us."

They chorused: "Just running."

"You understand now, you must never go there again. You see what can happen when you go too close and step in."

Again they exchanged glances and there was no laughter.

Nat had not appeared at the house until supper-time. He was a mass of bruises. One eye was swollen shut. He had, it seemed, already had his beating. Ase was cold to his marrow. He took the boy aside.

He asked: "Why did you take the gypsy boys near the bog? Have you forgotten the calf this spring?"

Nat scuffled his feet.

He said sullenly: "I didn't take them. They oughtn't have blamed me."

"But you were the one knew the danger. You could have stopped them. Before they got close enough for one to step in."

Nat looked at his father with an odd glint in his eye. Amelia came into the room.

"Asahel, leave the child alone. He's already told me what happened. He should never have been allowed to play with those wild animals. He could have been the one to fall in. I wouldn't put it past them for one of them to push him in."

Nat shouted. "I tell you, it wasn't my fault. We were just running."

The words were the same the gypsy boys had used. Ase turned away.

"Very well, Nat. Never let this happen again."

He had gone back to the gypsies that evening with foreboding. They had greeted him gaily as always. If the elders had done any questioning they were evidently satisfied. He had almost forgotten the incident. Now, with Nat's retreat, his fears were with him again. His heart was as heavy as his milk-bucket.

The camp supper was ready. The fires had died down and slow spirals of blue smoke arose, to disappear against the setting sun. Low shafts of golden light slanted under the apple trees. The birds twittered sleepily and the bees flew drowsily home to the hives. The Old One motioned Ase to sit beside her. Elissa filled his bowl from the stew kettle and brought him a dripping square of roasted lamb. The Old One patted his knee.

"Eat now," she said. "Throw away the sad face. Later, I tell you your troubles in the palm."

The gypsy band ate leisurely in spite of their appetite, taking time out for arguments, waving pieces of meat in the air to accent a point, falling to the food again, the argument ending as unexpectedly as it had begun. The children gnawed on bones sideways like young foxes. The highly seasoned stew burned Ase's throat, but he had always liked it. He had a second bowl, refusing Nellie's familiar dishes. The women praised her cooking. The children could not get enough of the sweets and the warm creamy milk. The orchard was probed by a rosy light, was abandoned by it. The twilight was the blue of the hickory smoke. Then it, too, drifted across the valley, trailed over the hill-tops and was gone. There was a time of dusk that was never darkness. The men threw themselves on their backs in the soft grass and stared at the night sky. Stars were tangled in the apple branches. A gleam in the east became the crescent moon. Pav studied it.

"No rain," he decided.

The women stirred. They stowed away the quantities of uneaten food and washed the bowls and utensils at the flowing spring. They packed Nellie's hamper with her clean pans and platters. The boys built up the camp-fires. Pav passed a jug of a fiery sweet liquor tasting of peaches. He brought his zither, another his guitar, one an accordion.

Pav said: "We eat too much. Tonight we sing and play. No dance."

Ase leaned on one elbow to listen. The first tunes were

124

sad and no voice sang. They were laments without words from long ago and far away. There was a home-sickness in them that broke the heart. Ase wondered if these people, rovers by choice, longed yet for forgotten hearths of centuries ago. And had some necessity other than the one within themselves first set them to wandering on the highways of the world? Pav swept his strong brown fingers across the strings of his zither. The other instruments fell silent. Pav sang. He sang love songs of such sweetness as the thrush might envy. They were songs of trysts, of love achieved and love betrayed, or cold at last.

The eyes of the Old One's daughter flashed in the firelight. Her nursling was asleep in her arms but Ase felt the old spark leap between them. There had been a time when it had been a spark bright as a star. He had loved Nellie always, but she had been Ben's girl. His youth had yearned to the gypsy girl. The Old One had encouraged it. The summer before Benjamin had gone away he had danced night after night with Elissa and felt her heart beat hard against his own. The Old One had watched.

She had nodded and said to him: "Elissa bring great gift of love. You have good life with us. Some day, you be gypsy king."

The thought of the open road had stirred him and he was tempted. The girl tempted him. Something held him back. He had made no answer. When Benjamin had left him Nellie and she had offered herself, for it amounted to that, he forgot Elissa, he was lost in Nellie. Now, tonight, his flash of desire for the gypsy made him feel for an instant disloyal. It seemed a natural thing for Ben to move casually from one woman to another. It was not natural for him, he thought, who had given his heart once and for all. Well, and so he had. He recognized that the male impulse was a thing almost apart, it responded as simply and instinctively as a singing bird to daylight. He smiled at Elissa with friendliness. All she did, he realized, was to make him feel more the man.

Pav cried: "Enough sad! Now, Asah, the flute!"

Ase brought his flute from inside his shirt. Pav lifted a finger. The instruments broke into a favourite dance tune, merry and shrill as a flock of starlings. The rest of the night's playing was lively, ending with a wild thing Ase had never heard before. He tried to follow it. It was too fast, too intricate, and though they played it several times for him, more slowly, he was unable to pick it up. Pav laughed.

"Only real gypsy can play that," he said.

The children had fallen asleep under all the tumult. The women threw blankets over the older and carried the younger inside the wagons. The men inched closer to the fires and yawned. They would sleep on the ground on a fine June night like this. The Old One took Ase's hand and turned the palm to the light.

"No. Tomorrow. Before we go."

The camp-fires were like bivouacs under the apple trees. The sky was a blue net filled with silver fish. Ase found Nellie sleeping soundly. He longed to rouse her, but she had seemed so tired today. He fitted his gaunt body around the curve of her back and rested one hand gently over her breast. She did not stir.

The queen herself returned the hamper at sunrise. Ase had been restless all night and was up early to start the kitchen fire. Curled in the bottom of a china bowl was a golden necklace of antique design. The Old One hushed him as he tried to speak.

"No, no, is nothing. Now come with me."

The wagons were hitched and nearly ready to go. Ase marvelled that the men had driven in the horses so silently that he had never heard them. The Old One led him up the back steps of the leading wagon. It was immaculate. Copper pots hanging along the walls caught the first glint of the sun. The lace curtains at the window were snowy. The floor was carpeted. She motioned him to the bunk beside her. He held out his hand. She waved it away.

"I tell from the heart today, not the palm. You worry. I know you since little boy. You worry, your son, the Nat one."

She watched his face. He nodded.

"Is not quite good boy. Is not quite bad. Is too young be sure. Is all think for the Nat. Not big inside, like you. I tell you this. Now stop worry."

She laid her hand with its mass of gold rings over his.

"Now this. This, yes worry. Have seen your brother."

Her hand tightened as she watched him.

"Where is he?"

"Move now. Last snow, we go far that way." She pointed to the south-west. "See your brother there."

His throat was too dry for questions. She spoke rapidly.

"Is well, is strong. No worry there. Women?" She shrugged her shoulders. "Sure. That's all right, is natural. Drink? Not too bad, maybe. Now. Is gamble bad. Is lose money. Is got coat to back, is all. I feed him two times, then he slip away."

Ase managed to ask: "Can I write him anywhere? Can you take him money for me?"

"We not like ever see him again."

She put her hand inside her bright embroidered blouse and fumbled for something.

"I find girl he knew. She write this for me. Place he think he be when next snow fly."

She brought out a crumpled piece of paper. An illiterate hand had printed in pencil the name of a town in Nevada. He stared at it.

"Did he—send us a message?"

She shook her head.

"Did he—ask about us?"

"Ask, yes. I tell him, mother fine, wife, three childs, all fine."

She hesitated.

"He say: 'Ase fool stay on farm, raise crops and kids.' He go away laughing in ragged coat."

She sighed.

"Now have tell you all."

He turned the paper over, and back again.

"Why didn't you tell me this yesterday?"

"Give you one happy night. Yes? Worry not so bad in good sun."

He stumbled down the steps from the wagon. Pav clapped him on the shoulder. The last children piled into the wagons, the steps were drawn up, the doors closed. Pav leaped to his seat and cracked his long red-tasselled whip over the leading team. The wagons rolled. The children waved from the lace-curtained windows. He watched after them down the easterly road as far as he could see them. They took with them the thing they shared with him, the knowledge of freedom.

He walked slowly to the house. Ben was well and strong. His mother would rejoice in that. Ben had asked about them all. Ben was on the move again. He might be in Nevada when winter came. All this he could tell her, could try to make much of it as best his awkward tongue allowed. He could not tell her that Benjamin had gone as a hungry beggar to the gypsies. He steadied himself outside the kitchen door. He opened it. Nellie was fastening the gold necklace around her plump white throat. Her eyes were dancing. He could not tell even Nellie that Benjamin had gone away laughing in his ragged coat.

★ 18 ★

ASE moved blindly through the morning's work. Nellie's pleasure in the necklace spared him her recognition of his anxiety. He avoided his mother. He needed the full day to prepare himself for passing on the news of Benjamin. He wanted to give it in the quiet lull after supper when the children were in bed. He wanted to have ready for Amelia, as well, some suggestion, some practical plan, for reaching Ben. Otherwise, she would burst into the hysteria that was close to insanity. She had been almost normal since her return from Indiana. She had begun brooding only lately. Ben's 'fiancée,' with whom she had been corresponding, had never heard from him again. In her last letter, the girl had given up all hope.

Shovelling manure from the cow barn to the compost heap, Ase thought that if Hulda's brother Eric would come as hired man, it was not too late to plant an extra acreage of potatoes for a cash crop. The apple orchard was in full heavy bearing. The fruit should bring a good price among the townsfolk. If the autumn harvest brought in enough money, there was no reason why he should not set out for Nevada in, say, November, to find Benjamin. Planning for the help of Eric reminded him that the coming of the gypsies

128

had prevented his seeing the Svensons to ask about Hulda for Nellie. He finished cleaning out the stalls and went to the house to wash. Nellie was not in the kitchen, although it was the time of morning when she usually began cooking the noon dinner. He found her lying down in their bedroom. She was pale. He sat on the edge of the bed and took her hand.

"Tired, Nellie?"

He stroked her hair.

"Been sick as a stuffed pup. Can't make it out. I felt good when I was carrying the others."

"Maybe we started this one too soon after 'Melie."

"Maybe so. Fine time to think of it."

They smiled at each other. The memory was still strong in them of that warm and windy April day under the hemlocks on the south hill. She had brought him fresh cake in mid-afternoon. She was wearing a blue gingham ruffled sun-bonnet and a blue gingham dress. She had pushed back the sunbonnet. She had her curls twisted and piled on top of her head, as was suitable for a young matron. Ase had taken out the hairpins and shaken the curls down around her shoulders. She looked to him like a ruffled blue gentian and her breath was sweet with wintergreen leaves she had gathered on her way. The hemlock needles were a soft and fragrant bed. The April breeze had lifted the hemlock boughs in a rocking motion, the earth had spun under them in one direction and the blue April sky had reeled over them in another. They had been almost too dizzy to stand.

He said: "I'm driving over to Svenson's to try to get Hulda and Eric both. Come, go with me."

Ordinarily she dropped any work she was doing, from churning through washing to baking, to ride with him on his errands. She shook her head.

"I couldn't sit up right now if my life depended on it. You'd better eat with them if they ask you."

"They always ask. I'll take the boys along."

"That'll be good. Get them out of my way. Your Ma can fix herself and 'Melie a bit for once. Don't take the boys off dirty, those Swedes are deadly clean."

Her eyes twinkled through her misery.

"Tell Hulda I promise not to scare her again. I do need her if I'm going to cut up like this."

Ase changed his clothes. He found the boys playing in the haymow and so, comparatively unsoiled. They needed only a face and hand washing and hair brushing to be presentable. The sweet hay had even made then smell fresh, instead of like a nest of mice. They whooped ahead of him, excited that they were to ride in Nellie's rubber-tyred buggy behind Prince, who sometimes made life worth while by running away. They jostled each other and chatted and quarrelled amiably. Ase retired again into his thoughts. They drove unseeing past the June hedges and fields until Nat's sharp greedy nose caught the scent of the first wild strawberries. Ase waited patiently while they rushed over a stone fence into a field, to plunder and pull and cram their young maws. Nat was still eating when Ase was obliged to call them in, but Arent brought his father a handsome spray. The boys' hands, faces and morning-clean blue cotton shirts were a mass of stains. Ase stopped at the next brook and cleaned them up as far as possible with his pocket handkerchief.

The Svenson place on the main north road of Peytonville was small as to house and acreage, but brought to full production with Scandinavian genius and energy. The family had arrived on foot not too many years ago, owning no more than the bundles they carried on sticks over their shoulders. The natives had kept away from them, complaining of the intrusion of foreigners. Ase had been among the first to call on them, to offer help in home-building, or the loan of horse or cow or implements. The family had been already a large one, the older children had hired out at once, and the Svensons had prospered.

'We were all foreigners to begin with,' he thought.

Only the Indians were born Americans. A few years of the little red school-house turned the Swedish and Norwegian boys and girls, the German, the Irish, all of them, into children indistinguishable from the native-born, except where a mop of straw-coloured hair like a thatched roof, a round bullet-head, or a pair of smoky blue eyes revealed an older nationality.

The Svenson door was wide open to sun and air. Dinner

was being put on the table and the Lindens were made welcome. There was not the variety of Nellie's table, but the food was ample and good. Ase spoke of his business before Mrs. Svenson began with Hulda and the other girls to clear the table, for he had found her the dominant element in the family.

"Mrs. Linden said to tell you she won't scare you again, Hulda," he finished.

Hulda snorted and giggled.

"That Mis' Linden! I t'ink I die. Hide behint garden gate when I go at dark for lettuce and raise up cabbage-head on stick. I t'ink it devil himself."

Ase said soberly: "She's not feeling up to her tricks these days. She was very sick this morning."

Mrs. Svenson asked: "She expectin', then? How long? Two-three months now? Yah, Hulda, you go. Eric, what you t'ink for you?"

The big powerful eighteen-year-old studied his rough hands.

"Yes. If I go training school next year I need the money."

"Crazy boy, Mr. Linden. Wants to work wit' machine, not farm like his Papa. Maybe he see good money you make, change his mind. All settled then. We bring Eric and Hulda tonight, bags and baggages."

Ase walked with Svenson and the older boys around their farm for the polite time of conversation, made his thanks for dinner and took his leave. At the fork in the road he stopped and had Nat hold the reins while he counted the money in his wallet. His credit was good anywhere in Peytonville but he preferred to keep it so, against a day when it might be needed. He had enough cash and continued on the road into town. Will Peyton had a new brand of seed potatoes on hand, highly recommended for quick growing, and Ase decided on these because of the lateness of the season. He estimated the acreage he would plant and the sacks of potatoes were stowed in the small open compartment behind the single buggy seat. He had a dozen or so pennies in change in his snap-purse. He went to the glass candy counter for a treat for the children.

Nat said: "Let me pick my own, Pa, gimme the pennies."

Ase divided between the two. He bought a bottle of tonic that Peyton assured him was unfailing for settling a lady's stomach when she was delicate. He looked around for some delicacy for Nellie and settled on a package of sultana raisins, then added a bottle of rose water. It was mid-afternoon and he hurried Nat over his decision as to which candies gave him the most for his money. Nellie was up, and in the kitchen, when they reached home. She looked herself again, and rested.

"Nobody but you, Ase Linden, could take all this time to ask the Svensons a simple question. Eric and Hulda coming?"

He nodded. It was too laborious to tell twice of his plans, of his trip to Peytonville for seed potatoes. He changed his clothes without comment and went about his evening chores. He called the boys to feed the chickens. The hogs were rooting in the woods now and needed no more than the swill and the skimmed milk. He was anxious to finish supper early, to hold the family conference before the Svensons appeared. Supper was ready ahead of him. Amelia sat daintily at table, in a fresh frilled dress of Nellie's washing and ironing. But perhaps she had given Nellie a little help today when she found her ill. The excitement of the day had used the boys' energy and it was not difficult to persuade them to bed when they were allowed to take their half-eaten candy with them. They divided reluctantly with 'Melie, who went to bed too with her share.

Nellie asked idly: "Svensons gave them the candy?"

"I had to go to Peytonville. They got it there."

He went to his coat and brought her the tonic and raisins and rose water. Amelia lifted her heavy eyebrows. He realized he should have brought her too at least a token.

He said: "I have news for you, Mother."

Nellie looked at him sharply. He must have news indeed when he volunteered to open a conversation. They watched him expectantly. He cleared his throat. In spite of his rehearsals it seemed impossible to begin. He must not permit any trace of his own anxiety to show through. He saw his mother frown, saw her mind begin to work towards various suppositions.

Nellie said: "Out with it, Ase. Is it about Ben?"

He said gratefully: "Yes."

Amelia jumped from her chair and came to him. She clutched his shoulders with hard, probing claws. She shook him angrily.

"Stupid ox! How is he? Where is he? Is he coming home?"

Nellie said: "Leave him alone, Mother Linden. Now, Ase, just begin with how you got the news and go on from there."

That was the way he had planned to do. He seized the cue as he would a life-line. He swallowed. He spoke by memorized rote.

"The gypsies saw him last winter in the south-west. The Old One never saw him looking so well and strong. He left ahead of them. He had prospects in Nevada for this winter. I have the address."

He touched his shirt pocket.

"I'm planting five acres or more of potatoes. If I make enough on the crops, I thought I'd try to meet him out there when the harvest's in. I thought I'd ask him to come back for the winter, if he can leave his business."

He faltered. Amelia's black gimlet eyes bored into him.

"What else about him?"

"The last the Old One saw of him, he was in fine spirits. He went away—laughing."

"Is that all?"

"That's all."

"Give me the letter from my son. How dare you hold back his message to his mother?"

He was trapped in spite of his precautions.

"I forgot, he inquired of all of us."

"Give me the letter in your pocket."

He said gently: "There isn't any letter, Mother."

He drew the rough printed paper from his shirt and gave it to her. She turned it over and over, as he had done.

"You swear this is all?"

"That's all."

She was a dark cedar struck by lightning. She stood blasted. As though the life sap oozed from her, tears seeped from her eyes. They collected, flowed down her face.

She dropped the paper to the floor and groped to her door, closing it behind her.

Ase had expected her to go mad with excitement, to insist even that he set out for Nevada at once, harvest or no. He had not been prepared for this. News of Benjamin's death would have been more welcome to her, if it might preserve the illusion of his love.

Nellie said: "Queer old girl, isn't she? Now if I were you, I'd write Ben to both places. The one he left and the one where he's going. Tell him it won't kill him to write his Ma now and then."

She asked suspiciously: "Has he done something he's ashamed of? Is he making money, or down on his luck?"

He looked at her imploringly.

She said: "Well, Ben'll always come out all right. He doesn't give a tinker's damn if he don't."

She had given him the only comfort possible. It was true, Ben didn't give a tinker's damn. He looked through the bay window. The sun had set but the sky was saffron and gold. Slowly though he wrote, with more assurance than he spoke, there was time to write Ben before the Svensons came.

Nellie said: "I've got to get to bed. Something's wrong with my legs. Put Eric in the room over the woodshed. Hulda can have her old room at the back corner. Tell her to go ahead and make breakfast if I'm not down ahead of her."

She tousled his black hair, passing him. He caught her hand and held it against his cheek.

"You're turning into an old man, worrying," she said.

The room was quiet. Only the old clock ticked away with a sound of importance, as though time would stand still without its alertness. He brought pen and ink and paper to the round baize-covered table near the window. A thrush sang flute-like its evening song from the grape arbour, flew to the garden gate, then on to its sleeping place in the hemlocks. A cow mooed caressingly to her calf. The sheep in pasture bleated to one another. The creature world fell silent. The scent of yellow roses on the garden fence eddied through an open window. The June twilight was blue. Ase shifted his paper. He dipped his pen and began to write.

'Dear son and brother:

I am writing you from all of us——'

AMELIA kept to her room for a week. She allowed Hulda to set trays inside her door and come for them again. Nat whined outside for entrance and at last she let him in. She appeared at the dinner-table one noon without comment. She was haggard but her manner was cheerful. Insisting as always that she had no appetite, she ate with the heartiness of Eric.

The young Swedes were good-natured, with little to say, but the family table lost its cosiness for Ase with the presence of the hired man and girl. Fortunately, Hulda was always anxious to get back to the kitchen to begin washing dishes, and Eric to get out of doors to smoke his pipe. There was left a pleasant interval when the family could dawdle over dessert and talk of private matters.

Amelia said brightly: "You'd think I'd lost my senses. It came to me that I couldn't expect that dreadful gypsy woman to take care of Benjamin's letter to me. She lost it, of course, if she didn't just throw it in the first pond she came to."

She helped herself to another wedge of cherry-pie.

"It's a wonder she managed to hang on to his address. I'm writing him that he mustn't be so trusting, turning over his precious letters to people like that. No telling how many he's sent that way. All lost, all lost. And what he must be thinking of me for never answering. From now on, until he comes back to his own home, he must use the regular mails. I intend to be quite firm with him. Put out that address for me, Asahel, before you go to the field."

Nellie said: "Ase wrote him, Mother Linden. A week ago. If it reaches him, maybe we'll be hearing by the end of July."

"I shan't wait to hear. I want him to have a good scolding right away."

She was flushed and self-satisfied. Ase's eyes met Nellie's. He left the table.

Hulda said: "Dinner all right, Mr. Linden? I don't cook good like the Missus, but I try."

"It was fine, Hulda."

He wanted to thank her for doing so much more than was

135

expected of her. She had kept Nellie in bed for two days, had slipped in an enormous washing and ironing by herself. She insisted on doing everything that was heavy or laborious. Nellie was feeling quite well again.

"It was fine," he repeated.

Eric sat in the sun with his back against the woodshed. The smoke from his rank tobacco came in quick puffs out of the porcelain pipe bowl.

"I think it's time to try something, Mr. Linden," he said. "That acreage of potatoes is too much to try to plant by hand, just the two of us. I made this."

He pointed to a small contraption, a wooden box with handles and a front wheel from an old wheelbarrow. The box had a slit in the bottom, and a lever.

"I saw a mechanical seeder when I was in Trent. This won't work as good for potatoes as for seeds, the chunks are apt to jam, but if it works at all we'll save a week anyway. Getting mighty late for potatoes."

Ase studied the planter and marvelled at the boy's ingenuity. He found himself marvelling, too, how quickly these young aliens lost their foreign accent and idiom. The first generation never did. Even Hulda, too old for school when the Svensons had arrived, would always say 't'ank' and 't'ink' and avoid connecting particles. Eric had had five years in the Linden schoolhouse. Ase smiled at him.

"Guess you were born for machinery, all right," he said.

Eric led the way to the new acreage proudly. It had had to be readied from scratch, the rank pasture grasses turned under, the field harrowed, the rows lined off. Yesterday had been heart-and-back-breaking, dropping the cut pieces one by one in the hilled furrows. As Eric predicted, the planter did not work smoothly for long at a time. One chunk of potato too large or uneven for the slot jammed everything. Yet for half a row at a time, the little implement rolled along, the pieces dropping spaced and evenly. It was a one-man job.

Ase said: "You should have made me one, Eric, too. You go ahead with it. I'll begin at the other end by hand."

They worked steadily. Eric's face was bright, his pale hair gold in the sun. Ase was surprised that Svenson had been willing to release the boy for the summer. It would make a man lighthearted to have such a son labouring beside him.

A day and a half completed the potato-planting. A good night rain soaked the earth. Green sprouts appeared within a week, then crinkled leaves. The bean-blossoms dried, the young beans were infinitesimal pointed swords. Sun and rain alternated, the beans matured rapidly. The winter wheat was ripening. Any breath of wind made it ripple like tawny flowing hair. The summer apples were sweetening under their thin rosy skins. Wild strawberries had been eaten with thick golden cream, made into extravagant tarts and shortcakes, preserved in the sun, and were now done with. Huckleberries and blueberries made puddings and pies. The hedges were thick with blackberries and the birds quarrelled with the Lindens over their gathering. Wild raspberries were ripening in thick and almost inaccessible tangles.

Buttercups were gone. The last of the daisies met the first of the wild roses. Wild chicory in flower was the blue of Nellie's eyes. There was no use for Ase to gather it to take to her, for the blooms closed tight the moment they were brought into the house. Nellie was again not well. Her ill-health was as unnatural as the failure of the sun to rise, and for Ase as disturbing. The road doctor stopped one day and Ase engaged him to stay a few days to examine and treat her. Her swollen legs indicated a kidney disfunction and the doctor gave her a diuretic. She was relieved for a time, then relapsed, and was obliged to keep to her bed for several days at a time. Hulda was a tower of strength.

The last week of July was hot and dry. The corn shot up overnight. Its joints creaked like those of a growing boy. The wheat was nearly ready for cutting and threshing. Ase drove around the countryside to arrange for the harvesters. Old Grimstedt owned the threshing machine. Each grower of grain paid a rental for its use. Labour cost nothing, for when the neighbourhood schedule was worked out, every man joined the crew. Machine and men moved from farm to farm as agreed in advance, according to the ripening of the grain. The wheat in particular was stout stuff and could wait a week or two if crops overlapped. Ase's was the earliest this year. The threshing would begin with him the following Monday, move on in mid-week to the Wilsons and make a circuit, ending with Grimstedt himself, whose wheat was latest of all. Ase drove to Peytonville on Saturday. His weekly paper, *The Farm Journal*, was the only mail in his post-office box. There had been more than time to have an answer from Ben. As he turned away, the postmaster called him back.

"Just finished sorting a sack, Ase. Here's two letters for Lindens."

Ase's hand trembled. The post office at the rear of Peyton's store was dark. He took the letters to the light. They were the two he had sent his brother, one to the Arizona town, the other to Nevada. Both were stamped 'Unknown'. He tore them into small bits and dropped them in the ashes of the cold stove of the store. He would do the same when his mother's letter was returned. She could endure a long time on her hopes and illusions.

Driving home, hunched over the reins, he himself took hope. Ben had of course not yet reached Nevada. He was somewhere between the two states at this moment. It was foolish to have written him so eagerly when his whereabouts were not known. It seemed to him that Ben existed not between two states, but between two worlds. He had a moment's panic in which he thought he would never find his brother, that he would hang for ever suspended between Arizona and Nevada. He straightened, slapped the reins over Dan's back. He would write Ben in Nevada again in October and mark the letter 'Please Hold'. Whether he had an answer or no, he would go west in November.

The harvesters' coming had the household in such a bustle that his brooding went unnoticed. Nellie and Hulda were cooking feverishly as far ahead as possible. Harvesters' appetites were proverbial. Because of the heat, meats could not be cooked in advance, for even the cool stone cellar was subject to the spoilage of August. Pies and breads, cookies and tarts could be baked and stored on the cellar shelves. Gallon crocks of baked beans would keep until Monday. Nellie was a fanatic about cakes and doughnuts and would make these fresh each day. Ten of the men lived at a distance and must be put up of nights. The others would have their breakfasts and late suppers at home and return there to sleep. There were still two vast meals to be provided for some twenty-five men for two or three days. Amelia kept fastidiously away from the kitchen preparations.

On Sunday, Nellie and Hulda made dishpanfuls of potato salad, pickled eggs, coleslaw and one batch of doughnuts, a washtub full. Eric had no scruples against Sunday work, as had the previous hired man. In the afternoon he helped Ase to butcher a hog and two spring lambs. The dressed carcasses were hung in the smoke-house. The family ate as sketchily as was possible for Nellie, not to save food, for there was an abundance, but for lack of time. Nellie went to bed as early as the children. Eric and Hulda, untired in the strength of their Swedish youth, borrowed the second-best buggy to make a Sunday evening visit home.

Ase went alone to his wheat-fields in the long summer twilight. The wheat-ears were so heavy that the stalks bent towards the ground. He studied the sky. A downpour of rain at this time would beat the grain to earth. The skies were clear. The evening star shone golden. He was always anxious for his crops, not so much for their money value, as because they were a part of him, something like his children. He had brought them into being, nursed and tended them, and it seemed to him a betrayal of them, of the land, when they did not thrive. Their failure was his failure. He thought of Nat. Somehow, he was failing with him, and he could not put his finger on the reasons. Arent was a mild boy, perhaps too mild, and gave no trouble. He followed Nat like a puppy. 'Melie was merely a little girl, except that now and then her black eyes, so like Amelia's, flashed with her grandmother's temper.

He cupped a bundle of wheat-heads in his big hands, testing their weight. He should have an enormous yield. Wheat prices had not as yet been quoted. For the first time, he was concerned to make as much money as possible. He would need a considerable sum to make his autumn trek, not knowing what he would find at the end of it. He stood waist-deep in the wheat, tall and brooding, a gaunt, lonely figure like a scarecrow in the twilight.

He was up at three in the morning to do his chores. The

summer world was dark and hushed. The cows rose lumbering to their feet, lowed softly in protest at being roused for milking. The horses in pasture snorted at sight of the lantern flickering so early in the morning, galloped to the fence to investigate. Streaks of bronze were showing in the east when the threshers began to arrive. There was a commotion of greetings, of questions, for the entire neighbourhood met only a few times a year. Teams were unhitched, the horses turned into pasture, except for a mare who had gone lame on the way and was rubbed down and stabled. Grimstedt arrived with his two surly sons and the threshing machine. They began to tinker with it. A large pile of chunk wood was heaped ready for its firing. Eric with a helper drove an open wagon to the lake to fill barrels for the machine's boiler. Ase kept his own horse-drawn reaper. He hitched up Moll and Toby. Moll was old, but Ase avoided using Prince the carriage horse for heavy work except in an emergency. He enjoyed keeping Prince sleek and round for Nellie's driving.

The dawn sky turned rosy, there was enough light to begin the reaping. Ase turned the team into the wheat-field and released a lever. The gears ground, the knives clicked, a wide swathe opened behind, a tawny road through a golden sea. The bundlers followed on foot, gathering the sheaves and stacking them. The sun was above the horizon and Ase had made his second turn when he heard the threshing machine make its sputtering starts. It spat and stopped, spat and stopped. Jim Wilson's crew began loading the sheaves of wheat on the hay-rick. The threshing machine caught with a roar, the steam whistled, the chugging settled down to a steady rhythm. For an hour Ase cut his swathes, the bundlers stacked, the loads of sheaves were taken to the busy maw of the threshing machine, the chaff blew far and wide, the tall funnel poured out its stream of shining grain.

There was an irregular puffing and the machine stopped dead. There were cries of "Breakdown! Breakdown!" Men with a mechanical bent or interest, or those always ready for a halt in work, hurried to join the Grimstedts. Ase remembered that he had eaten no breakfast. He tied the team loosely to the fence and joined the group to ask the seriousness of the machine's failure. It would take half an hour or so, they agreed, to make repairs. He started for the house. Tim McCarthy joined him. In the confusion at daybreak Ase had not seen him arrive.

Ase said: "I'm going for breakfast. Hadn't got around to it."

Tim chuckled.

"I'd of got around to mine," he said, "but the Boss's wife isn't the one for rising in the darkness. I'll be ready for the Nellie's fine dinner, and no joking."

"Come go with me, then."

"And gladly. A belly's a poor thing for work and it empty."

The little man looked peaked and old. Ase wished again that he had Tim under his wing. It was a sorry housewife who would send the hired man off to a day's threshing without his breakfast. Nellie frowned at sight of Tim.

She said: "You'll have to take what I can scrape up in a hurry. I've just got the kids fed and out of the house and now your mother wants a tray in her room."

Hulda said from the stove: "You go on wit' the tray, Missus Linden. It take me yiffy fix two men only."

She pulled the griddle to the front of the range and stoked the fire-box.

"Kids finish op oatmeal, but I stuff you wit' panny-cakes so you run over."

Tim said: "Ah, my beautiful Hulda. Now if you'll be laying me a pretty tray, too, with a posy on it, and be serving me in the front room, whilst I watch the others stirring."

She giggled.

"Get along wit' you, Mister Tim."

Nellie plopped the teapot on Amelia's tray and trotted off with it.

Hulda said: "No disrespect, Mr. Linden, but t'reshing day, would t'ink dat old one could come to table."

She ladled spoonfuls of pancake batter on the smoking griddle. Bacon sizzled in a skillet. Strong coffee simmered to greater strength at the back of the stove. She poured big china cups of it, set down a pitcher of thick yellow cream and one of maple syrup, a fresh pat of butter, and served the first stacks of cakes. She kept baking and turning and

141

serving until a wheeze from the threshing machine told of work ready to go forward again. Ase and Tim hurried back.

Tim said: "A man cannot live by bread alone, 'tis true, but he'd not need much else than Nellie's pancakes and syrup."

He added: "And the Hulda not begrudging of the batter and the baking."

Ase wondered if Tim had noticed Nellie's trace of a frown.

The threshing machine puffed steadily all morning. Eric kept the boiler filled, the huge pile of wood diminished, Nat, with Arent dogging him, carried buckets of spring water to the harvesters for drinking, machine and men sweated and thirsted and drank, and among them poured the vast flow of wheat on to the barn floor swept and scrubbed to receive it. The sun was high. The men were hot and prickling. The chaff filled their hair, their ears, and crept down their backs and chests from open shirts. The work was slowing. The iron dinner-bell above the carriage-shed rang out over the fields and barns, falteringly at first, as Hulda gripped the heavy Manila rope, then strong and welcoming, sweeter than any church bell. The men whooped and dropped their various tasks. The threshing machine coughed and stopped. The harvesters trooped to the house, to the outside wash-bench, laying back their shirts to the waist to be rid of some of the chaff, taking turns at the two water-basins and the roller towel, combing wet hair. Ase was the last to arrive, because of stabling and watering his horses, pitching down hay to the stalls for a noon meal for them, too.

The harvest hands were seated at the dining-room table, stretched out to its last extension leaf. The table was piled with foods more thickly than at Christmas. Nellie and Hulda bustled back and forth with hot dishes. Manners were of no importance, and men reached across the table to spear pieces of crusty fried chicken, lamb and pork-chops, to scoop up helpings of baked beans and stewed tomatoes. They wolfed down the food without speaking. Nellie and Hulda replaced empty dishes with full ones, kept the biscuits coming, made room on the table for the salads, the cucumbers and sweet onions sliced in vinegar, the quivering jellies and the pickles. The famished stomachs were a little appeased, the men insisted they did not need clean plates for the sweets, for they had already cleaned them, they roared with laughter, but Nellie, fastidious, ordered Hulda to remove the used plates and bring fresh ones while she loaded the table once again with manifold sweets.

It was a time of pride in a season of abundance, and apple dumplings and blackberry puddings and wild raspberry shortcakes jostled the pies and the layer-cakes for attention. The block of lake ice from the sawdust of the ice-house was chipped into more iced tea, more coffee was poured, the greediest man of all could hold no more, and the table was bare.

The cry went up: "Clean the table and kiss the cook!"

Ase remembered the first few years of their marriage, when Nellie relished the ceremony. He was pleased by her popularity with the men, by her fast growing reputation as the best cook in the township, but he did not enjoy the rough handling of her by a couple of dozen of sweating, shouting harvesters. Today she had made her preparations. Before the first man could leave the table to seize her, she rushed in a heaped platter of hot apple fritters, Hulda tittering behind her with pitchers of maple syrup. The men groaned.

"No fair, Nellie! No fair! We ate the table clean."

"Clean this up and see if you still feel like kissing."

The fritters were feather-light and delicious, but although Fatty Edmons managed four, a dozen remained on the platter. The harvesters accepted their defeat. They patted their stomachs and groaned again. They wandered out of doors to pick their teeth and smoke and stretch their legs. Hulda's strong back was wet with sweat. Nellie mopped her flushed face. Ase offered to help clear the table and was refused. He saw his mother peer from her room, then mince to the table. She laid a fresh napkin at her place over the ruined damask cloth and waited for Nellie and Hulda to bring plates and food for the three women.

"Oh dear," she said, "those pigs have eaten all the chicken livers."

Nellie said: "I've saved some back for you, Mother Linden. Here."

Ase joined the men at their brief rest. They were as anxious as he to have his threshing over and done with, if the community schedule was to be maintained. They went back to their work. The threshing machine broke down once again in the afternoon, but nearly a third of the wheat-fields lay shorn. It was agreed that by working later than had been planned the threshing could be finished in two more days.

Ase sent Nat with word to Nellie to hold up the supper. Towards sunset the men stopped, hot, exhausted, and inclined to be quarrelsome. It had been a hard fourteen-hour day.

The spring-fed lake a quarter mile away was irresistible, for all their fatigue. They stumbled to its grassy bank, stripped off their clothing, and plunged in. The crystal water was ice-cold, the shock almost unbearable for a few moments. The men who could not swim splashed from a shallow rock ledge. The others swam about with a certain bravado, for the bodies of three men and a boy who had once drowned there had never been found. Hank Wilson soon returned to shore.

He said: "They say drowning's quick and easy, but I always planned on a real nice funeral, and that's not possible without the corpse."

Only Tim McCarthy dared not go into the reviving waters. He busied himself with rinsing out the men's sweaty and chaff-filled shirts.

"They're wet, anyhow," he called. "I'll be making them a clean wet."

The harvesters pulled them on gratefully. The heat of the evening had them nearly dry by the time they reached the Linden house and sat down to the supper-table. Even those who lived near-by remained to eat, as their women-folk would not be prepared to serve them, so late, anything more than a snack. Except for coffee, the supper was of cold dishes. These were ample and tasty, but the men were too tired to eat with their midday appetite.

The threshing machine hit its stride and the job was finished on the third day without interruptions. The Wilsons were next on the list. In helping there, and at the Elkton farms beyond, Ase and Eric were able to keep up with their own home chores night and morning. After that, the distances were too great for going back and forth each day. Most households had boys old enough to leave behind to feed the stock, do the milking, and bring in wood for cooking. Tim McCarthy had given out completely on the second day of Ase's threshing. Even Nellie and Amelia were relieved to have him stay at the place for the two weeks that Ase and Eric were obliged to be away. Stove wood was no problem, for the woodshed adjoining Nellie's kitchen was stacked to the rafters. Tim could manage the milking and the care of the stock. Ase drove away well pleased. His wheat yield was enormous. His week's *Farm Journal* quoted the price as two dollars a bushel. Aside from the other cash crops, there was already money in sight for his trip before the snow flew. He believed as well that gentle little McCarthy would ingratiate himself in the meantime with Nellie and Amelia. He could not give up his hope of having the old man with him in his few years remaining.

Rain threatened over the first week-end and all hands worked through Sunday, so that Ase was not able to return home. When he reached there the following Saturday night, he found that Nellie in her exhaustion had come close to losing her child. She was on her feet again, but thin and pale, with blue circles under her eyes. He was disturbed that she had not sent word to him.

"Nothing you could have done," she said. "A man can't walk out on his neighbours' threshing just because his wife has to take to the bed."

The code was indeed rigid, yet he knew he would have risked community displeasure to be with her in her illness.

"I'm all right now," she said. "Pull up that long face. You look as if your pants were falling down."

The most important job of the moment was to haul his wheat to market while the price was still high. If the crop in general had been heavy, the market would soon drop. He made five trips to Trent, twenty miles away, with the loaded wagon. Usually Nellie enjoyed going with him on his business, but she dared not risk the jouncing of the springboard. Several miles of the journey were over an ancient plank road. The wheat brought two and a quarter a bushel because of its quality. His strong-box was crammed with good green notes. He counted the money again and locked the box. The baby was due in late December or early January. He decided to leave early in November, regardless of weather, to wait if necessary for Ben's arrival in Nevada, so that he might have plenty of time to return home for the birthing.

The dried beans on the vines had been ready for gathering and shelling for market some two weeks, but lack of rain had kept them safe. Eric copied a hand-turned shelling machine he had seen. The beans were gathered, shelled and sacked. These too brought a good price in Trent. The vines made fine winter fodder for the cows and sheep.

August burned itself out. A light frost in September touched the potato blossoms. The potatoes were not as large as a little longer growing would have made them, but it seemed best to dig them at once for fear of heavier frost. A soaking rain on top of that, as often came this time of year, would rot them almost overnight. Ase put down a generous supply in the root cellar for the family and sold the bulk easily in Peytonville. The town folk usually had small vegetable gardens of their own, but seldom used space for items like potatoes.

His buckwheat, barley and oats crops were not unduly large. He and Eric threshed these by hand on the barn floor. He made several trips to the miller at Burney's Dam to have wheat and buckwheat ground into flour for the year's use, paying a tenth in grain for the stone-ground milling. The last trip was with three sacks of buckwheat. These would fit into the back of the rubber-tyred buggy, and Nellie rode with him on a crisp September day.

The sumac was red, a few maple leaves were turning, the hawthorn berries in the hedgerow winked like bright eyes. Nuts were plentiful. Not yet ripened, the squirrels were already eating them wastefully. Their chatter rattled over the chirping of birds. There were no signs of migration. Nellie drew long breaths of the clear air. Her eyes brightened. She made a note of the thickest clusters of wild grapes for later gathering. She was herself once more. The good early

146

days were with them again, when she had ridden so often with him, often snuggled close against him. He put his free arm around her. There had been little of love, between his fatigue and her illness.

She prattled to the miller and asked for a closer grinding of the buckwheat. She watched the great mill-wheel roll over and over, spilling its load of water to foam away into the pool beneath. She dropped in leaves to see them spin. She tasted the raw buckwheat flour, still warm from the crushing millstones. She was little Nellie Wilson, and it was as though their children had never been, no memory of all the household toil and cares. On the way home, she pointed out the grapes.

She said: "Now this winter you can just get out in the woods and kill me some game to go with wild grape jelly. We haven't had either for two years."

Amelia was pouting at the length of their absence. She was fond of Nat, but she made it plain that the care of the two younger children for even a few hours was martyrdom.

Nellie said: "Oh, hush, Mother Linden. I'm going to make apple cobbler just for you."

The corn matured, the shocks stood like tepees in the field, the pumpkins were enormous around them, the Hubbard squash big and noduled and firm. Squash, pumpkins, turnips, beets and carrots went to the root cellar. Cabbage was shredded and put down in five-gallon crocks to make sauerkraut, made into a relish, stuffed inside green peppers put down in herb-seasoned cider vinegar. Popcorn was hung in bunches festooned on strings on the upper floor of the carriage-house. Hogs were butchered, lard and sausage made, hams and bacons hung in the brick smoke-house over slow hickory coals. Nuts were gathered, hickory, hazel, black walnut, beech and butternut. They lay in piles under the popcorn to make a delight of winter evenings before the fire.

The apple trees were loaded. Long-keeping varieties were stored in barrels in the cellar. Nellie made crock after crock of spiced apple butter, put up canned apple sauce and apples quartered in thick sugar syrup. Ase pressed cider for immediate drinking and for gifts, set away a barrel to turn hard and potent for winter entertainment. The rest of the crop sold like hot cakes in Peytonville. Ase and Eric cut cord on cord of wood. Hay-mow, grain-bins, smoke-houses, pantry, larder, cellar and root cellar were overflowing with food for all, until the earth's rotation should bring another season of growing things.

Eric drew his summer's pay and Ase added twenty dollars extra by way of thanks and good measure. They shook hands gravely at parting. October was over and done, the more anxious birds were winging south, ducks and geese stopped for rest and feeding in the marshes beyond the willow-bordered stream. The poplar trees were last to loose their leaves. They quivered in anguish above the yellow piles that blew here and there in the harsh November wind.

★ 20 ★

THE earth was stricken. The out-cropping granite in the bare pasture was the bones of the earth gnawed clean by the wolfish winds. Maples and oaks, hickories and willows were shivering skeletons. Pines and hemlocks were black and ominous against the grey November sky. Crows stretched evil wings on the ridgepole of the sheep-shed, waiting for a lamb to die. No snow had fallen to hide the nakedness of the year's old age. The sprouts of young winter wheat shrank in the cold, would die if not soon covered with the white protective blanket. Smoke from the Linden chimneys was torn as it lifted, scattered like ash across the low scudding clouds.

Ase was two weeks late in preparing to leave for Nevada. Nellie, monstrously swollen of legs, had been ill and delirious. She recovered, was cheerfully up and about again, insisted that he be on his way. Then Tim McCarthy, who was to take over the chores in Ase's absence, had overlapped with a return of his chest ailment and scarcely escaped pneumonia. Tim appeared, shaken and coughing, with his green flowered carpet-bag, ready and able, he swore, to free his friend for the journey. Ase packed his father's old Gladstone with the few belongings he would need, his second-best suit, extra shirts and woollen underwear,

148

handkerchiefs, razor, comb and toothbrush. He now planned to spend no more than two days with Ben, whatever the circumstances in which he found him. Tim had followed him to the bedroom.

"Supposing the Benjamin is not yet come when you get there?"

"I've thought of that. I daren't leave Nellie long too close to her time. I'll leave a letter and money with the sheriff, give him something for himself to watch out for Ben. Sometimes I think Ben doesn't go to the post office at all."

"No answer to your last letter?"

Ase shook his head.

"Supposing the Nellie is took before you're back?"

"I've spoken for Aunt Jess. She'll come the middle of December, anyway, ahead of time."

"That relieves me. I've done many the strange thing in me day, but bringing childer isn't after being one of them."

Ase smiled at his friend.

"I'll only be gone through the first week in December. You've got Hulda. And my mother."

"Ah, your mother is giving no thought at all to the new life coming. Her mind is far away in Nevada. She's fair daft, looking for you to bring back her Benny under your arm like a lost lamb."

They went down the stairs together. Hulda's voice split the air with a scream.

"Mr. Linden!"

Hulda was clumsy and had probably managed to scald herself again.

Amelia snapped: "Hush that hysterical Swede."

Ase and Tim hurried to the kitchen. Nellie lay on the floor. Her eyes were rolled back in her head. There was evidence of dire things occurring. Hulda began to sob.

"It happened just that quick, Mr. Linden. What's to do?"

Ase lifted Nellie in his arms and stumbled to the back downstairs bedroom. She moaned and arched herself on the bed. Amelia peered in wide-eyed and ran to shut herself in her own room.

Ase called: "Tim! Hitch up Prince to the light buggy."

"Will I go then for the midwife?"

149

"Later. The new doctor in Peytonville. Bring him with you. Use the whip on Prince both ways."

Tim dragged on his coat and ran.

Ase fumbled to undress Nellie. Her body was shaking and he pulled a down coverlet over her.

"Hulda!"

The girl came, wiping her eyes with her apron.

He said: "She seems cold. Do you think hot cloths on her stomach?"

She recovered herself. She shook her head.

"I'm t'inkin' hot is wrong. Ice more likely, to stop t'ings."

Her judgment was probably better than his own. He nodded. She hurried to the ice-house with pan and pick. Ase sat on the side of the bed. He chafed Nellie's numb hands between his own until they lost their blueness. He took her small feet in his lap and rubbed them until they no longer seemed made of marble. She roused and cried out in pain. Hulda's towel filled with crushed ice seemed cruel, but he laid it across Nellie's lower abdomen and drew the coverlet close around her neck. He stroked her hair. She opened her eyes and looked at him wildly. Her eyes were like those of a mare he had once lost in her foaling.

He said: "The doctor's coming. Easy now, easy."

His voice was soothing, as when he spoke to his animals. She twisted in a convulsion and then another. He was racked with her, his intestines were adders striking. He felt a vast nameless guilt. She would surely die if the doctor did not come soon, perhaps in any case she would die, and he himself could not help her, could only hold tight to her hands, straighten her legs when a convulsion had passed, smooth back her damp hair. He was a man to whom physical pain was as natural, as accepted, as wind and snow. His own scythe, glancing off a hidden boulder, had once sliced him to the bone; he had lain again for hours with a crushed shoulder under a dead-fall; the pain was severe. These things were nothing. He raged with a helpless fury that this strange agony should come to Nellie because of his love.

He looked at his watch. Tim had been gone an hour. Prince under the whip should have covered the road by now. Perhaps the doctor was miles in the country in another direction, tending some other woman in distress, and if so, would he be able to make a choice of duty, would Tim be able to tell him of Nellie's rareness, that because she was Nellie, she must not die? He heard quick hoof-beats over the wooden bridge, the rattling of light wheels. Tim turned the buggy into the driveway. Ase knew a moment's surprise and relief that the man who jumped down with a black bag in his hand was middle-aged. Because the doctor in the small town was new, Ase had assumed he would be a youngster fresh from training.

Tim spoke from the door: "I've winded Prince. I'll change to the mare to go for the woman."

Ase nodded to the doctor in greeting. He led him in to the bedroom. He retired outside the door during the examination.

"When did this begin, Mr. Linden? Has she had trouble with the pregnancy from the beginning?"

Ase gave his information briefly.

"This is extremely serious, Mr. Linden. The child will come of itself within a day or two, but we can't wait. Have I your permission to take it, to save the mother? It will probably be impossible to bring it alive."

Ase stared. It was a miracle that the man was here, since he did not understand about Nellie.

The doctor said impatiently: "I can't answer for the woman's life if you choose to wait for a normal birth. I can't answer for it, anyway. The kidney affection causing the convulsions has gone far."

"Why," Ase said, "nothing matters but my wife. Nothing at all."

"Good. Send me the girl from the kitchen."

The doctor gave rapid orders to Hulda. She was stolid again, braced to be of all possible help. The bedroom door closed against Ase. He sank into the sleepy-hollow chair by the bay window. He put his hands on his bony knees and looked unseeing over the bleak fields. Tim drove in with Aunt Jess. She spoke, threw off her coat and bonnet, whipped a large white cover-all apron from her bag and washed her hands. She went through the ominous door and shut it quietly behind her.

Ase heard the occasional murmur of her voice, of the doctor's. When screams came from Nellie, so different from her stoicism in childbirth, they tore like claws through his mind and flesh. He stepped outside the house, through the garden gate, wandered blindly up and down the dead brown rows, until he was more frightened to stay away than to listen. There was only silence when he entered the house again. The door was still closed. He heard Aunt Jess's heavy feet scuff across the bedroom carpet. He heard her speak with excitement. He heard the doctor's answer.

"Do what you can. I've got my hands full. This is nip and tuck."

Ase dropped into the sleepy-hollow chair. His legs would not hold him up. He bowed his head in his hands.

"God, help her, save her."

A gust of wind rattled the shutters, blew a whorl of smoke backward down the chimney and into the room. His answer was the November wind. He was presumptuous in his prayer. Who knew better than he that a man and his beloved, one man and one woman, were one mated pair among uncounted millions of all the animal world?

There was life, the mysteriously held together molecules, turbulent within themselves, in the very leaves of a tree, and the leaves fell and withered and were blown away, of as much or little consequence as he and Nellie. They were all too tightly bound together, men and women, creatures wild and tame, flowers, fruits and leaves, to ask that any one be spared. As long as the whole continued, the earth could go about its business. And if the sun's work was one day done and the earth cooled to desolation and all its folk and foliage with it, somewhere on or in or among other suns and earths and stars the life pulse would continue, indestructible, eternal, the Life to which men gave the name of God. Of this he was certain. He was not comforted. This was Nellie.

He stood up and stared out of the window. The bedroom door opened. Aunt Jess called to Hulda for a soft blanket warmed in the oven. An hour passed. The midwife joined him.

She said: "Ase, the baby's alive. Six weeks early, isn't it? A little girl, no bigger than a rabbit, but well formed. I think she'll pull through. Soon as Dr. Holder knows what else he needs from his office, you or Tim must go to town. We'll want nursing bottles and nipples."

The living baby had no reality. His sunken eyes questioned her.

She said gently: "Don't ask me about Nellie. We don't know. That's a good man in there, best I ever worked with. Something queer about him, though."

At noon Dr. Holder left the bedroom. He gave Ase a list of needed items. He ate Hulda's meal quickly and with abstraction. Ase could not swallow. He longed for the activity of the drive to Peytonville, but dared not leave the house. He sent Tim off on the errands. The afternoon passed and the evening. Dr. Holder asked for a cot to be put for him in the bedroom.

Ase said: "Can I see her?"

The doctor shook his head.

"Better not. She wouldn't know you, anyway."

Hulda returned from Amelia's room with her emptied supper-tray. His mother had not appeared all day. He wanted to ask her to move upstairs so that Aunt Jess might be near at hand. He had hoped she would make the offer herself.

Aunt Jess said: "Ase, I can use the couch in the living-room."

He was unwilling to be upstairs out of sight and call of that closed door.

He said: "I won't be sleeping. You go upstairs and get some rest. I'll call you when you're needed."

The couch was as poor a fit for his length as for Aunt Jess's breadth. He stoked the round-bellied stove and sat all night by the light of its red glow. Dr. Holder called twice for Aunt Jess. The morning came grey as ashes, the wind veered and turned to a gale. Tim McCarthy helped with the chores. The doctor joined them for a silent breakfast. Amelia appeared.

She said brightly: "I hope I won't be in the way now. Is everything all over, everyone all right?"

The doctor stared at her.

Ase said: "Excuse me, Dr. Holder, this is my mother."

Amelia inclined her head. The doctor finished his study

of her and made no answer to her question. He lifted his coffee-cup to his mouth.

She said: "Well, a boy or a girl? Naturally, a grandmother is a little curious."

Aunt Jess said bluntly: "A premature rag of a baby girl, still breathing, but Nellie scarcely."

"Why, that's not like Nellie. She usually has her children as easily as a cat. All prettied up in lace and ribbon an hour after."

The doctor slammed down his cup and went back to the bedroom. Aunt Jess followed. Tim kept his eyes on his plate. Ase watched his mother's bland face. He could not conceive of what thoughts lay behind it. Surely, if she still nourished a secret hate for Nellie, she could not think of losing her with indifference, if for no other reason than that she would never consider the care of orphaned children. Amelia ate heartily, chatting at random.

She said: "This will be quite an expense, Asahel. How long do you plan to have this doctor stay?"

"As long as he's needed, if he will."

"Didn't he give you any idea?"

"I'm sure he doesn't know himself."

Tim left the table abruptly.

He said: "Ase, I'll be up in the carriage-shed cleaning harness. Call me for anything."

The day was as long as a week. Dr. Holder appeared for snatches of food and coffee and once went out of doors to walk around and around the house, deep in thought. There was indeed something strange about him. He was a gaunt dark man, almost as silent as Ase. His black hair was streaked with grey. His eyes were deep-sunk and haunted. There were pouches under his eyes that seemed of more than fatigue. His face was seamed and of a grey-green colour. His long delicate fingers twitched constantly. He offered no information on his patient and Ase understood that it was of no use to ask. The alien physician was fighting as grimly for Nellie's life as though he treasured her as greatly as her husband.

On the third day he had Ase send Tim to Peytonville for fresh personal linen.

He sent as well the message: "Tell my housekeeper to turn everyone away."

The days went by in a slow nightmare. There were scurryings in the bedroom when the battle was close and fierce. Dr. Holder permitted Ase to go once into the bedroom. Nellie lay in a drugged sleep. Her small face was as sharp and bony as that of a fox. Her opened lips were blue. Her faint breath came irregularly, seeming more like sighs. Aunt Jess drew a cover back from the cradle and showed him the child. It, too, was blue, so tiny and fragile that he dared not touch it. He stumbled out of the room.

On the eighth day Holder came to him.

"We've made it. She'll come through."

Ase noticed his mother's beckoning to the doctor. They were in conversation only a few minutes. He heard the staccato voice like icy hail against Amelia's low smooth speech. She dismissed Holder and called Ase to her.

"My dear Asahel, you are so secretive. But I got it out of that disagreeable man that he expects Nellie to recover, as of course I have known all along. However, it does seem that she will be ailing for some time to come. Surely, you are not still planning to leave her to go to Nevada."

"Why, no. I put that out of my mind the first day."

"I assumed so. And of course your duty is here. Mine is otherwise. If you will kindly give me the money you expected to use, McCarthy can drive me to the west-bound train this evening. Benjamin will come home with his mother where he would only laugh at you."

This, then, was behind her indifference to Nellie's living or dying. Nellie's danger had been for her a God-given opportunity. His shoulders sagged under an almost intolerable burden.

He said: "Mother, it's a long, difficult journey, with many waits and changes. We don't even know whether Ben is there, or will be."

She stamped her foot.

"How will we ever find out if someone doesn't go? I should always have been the one to do it. Get me the money."

He brought the cash-box and counted out for her more

than he had planned to take himself. He made up a separate envelope.

"This is to leave with the local sheriff for Ben if he shows up later."

"I shall wait until he does show up. Benjamin would never have given anyone a definite address if he hadn't meant to go there. But I'll take the extra money for him."

Her luggage, he saw, was packed already. He understood that nothing Holder said would have mattered, nothing would have stopped her. He marvelled that she had restrained herself so many days. He saw her off in the buggy with a deep anxiety for her, an ageing obsessed woman going alone into a rude land. He recognized her necessity and admitted to himself his relief. Nellie could convalesce in peace.

Dr. Holder announced that it was safe to leave Nellie in the hands of Aunt Jess. He would call every few days in his own rig. He must be sent for if there was a relapse. The man's manner was exuberant. Ase brought out his cashbox.

He asked: "What do I owe you, Sir?"

The thought was between them that the services for so many days, day and night, ignoring other patients, could scarcely have a price set on them. Holder named a figure that was high, yet under the circumstances entirely reasonable.

He said: "If you can afford it, Linden. Otherwise, whatever you wish to pay. Or nothing at all."

Ase opened the box and counted out the notes.

"I should give you everything I have."

"It was one of my successes, yes. It makes up to me for some of my failures."

The man frowned. He held out his hand. Ase shook it warmly.

"I don't know how to thank you. I guess you understood—Nellie——"

His voice broke.

Holder said: "I assure you I had no sentiment about it. It happened to be a challenge to me."

Ase watched after him in the buggy beside McCarthy. Aunt Jess joined him at the window.

"I should have known at the first," she said. "It's drink. He began on it this morning."

Ase was startled.

"Was he drinking while he was working with Nellie?"

"By the grace of Heaven, no, or you'd have no Nellie now. He was nearly crazy, times, without it, but I didn't realize. He was man enough to stick it out until he'd finished his job."

The whole man was suddenly explained. He had been obliged, driven by others or by himself, to begin a new life in a small village, far from his sources and his roots. Ase could not guess what tragedy Holder might have brought some other man's wife, losing her in his cups, as he might have lost Nellie. Ase shuddered. He felt at the same time a vast pity for the man, wondering what had turned him to his desperate escape.

In spite of his promise, Holder did not call in the next week. Nellie thrived and had no need of him. Aunt Jess propped her up with pillows, brushed and combed her curls, was able to give her the first thorough bathing. Nellie began to have a little appetite, and Hulda, delighted, turned to the making of creamy custards and rich egg dishes. Ase could scarcely bear to leave the bedside. He sat for hours in silence, devouring the sight of her, holding her thin hand until she tired and drew it away and fell asleep.

Aunt Jess devoted much of her time to the tiny baby. Cow's milk was too strong for the infant's stomach, and the nurse experimented with water dilution, first with a trace of sugar, then of mild clover honey, and was not satisfied with the results. Tim McCarthy was sent to the Svensons for goat's milk, and this, diluted, proved the answer. The Svensons insisted on lending the milch goat itself, to save the long trip daily.

The first snow fell, soft and feathery. Nellie was moved into Amelia's front downstairs bedroom, where Ase kept a fire crackling on the hearth the clock round.

She asked in wonder: "But, Ase, where's your mother?"

"She went to Nevada in my place."

"Oh."

She smoothed the counterpane. She nodded.

"It will satisfy her better, whether she finds Ben or not."
Her eyes twinkled.

She said: "Too bad I'm laid up, with the old girl out of the way. We had our best times when she was in Indiana. Remember the night on the couch?"

He was horrified.

"Don't even think of such things, Nellie."

"Fiddlesticks! Doc said a mess like this will likely never happen again. I'm not going to be done out of my fun."

She was ready to see the children, to let them play in her room and sprawl on the bed, to beg mouthfuls from her special dishes.

She was able to sit in the sleepy-hollow chair by the living-room stove. Aunt Jess stayed until she was on her feet, and Hulda had learned the variations of the baby's care and nursing formula. Ase paid the midwife. His gratitude was awkwardly spoken but she understood.

"I take no credit for Nellie, but I will say, Ase, you owe the child to me. Doctor was ready to throw her away like a still-born kitten."

He said: "We'll name her after you."

"I've never liked the name of 'Jessie'. But let me name her anyhow. She's such a bit of a china thing, I'd call her 'Dolly'."

He was pleased. The name was close to 'Nellie', which had been his private choice. The baby showed signs of resembling her mother, the eyes deep blue, the wisps of hair were chestnut-coloured and curly. Aunt Jess hugged her to her big bosom and was off, for a bit of rest, she said before she took another case. Nellie approved the baby's name.

She said: "I suppose, after all this, she'll be rotten spoiled."

He kept Tim on, and Nellie did not seem to mind or notice. The old man freed him to spend more time with her. Christmas was spent quietly. Ase made a trip to Peytonville for gifts and holiday extras. The Wilsons came with presents but did not stay for dinner. Nellie had reminded him in time to mail a gift to his mother in Nevada. They had had only a note from her, telling of her safe arrival.

In early February the postmaster had a thick letter for

Ase from Amelia. She described the town, only a way-station in the desert. She was boarding with the station-master's wife and, while things were rough and crude, she was comfortable. The days were hot and sunny, the nights turned sharply cold. There was much more sky than she was used to. The town was a gathering place for the silver-miners. Benjamin had not yet arrived. She would stay until spring. He was likely to come with or ahead of the April rush. She was well. She hoped all was well with the family.

In March she wrote for more money, as she had been obliged to use the money saved for Benjamin. She had also engaged a man to go back to several towns between Nevada and Arizona, where Benjamin might have stopped to work and winter. The miners were not striking it rich, certainly, but prospects were good, and Benjamin had perhaps already made his pile, as they called it. She would need money to pay her scouting messenger. In April she wrote for money again. The family cash-box had shrunken from its bulging fullness to a few hundred dollars.

At the end of May Amelia stepped unexpectedly out of a Peytonville hired rig and stalked into the house. Her black eyes were sunk in their sockets. Her hair was untidy, her black silk dress rumpled and spotted. She looked like a sick witch. She jerked her head in greeting, walked into her room and closed the door.

★ 21 ★

ASE was awakened by thunder growling in the south. The summer dawn was scarcely lighter than the night. The air was still and close. The bedroom was shadowy. Lightning flashed, the polished highboy leaped into focus, the thunder crashed, the room was dark again. Nellie was up ahead of him and about her business. He turned his head towards the east at the next flash and caught a glimpse of her in the garden, picking the day's fruits and vegetables ahead of the storm. In the rumbling he did not hear the opening of the door. There was a soft running sound over the carpet, a leap like that of a kitten, and Doll was on the bed, her fingers in his hair, her warm cheek against his.

"Bear hug," she said, and he squeezed her, her own small arms tight around his long neck.

She was four years old, and every day of her life was a miracle, for she was fragile as a windflower. She was a tiny replica of Nellie, with the same blue eyes, the same white skin and wild rose colouring, with pale curls already turning to Nellie's darker gold. There was miracle as well in her closeness to him. She was a fragment of himself. Their edges were raw with recognition, so that they must constantly be fitted together, else in the separation there was pain.

She brought her clothing for him to help with her dressing. Unsteadily, her pink tongue between her lips in concentration, she put one foot and then the other through the legs of the diminutive ruffled drawers, was trapped by the doll's bodice and petticoat, was rescued, sighed and turned her back in a pink frilled pinafore to be buttoned up. The infinitesimal pearl buttons slipped from under Ase's big knotted fingers, slid like mercury away from the buttonholes, he was in a sweat before the labour of love was finished. He marvelled newly at the speed with which Nellie whisked the children in and out of their garments.

Doll announced: "Now I'll help you."

This too made for a delicious delay, a great and serious pretence of helping on with his socks, a reaching on tiptoe to help fasten the buckles of his overalls, her hands like white moths against the coarse denim. He swung her to his shoulder and carried her downstairs. Hulda had breakfast nearly ready. The amiable Swedish girl was a family fixture now the Lindens had prospered.

She said: "Best eat before chores, Mr. Linden," but he shook his head.

He would not relish his breakfast with the creatures waiting, unmilked, unwatered, unfed. Nellie came in with her overflowing basket, a ginghamed goddess of plenty.

She said: "Ase, I swear you've fooled around on purpose. You'll get soaked any minute and I think you like it."

He smiled and kissed the tip of her nose.

Doll said: "Da and I had an awful time to get dressed."

"I'll bet you did. Probably spent half the time hugging. Ase, for the Lord's sake go on and milk. No, Dolly, you can't go with him. One of you sopping wet's enough."

The summer storm broke before he was through at the barns. The rain poured down, a solid deluge as though a river dam had been swept away. He came into the woodshed with the foam of the milk pitted with the rain. The rain pipes were gurgling, the water rushed noisily into the deep cistern. He was soaked through as Nellie had prophesied, and, as she thought, enjoyed it. Nat and Arent and 'Melie and Nellie laughed at the sight of him, his black hair plastered to his head and neck, water dripping from his long arms, from nose and chin.

"Send out a man and get back a wet crow," Nellie said.

He took off his jacket, shook it and hung it in the woodshed. Doll watched over him as he stood by the kitchen range drying his hands, turning himself around before the heat, Nellie remarked, like a partridge on a spit.

Because there was a cosiness in the dark rain-swept morning, the family was breakfasting at the kitchen table. A lamp was lit on the warming-oven over the range. They had eaten, but helped themselves again, for company, while Hulda piled his hot plate with savoury fried ham and eggs and fresh blueberry muffins. The pot of redolent strong coffee was emptied and Hulda made another. They dawdled over doughnuts and sugar cookies piled with slabs of apple-blossom honey. Nellie had a notion for a raspberry tart with her third cup of coffee and the children must then have tarts, too. Willis, the baby, managed in an unwatched moment to cover his face and bib with the red jam. Ase, sitting next to his high-chair, made the domestic error of swabbing him with one of Nellie's linen napkins instead of turning him over to Hulda for cleaning with a wash-cloth.

Nellie's sputtering subsided and Ase smiled in reassurance at the little boy. Willie was not quite two. Nellie had borne him without the complications Ase feared. He was not fragile, like Doll, true, but something was lacking in his spirit. He was quiet, as even Arent had never been, with a gentle smile that seemed detached and lonely. It was as though Nellie's vitality had been too much expended on birthing Dolly, or the strength of Ase's seed had somehow been diluted. Ase yearned over the boy, he had room for him in his heart along with Dolly, but the child, smiling with shy courtesy, withdrew. His father could not reach him.

Nellie said: "Hulda, go see if Mother Linden wants anything more."

The girl giggled.

"Has already eat breakfast like horse. Maybe she eat two horses. I take more muffins."

"We've all eaten like pigs this morning. I was going to have the tarts for dinner. Well, I'll make cup-cakes."

Among her many famous dishes, one of Nellie's most special was her cup-cakes, for she made them in great variety with the frostings in a veritable rainbow of colouring and decoration. For serving, she arranged them on a huge iron-stone platter in a design, then complained that as they were taken one by one the platter looked untidy. Ase had begun a private project as solution that he thought might please her. This was the morning for finishing the cake tree.

The rain beat against the window-panes. The garden was a garden at the bottom of the sea, the feathery carrot tops waved in the wet greyness like seaweed. The barns across the road were scarcely visible. The log cabin had been turned over to the children as a play-house, where they kept their treasures and played long games, but Nat decided for them that a dash there through the rain was not worth while. He had a love of bodily comfort not quite natural in a healthy boy of twelve. It was simply that whatever happened to Nat was important, and Nat preferred not to be wet or cold. His decisions were the last word, although 'Melie, losing in the end, often battled him in a temper. This morning, he announced, they would play in the attic. They would make tents of Nellie's winter quilts and be Indians in a siege.

"Come on, Doll. You'll be a white child we capture."

She shook her head and slipped her hand in her father's. She would go with him where he intended to go. Nat scowled, then ran up the back stairs with a war-whoop, Arent and 'Melie behind him. Nellie sent Hulda to bed-making and sweeping and dusting and brought out the sacred vessels for her baking. Ase wrapped Dolly against the weather, put his wet jacket over his head and went with her across the driveway to the upper floor of the carriage-house. The place was dusky, odorous with hanging harness, piled nuts and festooned popping corn.

He liked to work with wood. He kept blocks and boards of wild cherry and black walnut seasoning, maple and poplar, butternut and pine ready to his hand. There was something of the satisfaction in carving and joining that he had from the flute. The intangible came to life, beauty was seen, was heard, no longer secret under his muteness. The grain of wood pleased him, the shaded laminations and the whorls. He moved aside an unfinished cherry table and picked up the sections of Nellie's cake tree. The problem had been to make it at once delicate and strong, utilitarian but not grotesque. He had made a previous one that resembled the skeleton of a toy Christmas tree stripped of its needles. It would have served its purpose, but its ugliness disturbed him and he broke it up for kindling. Then in his encyclopaedia he had found his model, a picture of an ancient candelabrum, many-branched, graceful and aspiring. He copied it in hard maple, modified it, struggled with the flinty wood where the slim round arms must make their acute angle. The base was a disc, smooth and substantial. The central trunk rose from the centre, two feet in height, tapering to a point at its peak. Now he lit a fire under his glue-pot. He fitted the branches into their proper holes; they extended widely at the bottom, narrowing towards the top, so that in silhouette the cake tree was a triangle. Each branch turned upward a few inches from the tip; the tips were sharply pointed, ready not for candles but for Nellie's sacramental cup-cakes.

Dolly was enchanted. She was in on the secret, the only one of the children who did not run tattling to Nellie. Ase put away his tools. The morning had passed in his absorption. He took Doll by one hand, the cake tree held high in the other, as though he lifted a light for her path. The rain had stopped without their noticing. They stood in the driveway and looked to the south. The hills were the blue of indigo. From the valley rose drifts of white cloud like smoke from Indian camp-fires. The drifts rolled slowly, were torn, vanished above the hemlocks into the freshening air. A ray of sunlight touched the indigo with a single silver finger.

Ase and Doll listened at the kitchen door. There was only the sound of Hulda humming. They looked inside and motioned to her. Nellie was talking with the children in the dining-room. Dinner was ready. Ase whispered and Hulda nodded. She brought the great platter of cakes to him, chuckling.

Nellie had outdone herself on the frosting of the cup-cakes. There were chocolate icing and white, caramel and peppermint, coconut and lemon. Some of the chocolate were sprinkled with silver pellets, the white were decorated with red cinnamon drops or stars of citron, the caramel were indented with halves of butter nuts. Ase and Dolly set them on the smooth sharp points, the finished pattern a bouquet of flowers. Hulda bobbed her head from the door.

"Best hurry op, Mr. Linden, or she come, then surprise on other foot."

They left their handiwork on the milk-shelf and joined the family. Doll was demure, her eyes shining.

Nellie said: "What have you two been up to? I was just going to send Nat to hunt for you," and helped Hulda cover the table with the smoking dinner dishes.

There was fried chicken, which Nellie did not believe in saving only for Sundays. There were sweet corn and small new potatoes, wax beans swimming in butter and cream, hot biscuits and sliced tomatoes, cucumbers in vinegar with rings of onion, and the usual assortment of relishes and jelly. The noon of the day had turned fresh and cool. The white curtains blew from the open windows. Full sun broke through and streamed across the damasked table.

Nellie said: "Save room for the dessert now. Took me all morning to make it."

Hulda began to clear the table and winked at Ase and Doll. Nellie followed with a stack of plates and they left the table, slipping behind her into the woodshed. They heard her shriek.

"My cup-cakes are gone! Nat! Did you kids go off with them? Ase, is this what you and Doll were up to? Having a party in the barn, I'll bet. Ase, where are you?"

He sent Doll ahead of him with the cake tree, one hand ready to steady it if she faltered. Nat and Arent and 'Melie had rushed to the kitchen commotion. They turned and stared and Nellie stared.

"For the Lord's sake, Ase!" she said. "A pretty trick for a grown man to play."

He felt as foolish as old Shep caught lapping the cats' milk.

Her calm restored with the cakes, Nellie was delighted with her gift. She set aside the flowers and placed it in the centre of the dining-table beside a bowl of floating-island custard. Nat grabbed the first cake. Little Willis reached out his hands, but in pleasure, not greed.

Nellie said : "Couldn't be nicer, Ase. I like the way you waxed it so the cakes don't stick. First I've known you had any imagination."

He was relieved that she had no fault to find. She made their daily living gay and casual, but her domestic perfectionism sometimes had him in hot water, along with the children.

Hulda had taken a heaping dinner tray to Amelia's room.

Nellie said: "Bring me the rest of the cakes, Hulda, and I'll fill up the stand again for Mother Linden. She likes things nice."

Ase looked at her gratefully. His mother's madness was a quiet thing for the most part, she had only withdrawn farther and farther into her fantasies, keeping almost entirely to her room. Nellie insisted that she was only sulking, cutting off her nose to spite her face. Yet Nellie was all graciousness to the dark unhappy woman, pampered her in every way.

Young 'Melie said: "I want to take the cake tree to Grandma. Doll's had her turn carrying it."

Ase was aware of the jealousy of the other children towards Dolly. It was difficult to account for, since Nellie made no distinction among them, except for her long-accepted preference for Nat. If his children cared for him, Ase thought, it would be reasonable for them to resent his absorption in Dolly, but they were indifferent to him. Perhaps the jealousy was part of their general avarice, wanting anything and everything for themselves, as Nat had seized first choice of the decorated cakes. Nellie had not corrected him, she had been amused. Ase felt he should have spoken.

The early afternoon was sparkling, tempting all the family out of doors. The grass was wet, sweet-smelling, and Nellie allowed the children to go barefooted. She watched them curling their toes over the green blades and suddenly pulled off her own shoes and stockings. Her hair was loose and in her frilled gingham she seemed a child among them. 'Melie still played with dolls, especially when she was at odds with Nat. She disapproved of his plan now to continue the game of Indians over the hill, for he and Arent always ended by running away and leaving her. When Dolly appeared around the corner of the house with the old mother cat in her arms, 'Melie fetched her doll-clothes and doll-carriage and struggled with dressing the tabby and forcing it under the coverlet. The cat was passive briefly, became annoyed, yowled and clawed her way out of the cap and dress, and escaped to the barn in outrage.

Nellie was sitting on the garden gate, swinging her bare legs.

She called: "Try the baby pig."

A small pink-and-white porker of a recent litter had wandered across the road from the barn, snuffling the ground of its new world. Nat captured it and held it while Doll and 'Melie put its forefeet through the arms of the long doll dress and tied the strings of the doll bonnet under its snout. Its squeals shrilled out of murder and the mother sow came grunting on the run. The sow trotted along the garden fence. It passed the gate and in an instant Nellie had dropped astride its broad back. She gripped the hairy ears and was off on a mad ride across the lawn and down the road, her plump buttocks thumping up and down. The sow spilled her off beyond the bean-field, where the road began to dip towards the bridge over the stream. She returned on muddy feet, her dress stained and torn, pink-cheeked and laughing. The children rolled on the grass in hysterics and Ase was chuckling, too. She might easily have hurt herself, but she came unscathed from all her pranks. She went to the house to change. 'Melie and Dolly undressed the piglet and turned it loose, for the mother was to be heard coming again. They agreed to join the boys in the hay-loft and went to the house to put away the dolls while Nat and Arent went to the attic for the Indian gear. Ase moved Willis inside the garden gate and brought a hoe to weed the vegetables. The Linden world was quiet for a few minutes.

It was shattered by shouts and shrieks from the rear of the house. Ase dropped his hoe and ran. In the woodshed door stood a suspiciously small tramp. It was dressed in what he recognized as a pair of boy's overalls and a ragged sweater and wide-brimmed black hat left behind by Tim McCarthy. The back of its neck was white, but as he came near he saw the face, well sooted with lamp-black. The shoulders were shaking with laughter and the arms were crossed over the head against the thwacking of a broom in Nat's hands and a feather duster in 'Melie's.

Nellie gasped: "All right, kids, that's enough. It's me."

Dolly ran to her mother with a cry of anxiety. Nat and Arent and 'Melie stood gaping, then Nat frowned sullenly, and Arent at last grinned. They were not so amused this time. Nat could not endure any joke at his expense. Ase was not amused at all. Nellie and his mother had taught the children a fear of tramps, who were plentiful on the roads in summer, and his loaded gun stood in the woodshed corner. Nat might well have lifted it instead of the broom. Yet he did not want to make too much of it with his gravity.

He said: "A pretty trick, Nellie, for a grown woman to play."

She said, laughing again, wiping her sooty face with an arm of the sweater, "I never dreamed I'd fool them so. I thought they'd know me in a minute."

Nat said: "The voice fooled us, Pa. Sounded deep down just like a man. I'd have known her all right if I'd got the hat knocked off. It was way down over her face."

She did indeed have an amazing talent for imitation. She had a talent too in her mischief, so that it was always effective, where his own attempts at mere 'surprises' fell entirely flat. He would never again make himself foolish with anything like the cake tree. She took over the cooking of supper from Hulda. She was still restless, and he knew that he would be allowed little sleep this night. Her intensity built up like a volcano, she expended a portion on her pranks, and was left still boiling. She would be calmer again tomorrow. He was conscious of a slight dread shadowing the pleasure of his anticipation. He could never accustom himself to the loneliness that swept over him when she turned afterwards away from him.

The family was tired from the day of play. Even Nat went to bed early without protest. Dolly came to Ase to say good-night. She clung to him, her lips like a butterfly on his bony face, her small arms tight around his long neck in a passionate reluctance to leave him. Her caresses nourished him, it was almost as though Nellie returned his love.

★ 22 ★

DOLLY, still small and fragile, celebrated her sixth birthday. Nat and Arent and 'Melie were lofty from long experience with birthdays, but with little Willis held out their plates for second slices of the cake. Nellie looked over her brood.

She said: "Doll, when you were born, we didn't think we'd ever raise you."

Nat said: "I remember. She was about as big as a barn rat and sort of blue. Aunt Jess said she had to breathe down her throat."

Nellie said: "Ase, isn't it funny? Look how things change in the years. The time jumps like a rabbit. Thinking we'd lose Doll, and now she's a big girl. You worrying about me, and Willis making no trouble at all. All of it in jumps. I suppose some day it'll seem as queer to have grown children as having new ones."

He was troubled by his feeling about time. It seemed to him that he had always known that he and Nellie would have children from their love. He had seen them from babyhood to manhood and womanhood as a consecutive flow, like the stream that ran from Pip Lake, under the willow trees and the wooden bridge, to join Long Lake, to flow in turn to the Meshawk River, which, he knew, joined other rivers and ran at last to the sea. He stood off at a distance and saw his remotest ancestors side by side with his farthest descendants.

He wondered if he had an unnatural point of view. Time for him was not marked off in jumps, as Nellie expressed it. It was not clearly marked and definite, it was all one, sometimes relative but for ever whole. All life seemed to him contained in the beginning and the end, if there had ever been a beginning and if there would ever be an end. Time was, must be, timeless. As from a great enough height a landscape would show no detail, so from a far enough distance all time would be seen to exist simultaneously. He felt this in his inner mind and spirit.

He ate Doll's birthday cake absent-mindedly. It was six years now since the terror of her birth and Nellie's danger, almost six years since Amelia had returned stricken from Nevada with no word from Ben, since his mother had retired to her room, a living dead woman.

He said: "Maybe Mother would eat a piece of the cake."

Nellie said: "You'd better take it to her. I thought I'd treat her yesterday with apple dumpling and she threw it on the floor."

She cut a slice of cake and laid it on one of the new Haviland china plates, one of her best linen napkins at the side. Ase went to his mother's door and rapped.

"Who is it?"

"Asahel, Mother. I have something for you."

Amelia opened the door. He was perpetually shocked at the sight of her. She kept a certain tidiness, but her hair was uncombed, her eyes vacant.

"Doll and I wanted you to have a piece of birthday cake, Mother. She's six years old today."

"Who's Doll?"

"You remember Dolly, Mother. She was born just before you went to Nevada, looking for Benjamin."

He was deliberately specific, wanting to shock her back into reality.

"Nevada? Benjamin? You refer to my son. You and Tim McCarthy and the gypsies, you're keeping my son Benjamin away from me. He writes me letters and you hide them."

Perhaps it was as well, he thought, to leave her alone with her fantasies. They were harmless. In her darkness they must be even of some comfort. He wondered if he dared have someone, Tim McCarthy possibly, write a letter as though it came from Ben. He decided against such a deceit. She proved astonishingly shrewd at times. If she sensed the forgery, her suspicions would be confirmed. If she accepted it, she might become uncontrollably hysterical with hope, might demand to set out on another disastrous search. In any case, the truth had always seemed to him more vital than happiness.

"Doll, eh?" she said. "Dolly. Yes, I remember. What a silly name. You stayed behind for her birth, when your duty was to find your brother. And then you sent me away instead. You hoped to lose me, too."

It was of no use to remind her of her own insistence on that fatal journey. Nothing was of any use. She eyed the cake on the fancy plate.

She said: "I'll have my cake at the table with the family. You keep me shut up in my room like a prisoner. I've scarcely seen my youngest grandchildren. This 'Doll' now. I hear, oh, I hear things, she's your pet. She was your pet before she was born. This 'Dolly' lost me my Benjamin."

"It was Nellie I stayed behind for. You've forgotten how close she came to dying."

"Nellie, Dolly, it's all the same. Why do you dote so on the child?"

He could not speak the truth to this woman, his mother. Doll was as close to him as his own skin. She lay as deep in him as his very seed. With her, he felt himself complete, often actually articulate. He puzzled over this relationship of parent to child, of human to human, so that one spoke to another with understanding and in turn was understood. It seemed to have nothing to do with the blood relation, but only with some spark that flashed rarely, that said: "You and I together share a bright secret flame. Perhaps, as one, we may find the answer to all that torments us and is hidden." It seemed to him that no man could find it for himself, alone.

He said: "Come, Mother. We all want you to share in Doll's birthday."

Amelia stood starkly by the festive table.

She said: "Dolly?"

The little girl held out her hand.

"Grandmother, come have a piece of my birthday cake."

Amelia said: "Why, yes. Yes indeed."

She studied the child. She sat down and ate, nibbled, rather, as though a cannibal found a certain flesh distasteful.

She said: "Nellie, your husband has been cruel enough to remind me of the circumstances surrounding the girl's birth."

"Now, Mother Linden, be sensible. I knew Ben better than you did. You were foolish to go out looking for him. He didn't want to be found. Ben was Ben, he wanted to be on his own. If he wants to show up here some day, he'll come. Leave him alone."

Amelia rose from the table.

She said: "I will not be outraged in my own house. Never forget that it is mine."

Her door closed behind her. The subdued children slipped away. Nellie frowned.

She said: "Your mother keeps harping on her owning the farm. She's just crazy enough or mean enough to have done something queer about it. I've made the children be nice to her, so she'd feel they're her own blood as much as her precious Ben. Lord knows I've done my best for her. I've often thought what a pretty pickle she could put us in."

Ase was unwilling to believe that her years of kindness and patience towards his mother had been a matter of calculation. He smiled.

"Tim McCarthy said that to me when we were first married, Nellie. You see, nothing's happened."

"Well, she's getting crazier all the time. You talk to Judge Simmons. I'm thinking of the children's future. You want to give them all a good start in life, don't you? Make things easy for them?"

A good start in life, yes, he thought, if by that was meant strong bodies and seeking minds, and something else that

171

only Dolly seemed to have. An easy start for them, no. The two surely were not the same. He heard and read much these days of giving the younger generation 'advantages' and 'opportunities'. Where this concerned a better education, he agreed, with the deep yearning of his own to know the things he had never known, to learn not only facts and wisdom, but the truth, and beyond that, the very nature of truth. Where it seemed to mean a blind leaving of the farms for the cities, a seeking of less arduous labour, the going into the businesses and industries that were making great fortunes, for the sole purpose of making a fortune, he could see not advantage, but loss.

Yet he would not discourage any of his children if what was called the new 'progressive' America attracted them. Nat certainly would never make a farmer. In his adolescence he had a profound distaste for all of the farm life and work that was far more than a boyish laziness. Nat wanted frankly to make money, for what reason he could scarcely know. Arent, Ase imagined, would follow where Nat led, as he had always done. It was too soon to know about the girls, or about Willis. He felt a certain panic at the thought of more children, hoped there would be none to prove as cold and ruthless as Nat, as blindly following as Arent, as hard and snappish as 'Melie, as aloof as Willis, as vulnerable, yes, that was it, as vulnerable as Doll. Children came into the world with characters infinitely more unpredictable than those of the creatures, from whose breeding and blood lines much could be prophesied. Well, he thought, that was part of the glory of human beings, that each was only himself.

Nellie said sharply: "Ase, I asked you a question. You never listen to me. I say something or ask something and you just sit dreaming."

It was impossible to explain that her question had started a long train of thought, the thoughts futile, he must admit. She was right to call it dreaming.

"Are you going to talk to Judge Simmons?"

"Why, yes, Nellie, I'll talk to him. But, whatever the law, we're all right."

"The trouble with you, Ase, you don't have any ambition."

He heard that word often, too, and again, as with 'advantages' and 'opportunities', 'ambition' seemed to mean the avid desire to make money for its own sake.

He said mildly: "I guess not. But Nat does, the way you mean it."

"I'm glad you think so. I've tried hard enough to make him ambitious. I must say, your mother's always backed me up there."

Nellie said: "I wonder now. Maybe we ought to have Doc see what he thinks about your mother."

"There's nothing wrong with her health, Nellie."

"You can bet your boots there isn't. She eats like a horse. Her mind, I mean. A crazy person's will wouldn't be worth the paper it was written on."

He stood up from the table. To an extent, he could understand Nellie's concern. He knew that never, whatever mad or spiteful act his mother committed, could he quarrel over the disposition of the Linden land.

23

THE afternoon in late November was brooding, making ready for the first snow. The yet unfrozen earth was grey. The winter wheat was a brave pale green before the dark of pine trees and of hemlocks. The snow-containing sky was grey, the copper streaks the colour, Ase thought, of Mink Fisher's skin when he had first known the Indian. He wondered why he thought now of old Mink, and then remembered. It had been at this season, with sky and earth so coloured, that he had once helped his friend to begin the running of the trap-lines. He longed suddenly for Mink's presence, since the fur-bearing animals, after years of unmolested breeding, were back in numbers. Also, he realized, his present content was so great that it needed only Mink to complete it. The need of his brother was a steadier, more constant pain.

Ase turned his rig into the barn for unhitching, marvelling at his felicity. All his crops had prospered. Severe cold had held off, so that when the impending snow should fall, his increased acreage under winter wheat would yield sufficient in spite of anything but unforeseen catastrophe. The new barn, called for by his expanding crops, had been raised, with the help of the neighbours. Nellie was allowing him to have Tim McCarthy with him for the winter.

He fingered the cheque in his pocket, walking in the not entirely cold air to the house. He had shipped his apples, his surplus barley and potatoes, his summer wheat, by the new freight line to a more eastern market. The returns seemed to him fabulous. They would finish paying for the new barn, they would assure Nellie of Hulda's help for a long time, they would provide as many hired hands as he might need for the coming spring and summer, for he saw how he might enlarge his money-acreage by developing his wood-lot near the wintergreen bog, and turning the old north-west wood-lot into other and more profitable crops. If and when Benjamin returned, he would be able to hear his brother say: "Well done."

Hulda was doing the washing in the woodshed. Her strong fair arms moved briskly up and down on the washboard. He wondered why she had not married, for all her square-faced plainness, in this country where a man needed a sturdy wife more than a handsome one. He recognized again his good fortune in Nellie, capable and busy as a mother wren, and still the prettiest woman in four townships. He wanted to say something to Hulda, to let her know that he appreciated her, beyond her wages. He cleared his throat, to bring the always difficult speech.

"Hulda, what's the matter with the men around here? Somebody's missing a good wife."

She drew a soapy hand across her face and flushed. He was surprised to see tears come into her eyes.

"Oh, Mr. Linden, dot's the trouble. The one I wanted, a good-lookin' girl she got him. D'odders, all dey want is cook, clean, wash, for free. Better I save my wages."

She said bitterly: "Maybe some day I buy me a hoosband."

He was sorry he had spoken. He had thought of Hulda as stupid and contented. He was appalled to think how little one human being knew of another. Any man or woman might live with a steady heartache and there would be none to know or console. His mother, true, announced her grief as though she beat blatantly on a bronze bell, but it was her nature to do so. But the others were silent: the physician Holder, driven by some tragedy unspoken; Tim McCarthy, a sad-gay little man taken to drink and never telling who or what had wronged him; he himself, Ase realized, keeping secret his concern about his mother and his brother, keeping privately above all his loneliness in the midst of love and plenty.

And Nellie? She went about her family affairs gaily, playing her tricks now that she was well again, her passion not so insistent as once, yet he feared in her secret heart she still longed for Benjamin, the wild, the glamorous, or for some remote satisfaction beyond his understanding or capacity. He wanted to comfort the Swedish girl. He could not think of anything to say. He wanted to put his hand on her muscled arm by way of solace. He wanted to give her his recognition of her value as a woman, even, her solid charm.

He said: "You've turned into as good a cook as Mrs. Linden."

"Yah. I know. I help cook soon as I finish washing."

Nellie and Amelia were in the sitting-room. Ase was glad to find them together.

He said, knowing it would please them both: "Here's the cheque."

He laid it before them on the table. Nellie examined it briefly.

"A lot more than you thought, Ase. Tell you what I want now. A windmill for the well, so we can have a bathtub, and not have to pump water for the house."

Amelia fingered the slip of paper.

She said: "Asahel, I've been lenient about our division of money. I think that from now on you should give me my share."

He could not understand why she wanted her 'share', as she called it, for she had always had access to the family cash-box. When she had gone to Nevada in search of Ben she had nearly depleted their joint monies.

He said: "Of course, Mother. I thought I'd start an

account in the new bank in Peytonville, but take whatever you want."

Nellie said: "Ase, you've got bills to pay out of this."

"I know."

"Mother Linden, we've got to save for the children's future. They'll be needing all sorts of things. You can't hold money out against them."

Amelia said blandly: "I am saying only that we must divide properly. You forget my own child, robbed of his inheritance."

Ase said: "We'll divide, Mother, any way you say."

Amelia went to her room.

Nellie said: "Ase, you're a fool. She'll ruin you if you let her."

He was sickened. He could not eat the good meal Nellie put on the table.

He asked: "Where are the children?"

"Playing in the old log house. I gave them stuff to take with them to eat. If you don't have much to do right now, try to keep them out of my way."

He went to the play-house. It held remnants of the early furniture, tables and stools and rawhide chairs, and enchanting cupboards and crannies where the children could store their treasures. He rapped on the heavy door with its shoe-string latch, for it was part of the fun that no one might enter without knocking. 'Melie opened for him. She was nearly as tall as Nellie and was wearing one of her mother's aprons. She was maternal and officious.

The children looked up indifferently. He felt an intruder. Nat, who had a passion for knives, was throwing his pocket-knife at a target on the wall. Arent was sorting over his collection of birds' nests and eggs. Nat had never been interested in birds, except to aim at them with his slingshot. 'Melie had tiny pancakes baking on top of the stove. Her large assortment of dolls was arranged on chairs around a table, waiting to be fed. Willis sat in a corner, holding one of the reluctant barn cats. Only Dolly ran to her father, clasped her thin little arms around his long legs. He swung her to his shoulder.

"What's my Doll doing?"

"Oh Pa, I wanted to help cook, but I'm not any good."

'Melie said, flouncing herself: "She just gets in the way. Ma says some girls are born cooks and some aren't. Dolly's plain stupid."

Ase patted the child on his shoulder. He was aware of a subtle cruelty here and did not know how to cope with it.

He said: "Doll can do other things. She can sing."

'Melie said: "Don't be silly, Pa. Who wants to listen to singing when we're busy?"

Ase tried to recall where he had heard this comment before, for it was not 'Melie's own. Yes, it had been a year or so ago at threshing time, when Tim McCarthy had offered to sing and play, and Nellie had stopped him curtly. Dolly buried her face in his hair.

"There now, Doll, we'll sing at Christmas."

He felt the child trembling. He wondered to what extent 'Melie over-rode this sensitive creature.

Nat said: "Who cares about Christmas singing? I hate Christmas. I never get what I want."

Arent said: "Nat, you've forgotten. You wanted your pocket-knife and you got that."

"Yah, I wanted a gun, too, and I didn't get it. Don't you tell me what I want."

Arent echoed: "That's right, you didn't get a gun."

Ase had told Nat that he might not have a gun of his own until he was fourteen, some six months hence, and not then if he did not curb himself on random inaccurate shooting. In practising with his father's gun, Nat had merely banged away, indifferent to the wounding of game, seeming to want only to fire, with whatever consequences.

Ase said: "Nat, you'll get your gun when you shoot better."

"I've got to have my own gun, to shoot. Nothing's any good unless it's your own."

Ase set Dolly down gently and left the cabin. He supposed Nat was right, to a degree. A boy with his own gun would surely work harder towards accuracy. He found McCarthy in the new barn. He wanted to ask the old man's advice about Nat's trait of possessiveness but felt it would be disloyal to his son to do so.

177

Tim said: "It's a fine harvest you've had, Asahel my friend. Things go well for you."

Ase touched the old man's arm.

On an impulse, he asked: "Have you heard lately from your brother?"

"Indeed, I have that. He's selling of apple trees all over the country. 'Tis rich he'll be if this continues. Privately, I think, he's no more than eating regular. You know, Ase, he minds me of your brother Benjamin that way, a-bragging and a-bumming over the earth's surface. But good lads, both of them, good lads. A-doing of the thing they want to do, and that's important for a man, is it not? And I've not done it."

"What did you want to do, Tim?"

McCarthy scratched his grizzled head.

"Now, my friend, you do put up a problem. I'm after being a man of simple needs. I suppose I wanted a sort of safeness, a loving wife and childer, knowing where the next meal was coming from for all of us, and independence on the side. Yes, that, to be me own man under any and all conditions. None of that I've had."

He turned to Ase.

"So now you're questioning me so sharp, what is it you've wanted to do and have not? What is it you've been after needing?"

Almost, Ase thought, he knew. He loved the land he tilled and all its products. He wanted to know other lands and other products, to feel strange soil under his feet, to draw strange grasses between his fingers. He loved the changing seasons in this place, from the first blood-root pushing through dank mould, to the last yellow poplar leaf bedded beneath the snow. He loved the March winds, the soft grey rain of April, the summer heat that shimmered visibly over golden wheat, the bleak gales of autumn, the winter ice that closed like a clean crystal death over field and wood. He wanted to know the seasons other-where, a wetter rain, a stronger sun, more sweeping storms and colder ice.

He loved his Nellie and his Doll, felt pity and concern for the strangers in his family, his mother and his other children. Yet he was desolate without his brother, and it

178

was with him he wished to roam far away. And after he had known all possible of this earth, he longed to know still others, to walk like a god to the starry sky. The sky itself could scarcely satisfy, it was infinity for which he yearned, to be absorbed in it, never again lonely, the cosmos filtering through his conscious being, and he in turn returning to the cosmos his own awareness.

It was not that he willingly veiled his mind and his heart from his friends, but only that, mute and puzzled, he could not answer.

"Tim, I don't know."

The old man nodded.

"There's things no living soul can speak to another. I understand. I'd give you your heart's desire, if 'twas in my hands and not the hands of God. You're a good man, Asahel Linden, and I grieve for you, for all your plenty."

Ase thought, this is a rare thing, the understanding of this old ragged farm hand, perhaps it is he who is after all my brother. Yet with his brother surely a man could speak out. He remembered that he had been equally mute with Benjamin.

He said recklessly: "You're not to leave here this time. You're to stay."

"That has been me own feeling. I doubt I'll burden you too long."

The twilight was closing in. They did the evening chores. Tim was as gentle with the stock as Ase. The sheep had not yet been brought into their winter quarters, the weather continuing so mild, but Ase sent Tim to the pasture with salt and extra feed. The children came in from their play at the cabin, washed faces and hands with the usual reluctance, as though imposed on. Amelia, surprisingly, helped Nellie to serve the supper. She gave an extra portion of her sweet to Dolly, stroking the child's fair hair.

Dolly said: "Grandmother, I used to be afraid of you, but you're so good."

"Thank you, my dear. I have never been understood."

The evening meal was pleasant, and all went early to bed.

179

24

SNOW fell softly all the winter day. The world was an
inverted paper-weight, the snow filled the round atmosphere,
it was the atmosphere itself, shredded into these cool white
patterns. Layer on layer piled on the tree limbs, extended
like arms for garments, so that the trees were dressed and
shapely. The roofs of houses and barns and sheds were inches
deep in eiderdown. In late afternoon Ase heard the sleigh
bells ringing, the clatter of horse hoofs, bringing the children
home from school.

Ordinarily the three of school age, Nat and Arent and
'Melie, walked the two miles each way to the one-room
Linden school-house, but in times of heavy snowfall he sent
them off in the cutter, now that Nat was old enough to
drive. He himself had never had the use of a rig for school,
and he remembered the agony of walking, fighting against a
bitter wind, his feet slipping backward, half crying in
exasperation, the miles taking an eternity to cover. He had
done his chores early, for there were signs of the weather's
worsening. He waited and helped the boys unhitch and stable
and feed and rub down the horse. The lamps were lit in the
house when he went to it. The windows were golden. Firelight flickered orange and was reflected on the snow. The
house was a white-banked haven. The kitchen door opened
into a place of warmth and comfort and savoury supper
smells. Doll ran to meet him. She brushed the snow from
his coat sleeves. Supper was early. If the children finished
their homework quickly, Nellie said, they might pop corn
or make pulled taffy, or both. They begged to do it now, to
have the solace of munching while they studied. Nellie
laughed and agreed.

"It'll get all the muss out of the way at once, anyway,"
she said.

'Melie boiled the molasses syrup while the boys shelled
popcorn and popped it all over the fire in the living-room.
Nellie melted a dipper of butter for it. Ase picked out a
cupful of butternut meats for a portion of the candy. Doll
helped him until she pricked her finger. Her hands were so
tiny, it seemed to him they should be used for nothing but

to hold a few thornless flowers. It frightened him to think that she might ever have to use them for anything harsh or heavy or unclean. The taffy was cooled and pulled, 'Melie dictating its breaking into chunks. Nellie warned against soiling the school books with buttery and sticky fingers, and the children licked faithfully before turning pages. Doll climbed into Ase's lap for her own lessons.

She was actually, at six, old enough for school, certainly bright enough, but because of her frailness Ase was unwilling to toss her into the rough and tumble of country school life, where the pupils were sometimes as old as sixteen. Young as Doll was, she shared with him the wonder of books and letters, and he must be for ever reading to her from his inadequate and unsuitable volumes. She knew her alphabet and could already read and write a few words. She wrote now with concentration, her little pink tongue at one corner of her mouth. Ase corrected her spelling and gave her three new words to learn. Amelia had had her supper in her room. She opened the door.

She said: "You've all forgotten that poor old Grandmother likes popcorn and taffy too."

Nat mumbled: "Got a mighty good nose, to smell it through the door."

Doll said: "We didn't forget. We'd have saved you some."

Nellie brought the plate and bowl. Amelia sat down in the Boston rocker by the fire. She spread her handkerchief daintily over her lap.

Nellie said: "You know popcorn gave you a stomach-ache the last time, Mother Linden. Better not eat so much again."

Amelia's sly greed for food was indeed a puzzling thing. It was as though, feeling cheated by life, she would compensate herself in this fashion. Surprisingly, too, she remained lean, where Aunt Jess the midwife, who ate half as much, grew yearly vaster. The consuming flame in Amelia seemed to burn up the aliment as fast as she took it. She ate mincingly and steadily of the popcorn and taffy.

Doll spelled her new words correctly and was praised.

"Now read to me, Da," she commanded.

Ase had exhausted the Bible stories comprehensible to a child, unless he underestimated her understanding. His

Shakespeare was of course beyond her, but he looked forward to the time when she would read aloud to him the rolling rhythms, where his own tongue could only stammer. He brought a volume of his disappointing encyclopaedia and searched through it for items of interest. He turned to the gems, and recalling his own comparison of them to Nellie's jewel-like jellies, passed on his conception to the little girl. She was delighted.

She said: "But, Da, nobody can eat them like jelly, can they?"

"No, Doll."

"Then what are they good for?"

Amelia brushed a crumb of candy from her flat breast.

"They're ornaments for rich and pretty ladies, Dolly," she said. "They dress you up and show that you have lots of money."

Ase felt a slow anger spreading through his veins. He remembered the taint his mother had put on old McCarthy's gift of a silver piece to Nat. He could not allow her to pass corruption to this beloved child. He struggled for words. Doll nodded.

"Just something pretty to look at," she said. "Like flowers. Da, this one, the ruby, is that right? It's the same colour as Mama's red roses."

It came to Ase in a wave of relief that perhaps Doll was incorruptible.

"That's it," he said. "Just something pretty to look at, like flowers."

"Read me some more, Da."

He searched for something with which to feed her imagination. All the pages seemed dull. After 'gems' he came on 'genie' and tried to explain as best he might. He turned pages back again and found 'Gemini', the stars, and here he was more at home. He found courage along with speech and, fumbling, told of Mink Fisher, only a little, but of the Indian's taking him so long ago across the Milky Way. Doll's eyes were wide, as starry as the sky he attempted to describe.

"Da, you couldn't really walk on it, could you? You just have to think about it."

He became aware of his mother. She had risen from her chair.

"Haven't you done enough damage, Asahel, without passing on these savage superstitions? To this child in particular, whose birth kept you from your brother?"

The children were gaping. Nellie laid a hand on her arm. "Be quiet, Mother Linden."

Amelia said in a loud voice: "Don't you try to quiet me, you sly one. I know you, trying to get a claim on this place."

Ase said: "Come, Mother. You'd better go to bed."

He led her away and closed the door after her. She had frightened Willis.

Nat said: "Say, I think Grandma's crazy."

Doll was thoughtful.

"She's very sad, isn't she, Da?"

He nodded, amazed at the child's perception.

Nellie said: "Don't any of you cross her when she's like that. Just agree with her."

Nat asked, frowning: "What did she mean, talking about a claim? It's our place, not hers, isn't it?"

Ase and Nellie exchanged glances. She shook her head at him in warning.

She said easily: "Of course it's our place. Don't pay any attention to Grandma's talk. She's an old lady and not responsible."

Ase was obliged to agree tacitly on reassurance for the children. He wondered unhappily if Nellie and McCarthy had been right, after all, if years ago he should not have had the matter out with his mother, have arranged at least some definite division. Nat sat rocking back and forth, his hands clasped over his knobby adolescent knees.

"Pa, will you sell the place some day and divide up the money?"

Ase stared at the boy.

"Why, I hope not, Nat. This is our home. Wouldn't you like to have your own children here some day?"

"Nah. No old farm for me."

Arent echoed: "Me either."

Nellie ordered them all to bed. Doll tugged at her father's coat.

183

"Da, why is Grandmother sad?"

"You've heard us talk about your Uncle Benjamin. He's been gone since before any of you were born. Grandmother worries about him."

"He's lost?"

"Yes, Doll, he's lost."

He stroked her soft curls, so like Nellie's.

"But she has all of us."

He could not explain the uniqueness of love, so that, out of the largest household, one only might fill and ease the heart.

"Suppose I lost you, Doll. The others wouldn't make up for it, would they?"

Grief and panic struck her, as though untimely hail crushed a windflower.

She sobbed: "Don't ever lose me, Da. You won't ever lose me?"

He took her in his arms to comfort her.

Nellie said: "That's what you get for talking to her as if she was grown up: her grandmother had her scared to begin with."

She took the child away to bed. Ase brought in extra wood to the kitchen, for the temperature was dropping rapidly. He supposed he should not have attempted to answer Doll's question, yet she drew honesty from him always. There seemed no limit, he thought, to her ability to understand him. They were like two streams meeting to make a river, so that it was impossible to tell where one flow ended and the other began. He lay awake a long time. The snow had stopped falling. In the increasing cold the house timbers groaned and cracked. Lake Pip rumbled as its ice thickened. The bitter air was a vacuum. The night, he suspected, was a weather breeder.

★ 25 ★

ASE scarcely knew when morning came, for the grey of daylight did not alter from the grey of dawn. There was no wind. The world was hushed and still. There would be snow again, he was certain.

Even Nellie overslept in the deceptive light, and there was a bustle in the kitchen, a hurried eating of breakfast and packing of lunch-baskets, so that the children would not be late for school. When the house had quieted, Amelia appeared, to ask for breakfast on a tray before the living-room fire. She was bland and amiable, as though her out-break of the night before had never been. She called Dolly to her and made her a cup of cambric tea from the tray.

Nellie murmured to Ase: "Wouldn't you think the child would be frightened to death to go near her this morning? I suppose she's forgotten all about it overnight."

It seemed more likely to him that Doll's gift for com-passion was endless. He saw her straighten the lace at her grandmother's throat, then feed her a bit of sugar cooky dipped in the cambric tea. They made a gracious picture together, the dark old woman and the pale, lovely child.

He dressed warmly to go to the sheep-shed. He turned down the ear-flaps of his fur cap and tied a woollen muffler close. He had not heard the wind rising, but when he stepped outside it met him from the west, a pack of wolves springing for his throat. Driving particles that were more ice than snow bit at his face and hands like teeth. If the weather thickened, there would be a blizzard. He wished he had kept the children out of school today. He was relieved to shut the door safely on the rest of his family. The woodshed held fuel for warmth for weeks, cellar and pantry and attic were stocked with food for months, the winter, even. If the blizzard came, he would keep the children home, would put old McCarthy at house chores, at stoking the fires, and would make his way back and forth alone to care for the stock in the barns. His house was in order, ready for a siege. He had made with his own hands this protection for his own. He felt the deep male satisfaction of the provider.

A young ewe had been bred too early and showed signs of lambing. He sought her out among the flock. She stood gently as he felt her belly. Life was stirring, the lamb lay low in her womb. It would be born perhaps at nightfall. The ram came nosing, spoke to him, then returned to his munch-ing of clover hay. Ase brought extra loads of bedding straw to the shed. The sheep stood knee-deep in its warm sweetness.

He filled the feeding trough with the best wheat middlings, pumped bucket after bucket of water from the barn-yard well. McCarthy was at the same business in the barn. He was pitching down hay from the loft. Ase moved on to the barn stalls.

McCarthy called: "'Tis a bad storm we'll get, I'm thinking. We can make all snug and then keep to the house our own selves, save for coming to the milch cows. Would you consider, now, turning the calves in to suck, do we have a few desperate days of it?"

Ase called back: "No. I can always get through."

McCarthy came down from the loft and chuckled.

"You're a man in a thousand, Asahel Linden. I was hired hand to a devil once. 'Twas in Ohio in a flood-time, and rather than wade to his waist only, he lost a heifer beautiful as an Irish queen. Most others would let the calves suck and ruin the bags for the too-fullness."

Ase took a pitchfork and divided the hay among the stalls. The cows had already come into the barn from their outside lot in animal prescience. A sudden gust of wind shook the building. The snow, hard and bitter, pelted the roof. The day was so grey that the interior of the barn held almost the darkness of night. McCarthy joined him to fetch oats and bran and shelled corn. The cattle could be trusted not to over-eat, confronted with a three days' supply of food, but the horses would not be so cautious. He would have to bring them water in any case. He piled their surplus grain in a corner, to be doled out to them when he came for the milking of the cows.

The wind that had been coming from the west veered to the north-west. This gave a greater protection, especially for the sheep-shed, which was partly open on the southern side, yet it indicated altogether too definitely the blizzard. The snow now swept in thickly, it was heavy and ominous, with none of the feather lightness proper to the season. It seemed to Ase that snow resembled human beings, after a fashion, with an equal capacity for good or evil. It was necessary for covering the winter wheat, it was needed for winter moisture, to supplement the spring and summer and autumn rains, for without water neither man nor stock nor vegetation could survive. Yet when it came, as now, it was malevolent. He recognized in the same instant that he was being unjust in his conception of the snow, for it was a casual, an indifferent, force of nature, whereas mankind surely had a choice.

He said to Tim: "We'd better finish here and not go in for dinner."

"Right you are. The dear Nellie's food will be that more delicious in the afternoon. Listen now, there's sleigh bells; isn't it your light cutter coming home from the school?"

The sleigh turned in. The teacher had sent the children home ahead of the storm. Ase helped Nat and Arent with the unhitching and sent them with 'Melie to the house.

He said: "Tell your mother please to save dinner for Tim and me until a little later."

The children ran to the house, cupping their hands over their faces against the cutting snow and wind. Ase and Tim worked into mid-afternoon, preparing comfort for the stock. The sheep, the cows, the horses, the poultry, the barn cats, all snugged down, content with the amplitude of food and of warmth.

McCarthy said: "'Tis good to have things right and proper. No doubt the Nellie will be after rewarding us with her good ham and succotash."

They were obliged to bend low against the wind to reach the kitchen door, scarcely visible in the murkiness. Ase pulled it open and it flew back, straining against the hinges. He drew it shut after them. In the woodshed they brushed the snow from their clothing, stamped their feet and came into the kitchen. Nellie was waiting for them, their dinner ready. The two men ate ravenously.

Ase asked: "Where are the children?"

"They wanted to play in the log house, but I told them it was too cold, so they're upstairs in the carriage-barn, with the stove going. I gave them stuff to eat there. The blizzard's like a holiday for them.

"Where's Mother?"

"In her room. Didn't want any dinner. She went out for a walk in the snow, she said. She wasn't gone long."

The carriage-barn could not be too warm at best. He went there to the upper storey where the stove was burning bright, where the popping corn hung festooned over the piles of hickory and butternuts. Nat and Arent, 'Melie and Willis were finishing the picnic food Nellie had prepared for them.

Ase sensed rather than saw that Dolly was not among the brood. He checked them over, looked around the long bare room for the child. The room was warm at the end where the stove glowed red and the children cooked and ate and played. The other end was cold and empty. Beside the open stairway hung the heavy rope for ringing the farm bell above the roof.

He said: "Where's Doll?"

'Melie said: "That the first thing you always ask, Pa. 'Where's Doll?' She didn't come with us, that's all I know."

She served more food in her officious way. Ase had a feeling of guilt. It was true, Doll was his first concern. He should not so reveal himself, to the extent of making the other children resentful. Yet ordinarily they seemed scarcely conscious of his presence, or, he was sure, his absence.

He said: "Why don't you pop some corn?"

Nat said, with his mouth full: "Have to wait for baby Doll for anything special."

Ase turned away down the narrow steps, across the driveway through the blinding snow, through the woodshed and into the kitchen. Nellie had finished her work there. McCarthy was nodding in a rocker near the range. She was not in the living-room nor was Doll in sight. He found Nellie finally in the attic, taking woollen clothing from chests and trunks.

She said over her shoulder: "Never saw it so cold. House doesn't seem to warm up. Thought we'd better have extra flannel underwear. The kids getting enough to eat?"

"Nellie, Doll isn't with them."

She said: "Come to think of it, she wasn't with them when they went out to the carriage-barn. Why pshaw, she must be with your mother in her room. Go get both of them and make them eat something. They haven't had a bite of dinner. There's plenty in the pantry."

Ase rapped on Amelia's door. There was no answer. He rapped again.

"Mother, it's Ase."

188

He heard her rise, pushing back her chair, heard her slow walk to the door. She opened it.

She said: "I was having such a nice nap. You shouldn't have disturbed me."

"I'm sorry, Mother. I'm looking for Doll. Nellie said she must be with you."

"Doll? Oh, yes. Dolly. She's not here. Why do you ask?"

"She isn't with the other children."

"She isn't? Really, Asahel, you can't expect me to know all these things. She went with me on my walk in the snow. I love the fresh snow, I've always loved it, it's so clean. It makes me feel young again. You've done such dreadful things to me, but when Dolly and I walked in the snow together, really, I forgave you."

He took her by the shoulders.

"Mother, you say Doll went with you in the snow? It isn't snow now, it's a blizzard. Where is Doll? Where did you go?"

She smoothed the front of her black satin dress.

"Why, we went for a little walk. I wanted to break some hemlock boughs, to make a sweet-smelling pillow for my bed. The needles smell so wonderfully in the winter."

He shook her roughly.

"Mother, where is Doll?"

"My son, how should I know? She had the idea that if she lay down, the snow fairies would come to her. So, I left her lying in the snow. A stupid child, to think that, I should say. I told her it was not to be expected."

"Mother, where did you and Doll go in the snow?"

"Over the hill, my dear, over the hill. Somewhere."

He roused McCarthy by the kitchen range.

"Hurry, Tim. Doll is lost in the blizzard."

The old man shook himself.

"Mother of God. Where do we begin the searching for her?"

"Over the hill."

"Would that be by the wintergreen bog?"

"We'll see."

Surely no child could stand against the wind. Through the driving snow the barns were invisible from the road. Ase vanished from Tim's sight at a distance of six feet and the old man called out to him to wait, else he should be lost, too. They groped their way to the lane gate. The lane was fenced to beyond the top of the hill. They took a moment to consult, agreed to stay within the lane, to take with them all the rope available. They gathered plough-lines, pulley-ropes, in feverish haste, all they could lay their hands on. Inside the barn the gale was a little muted.

McCarthy panted: "What on earth took the child away? And no one to see her go."

Ase did not answer. He could not face questions, least of all his own, not now. He led the way up the lane, bending low against the white, dispassionate fury that was the blizzard. He blundered into the fence, first on one side, then the other. McCarthy kept hold of his coat-tail. He tugged at it for attention.

"Why are you thinking first of the bog woods? She never went there except for flowers, and never alone."

It must be told sooner or later. The wind whipped the words from his mouth and flung them back at McCarthy.

"My mother took her over the hill somewhere to break hemlock boughs for the needles."

"In the name of Heaven! A day like this."

Towards the end of the lane they slowed and searched back and forth across it. More than two feet of snow had already fallen. The old snow and the new were piling in drifts waist-high. A small body would be hidden under them.

McCarthy shouted: "Pray God the child's kept moving. 'Tis the one thing would save her."

But she had lain down, Amelia said. So that the snow fairies would come to her. He had told her no such fantasy. Had she then made it for herself, or had it come from the dark arctic mind of a madwoman? And from madness only? He lurched into the gate that opened into the hill pasture. He tied one end of a rope to a gate-post. Shaking in the cold, he knotted rope to rope, line to line. With luck, the lengths should reach to the hemlock wood, almost to the near limits of the bog. At least the bog was frozen. There was not that horror to be faced, more ominous than ever since the day the gypsy boy had fallen in. Or been pushed. Ase felt a spasm through his body that was of more than the cold.

It was impossible to keep a straight direction when there was no landmark, nothing at all to be seen but a whirling chaos, like nebulae in collision. There were a few more yards of rope remaining. He crashed head on into the trunk of a tree. He girthed it with his arms. It was the largest hemlock of all, standing somewhat left of the entrance to the wood. He felt of it again, to make certain, stripped a few needles from a low bough abstractedly. The crushed wet fragrance was strong and pungent. But there had been no such scent in his mother's room. There had been in her room no hemlock boughs at all.

The trees gave some protection, the ground could be seen and searched within a radius of some forty feet. No deep drifts were here as yet. The bog indeed was frozen, harmless for once. They fanned to the limits of the rope to the left and to the right. No child was here. The trees lashed their boughs and complained.

McCarthy said: "The only other hemlocks would be the few ones by the north-west wood-lot."

So they would be, Ase agreed in his mind, if his mother had truly gone in search of them. And if not, where else might she had led his Doll, to leave her lying in the snow?

"She wasn't gone long," Nellie had said.

He tried to reconstruct his mother's habits. She did wander away occasionally in her desperation. Where was it he had seen her go, from where had he sometimes found her and led her home again? It was most often from the willow trees along the stream. He remembered once finding her on the wooden bridge, stark as a statue.

"My Benjamin left me over this bridge," she said.

McCarthy cried: "Asahel my friend, we'll freeze like the child if we stand here. The ropes will not be after reaching clear to the wood-lot from the west fence, but leave us be trying as far as possible."

Amelia had surely gone to the willows.

Ase shouted, the wind and snow again overwhelming: "We'll try along the brook."

McCarthy repeated, shouting, too: "No, no, the north-west wood-lot, the only other place of hemlocks."

Perhaps Amelia had set out to gather boughs and had then forgotten her errand. One place was no more hopeless for searching than another. He had a despairing sense of haste. Doll might perish in the very moments wasted in the wrong direction. He worked his way back down the lane, stumbling in his hurry. Perhaps she had found a shelter somewhere. Why, perhaps she had even made her way to the log cabin. A child's sense of direction was sometimes as uncanny as an animal's. Hope warmed his numb body. In the deep snow of the road itself he managed a plunging trot, his long legs breaking something of a trail for the little man following half blinded behind him. He found the split-rail fence along the apple orchard and kept to it, tearing hands and knees against its projecting sharpness. The fence ended. He groped for the cabin in the clearing, decided he had missed it, when he crashed into its wall. He felt around three sides before his fingers recognized the door. The latch was stiff and heavy. He had to throw his shoulder against the door to open it.

Tim, holding to him, yelled: "A child could not have entered."

Perhaps through a window, Ase thought, unable to deny himself his hope. The cabin was murky. It must be already twilight of the day, indistinguishable for the storm. He found a candle on the mantel over the hearth and lit it. Their shadows moved like ghosts against the walls. The candle-light sought out every corner, reached under the ancient bunks, into the cupboards, empty of all but children's toys and knick-knacks. A battered rag doll that was a favourite of Dolly's blinked its shoe-button eyes. This was a good omen, surely. She must be in the cabin. He opened the door into the one small bedroom where his mother had slept as a bride. No child was here.

The blizzard assailed the cabin. Snow hissed down on to the bare hearth. The wind screamed down the chimney in a high treble wail. McCarthy shook him.

"Man, we're losing time. It's the wood-lot next and then the stream. Leave us stop by and ring the bell."

The cabin door swung unlatched after them, the snow and wind marched in, the rag doll with the shoe-button eyes

192

was blown to the wide-planked floor and was drifted over.

It was nearer night than twilight, and a cruel thing to ring in the neighbours now for such a dangerous search. By crossing the road and meeting the north-side rail fence, they made their way back to the house driveway and into the carriage-barn. It was nearly dark inside, but Ase found the bell-rope and pulled, and pulled again desperately, leaning back almost as far as Nellie had done in her days of clowning. The great bell reached four neighbouring farms, including the Wilsons' and, except when rung at the conventional hours for calling the hands to table, was an understood signal of dire need, to which all within hearing responded. Tolling the bell, it occurred to Ase that it was fire all would be expecting, yet they would come the quicker in country dread of that. But the blizzard so muted the sound of the bell that it was only the Wilsons who heard it faintly, and agreed among themselves that it was another illusory voice of the storm, speaking its various and evil language. Nellie heard and called from the woodshed door. The two men reached her. They huddled a moment in the welcome shelter.

She said: "Ase, I can't get a word out of your mother, but Doll must have gone with her."

"She did."

"Better come in and have hot coffee before you go on looking. Maybe she found a place to hide."

He thought, there is no place to hide from death when it reaches out its cold definitive claws.

He said: "I can't come in. Tim, go in for coffee."

McCarthy said: "I've not been much of a man, my friend, but I'm staying with you wherever I'm needed to go."

"All right, Tim. I want to go to the stream."

Now it was dark indeed. The night had truly come. Ase lit two lanterns. Again, the two friends followed the rail fence, down the road, to the wooden bridge. Ase turned off to the south. He dipped his hands into the snowdrifts, scuffled with his feet, in search of the unspeakable.

McCarthy called: "'Tis a wild goose chase, Ase, you must know that."

The willow trees were weighted with snow. Their slender branches were too burdened. Ase felt something under his foot. He bent down and dug feverishly in the snow. The object was only a granite rock. He went on. Now he thought that Doll was somewhere near. His groping hand met a small hardness. He pulled on it and pulled again. He did not lift his lantern, yet as he drew the stiff and frozen thing from under the snow, he knew that it was Doll.

A knife went through him, it was a thick knife, jagged and dull, not cleanly sharp. It turned over and over inside his stomach, his loins, his breast, until there was no part of him that was not bleeding. McCarthy heard the low groan of pain and touched him. Ase handed him his lantern and stooped to lift the weightless body. It had frozen in the curled and sleeping position of the embryo. McCarthy led the way with the two lanterns lifted. The tears froze on his seamed old face as they fell. There was no word of comfort he could ever say. He could only hold his lanterns high to light the road for the feet of his friend.

He went first into the house to send the children away upstairs. He spread a quilt on the couch in the living-room, made a sheet ready. Nellie's shrill cries offended him.

He said sternly: "Hush now. Do you not be adding to the terror for the others."

He could not control her. Her grief was primitive and female. It would heal, he knew, and was no greater and no less for the one child than it would have been for any of the others. Ase, he thought, might better have lost his eyes, they were not so much a part of him as this child. He dreaded to speak, but it was necessary.

"Asahel, my friend, the thawing of the little limbs——Leave me be doing the straightening, to spare you."

Ase shook his head. He knelt by the couch and stroked the tiny arms and legs until they warmed into their final coldness. He forced himself at last to draw the sheet over her face. This was a nightmare, surely she was only sleeping. Her mouth held a faint smile, as though in that last sweet and drowsy moment she may have glimpsed the snow fairies for which she waited.

McCarthy said: "I'll try to be making it to town tonight,

if you'd rather. Or get in some of the Wilsons. They could not have heard the bell."

Ase looked at him blankly.

"Why, no," he said. "There's no hurry now."

"In the morning, then, if the blizzard's lessened. I doubt a team could make it else."

Nellie had exhausted herself with sobbing. McCarthy induced her to leave, to go to bed. He knew his friend's need to be alone, knew when they were gone he would draw away again the sheet, to fill his memory, quite needlessly, with the small face. He laid his hand a moment on Ase's head, with all he could give to it of blessing. He turned away, trudged with his old man's slow gait up the back stairs to his bedroom. He found himself coughing. He longed for a pot of scalding tea, but was unwilling to make a commotion in the kitchen.

Ase sat all night by the side of the couch. The fire died down and he was not aware that he was cold until suddenly his fingers were too numb to move to touch the child's marble forehead. He thought in a panic, he must keep the room warm for Doll. He built up the fire again. The blizzard shook the house. It came inside, trampled him under iced and silver hoofs. He thought irrelevantly of the ewe about to yean, she would perhaps not own the lamb, and then he would bring the woolly orphan to a box behind the kitchen stove and raise it on a bottle. He had promised Dolly the first orphan lamb for her own. The knife turned in him again, the pain rose to his throat so that he was suffocated. Sweat stood on his forehead. He clenched his fists against the anguish tearing out his vitals.

The wind cried high and thin as in the cabin.

All night it cried: "Don't ever lose me, Da! Don't ever lose me!"

★ 26 ★

THE lilacs, growing bold too long, had over-reached themselves. In their eighteen years since Nellie had planted them, they had grown faster than Nat, now nearly as tall as his father. The mass of lavender panicles made a hanging garden of its own, the fragrance almost too much of a sweetness, so that Ase Linden shook his head to free his nostrils. Slyly, through the years, the lilacs had sent out insidious suckers. Ase saw with surprise that the young shoots had not only encroached on a portion of the gravelled driveway and on the smooth lawn, but were flourishing in a veritable thicket beyond the west fence, and into the field which he planned to plant this spring to buckwheat.

He brought a grubbing-hoe and set to work to rout them out. They were tough, resistant. He felt the landsman's dislike for the growing thing that ran wild beyond control. A shower of morning dew sprayed over his face from the pendulous bloom he jostled. He took it for reproach, for there were many things that spread as carelessly, but that delighted him: mint and water-cress along the willow stream, wild strawberries, even buttercups and daisies. He loved flowers as Nellie did, and with an added awareness of the mystery of their haunts, the magic of snowdrop and blood-root and arbutus coming to blossom on the very heels of the retreating winter. Yet the lilacs had always disturbed him. He leaned on his hoe. Of course. He remembered now. He had awakened to the scent of Nellie's lilacs so long ago, when he had been frightened for her, giving birth to their first-born. It was he who was unreasonable and not the lilacs. When he was done with his hoeing, driveway, lawn and field clear of the suckers, he broke an armful of the flowers in something of apology. He divided them, took one bouquet to Nellie in the kitchen, and rapped on the door of his mother's room to present her with the other.

Amelia's voice called weakly: "Come in."

She lay propped against her pillows. She seemed so old, so old. He laid the lilacs on her knees, bony under the coverlet, and took one of her withered, blue-veined hands in his gnarled one.

"Lilacs, Mother."

"Yes, I can smell them. Nellie's lilacs. I remember when she brought them here."

So she too, he thought, had been going back into the past on this fair April morning. Her hands plucked at the

196

bedclothes, as though she picked over the rags of memory.

"It seems just yesterday," she said.

"It was eighteen years ago."

He released her hand and sat in silence, counting. Why, his mother was not old at all, as age went in this sturdy country.

"Let me think now, Nellie and I are forty years of age, or thereabouts, my mother is something past seventy, and that is nothing."

Old Grimstedt, who thought to cheat Pav the gypsy, was in his nineties, still taking his turn at the harvesting. The two foreign brothers down the road, who kept to themselves and made coffee of their barley grain, they were men near eighty, still working their land alone and prospering, hiding their wealth, folk said, under their mattress.

No, Ase thought, my mother is not old, not old enough to lie like this against her pillows. Yet what was it that aged a man or a woman? Nellie was often as young and blithe, as mischievous, as in her girlhood. As for himself, it seemed to him that he had been born old. He recalled all that had tormented his mother, to make her old before her time. She lifted the lilacs to her face.

Holder the physician had been right about her. Ase leaned back in his chair and revived in anguish the day of the burying of his Doll, the child who was alone blood of his blood, flesh of his flesh, bone of his bone. He was back in that day, completely vivid again, and it was a day in and of eternity.

It had been necessary to wait to bury Doll until the blizzard ended, until the frozen ground thawed enough to dig her little grave. He remembered that as the tiny coffin was lowered into the dark and final earth, he had thought that after all, Doll would never need to use her delicate hands for anything more harsh than the holding of thornless flowers. He thought of the second grave, the larger coffin. He had lost Tim McCarthy, too, a few days after Doll. The exposure during the search had finished the old fellow. Tim and Doll were laid side by side under the ambiguous earth, an earth that gave and an earth that received. Ase had been conscious of Nellie's satisfaction, under her grief, that

McCarthy was proving so little trouble after all. He recalled the vacuity of the double funeral sermon, for there was as little the man of God could find to say of the one as of the other, the child dead untimely, the old man, the preacher intimated, having lived a life as wasted. The death of Tim had been a muted thing. Against the diapason of his agony, the lesser note was for the moment lost.

Doll and Tim, he could think of them now together, a linked thread in the pattern of pain. Yet when first the larger grave had been covered over, and then the smaller, Tim's had been the shadow and Doll's the substance. Amelia's stark reality had remained as always, but now sharply to be questioned.

He himself would not have known how to raise the question about his mother. Returned home from the burying, he sat numb. Dr. Holder and Nellie had asked him to choose between two various ways of tearing himself to pieces. Nellie had begun it.

She had said: "Ase, I've asked Doc what we ought to do about your mother."

Holder had said gently: "I know this is painful for you, Linden, I know it's difficult for you to speak, but we have to get down to bed-rock. Nellie told me about your mother's taking the child out into the beginning of the blizzard and leaving her there to die."

The words rang in his ears with the metal clangour of the tolling bell no neighbour had heard or, hearing, understood and heeded.

"The first question, Linden, is whether she knew what she was doing. The next, in which case is she most dangerous?"

Ase had not answered. Holder had continued with the physician's ruthful mercilessness.

"If she meant to do it, she may be no longer dangerous, for she seems to have hated only the one child. Yet still, that's murder, and my duty would be to certify her as criminally insane. On the other hand, if her mind was merely wandering and there was no evil intention, she might easily, another time, lead Willis into some similar disaster. To your famous bog, for instance. Have I laid out the issues fairly?"

Ase had nodded. He was cold to the marrow of his bones. "Well, Linden, what's your feeling about it?"

His feeling? Why, it was only of nameless horror, deep and black as the bog, enveloping as the blizzard.

Nellie said wearily: "Doc, you can't ask the man to pass sentence on his own mother. I'm willing to leave it up to you, if he is."

Ase had stared a long time out of the window, across the grey hideous slush the thaw had made of the snow. It was asking too much of the physician, too, he thought, to pass judgment on a human soul. That was a function of God. Or was each soul supposed to judge itself, was that the ladder by which it climbed towards godhood? And if so, where and whose was the responsibility when a soul like Amelia's had lost, apparently, all power of judgment? Did it then lie in the opaque and timeless hands of time?

Holder persisted: "Would you like to call in some of Nellie's people? Other doctors, perhaps, or your friend the Judge, a home-made jury, shall we say, if you're unwilling to pass on your mother's guilt?"

Tim, Ase thought, only Tim might now have helped him. Nellie spoke sharply.

"Keep it in this house, Doc. Gossip about it's not right for the children. Unless she has to be put away, then everyone'll know, anyhow. Ase, you have to say. Either what you know or think. Or will you leave it up to Doc?"

He saw his mother behind tall barred windows, the screams of maniacs picking at her like carrion crows. It would take but a little of this to kill her. And if she were better dead? He saw her roaming over the pasture hill, another of Nellie's children by the hand, moving towards the bog.

As though he bowed indeed to God, he said: "Whatever you decide, Doctor," knowing he was frightened.

Holder drew a long breath.

"Very well. It's a risk for all of us, but let's keep her here for the time being. Watch her closely. Warn the children that she's not responsible. If she shows any peculiarity she hasn't had before, let me know at once and we'll make another decision. I think this is the way you want it, Linden. Nellie?"

She passed her hand over her tear-swollen eyes, brushed back her curls from her forehead. She spoke directly to her husband.

"I can stand her around a few more years, if you can bear the sight of her."

Ase laid his hand on hers.

He said: "You're so good."

Sitting at his mother's bedside now, Ase brought himself back from his memories of that day. It had seemed a long time, as time went for one family, with the children growing fast, and Amelia only fading away, turning to skin and bones in her bedroom. He was obliged to ask himself again if she had truly murdered Doll, had been terrified, after, by her act, and so had quieted. He put aside his panic at the thought. In any case, Holder's judgment had proved correct. She had given no trouble of any sort, had turned almost gentle, lying in her bed against her pillows, even smiling sometimes at Nellie when her tray of food was brought her. Nellie's patience had been inexhaustible.

"Shall I put the lilacs in water for you, Mother?"

"That will be nice. On the mantel, where I can see them. So pretty. Dear Nellie's lilacs."

And was this, he thought, another spurious thing, was his mother hiding behind the lilacs? But she had been always hidden. He brought a vase and arranged the flowers awkwardly.

Nellie had shortened the stems of the lilacs he had taken her and made a low bouquet for the dining-room table. The day was Saturday, so that the children were home from school.

Nellie said: "Goodness knows where the boys have gone to, you'd better ring the dinner-bell."

He went to the carriage-shed and tolled the bell. He was annoyed with himself for being reluctant to ring it, as he had been ashamed to find that he had blamed the lilacs this morning. Yet ever since the twilight of the blizzard, when he and Tim McCarthy had rung the bell, and no help had come, he had hated the bell as he hated the lilacs. If the bell had been heard, been recognized, the Wilsons would have come, and the other neighbours, and Doll been found in time to save her. How could a man escape his self-centredness, he pondered, how divide the inevitable from his private destiny, from his own failures and stupidity? For he would never be done with his sense of guilt at losing Doll. He should have asked for her earlier, he should have been constantly aware that a life as precious as hers was always menaced, if not by Amelia, by some other obscurity that disliked perfection. As the last stroke of the bell died away, he heard Nat and Arent and 'Melie and Willis running to the house, children of his loins but not his heart, to Nellie's bountiful table. It came to him that the one strong family bond was Nellie's food.

Nellie said: "Quiet down, you kids. I won't have a racket at the table."

Ase thought, half smiling: 'Mrs. Joshua, you might as well tell the sun to stand still.'

Nat at seventeen was half man, half boy. He was nearly six feet tall and was not done growing. His shoulders were broad and he would make a bulkier man than his father. His colouring after all had not resembled that of his Uncle Ben, but that of the male Wilsons. His smooth hair was sandy, his eyes were pale and cold. His beard was sprouting, so that a weekly shaving came at once too often and too seldom, which distressed him. He was particular about his cleanliness and his clothing, complained that he was not well enough dressed. Yesterday, in preparation for the Friday night school dance at the Academy in Peytonville, he had doused himself with Nellie's lavender toilet water, was in a rage to find the scent, too late, unsuitable. His adolescent surliness had hardened, he was a crude block of stone the sculptor had not yet finished. Yet the chisel-marks, his father was unhappily certain, already indicated an ultimate ruthlessness of character.

Ase helped himself to the home-corned beef and passed the platter to Arent, sitting next him. Arent passed the platter to Nat before helping himself.

'Melie snapped: "Hurry up, you greedy pigs. Ladies first."

Nellie said: "Behave now, all of you."

Ase was ashamed that his lack of affection for 'Melie came so close to actual dislike. She was the image of his mother with the same spare frame, the same close-set black eyes and sleek black hair. For better or for worse he loved his mother. He could not bring himself to love this girl, so officious, so unduly maternal, so sharp and cruel of tongue. 'Melie and Nat had always sided together against the others. They shared a common hardness, a similar and as yet unrevealed purpose. Ase sighed, eating steadily without notice of what he ate.

Thank God, Ase thought, Nellie was done with child-bearing. She was more precious than the whole raft of them, except of course for Dolly. The old gnawing pain assailed him. He was aroused by laughter all round the table.

Nat said: "Pa, we've been holding the pie in front of your nose for ten minutes."

Nellie said: "Now you know how your father is. He goes off into a trance and isn't thinking at all, just dreaming about nothing."

Ase felt a slow anger. He had an impulse to raise a great paw like that of a bear, to brush them all aside. Then he was ashamed. A father at table should join himself to the others, whatever his private concerns. The breaking of bread together, the sharing of salt, the eating of meat, was a sacred thing, one small community against the outer darkness.

He said: "I'm sorry," and cut a wedge of pie, and could not eat it.

He left the table and walked across the road. The apple orchard was mature. Spring was early, the orchard was as he had dreamed of it before its planting, as a parent dreams of an unborn child, then finds the mien and character fulfilled. The pink and white bloom was a sea. It spilled over the hillside in rolling waves. The fragrance poured over him. He breathed of it deeply, feeling cleansed. This too he had helped create. It was beautiful and good.

★ 27 ★

FROST came on the first morning of October. Ase felt the clean sharpness prick the hairs of his nostrils. Dolly had learned to sing in her birdlike voice: "Jackie Frost, Jackie

Frost, comes in the night——" He hurried out of the house, as though he might catch sight of that droll fellow Jack going away over the hill, scattering from his paint-brush the last of the white crystals. He would have enjoyed living in pagan times, he thought. He had read again and again in his encyclopaedia of the ancient myths, had found himself nodding in half agreement. It seemed a natural thing to personify the seasons and the elements.

He stood at the edge of the road between the house and the barns. He looked out over the fields, the meadows, the planted crops. The sky was of a denim blue, the frost was melting under the golden sun, the corn was golden, too, the pumpkins orange, and all his land was brilliant in a great glory.

He did his chores at the barn. He had not engaged a hired man this summer, paying, instead, the wages to Nat and a lesser amount to Arent. He had also given Nat the use of one of the best fields, to raise a bean crop for himself, to add to the available cash for his entrance this autumn to the state university. It had been hard to give up his hope that Nat would study agriculture, having rejected the arts and professions, for the Linden lands were proving more and more profitable, so that there could be a good living here for all. Yet Nat had insisted that he would consider nothing except a business course. Well, Ase thought, every man must work out his own destiny, and Nat was almost a man.

He took the milk to Nellie at the house. Nat and Arent were finishing their breakfast. He sat down at the table for his own.

Nat said: "Pa, I can't get those damn beans shelled and sold in time to get to the university. You expect too much of a fellow."

Ase took a mouthful of sausage. Nat should be grateful, he thought, that the bean crop had been so heavy. It would mean that he need not, his first year at college, do outside chores to pay for his living, beyond the tuition for which Ase was paying. There was a taint on Nat, he could not put his finger on it, but it seemed to him that Nat asked for a great deal in return for nothing. Ase thought of his own long years of toil, he recalled his own meagre schooling. More schooling, more education, access to more books, that must be the answer, so that a man learned all there was to know of the world, of mankind, of ideas of the relation of man to the outer cosmos. If Nat could learn the things that had been denied to him, Nat could go on where he had been obliged, because of his ignorance, to leave off.

Nat repeated: "You expect too much."

Ase lifted his head. He studied his son, his first-born. The boy's face was clouded and surly. No, Ase thought, it isn't that at all, I have asked too little. It seemed to him a crucial moment. Yet there had been others, and each time the moment had eluded him. But he could not find the words with which to speak, he had never been able to find them. And if he had ever and always spoken, would Nat have ever listened? Was each individual character implicit, fixed even before birth, so that every man went his own tormented way and could never be guided by another, equally tormented, towards the truth? He could only help his son at this moment in an entirely practical way.

"Why, Nat," he said, "I can give you a hand today. I can spare Arent to help you, too."

They left the breakfast-table together and went to the barn for the shelling, in Eric's home-made machine, of Nat's crop of beans. The beans were shelled, were put into sacks, were ready to be hauled to market. The crop was large indeed. Nat's first year at college was assured.

Nat was excited and happy at the supper-table. He talked sensibly of his plans. Before his eyes Ase saw the cracking of the shell that was the boy, saw the man inside, as the hard chrysalis splits to release the locust. 'Seventeen-year locust,' Ase thought, and smiled to himself. Nat was possessed of power. Ase felt a moment of relief for his son. However the boy used himself, he was one who would make his way. The world would never swallow him as it had swallowed Benjamin.

Nat said: "Pa, if we take the beans to Trent tomorrow, why can't I take the train straight on from there to the college? I'll need a few days to buy things and get settled, find a room. I'd like to size things up a little ahead of time."

Ase had already been thinking over Nat's transportation. He said: "No reason why I can't take you all the way."

Nat frowned.

"Thanks, Pa. I'd rather sort of go in alone. That's not so, well, countrified."

Nellie said sharply: "See here now, Nat Linden, I won't have any boy nonsense about acting ashamed of a farm. Or your father. When he's dressed up, he's a fine-looking man, good as any banker I've ever seen."

It was true, in his Sunday best Asahel Linden was distinguished. Being unconscious of his appearance, he wore his black gabardine, starched white shirt and black string tie casually. Nellie saw to it that sleeves and trousers were long enough.

Nat said: "Oh, I know, Pa's all right, but, shucks! imagine driving up in a wagon."

He grinned at his mother.

"Don't suppose you'd let me have Queenie and the rubber-tyred buggy, would you? And the light sleigh later? Come on, Ma, you won't be using them much this winter."

She hesitated.

"Tell you what I'll do, Nat. If you make good marks and behave yourself, maybe when you come home for Christmas."

"You know," he said, "I don't suppose you remember, but when I was about knee-high to a grasshopper you and Grandmother told me that when I made enough money, I could have a horse and buggy of my own."

"No, I don't remember."

Ase remembered. He remembered very well indeed.

'Melie said: "Nat, you going to college to learn to make money, or to drive girls around?"

"Maybe a little of both."

The family laughed together. Ase was disappointed not to be taking Nat all the way.

Nellie worked late into the night, washing and ironing and mending odds and ends of Nat's clothing. In the end, he left most of it for Arent. One portmanteau held all he considered fit for his new life. Ase watched the packing, feeling the need of making his son some special gift, tangible or intangible. There was advice he should offer him, perhaps, but he could think of none worth giving or that Nat would accept. At breakfast, he drew from his pocket his own father's heavy gold hunter's watch and laid it beside Nat's plate. Nat lifted it and balanced its weight on his open palm.

"Thanks, no, Pa. Nobody carries these old-fashioned things any more. Lot of gold in it, though. Maybe I could trade it in on a new one."

Nellie reached for the watch and handed it back to Ase. Nat shrugged his shoulders.

She said: "Now say good-bye nicely to your grandmother. You were always her favourite."

"She probably won't know me."

"She knows more than she lets on. Do as I tell you."

Ase wondered at Nellie's sharpness. Nat was her favourite, too. He decided that she was only shielding herself against the pain of his going, the first out of the nest. Since his trip today was to be only on business, and brief at that, in the dusty wholesale feed and grain warehouse at Trent, Ase was dressed cleanly and decently in his second-best. He hitched the team to the already loaded wagon while Nat paid his visit to Amelia.

Beside him on the seat, Nat said: "Grandmother thought I was Uncle Ben, going away. I guess you'll be in for it again."

The drive to Trent seemed to Ase unduly brief. Nat watched closely over the weighing of the dried beans and haggled for a higher price. He put out his hand greedily for the thick roll of notes.

"Damn," he said, "I haven't got anything but my pocket to keep it in."

Ase took out his new leather wallet and emptied it. His old worn one would do him as well. Nat accepted the gift with satisfaction, filled it with most of the money, stuffing a few small notes in his trousers pockets, and patted his hand over the wallet in his inside breast pocket.

"This is one country boy that isn't going to get his pockets picked," he said.

The original agreement on the bean crop had been that Nat was to have the net profits. The cost of the seed and extra manure for fertiliser bought from the Grimstedts had been not inconsiderable. Ase was unwilling to remind Nat of this. He was glad to contribute that much more over the crop itself, as well as the cash he had given him. Nat considered it a hardship, as it was, to do more than his usual amount of summer work, even though his father had paid him at a higher rate than for an ordinary hired man.

Ase said: "Ready to go to the station?"

"Don't bother, Pa. You start on home. I'll amble around town for a while."

He held out his hand.

"Tell Ma to keep the cookies coming. See you at Christmas."

He strolled away whistling. From the back, he looked very like Benjamin. Yet in the idleness of his gait there was purpose. Ase lifted the reins and slapped them lightly over the horses' backs and turned on to the road towards home. Perhaps some time he and Nellie might go together to visit Nat at college. Spring would be a good time, when they could use the surrey, and Nellie would do them proud in her Easter ruffles. It was foolish to have this yearning to see his son walk for the first time through the door of a great institution of learning. He had always pictured vast gates that swung silently wide to give a glimpse of glory. No doubt it would be like any other door.

★ 28 ★

THE Lindens sat at early supper on a sharp November evening. The sunset was reflected bronze and blue in the east. Lamps were not yet needed. Nat's absence had changed the character of the family for the first time since the death of Doll. There was no quarrelling at table. Young 'Melie's dominance over Arent and Willis was complete. Her orders and critical comments were accepted so meekly that their sharpness was dissipated like smoke up a chimney. It had been Nat, Ase realized, who always started the rows and trouble, 'Melie fighting him to begin with, then veering around to his side when any of the others attacked him with childish words or fists.

'Melie said: "Arent, for heaven's sake, sit up straight. You're lying down over your plate like an old sow."

He said sullenly: "I'm tired."

He was growing too fast, Ase thought. He could remember the fatigue of the mid-teens, when the vast quantities of food a boy ate pushed his bones daily almost out of their sockets, drove the rich and puzzled blood like a consuming fire through brain and glands, leaving him exhausted. There was something else. Arent missed Nat grievously.

Ase understood this, too. He recalled the first time Ben had left home, his own desolation. Yet Arent, oddly, had no actual love or even affection for his older brother. His loss now was negative, not positive. It was as though his own nature were empty, and the overflow of Nat's vitality filled and completed it. He was a shallow stream that had no existence without the deep spring to feed it. He was the shadow without the body. Ase felt a sudden anxiety for the boy, greater than for Nat, for up—or down—whatever rough or devious roads Nat might choose to make his way, Arent would be obliged to follow, a puppet moved by the strong hand of his master, a small soul born to be a henchman.

Ase looked at the unhappy boy, embarrassed by his flash of perception. Arent was nondescript of colouring. There had been no one on the Wilson or Linden side of the family so drab. He was more inclined to colds than the other children, but was healthy, and at fifty would probably look very much as he looked at fifteen, a man who would pass unnoticed in any crowd. Ase looked on down the table to 'Melie, officiously cutting up meat for Willis. She too, now nearly fourteen, would be little different at forty. Her resemblance to her grandmother was more striking every year, except that she would make a handsomer woman and if possible a harder.

Outsiders, even the Wilsons, all spoke of 'Melie as 'such a little mother'. True, she fussed and clucked over Willis, even over Arent, like a pullet with her first brood, but she seemed to Ase to be motivated not by any tender maternalism but by her need to dominate. To her own offspring, he thought, she might well seem more the stepmother of a fable. He could not even quite imagine her with children of her own. Like Nat, she would always, he felt, make her way, the same question applying to the way she chose. For Nat and 'Melie would do their own choosing.

He turned his study to Willis with puzzled tenderness. Young as he was, at ten, he had an odd independence, quite different from that of Nat and 'Melie, and with somehow a greater integrity. Yet he too stayed aloof from his father, with no antagonism such as Nat's, with, indeed, a casual friendliness, but giving the impression that he had looked to his father for something that was not there and now would look no longer. Ase remembered his advances to Willis, even in the days of his absorption with Doll. He recalled holding Willis on his bony knees, and the child's politeness, watching his chance to slip away and play with the endless kittens. It seemed, simply, that the strange flame of communication had never been lighted between them.

Nellie was determined that Willis should not be the spoiled baby of the family. She handled him with the firm but dispassionate wisdom she had given the other children. Her discipline was occasionally menaced by their taking her for accomplice rather than mother, especially after one of her madcap pranks. Ase sometimes thought of them as children together, she the eldest and most dearly beloved. But she was still all woman, her fire having subsided to a comfortable glow, rather to his relief. There had been many times after a hard day in the fields when Nellie had been almost too much for him.

He looked at her dotingly. Her added plumpness, the all but invisible touch of grey in her gold-chestnut hair, made her in his eyes more delightful than ever. He realized that her expression now was dangerously demure and that the children were giggling. For sweet, she had, along with the stewed damson plums, baked cup-cakes in frilled papers. He had a cake in his hand, ready for his mouth, paper and all. He dropped his hand and the children burst into laughter.

Nellie said: "Now you shouldn't have stopped him. When your Pa goes off into his trances, he isn't thinking about anything and he'd enjoy the paper as much as anything else."

Arent alone seemed not entirely amused. He shuffled his feet restlessly.

He said: "Pa, I don't see why I have to keep going to school. History, geography, reading and writing, all that stuff, it won't do me any good when I go into business with Nat."

He was parroting these words from Nat, Ase knew, yet Nat himself had been desperately anxious to go to the state university. Neither Nat nor Arent was a good scholar, but both managed to master the necessary subjects, Nat in particular. Ase had the unhappy thought that Nat planned deliberately always to keep Arent a few steps behind him, the better to use him later for his obscure purposes.

He wanted to say, 'Life is a difficult matter, and the more a simple man may learn of what greater men have thought and taught, have spoken and have written, the better can he cope with any sort of life.'

He was still pondering when Nellie said: "Ase, the boy's right. He doesn't like school, he doesn't like the farm, either. He can just as well get a job near Nat."

'Melie said: "Maybe Nat wouldn't want him tagging on to his coat-tails. Interfering with girls. He might be just a nuisance. Pa, you know it, I'm smarter than Arent, can't I go to college?"

Nellie said: "I'll give you all the college you'll need right here in this house, You've got to learn to bake a lighter cake if you're not to shame your husband."

"Maybe I won't get married. Maybe I'll be a school-teacher."

This seemed plausible to Ase, though again, he would feel sorry for her pupils.

He said: "You can go to college if you want to, 'Melie, when the time comes."

Nellie said: "A lot can happen to a girl in four years. You'll be having beaux by then, if you'll stop acting so bossy. The boys don't like that."

"Some of them do. You boss Pa, lots of ways, and he likes it."

Ase smiled his rare slow smile.

He said: "Child, your mother does it such a pretty way. There's the difference."

Arent returned doggedly to his theme.

"How about it, Pa? Can't I quit the Academy at Christmas and get a job near Nat?"

"No, son. Finish your high school and then we'll see."

Undressing for bed, Nellie said: "Ase, you might as well let the boy go. Ben finished the Academy and what good did it do him? Seems to me an education's no use if you don't want it."

He could not refute this. Yet a boy of fifteen knew neither what he wanted nor needed. Or did he, if he burned with such a secret flame as, for instance, had Dolly, who could never have enough of learning? Or as Eric Svenson, Hulda's brother?

As though she read his mind, Nellie continued: "Or take Eric on the other hand. He was hell-bent on college, and look what he got for his trouble."

Her reasoning was specious, for Eric had been the victim merely of incredibly bad luck. Ase had encouraged the young Swede, during his summer as hired man, in his ambition to graduate in engineering, in his dream for designing such bridges, such buildings, as had never been seen before. It was an architect he was meant to be, but neither the blond boy nor his grave mentor, so few years older, understood the distinction. Eric had moved on from the Linden farm, with his summer's savings and Ase's parting gift, to a factory job, there to make higher wages and larger savings towards his goal. A careless fellow worker had caught Eric's hands in a machine, crushing the fingers, so that factory work was as impossible as the dream of draftsmanship. Eric had returned of necessity to his father's farm, to till the land quietly and bitterly with his maimed hands. Ase had hired him occasionally. Eric worked for lower wages than the average, as there were many chores, such as milking, that he was unable to do.

Ase said to Nellie: "Very well. We'll let Arent go. I'll hire Eric again."

He drove Arent to the train the following Saturday. The boy showed more enthusiasm than his father had ever seen in him. Nat was the breath of life to him. It was touching, Ase felt, and he thought of his own vanished brother with the familiar pain. Perhaps he had done properly after all in letting Arent follow Nat. Yet he was again disturbed by the vacuity of Arent's nature, needing his brother not for love, but because without him he was nothing. Now he might never stand on his own feet. The relationship was even more dangerous for Nat. It seemed to Ase that he became increasingly harder and more arrogant as he fed on Arent's paler substance.

He lifted his hand in farewell after the train, but Arent did not look back from platform or from window. He was glad that he had brought Willis at the last moment, noticing the ten-year-old watching wistfully the preparations for departure.

He said now to him: "We'll miss the boys."

Willis said: "They won't miss us."

The comment was matter-of-fact, as though an old man spoke without malice of love's unrequitals. Ase looked down at the boy, surprised. Willis had always eluded him. In a surge of affection, he hoped it might still not be too late for communication. He forced himself to speak more fully than was usual for him, thinking that this unknown son was strangely adult, and he must so address him.

"It's been a disappointment to me that Nat only cares about business. I'm sorry that Arent doesn't want to go to school."

Long-pent ideas surged in him, of a man's need to learn all possible that may be taught, of the values of life, whereby a preoccupation with money seemed an ignoble thing to him, of the greater nobility of labour with the soil, of the dreams of men, to add to the force and beauty of all human living, those dreams too often, as with Eric Svenson, inexplicably destroyed.

"A man lives a short time, but a long time, too. He needs——"

He faltered, and as always, could not go on.

He gathered himself and asked: "What do you want to do, Willis? If you like farming, you can go to the agricultural college. You might want to be a doctor. A lawyer. Have you thought about it?"

The boy leaned forward in the buggy, examining his copper-toed shoes, retreating into his shell.

"It doesn't matter," he said. "Anything's all right."

He should question further, Ase thought—no, he should avoid questioning like the plague, should instead somehow stir this shy male child to a willing revelation.

He could only say: "I'll help you with anything you want to do."

Willis repeated: "It doesn't matter."

The buggy drew up at the Svenson house. Eric came to meet it.

Ase said: "I need you again, Eric. Can you come?"

He was shocked by the appearance of the man. His shoulders sagged, his lean Norse features were haggard, his once blond shock of hair was matted, and of the grey of dead seaweed, as though despair had washed over him in a last battering wave. He was five years younger than Ase, whose hair at forty was still raven-black.

He said: "Yes, sir. Be glad to."

Ase said: "Eric, would you like to stay this time, for good? I think I've lost Nat and Arent."

The unhappy eyes lightened, then were again beaten and cautious.

"I might as well. I'm not needed here, now the new crop of Svensons is coming along."

Of the large Swedish brood, Eric and Hulda alone had never married. There were nieces and nephews at work on the expanding farm. Hulda had not found 'a husband to buy', but Ase wondered why Eric was still a bachelor. He had been a handsome young man, and no loving and proper woman would reject him for his hands. The reason must be his fitful earnings, his inability to provide a roof over their heads, necessary to marriage, where love alone needed only a hedgerow. As occasional hired hand at other places, Eric, he knew, often slept in shed or barn. At the Linden farm he had always occupied a small room on the second storey of the house, above the wood-shed.

Ase said: "Eric, if you come to stay, there's no reason why you can't have the log cabin."

The man gripped his arm with a twisted hand in what seemed almost an attack.

He said: "Do you mean that, Mr. Linden?"

He answered himself at once.

"You mean it. You never say anything you don't mean."

He brushed a sleeve across his grimed and sweating face.

"I'd given up. There's a girl——"

He looked away a moment, into a past desolate space.

"Of course, she isn't a girl any more. She's a woman, she's as old as I am. She's turned grey, too. She's waited for me all these years. She didn't care whether we ate or starved, as long as it was together. There wasn't any way I could manage it."

He was fierce again, his face close.

"Your cabin, what it means—— She'll be with me."

He smiled in apology.

"But you know what it means."

Yes, he knew, but he could envy Eric the woman who would starve with him, if it was together. He decided to pay him full wages and to give him some breeding stock for his own, a heifer, pigs and chickens. There would always be enough Linden fruits and vegetables to share. It would be good to have Eric in the cabin, so long empty, so long haunted by bitterness.

Ase was surprised that evening to find Nellie snappish on the subject.

"You'll be over there half the time, jawing and yarning," she said. "I thought when Tim McCarthy died I was done with your chums."

He stared at her. Then he turned away his face, to smile. An ancient puzzle was explained. Nellie, astonishingly, for no female could have disturbed her, had been jealous of Tim. The male community was offensive, for into it no woman could ever enter.

✶ 29 ✶

THE only wonder, Ase thought, was that such a year had
been so long in coming. Catastrophe after catastrophe struck
the crops. A man working with the land might expect
disaster at any time. He had escaped it better than many of
his neighbours. His instinct for weather changes, streng-
thened by the lore of Mink Fisher the Indian, had often
led him to plant a crop earlier than was customary, or when
other landsmen said it was too late, and the seasons had been
harmonious with him and proved him right. Now there
seemed no benignity left in nature.

The spring came early. The apple orchard was a foam of
blossom. The wind veered one April day, the sun withdrew,
a norther roared down with sleet and bitter cold, and when
it passed, the orchard was a stricken thing, bereft of bloom
and hope of harvest. There would be no plums, no cherries,
no peaches. The winter wheat lay flailed to the ground and
would not rise again. Half the crop of spring lambs perished
in the sudden and unseemly cold. Eric worked through two
nights with him, saving the remainder. No hours were too
long, no labour too hard for him. The man was luminous
with happiness. His middle-aged bride had transformed the
dark log cabin into a house of bright Swedish reds and blues
and yellows. Her plain sweet face was as glowing as
his.

To compensate for the loss of major cash crops, Ase
doubled, working with Eric a twenty-hour day, his plantings
of beans, of potatoes, of corn. These were well sprouted
when two weeks of rain turned the fields to sodden mud, and
the young green sprouts and cotyledons turned yellow, then
grey, and merely disappeared. The previous winter's store
of root vegetables, of home-canned fruits and vegetables,
was eaten to the last crock of apple butter. It was necessary
to buy almost everything from Peytonville, even feed for the
stock, at new high prices. Ase sold everything he could spare,
lambs, calves, poultry, pigs. He replanted the drowned-out
house garden and fought through the wet summer for every
carrot, every beet and turnip. His cash reserves were dangerously depleted and life was almost a matter of immediate

survival. It was necessary to keep money aside for the next winter wheat. With no broad acres of crops to be worked and harvested, Nat and Arent took summer jobs in Trent.

The price of seed wheat soared. When it was paid for, allowing an extra acreage this time in an attempt to recoup, Ase checked over his balance in the Peytonville bank, the remaining currency in the tin box, and found himself perilously short. The family would not starve, it would not go cold or unclothed, but there would be no amenities, and Nat would have to finance his second year of college by himself. Eric's wages would be a steady drain. Dismissing him was out of the question. The log cabin was the rock on which he was building his life. Ase looked over his account ledger. He had not realized that Nat had called on him so often the past winter for extra money. Twenty-five dollars here, fifty there, it amounted to several hundred dollars. His mother and Willis had been sickly. Dr. Holder had come often and prescribed expensive tonics.

Aunt Jess the midwife had been ill and unable to work at her profession. He had taken money to her and arranged for paying a girl to stay with her until she should recover. There were other items, too, a contribution to the struggling high school Academy in Peytonville. He had said nothing about these things to Nellie or to Amelia. They made a considerable amount, more than he could afford. He pushed the ledger away and asked himself why he had not felt free to tell his wife and his mother that he was, actually, robbing them of their deserved comforts. He acknowledged to himself his fear of his mother's sharp tongue and greediness. Yet Nellie had been always so generous with stray tramps, with the gypsies, the bounty of her table was fabled, for any and for all. And she had sent Hulda home with the first tightening of his finances. He looked up from his ledgers. Eric stood in the doorway.

"Worse than you thought, isn't it, Mr. Linden?"

"We'll manage somehow, Eric."

"I shouldn't have let you pay me wages all spring. I'd work for nothing now, but I can't. But I've got things figured out. I can have a job hauling lumber at Peytonville, if you'll spare me the mare to ride back and forth. That way, I can give you a hand night and morning, and still make my wages outside, until things get better for you."

Ase said slowly: "That would relieve me, Eric. But I couldn't let you give me help without pay."

Eric's blue eyes twinkled.

"Then I'd have to pay you rent on the cabin, and I can't afford to. Elsa and I can't give it up. We're having a baby in November."

The man's delight was almost a tangible aura. There was something else, Ase sensed, beyond a normal pride in paternity. Eric had returned to his rightful share in man's hope. Life had failed him, but it would surely never fail his child.

Ase rose and shook hands gravely.

He said: "Good luck," having in mind the perhaps dangerous maturity of the mother in childbirth, the for ever dangerous fact of every new life, and Eric, understanding this, gripped tight and grateful.

"I'll begin the hauling job day after tomorrow, Mr. Linden."

July was perversely dry. The earth hardened and cracked. Ase and Nellie carried bucket after bucket of well water to the garden each evening. 'Melie and Willis doled it out around the plants with dippers, making a game, stopping to dabble in the momentary pools, so that Ase was usually obliged to finish the job himself before going late to his chores. The small garden fruits, the currants, the gooseberries, the raspberries and strawberries, turned shrivelled and seedy. Nellie complained of the quality of the jam. She used honey in making it, to save the price of sugar.

There were two days of bright sun towards the end of the month. The fodder grasses, the rye and clover and timothy, dried enough for mowing. On the third morning Ase hitched the team to the mowing machine by lantern-light, to be ready with the first nebulous grey before the dawn. Even the birds had not yet aroused from sleep. He made a round of the lower pasture field before the robins began their harsh twittering. With the first faint glow in the east, only a prescience of sunrise, as though someone approached from far away with a lighted lamp, the meadow larks took to the air, disturbed by the machine rather than the day, for which they were not ready. They circled but did not soar, spoke but did not sing. The grasses were heavy with the dew and made hard mowing. But the sun rose clear and golden, the mown grass steamed and would soon dry, and Ase clucked to the horses to move at a faster gait. They were almost too fresh from weeks of inactivity. They broke into a trot, the whirling blades of the mover could not keep the pace, became clogged. Ase was obliged to saw on the lines with all his strength to slow down the team, to save a fatal breakdown of the machine.

A cloud passed over the sun. It moved away to the south in a moment, leaving the light somehow less dazzling. Ase felt that he was racing the sun, an ant against an antelope. He would not take time for breakfast. At eight o'clock he tied the team to the fence, for rest, and went to the barn to do the chores. Nellie was there, milking. Her curly head leaned against the flank of the brindle cow, her hands looked to him like frail leaves fluttering under the big udder, but her small strong fingers were pumping milk from the teats in a steady stream. She turned her head and chuckled.

"Bet you thought I'd forgotten how to milk."

He tousled her hair.

"Go on to the house, Nellie. I'll finish now."

"I'm almost done. Eric did a lot before he left. I've got the poultry fed and watered. Go eat your breakfast. It's keeping hot on the back of the stove."

He had said nothing to her of the need for hurry, but she had understood and gone casually to do a man's work. The love in him for her swelled like the willow stream in flood.

"No, Nellie, let me finish."

"Look at your dirty hands. I'll be through with the stripping before you could get them washed. Go on, now."

He could not leave her. He would never again envy Eric his Elsa. He squatted on his haunches and watched her, saw the sweat come out on her forehead, and loved the dampening of her curls. He forgot for the moment his anxieties and his danger. She stood up from the milking-stool and wrinkled her nose fastidiously at her hands, holding them in front of her.

"I'll gather up the eggs, guess I won't get them smelly. You take the milk-buckets to the house."

"You can come back for the eggs."

"Want your breakfast dished up in style. I know."

It was not that he wanted his breakfast served, but that he could not spare her out of his sight, not just now. She darted ahead of him, and by the time he reached the kitchen with the milk and had washed up and combed his hair, his late breakfast was on the table. He coaxed her into sitting with him and she sipped at a cup of coffee.

She said: "Think you can get the hay in before it rains again? Weather still acts sort of peculiar."

He was jerked back painfully to the hay, to the weather, to the fractious team waiting for him. He rose from the table. He leaned over her and kissed her throat.

"Ase, for heaven's sake, we're getting to be old folks. Save it for bed-time, anyway."

"Little Nellie Wilson——" he said.

She would always be younger than he. It would offend her to know that what drew him to her now was not amorousness, but some deep need of physical contact, as for a mated pair of animals huddled together against a storm. He went back to the mowing of the hay. Nellie brought him food at noon, to save time, brought grain and water for the team of horses. The sun was strong all the afternoon. The swathes of grass fell in half-circles behind the blades of the machine, drew in the warmth and dryness, were ready to be taken to barn to nourish the stock through the coming winter. Ase kept at the mowing until the late summer twilight. If he had not been obliged to let Eric go, if Nat and Arent had been with him for help, the felled and valuable fodder would have been already raked into piles for stowing in the loft. The sun set angrily. Ase put away the team, the machine, did the evening chores, and went to the house for supper.

Nellie had a finer meal than usual for their time of dearth. She sent the children to bed early. She took Amelia her supper-tray and retrieved it shortly. Ase was torn between a sigh and a smile. He was exhausted, yet he gloried that he was still able to give her some portion of a meagre happiness.

He was up early the next morning to go on with the

mowing. On studying the sky, he changed his mind. He decided to rake as far as he had already mown. The hay-rake was a one-horse affair, and he could spell off the two horses, having overworked them the day before. The job took less than half as long as the mowing. The day was cloudy but dry. In mid-afternoon he called Nellie to help him begin to load. He needed badly a second man to pitch with him, but she could easily take the place of the customary grown boy who stood on the load and evened and trampled the hay. She put on an old pair of Arent's jeans and tied a bandanna over her hair. She pranced up and down the load. She could not help him when it came to pitching the hay from the wagon up into the loft of the barn. This was back-breaking work for a man alone, with no respite. The next day was Sunday, and Eric worked with him from sun-up to sun-down. Six loads were safe in the loft when night came, and with the night, again, the rain. Two days ruined the hay remaining on the ground. It turned black and soft and mouldy. The rains began once more in August. They opened gullies along the granite ribs of the sheep pasture. The brook rose high, foamed and boiled. The lower branches of the weeping willows were drenched and muddied, untidy as matted hair. The grasses grew rank. Wild blackberries were swollen and insipid.

The weather cleared and Ase mowed the short hay in the high pasture without trouble, but the amount would not see the stock through the winter. In early September he went to the marsh along the willow stream. The marsh grass was coarse and not too nutritious, but Mink Fisher had told him many years ago that it made good fodder in bad times. The Indians had often used it for their ponies. He moved slowly across the marsh, swinging the big hand-scythe rhythmically, cautious against deep hidden pools of water and against the equally hidden small rattlesnakes. These had once infested the marsh by the hundreds, and as a boy he had sometimes killed as many as thirty in one day. He smiled to himself, remembering that his father had paid him a penny a snake. He had been rich for weeks. Of late years, the hogs had kept the snakes down to a modest number. He stepped back as a triangular head lifted beyond his feet, then sheared it off neatly with his scythe. He hauled the marsh hay bundle by bundle, by hand, to higher ground, for availability in loading the wagon. He refused to let Nellie help this time, for a few rattlers managed to tuck themselves inside the bundles. These he killed with the pitchfork. The season's hay was all of poor quality, but it would see him through.

He went next to the sowing of the winter wheat. Eric gave him early and late hours of unpaid-for time. The weather immediately following was propitious and the grain sprouted and seemed established. The home harvest was better than he had expected. There were enough potatoes, carrots, turnips, cabbage, pumpkin and squash to make respectable piles in the root-house and in the cellar. The autumn crop of nuts was good. He and Nellie and the children made picnic outings on bright October days to gather the butternuts, the hazel and black walnut, the hickory nuts. He butchered hogs early and hung more than usual of hams and sides in the smoke-house. Nellie put down half a dozen large crocks of salt pork in brine. When the snowy slices were dipped in flour and fried golden brown, served with potatoes boiled in their jackets and rich milk gravy, the meal was savoured by all the family except Amelia. When Nellie had only such 'common' food she prepared some special delicacy for the querulous old woman. They would all miss the apples through the winter, but, on the whole, Ase felt a new hope that they would come through to spring not too uncomfortably.

Towards the middle of October Nat and Arent came home to get their clothes in order. Ase had warned Nat early that he could give him no help towards his second year of college. Nat had saved most of his summer's wages. Ase was relieved and surprised, for Nat had always assumed that his father could produce extra money when he really cared to.

Nat explained: "I decided I'd rather get the work out of the way this summer. I wouldn't like this business of waiting on tables and stoking furnaces for the rich fellows. They call the working boys slavies and stuff like that."

Ase said mildly: "Mr. Lincoln split rails while he studied. He made a pretty good name for himself."

Nat said: "Well, there must be easier ways of getting to be President."

He was sullen because he dared not use any of his money for a new winter suit. Arent had inherited his second-best suit and now he would have to wear his one good one every day.

Ase said: "If I get a good price for the young stock, maybe at Christmas——"

Nat's face lightened.

"Fine, Pa. Even twenty-five dollars will do me."

Thinking out his words beforehand, Ase talked with Arent to convince him that he should enter college, too. If his lesser amount of saved money was not enough, surely as a freshman he need not share Nat's lofty feeling against working on the side. The boy nodded.

"I guess you're right, Pa. Nobody notices me, anyway, when Nat's around."

He spoke more with pride than resentment. It was enough for him to trail behind his brother. Nat heard his name and joined them and questioned them.

He said: "I tell you, Pa, it's too hard work for one thing, to make a living and study, too. I've got a good job for Arent in town, in a store. We'll live in my room together and between us we'll have enough money to do things right. Why, I can teach Arent at night myself. The first-year stuff is easy."

The matter was settled. It was impossible to urge Arent further. The promise of continuing to live with Nat so elated him that he became deaf and blind to other arguments. Ase understood wryly what would happen. Nat would never think again of teaching Arent, was incapable of it in any case, and he would live well, making the show he demanded, with the help of Arent's earnings. As ruefully, Ase acknowledged to himself that it probably did not much matter. Arent's cup was not only empty, it had a hole in it. Even the modest education of the Academy had gone in one ear and out the other.

Ase had not entirely given up hope for Nat's development. The boy had made good marks his first year, especially in history and economics. Perhaps he would find a professor who would stir him, some wise man of books who would open for him, as he himself had been incompetent to do, the world of the mind beyond its commercial application.

"History certainly teaches you, Pa," Nat had said, and Ase had felt excitement mount in him, and had leaned forward eagerly to listen.

Nat had continued: "Why, you can see where business and political leaders made their mistakes. The depression wasn't necessary. Cleveland proved that. Even then, a smart man could have seen what was happening, and bought stuff low, and held it, and then sold it high. I tell you, I wouldn't take anything for history."

Ase had left Nat abruptly. What did he mean by 'stuff'? He used the word constantly. Yet it was gratifying to find that the boy had a good mind, as strong and vital as his body. He was young, he could change, and if not a man of letters, perhaps the right wife would tone down his stridency. Perhaps his own children would teach him a more basic humanity. Ase drove his two sons to Trent to take the train for the university city. The time was still clement, so that they went in the surrey.

Nat said casually: "You could just as well drive us all the way, Pa. See the college, too."

Some things, Ase thought, came too late. A year ago he had yearned to feast his eyes at least on the portals. Nat had not asked him and Nellie to come for a visit. Nat had been ashamed of him then, collecting the bean money from the old wagon. He was not ashamed of the surrey, as fine a carriage as anyone had. And Nat no doubt had in mind the saving of the two railway fares. No, it was too late, something was soiled.

Ase said: "I'd better reach home tonight."

He added, ashamed of his evasion, although the fact was so: "Your grandmother had another spell, I ought to be there."

Elsa bore her child in the log cabin in early November. Dr. Holder attended her with Hulda's help. Aunt Jess was past midwifery. It was a difficult birth, but Elsa made as light of it as Nellie had always done. The baby was a girl. Ase had wondered if Eric might not need and have wanted a son, further to have restored himself. He was immediately reassured.

Eric said to him, drinking a toast of hard cider in the cabin to the new-born babe, to the mother: "I'm glad it's a girl. A girl can't possibly be as disappointed in life as a boy."

It seemed as though Eric had always been a part of the family. Ase was comforted by his quiet presence, by the hour of help he gave night and morning, by the sight of lamplight in the old cabin, and smoke curling from the chimney.

November was cold and dry. There were wind storms, gales that ripped branches from the trees, but with them no beneficence of rain. December turned unseasonably warm. Rain fell, and the yellowing wheat shoots turned green again. There was no snow, none at all. Without its protective covering, the wheat was at the mercy of winter. Bitter cold moved in, the temperatures near zero continued for a week. The wheat froze where it stood in its nakedness. The soft snow that fell at last was wasted on the empty fields.

Ase and Nellie sat on the sofa before the living-room stove. The children were in bed. Amelia had been troublesome all day, calling from her room for unneeded attention, but now seemed asleep. Nellie turned the lamp low to save the oil. The belated snow hissed like snakes against the window-panes.

Ase said: "I'd better sell off most of the stock now."

"Won't bring as good a price as in the spring."

"I can't pay for feed through the winter, Nellie. Not with the wheat gone and nothing coming in. We'll just keep the brood stock."

"Ase, let's keep all the turkeys. Nobody raises them much for market. I'll set all the eggs early. They can feed spring and summer over the high hay-field where there's always so many grasshoppers."

"All right, if you want to bother."

Yet the problem was one of survival in the meantime.

He said: "I hate to disappoint Nat about money for his suit."

"You shouldn't have come so close to promising him."

"I know."

He put a chunk of maplewood in the stove. He had timber

224

to spare in both wood-lots. He should have thought of this before.

He began felling and cutting the next day in the snow. He hauled the wood by the cord to Peytonville and disposed of it easily. He sent the first twenty-five dollars to Nat and felt somehow free. He made charcoal from the smaller wood. This too had a ready market. All winter, when the snow was not too deep or the winds too fierce, he hauled charcoal and cordwood to Peytonville and peddled it from door to door. Nat was furious when he heard of this through Nellie's casual mention in a letter. To Ase it seemed as honourable a way as any for a man to make a living. All men sold or traded the products of their minds, their backs or hands, for subsistence. Wood was a clean thing, as vital as food to human life, to warm and comfort. He began filling his pockets with hazel-nuts to give the children on his route. They left their romping, their building of snowmen, to run to his wagon in welcome.

He enjoyed their shrill, friendly cry: "Here's the woodman!"

★ 30 ★

THE May sun forced the wet earth to give up its moisture. The soil steamed. Ase stood in the sparse shade of the new-leafed poplars before his house and looked out across his land. The blue mist rising in the valleys seemed more like smoke. It swirled and eddied, spiralled and lifted, and, almost as he watched, was absorbed into the pale gold light. He had finished the planting of all his fields. Spring had come early, as though to compensate for the past year's harshness. All signs had been of a continued blandness. He had fallen back on his long established but never used credit with Mr. Peyton, buying seed with abandon, since he felt certain in his bones of a fine growing season. He had planted summer wheat. The bean crop was in, the potatoes, the barley and the buckwheat. He had even risked so early a planting of corn, the oak leaves being the size of a squirrel's paws.

Easter vacation at the university had been late this year and Nat and Arent had come home and given him ten days of priceless help in turning the land, fertilising, harrowing and laying out the rows for the planting. A little money was left from the hard winter and Eric interrupted his job to give him two weeks of time. There had been enough rain and not too much, and any day now the rich brown fields would sprout with the blessed green of growth. He took a long breath of the sweet moist air. The Lindens had come through a perilous time. There was still meat in the smoke-house, the one milch cow he had kept was fresh, Nellie's chickens and turkeys were laying heavily. The fruit trees were ending a riotous bloom. The house garden was in, nursing secretly the good vegetables and berries.

It was mid-morning and there was no special thing Ase found necessary to do. It was a moment of waiting. He thought of his mother in her closed room. She was failing fast. She had been oddly difficult all the winter and early spring. She had become gentler in her increasing physical frailty, yet she called on him more and more to listen to her rambling memories, where Benjamin was sometimes confused with her husband, again, with Ase himself. He went to her room and found her rocking in her favourite chair.

He said: "It's a beautiful warm morning, Mother. Let me put your chair out on the grass in the sun."

"Benjamin? No, no, I see it's Asahel. The sun? Why, yes, everyone's kept me from the sun. Away from the sun."

"Come, Mother. Hold on to me while I move your chair."

He settled her under the poplars in half-shade.

She asked: "What time is it, Benjamin?"

He recognized that time for her, as for him, was not of the hours of the day.

"It's spring-time, Mother," he answered.

She was satisfied. He picked a spray of lily-of-the-valley from the corner by the house and laid it in her translucent hand. She sniffed it with pleasure.

She said: "Your brother Asahel gave me a bottle of toilet water once when he was a little boy. It smelled like this. Do you remember?"

He did not remember. He did not remember her when he

was young. Perhaps she had once been tender. He felt a sense of loss for the mother she might have been.

She said: "Sit near me, son."

He stretched his long legs on the grass beside her chair. A nesting wren dropped a straw. It fell on Amelia's head and he lifted it away and stroked her hair. He yearned to go back with her the more than forty years, to begin again. She closed her eyes and seemed to drowse. He drew her shawl around her shoulders and slipped away.

It was strange to have so little to do. Later, the days would not be long enough to contain his labour and he would out-toil the sun. He though of his flute. He had not played it since Tim McCarthy died. He was not sure where he had put it, it was not in the hay-mow, nor the carriage-shed, he knew. He found it at last in the bottom drawer of his dresser, wrapped safely in clean linen, and this was Nellie's doing. He looked around for her. He wanted to take her with him to a hill-top and play for her. He heard her voice, high and furious, then caught sight of her in the barn-yard, flapping her apron at an equally angry setting hen. It was no moment to approach her for what she called, in her spells of stern-ness, his moony nonsense.

He felt foolish in any case, but he polished his flute and ambled across the adjacent field to the rise overlooking the willow stream and the bridge. Perhaps he had forgotten how to play, or the flute might have lost its key, its tone, its sweetness. He sat with his back against a broad maple trunk. A turtle-dove mourned from the woods near-by. He put the flute to his lips to imitate the notes. The tone was as sweet as ever. He had not forgotten. He played to the dove and it seemed to answer. He played at random, careless phrases like the songs of birds. He longed for Tim McCarthy. On such an idle day in May they would have played their best together.

He was absorbed in his piping. He was not aware of the stumbling figure until it was almost on him, as though it had no previous existence but had materialized out of his tunes, drawn by his flute. He stood awkwardly. For an instant more the figure was a stranger. Mink Fisher lifted a hand to him.

No, Ase thought, he had never quite given Mink up. His reason had told him, that winter day so long ago, that he should not see his friend again. It was incredible that Mink had returned, yet he was not astonished. The old man wavered, fell on his knees and sprawled face-down at Ase's feet. Ase knelt beside him and turned him over gently. The breeze stirred the maple leaves. Light and shadow flickered across the seamed bronze face.

Mink muttered: "Too far."

Ase said: "Just rest."

The Indian's breath came heavily. His eyes were closed. Ase loosened the ragged blanket, fanned away a fly. Mink was old and worn past belief. He had seemed ancient that other year, but now he was more mummy than man. The skin was taut over the high cheek-bones, the black hair that had then been grizzled was now all the colour of soiled snow. Ase took Mink's wrist in his hand, to feel for the pulse, and it was as though he lifted the straw that had fallen on Amelia's hair. He put his arms under the emaciated body, rose easily with it, and carried it to the house. Mink seemed little heavier than Doll had been. The breath of life was almost the only difference.

He saw Amelia still sleeping in her chair under the poplars. Neither Nellie nor any of the children were in sight. He took Mink to the back downstairs bedroom and laid him on the bed. The house was cooler than the outdoors, and he drew a cover over him. Mink turned and moaned.

He mumbled: "Brother—— Son——"

Ase went to the kitchen stove, where Nellie usually kept a kettle of hot water boiling, to make tea or coffee. The stove was cold. He went to a cupboard that held the medicinal whisky and poured out a quarter of a cup. Mink's teeth were clenched, but he held open the old man's jaws and poured down the liquor.

Mink said: "Eat."

Ase felt the hair rising on the back of his neck. Mink was starving. He went again to the kitchen. There was no food there, but in the pantry he found bread and buttermilk. He mixed a bowl and fed Mink spoonful by spoonful. Mink took it greedily. A memory came to Ase of a trek he had made with the Indian in bad weather, when they were without food for two days. On the third day Mink had taken some small game, had cooked it for the boy Ase, saying he was not himself hungry. Mink had gone then without food for three days. How long had he been now without it? He dared not feed him too heavily at first. He set the bowl aside. He drew the blind at the window. He pulled a chair to the side of the bed. Mink tried to speak.

Ase said: "Don't talk."

The old man closed his eyes again. Ase sat watching him. He was torn by grief for him, with joy in the sight of him. A few days of rest, of nourishment, and Mink might yet recover to have a little while to sit with him in the sun, to talk together of the old days. He could more easily then see his friend's spirit return finally and peacefully into his forefathers' West from which his racked body had made its way.

He wondered if he should undress Mink now. Then he saw that he was sleeping. It was best not to disturb him. He heard Nellie come into the house, scolding one or another of the children. Her sharp moods never lasted for long. He would tell her later of Mink's presence. He left the bedroom and closed the door cautiously behind him.

Nellie said: "What are you prowling around in there for?"

He felt like a boy trapped at the cookie jar. He could not lie to her and simple evasion was almost as difficult for him. He stood sheepishly. She spied the flute in his shirt pocket. She laughed.

"You found it. I thought I heard flute music on the hill. Don't look so silly, it sounded nice."

She had shed her crossness as suddenly as the clearing of an April sky. He swallowed. his Adam's apple bobbing, to prepare to give his news.

She said: "Go get me a side of bacon from the smokehouse. I fooled with that dratted hen so long, I've got to fix a mighty quick meal. 'Melie, set the table for me, put on some raspberry jam. Hurry now, both of you."

He was grateful for the respite. He was shaken by Mink Fisher's arrival and by his condition, and now he would have a little time to think of words that might help, instead of worsen, the situation, for Nellie was bound to object. He brought the bacon, washed up, and went to the front yard to help his mother into the house. She was cheerful and rational.

"The sun did me good," she said. "I think I'll eat at table with you."

Nellie said: "You won't much like dinner, Mother Linden, but I was late and couldn't help it. I'll give you a piece of the cold chicken from yesterday. There's custard, too, and you always enjoy that."

Amelia seated herself and spread her napkin daintily.

"You're very sweet to me, Nellie," she said. "I couldn't have had a better daughter."

Nellie whispered to Ase: "Will the heavens fall? A compliment instead of a complaint."

She said loudly: "All right, children, both of you clean? Come on, Ase, old slow-poke. Pass the eggs before they get stone-cold. Sorry about the dinner. I'll fix something nice tonight."

For all the meagreness of the meal there were special touches—'Nellie's way', Ase called it—that made it more than palatable. She had added minced chives to the scrambled eggs, the creamed potatoes swam in butter, and she had opened one of the last precious jars of peaches to serve with the custard for a sweet.

Amelia said: "Very tasty, my dear, very tasty indeed."

Nellie cocked an eyebrow at Ase.

"Expect the roof to cave in," she said.

Amelia asked: "What did you say, dear?"

Nellie lifted her voice.

"I said we need some new shingles or the roof will cave in."

She winked at Ase. Sometimes she seemed to him a born liar, yet her untruths were always either in a spirit of elfin mischief or in the name of family peace. Willis finished eating and asked politely to be excused. Amelia went with young 'Melie to her bedroom. Ase and Nellie sat alone at table. He cleared his throat.

"Mink Fisher is here," he said.

Nellie stopped her coffee-cup in mid-air.

"Who's here?"

"Mink Fisher."

"Never heard of him. Who is he?"

"My friend. The old Indian. He gave us the wolfskin rug. He brought the mink and otter skins. You made a muff and tippet, and trimmings for 'Melie's coat."

"Where is he?"

"In the back bedroom."

Nellie pushed back from the table.

"You have that stinking Indian in the house this minute?"

He laid a hand on her arm.

"Nellie, please. He's sick."

She wailed: "Oh, Ase, you and your sick old men!"

She looked over the table.

"I suppose he's hungry."

"I don't believe he's eaten for several days, Nellie. Maybe longer."

"He picked a fine time to come here to get filled up. I'm not going to pitch in and cook for him, either. Take him the rest of the eggs, here, bread and jam, there's some custard left."

"Never mind the bread and jam. Too much would make him sick."

"Go feed him in the kitchen. I won't have him in the dining-room. You should have put him out in the barn."

He thought that Mink himself would probably have preferred a bed of clean hay, with mice and swallows for company. Ase went to the bedroom with the plate. The old man was too exhausted to know or care where he lay. His eyes were still closed. Ase spoke, and he stirred. He seemed more in coma than in sleep. Ase wondered if rest was more needed than food, but, studying the tight skin over the protruding bones, decided that nourishment was vital. He roused Mink and forced down most of the soft eggs and custard. The old man drowsed again, but the sleep seemed healthful, the breathing steadier. When he opened his eyes in mid-afternoon they were less clouded. They took in the room, the bed.

He muttered: "Me too dirty."

He had always been clean. On their jaunts he had plunged morning and night into lake or running stream, no matter how icy, or the time of year. His smell was of wood smoke, of animal pelts, of the leaves and boughs on which he bedded. Now there was another odour, something indefinable, and Mink must have smelled it, too.

Ase said: "Let me bathe you."

Mink shook his head.

"No time. Must talk."

He struggled to raise himself, then fell back.

"Come near."

Ase sat on the bed and leaned over him, to catch the half-mumbled words.

"Long time find brother, son."

Ase said: "I shouldn't have let you leave me."

"Not you. You never lost from me. Always here——," his skeleton hand wavered to his throat. "Other one. One you sorrow."

"Benjamin——"

Ase felt his heart pound.

"I find him. Almost give up. I find him."

He closed his eyes.

Ase said: "You spent all these years looking for Ben."

"Sure. One place like another for Indian now. You say maybe I see brother. Tell him send white man's word, Mother sorrow, you sorrow. Now, bring word."

His breathing was rapid. His nostrils spread, as though to draw in a thin air with which to continue.

"Long walk," he panted. "Sun rise, sun set, many times."

Ase said: "You could have had someone write us the news of Ben."

Mink opened his eyes.

"Sure. White man say to Indian, sure, I write word, I send word. Indian pay silver. White man write, Indian go away, white man laugh. No word."

He got himself up on one elbow and said fiercely: "Mink bring word."

"Lie quiet, Mink."

Ase could not push his friend's strength too far, however desperate he found himself for news of Ben. He heard a sound outside the bedroom. He turned. His mother stood in the doorway.

She said: "Nellie tells me there's an Indian here."

She made her way to the foot of the bed. Mink opened his eyes. He stared at the old woman holding to the footboard. He spoke a few words in his ancient tongue.

"It's Mink," she said. "What is he doing here?"

"He's brought news of Benjamin, Mother."

She looked from one to the other.

"Benjamin?"

She clutched at Ase.

"Benjamin! He's here!"

Her trembling alarmed him.

"No, no, Mother. Sit down. Mink will try to tell us. It's news, only news."

She pushed him away and gripped the footboard and leaned over it.

"You've kept it from me all this time. You and the gypsies. Tell me."

Mink lifted his hand in a gesture for quiet. He stiffened his shoulders, gathering his strength.

He said in a firm voice: "I hunt son, brother, far west, far north. I find him. Big timber land."

Amelia said shrilly: "He owns big timber? He's rich now? He's coming home?"

"Woman, be still. Son, brother, him cook in lumber camp. He say, world go bad for him, men cheat him, much trouble."

Ase watched his mother. Her face was grey. Mink clenched his fists and took a long breath.

"Son, brother, he say, tell you him have chance buy big timber rights. Make much gold. Him come home two-three years now. He say."

Ase caught his mother, falling. It was like catching some small wounded and broken bird. He lifted her in his arms to carry her to her bed. Her voice was strangely thick.

"I can't wait for him—any longer."

He called Nellie to help him with her. They saw a spasm pass over her. Her eyes rolled back in her head.

Nellie said: "Ase, I think she's having a stroke. Hitch up and go for Doc. Never mind, listen now, hitch up the light buggy and I'll go. It'd give me the creeps to be alone in the house with this pair of yours."

He stumbled to the barn, and led the fast mare to the carriage-shed, his hands all thumbs. Nellie had changed into a silk dress and was waiting.

She called from her seat in the buggy: "Guess I shouldn't have told her about the Indian."

She clucked to the mare and slapped the reins and was off down the road. Ase went to his mother's room. She lay immobile. He turned back the bedclothes and rubbed her hands and feet as he had done for Nellie when she lay in danger before the birth of Doll. 'Melie looked into the room, Willis wide-eyed behind her.

Ase said: "'Melie, come rub Grandmother's hands and feet a few minutes."

"Grandmother doesn't know anything, does she, Pa?"

He shook his head and went to Mink. For a moment he thought his friend had already gone away from him into the mist.

He called: "Mink?"

The old man's lips moved almost without sound. Ase put his ear close, to hear.

"In shirt."

Ase recalled the earlier gesture. He laid back the cover and groped inside the soiled white man's shirt. He found a dog-eared envelope, stained with sweat. He laid it against Mink's hand.

"Is this what you want?"

"For you."

He saw that the envelope was addressed to him in Ben's writing.

"Now I die."

The whisper was only a statement of fact. Across the continent Mink had sought Ben and found him, to bring back the wanted white man's word on paper. There was nothing more he could do for the boy he had taught and loved. He was done with life. He rejected it with contempt. Ase could call loudly to him, could beg him not to go. Mink might hear, but he would not listen nor ever answer. Ase slipped the letter in a pocket. He did not know whether Mink's breath ceased to come or whether he ceased to draw it. There was an instant when he sensed an unheard thunder and an

234

unseen lightning. Then the room was filled with a vast calm. He drew the spread over his friend's face and went out of the room.

He heard Nellie say: "Ase, for the Lord's sake, didn't you even notice Doc's trap drive up, and me behind him? Go unhitch both rigs."

It was a relief to use his hands, to rub down both lathered animals, to feed and water them. When he returned to the house, he met the children huddled on the lawn.

'Melie said: "Ma made us get out. She said children oughtn't to be in a house with death. Willis is scared, but I'm not. I wanted to see. Can you see death?"

He laid his hand on her shoulder. He was sorry that Nellie had made of their grandmother's dying such a thing, as though a thief and murderer had come through the window. It was a quieter matter, he thought, for one advanced in years; not that death comes, but that life goes. It was like the flowers in Nellie's garden in the autumn, done with blooming; only that the long-used life sap sank back into the earth, and so the roses, the asters, the marigolds, being deserted, died. He took the two children by their hands.

He said to Willis: "Come get some cookies. There isn't anything in the house that wasn't here before."

Dr. Holder nodded to him at Amelia's bedside.

He said: "Your mother's had a stroke, just as Nellie thought."

"Will she come through?"

"No. She's about gone now."

Holder leaned back in his chair. He frowned.

"Let's hope it's the end, anyway. I never told you, Linden, but I haven't had an easy night since I advised you to keep your mother here. I'd wake up in a cold sweat, wondering if she'd gone berserk again."

Ase stood mute. If his mother breathed, that breath was impalpable. Her face was grey as the granite in the pasture.

Nellie said: "I've been telling Doc about that sick Indian you put in my clean bed. The time I put in with that old Tim McCarthy, and now with your mother giving us some

235

peace at last, I suppose I've got to help nurse the Indian, too."

He felt a revulsion that roiled his stomach. Yet, he remembered, Nellie had been all kindness during Tim's illness and dying. Her sharp little tongue had nothing to do with the rest of her.

He said: "Mink Fisher's dead."

She said: "Well! That's a blessing, too."

Holder said: "Nothing I can do for your mother, Linden. Let me see this Indian. Nellie told me the shock it gave the old lady when he gave his news about that fabulous brother of yours."

Ase wanted to keep Mink inviolate from the professional eyeing and probing.

He said: "The Indians have superstitions."

Mink had talked many years ago of the spirit, which asked to be left alone for a decent period after the death of the body.

Holder said: "Dead men don't have any superstitions. Nellie says he was starving. Can't imagine an Indian starving to death."

Ase was unable to stop the intrusion. The doctor threw back the bedclothes.

"I'll swear. Skin and bones. You know, in all my years of practice, this is the first time I've ever seen an actual death from starvation. And it had to be an Indian."

He studied the sharp features.

"Handsome old fellow. Say, Linden, you look a lot like him. Sure he's not your sire?"

The doctor chuckled and left the room.

Ase stood over Mink's body. He stared at the still face. A great yearning filled him. No, Mink was only the father of his mind and spirit. He turned away, his eyes misted.

His mother's life left her at sunset with a quiet it had never known before. He could only share Holder's relief. His sadness was for the path they had missed together. He sat alone with her into the night, grieving over the destruction she had received and had inflicted. Nellie was asleep when he went at last to their bedroom, and he was grateful. He could not have endured her practical chatting about the funeral arrangements.

236

Dr. Holder stayed the night. In the morning he made a list from Nellie's dictation of such details as folk to be notified, the preacher to be called for the home service, the type of coffin to be ordered. The words penetrated Ase's brooding.

He heard her say: "I don't know what he expects to do with his Indian."

She seemed as alien to him as some woman stepping off the train in Peytonville. He went to the back bedroom. Mink, who had given and had not received, Mink the proud, would share his contempt, would ask never to be troublesome and unwanted, would thank him wordlessly, as always, for the boon of a final aloofness.

Ase wrapped the ragged Indian blanket tightly around the body of his friend. He reached for Nellie's hand-pieced quilt for further shroud, then dropped it as though unclean. Let Mink Fisher go to earth in what he had come in, as he would want it.

The long stiff body was awkward, but it was feather-light. Ase carried it cradled in his arms out of the back door. He circled the house at a distance and crossed the willow stream. He walked with long strides up the pasture hill, into the hemlocks, towards the dark, receptive bog.

★ 31 ★

THE gathering at the living-room table seemed to Ase like a flock of crows ringed around a mass of carrion. He considered the reading of Amelia's will a family matter, but Nellie had insisted that not only Judge Simmons but Dr. Holder must be present. Nat drummed his fingers on the table. Arent shifted in his chair, watching his brother for cues. Ase brought his mother's tin box from her room. They had been unable to find the key and the Judge prised open the lock. A thick sheaf of bank-notes lay on top.

Nat said: "Ah-hah."

The Judge laid the notes aside with a slow dignity. The next layer was of material concerned with Benjamin, his grade school and Academy diplomas, the few letters he had written his mother from his periodic absences in his youth, the illiterate scrawl brought by the gypsy queen that had proved of no use in tracing him. The Judge laid these too aside. At the bottom of the box lay the will. The Judge lifted it out, unfolded it with a crackling sound. The paper was yellow with age. The Judge looked it over.

"Hm-m. She had this drawn up in Trent. Odd, she didn't come to me." He read:

"To my beloved son, Benjamin Linden, I leave all my property, real and intangible——"

The Judge removed his spectacles and peered around the table.

"A strange arrangement, under the circumstances. Does this come as a surprise?"

Nellie brought her small fist down on the table.

"Not to me. I always knew she was up to something. Talking so mealy-mouthed about Ben's third, Ben's share, planning all the time to leave him everything. Something told me I was wasting my time being good to her."

Nat said sharply: "What's the date of the will? Everybody knows she was crazy as a bed-bug."

The Judge replaced his glasses.

"Nearly twenty years ago. Asahel, wasn't that about the time your brother went away and you were married?"

He nodded. The exact date was a week after his marriage to Nellie.

"Well, Asahel, she wasn't insane then. Or you couldn't prove it."

Nellie nudged Dr. Holder.

The physician said: "I believe you can. In my professional opinion, Mrs. Linden's unhinged mental condition can be definitely traced to the disappearance of her eldest son."

The Judge said: "Thank you, sir. Then, Ase, shall I file a protest, using that as the basis? The will is obviously unfair. You have carried the whole burden all these years."

Ase was recalling the November evening after his father's burying. He heard again the bitter words of the quarrel. He saw Ben scribbling out the relinquishment of his share in the farm and his mother at once consigning it to the bright flames in the stove. He shook his head. He heard again the implacability of her voice revealing her hate for him, her love for his brother.

"No. Ben signed over his rights in the farm and Mother put the paper in the fire. Her intention is perfectly clear."

"What do you plan to do, man? Go against the interests of your own family?"

Nat said: "The least you can do, Pa, is keep your mouth shut and let the Judge go ahead."

Nellie said: "Ase, sometimes I wonder if you aren't crazy, too."

Let them think he was mad, he would not scramble at law for Ben's property.

"We're making a living here. Having the deed in my name wouldn't make any difference."

Nat shouted: "It makes a difference to me. What's going to happen when you die? The state'll take the place, that's what, and nothing for me——" he corrected himself—"for the rest of us. That precious Uncle Ben's probably been dead for years."

Ase had not yet shown Ben's letter to his family. An obscure instinct of protection had kept it privately in his pocket.

He said: "Ben's alive. Mink Fisher brought the word."

The Judge said: "Ase, I almost agree with Nellie. You are not acting the part of a proper *paterfamilias*. I don't understand you."

The table fell silent. Nat reached for the sheaf of notes and began counting the money.

"Close to four thousand. Anyway, this is ours. It's what you've been giving the old witch all this time."

Judge Simmons said: "The lad is right, Asahel. This cash represents your own labour. Even, you might say, repayment for your mother's keep. I suppose she never paid you for bed and board?"

Holder said wryly: "Or for medical care. We kept her out of the asylum, or don't you remember?"

Yes, he remembered, and the sweat came in the palms of his hands. He did not answer.

Nellie said: "Ase, you're just being stubborn. All that stinking Indian brought you was his own story that Ben was alive and in his usual mess of trouble. You said we were making a living here, but it's been a mighty poor one lately. Don't be an idiot about this cash. It's yours, it's ours."

He had once as a boy in winter seen a deer surrounded by wolves. He had been young and unarmed and had been obliged to turn away in sickness of heart. Now he too was hemmed in by the enemy. Nat did not surprise him, nor the rest of the pack, but he had not expected from Nellie this subtle dishonesty. No, he thought, she was not dishonest, she was the eternal mother, the eternal bitch, fighting for her young and for family safety.

Nat said: "I don't see where there's an argument. Nobody but a dead Indian knows where Uncle Ben is."

Ase said: "I have something here from Ben."

He took from his pocket the letter Mink Fisher had brought him. He handed it to the Judge. Simmons read aloud slowly.

"Dear Brother Ase:

"This pesky old Indian of yours won't give me any peace until I write you what he calls white-man's-word-on-paper. Can't imagine how he happened to run across me. Have been waiting to write you until I made my pile. So I'm killing two birds with one stone, as think I have the big chance now if you or Mother can send me enough money. The timber out here would knock your eyes out. Douglas firs a hundred feet tall and six feet in diameter. The more you can send me the more timber rights I can buy and either re-sell at a profit or with enough cash set up my own logging camp and really clean up. Will cut you in on it fifty-fifty. Send an express money order, cheques no good out here and cash stolen before it arrives. Get the money out of Mother if you don't have it but by no means give her my address. Tell her this one is temporary, not a lie either, which you wouldn't tell her unless you've changed, I know you. I'll write her when I'm on my feet.

Affection to all, your brother,
Benjamin Linden

P.S. Have had a little bad luck but a hell of a good time."

There was silence.
Nellie said: "Well! This would have killed the old lady

240

if the Indian hadn't. She'd have wormed it out of you some-how, Ase."

He said: "I think this settles things."

The Judge said: "Yes. Unfortunately. We can only hope that Benjamin doesn't put you off the farm and have it sold. However, Asahel, any probate court would concede that you are entitled to share in the estate, for your mother's care."

"My mother didn't need to pay for her room and board. You forget, the farm was always hers."

"If you insist on looking at it that way, I suppose you consider yourself fortunate that she allowed you to farm her place and live in her house."

Ase was aware of the contempt in the voice.

Remembering his mother's greater contempt, he said: "I do."

Simmons lifted his hands to the air.

"Very well. Cut your own throat. I'll go ahead with the probate and have the money sent your brother as soon as the court permits. I shall charge a fee of three hundred dollars, since money means nothing to you, to be taken out first, along with the costs."

He gathered up the papers and left.

Nat's eyes narrowed.

He said: "You know, Pa, I sort of like the sound of Uncle Ben's proposition, thinking it over. He'll be surprised to get that much working capital handed him. Tell him fifty-fifty is all right. Tell him you didn't insist on a division of the cash here. I've been hearing about the big timber. There's bound to be a fortune in it."

Nellie snapped: "There's no fortune in anything in the world Ben Linden touches. If he does put the money where he says, there'll be a forest fire the next day and wipe it out."

Nat said: "Well, I'm for it. The big chance comes once to the unluckiest man on earth. All he has to do is recognize it. And don't think I won't know mine when it comes."

He frowned.

"Say, Pa, what kind of fellow is this Uncle Ben? Is he the kind to put us off the farm?"

Ase was half blind with rage. He stood up from the table. "No. He isn't."

"Ma, that right?"

Nellie hesitated.

"Yes, Nat," she said. "That's right."

Ase went from the house to the barns. They did not hold their usual comfort. He went to Pip Lake and stripped and plunged into the icy water to try to relieve himself of his feeling of uncleanliness. At supper he closed his ears to the chatter of his family and did not speak. He waited until they had gone to bed, then sat by the lamp and wrote at length to his brother. He dealt briefly with business matters. He gave the story of their mother's life and death. He gave the history of his children. He reported on the progress of the farm. He hoped that the cash would be enough for the desired timber purposes. He made no reproaches for Ben's two decades of silence. He expressed his love as best he could, and begged of Ben not to lose touch with him again. As he sealed and stamped the letter, he found himself with his mother's ancient hope, that the family news, the affection, would bring his brother home again.

Judge Simmons handled affairs promptly. The money order went west. Word was awaited by the probate court on the disposition of the Linden farm. Nat and Arent returned from the university. On a Saturday in July, Ase drove to Peytonville for supplies, and to trade in Nellie's eggs and butter, and to the post office for his weekly papers. The postmaster handed him a letter from Ben.

"Judge got one from Ben, too. Guess you'll want to see the Judge while you're in town. He hasn't told anybody how things came out. Even Miss Minnie don't know."

Ase could conceive the village curiosity over his mother's will. He smiled.

He said: "I'll tell the Judge to make sure Miss Minnie's the first to know."

The postmaster chuckled.

"He will."

The Judge welcomed Ase in the dusty office. He held out his hand.

"Glad you came by. Well, Ase, you knew your brother

242

better than I did. I'd have preferred a definite renouncing of claim, but this is good enough for the time being."

He pushed Ben's paper across the desk. It read:

To the Peytonville Township Probate Court and to Whom it may concern:

It is my wish that my brother Asahel Linden have full use of the Linden farm property as described, and any profits therefrom.

The paper had been notarized. A note asked to have the deed forwarded.

The Judge said: "My congratulations. Benjamin has more decency than I gave him credit for. I heard you have a letter, too. What does he have to say to you?"

Ase hesitated. It would seem ungracious, but he could not spread whatever Ben had written him before the Judge, the town and township.

"If you'll excuse me, I'll read it first with my family."

"Perfectly proper. Drop in next week if you have further news for me."

The letter was addressed to Asahel Linden & Family. He did not open it until the family was gathered together around the supper table. He glanced it over in search of one of Ben's typical indiscretions. There seemed none and he read aloud.

"Dear Bro. Ase & Nellie & All:

"Hard to imagine my kid brother with a houseful of children some near grown. That Nat sounds like a go-getter to me. Tell him to look me up if he ever comes west, it's the place to be. Wouldn't know what to do with a family myself but guess it's all right for an old slow-poke like you, Ase. Glad to hear you're still pretty, Nellie.

"Had an idea Mother would live for ever. I should have written her but didn't want her hounding me to come back.

"Well, folks, by the time you get this I'll be half-way to the Yukon. Suppose you've had the word. Gold. The news that's come back says Alaska makes chicken feed out of the California gold-rush. Stake out your claims and then just pick the nuggets up off the bare ground, some big as a hen's egg. Brings a hundred dollars an ounce and that's what I call money. Didn't make sense to bother with small potatoes like timber so I'm on my way tomorrow with that good cash they sent me safe in my belt and I mean safe, I've turned into a pretty good knock-down fighter. Had to pay five hundred for boat fare north, a good thing, too, it keeps out the pikers.

"Well, guess you won't hear from me again until I've made my pile. Nat, how about Uncle Ben coming back to the farm driving one of those new horseless carriages?

"Don't know just where I'll be, seems there's a good many rich lodes up there, plan to pick the best before I begin raking in those chunks of pure gold, so can't tell you where to write. Never fear, Brother Ase, you'll have word from me sooner or later.

> Best to all,
>
> Bro. Ben, bro.-in-law Ben, Uncle Ben."

Ase had a feeling of unbearable depression. In his heart, he recognized, he had expected Ben's return. Well, Ben had been generous about the farm. Yet he recognized his despisal of it, his eagerness to leave it behind. He knew further that the two of them equally despised property as property, both considering that such things were only meant to be used towards some other end. And if his end and Ben's were at variance, it had nothing to do with their tacit understanding that a precise ownership of the farm was irrelevant. He wondered whether Ben might not be off on another wild goose chase, but that did not matter, either. Nellie seemed to be speaking for him.

"What did I tell you, Ase? Ben's gone hog-wild again."

Nat's eyes flashed.

He said: "Now listen, Pa, you just don't know what's going on in the world. Uncle Ben's right. This is a chance in a million. I'm heading for the Yukon, too. Tomorrow."

Arent said: "Hey, you'll take me along, won't you?"

"Naturally. I'll have plenty of use for you."

* 32 *

Ase could not put a mortgage on property he did not own. He was reluctant to borrow on a personal note from the Peytonville bank, for the interest rate was ten per cent. He

244

could borrow ordinarily of an individual, as he had often loaned the use of money, at the less hazardous rate of seven per cent, but his farmer and merchant friends had suffered as serious reverses as he. His crops were thriving, but hail or storm at any time could finish his ruin. He asked Nellie in mid-August if she could make her supplies last a little longer.

She checked the larder and announced that she could manage. Her butter and egg money brought enough each week to trade for flour, sugar, tea and coffee, and the garden was abundant. If he killed an occasional lamb or shoat before he harvested his wheat, they need not go hungry. With Nat and Arent gone, the family seemed to eat no more than half as much. There were no longer Amelia's delicacies and strangely large appetite to be taken care of. The summer days being long, Eric insisted on helping for two hours night and morning, as well as all of Sunday. He was a new man, secure with home and family. Ase wished for the first time that the farm was his own, only in order to give to Eric the cabin and a few acres of land.

There had not been time to hear from the boys. He and Nellie had joined battle to persuade Nat to finish his college, but it had been like trying to rein an unbroken stallion with a cobweb. Nellie fretted constantly. Ase was less disturbed. His instinct told him that Nat's toughness would see him through, danger and hard labour would only give mettle to his steel. Nat would take care of Arent in turn because he needed him.

Ase walked through his wheat-field under a blazing sun. His yield, short of new catastrophe, would be as heavy as he had ever had. The crops of beans, of oats and barley and potatoes, were enormous. The apple orchard was in its prime, the heavy-laden trees grown so large their branches almost touched. The ten acres of peach orchard on the south-east slope above the lake had come into bearing. It was said that grains and fruits were scarce over most of the country and prices would be high. The bank would have loaned him any amount he asked for, but it was better this way, to depend only on the crops themselves, on himself, on Nellie, on Eric.

He crossed the road towards the bean-field. He heard a rumble of wheels over the wooden bridge. The planks kept rattling, so that there must be half a dozen heavy wagons coming towards him, and he knew it was the gypsies. They had not appeared in two years and he had missed them sorely. He waited by the side of the road. He lifted his arm high in greeting to the leading wagon. The driver was not Pav. The wagon came close. The driver was Pav's son. The line of wagons drew into the accustomed camping ground in the orchard near the spring. The back steps were lowered, the doors flew open, the gypsies hailed him as cheerfully as ever. The younger children had forgotten him and were shy. He looked anxiously for the Old One. Pav's son turned from giving his orders.

He said: "Our queen say you come to her first thing."

The relief was great.

Carlo said: "She go soon. Very soon. My father go snow before last."

Ase said: "I'm sorry. I loved him."

"I know. All love my father. All love our queen. All love you. Now come."

Carlo led him to the rear of the leading wagon. The Old One lay in her bunk. She was bright-eyed and Ase could not believe that she was ill or dying. She patted the bunk and he sat down beside her and took her brown old heavy-ringed hand in his huge ones.

She said: "I think I not see you again. I say, whip horses, I wish see our friend Asah before leave you."

He could not bear this further loss, he thought, not yet. He bowed his head.

"Now, now! Lift the head! Good smile! How long you think Old One like wear dress of life? Dress bright once, dance much, now old dirty rag, throw away! Is right."

She stroked his hands.

"Now I have wish, see you, have much tell you, you have much tell me, I decide not die today."

She laughed her ageless, rich, deep laugh.

Her face turned grave.

"I tell you first. Plague, smallpox, strike us like snake. My Elissa, her babas, all, big and little. Others. Old Pav."

246

He laid his hand on hers and she gripped it. She closed her eyes. They grieved together in silence.

"So. Now you tell me your much sadness. **Or** I tell you. Some things I know."

Her prescience, or her reading of his face, he could not know which, had always amazed him.

He said: "My mother died. My friend the Indian died. My two oldest sons have gone to Alaska to hunt for gold. My brother went there, too, before them."

"Something more."

He hesitated. The fact that he had little claim, only Ben's permission to work the land where he lived, that he was in desperate straits for the moment, seemed trivial.

"Tell me."

He shook his head. She shrugged her shoulders.

"Money trouble. New for you. Leave me now. We talk again tomorrow."

He went to the house and said to Nellie: "The gypsies are here again."

"Yes, I saw them come."

"What do we have for them?"

"Mighty little, Ase. I'm at the bottom of the flour- and sugar-barrels. There's plenty of vegetables in the garden, but they don't seem to use any, except to put in their stews. Fruit now, they like that. I can spare a pat of butter and some eggs."

He thought of the enormous hampers of food Nellie used to give him for his friends.

"Do the best you can. If you can stand it, I'll give them the spotted calf we planned to raise."

"Oh, Ase!"

She had raised the calf on a bottle and it followed her about like a dog. She wiped her eyes quickly and packed a small basket.

"Tell them I'm sorry it's so little. Take them the calf and get it over with."

He took the inadequate food, and the calf led by a halter, to Carlo. He could not butcher it himself.

He said: "I'd bring you more if I had it. The crops failed for two years."

Carlo looked at him with some of his father's old shrewdness.

"Is more welcome, friend Asah, because hard to spare. We thank you. Now you eat with us tonight, like always?"

Ase shook his head. Carlo laid a hand on his arm.

"I know. Is too much changed. No meat good when salt is sadness."

At their own frugal supper Ase told Nellie of the deaths among the Roms, of the Old One's soon-dying.

She said: "I always wondered about you and the gypsy girl Elissa. You were pretty sweet on her, weren't you?"

He looked at her imploringly. There was nothing he could say, in affirmation or denial. He wished she had chosen a less crude way of expressing it. She laughed.

"Oh, I know you didn't actually do anything. You're transparent as a window-pane. I'd have known."

He went to the front steps in the late twilight and sat watching the camp-fires in the apple orchard. He thought back to the days when he had danced with the gypsy girl. Why, she had been a princess, the daughter of a queen. Her black hair had brushed across his face like the wings of butterflies. He recalled the firm roundness of her flesh. He remembered the scent of her, made up of wood smoke, of crushed wild berries, or the flowers she was for ever gathering, sharp daisies and sweet hedge-roses. And though he had known her last as a plump matron and mother, he would think of her for ever as young and slim and lovely. For himself, he felt old for the first time in his life. Too much had happened in too short a while. For once, he lost his sense of the all-embracing unity of time and recognized a milestone in his life.

In the morning Nellie considered visiting the Old One with him and decided against it.

She said: "I haven't been near her the last ten years, better not bother her now. Tell her——" she hesitated, "tell her—oh, say something nice for me."

He thought miserably that he could not even speak for himself. Nellie's not going was a mixture of delicacy and of avoidance of difficult situations. He went to the leading wagon and called at the back for admission.

"Come, my friend."

He was surprised to find Carlo and several of the older men and women crowded in the wagon. The Old One held out her hand to him.

She said: "Friend Asah. Like I say, I go soon. Maybe tomorrow. Now I talk."

She seemed well and strong, yet if she was determined to throw off, as she had said, the dirty cloak of living, she would surely do so, as Mink Fisher had done. Where better for her to lie at peace than in the ancient Linden graveyard?

He said: "Stay here, now, and after."

"Pah! Where gypsy body lie, no matter, I go on. I like better some strange hill where no one ever know or see. Now. Listen, our friend. Is little something all agreed."

She looked around at the elders. They nodded their heads.

"I, Queen. King, my husband, die long ago. Pav, Pav's son Carlo, like prince, maybe, not king. I ask you years past, be gypsy king, marry my Elissa. Yes? Too late now, all too late. Because I ask you, you belong. Now. I have gold, much gold. I divide. I share. Most for tribe, little part for you."

She reached under her pillows and drew out an embroidered bag. She opened it. It was heavy with gold coins.

"This small much for you. Is my wish. Is wish of all."

He said: "No."

The Old One continued: "I know your trouble, in a dream. Now, Carlo tells me more."

He said: "No, I can't let you do this for me."

She said sharply: "No? So you make great gifts and take nothing? Too proud to take gift, eh? Hold head high, say, I am great man, I give, no gift to me from friend?"

He said: "It's too much."

"Too much, eh? What price you pay for friends? Gift is love. You hate love?"

He understood that this thing could not be refused. He inclined his head in thanks.

"Good, then. Little bag is for the wife. I make it long ago. Now, you see. Your luck change. All go fine now. And so, good-bye, my Asah. Never grieve for me. Only think some

249

time, when summer wind blow: 'Ah, the Old One, she speaks to me!'"

He kissed her cheek and turned away. Tears that he had not shed for his mother clouded his eyes. He watched the caravan move on until the last dust down the road had settled.

He went to the house. He turned out his inheritance on the baize-covered table before Nellie's wide eyes. He gave her the embroidered purse and told the story.

Nellie said: "Ase, I'll swear, I can't figure you out. Wouldn't lift a finger for your own money from your mother, and then take this from strangers."

She spread out wonderingly the pile of gold coins.

"Ase, there's close to a thousand dollars here. Well, our necks are saved, I must say. Count it."

He had no interest in the amount. He left the house and went to the comfort of the barns. He found no sharpness in his pain. The Old One's blitheness before life and death carried its own relief. He prayed that when his time came he would cast off the well-worn garment with a similar courage. He walked down the row of cattle stalls. They were empty except for one, where the spotted calf had been silently returned and tethered.

Nellie had called the gypsies 'strangers'. They were less of strangers to him than his own

* **33** *

NAT's letters to his mother were direct and often vivid. Ase was not offended that none was ever addressed to him. He had long accepted the bond between the two, and his own exclusion. He handed her the letter. Nellie ripped open the envelope, scanned the first lines, then thrust the letter at Ase, saying: "Read it to me."

She rocked back and forth in the Boston rocker, her hands crossed over her plump stomach, as he read slowly aloud. Her satisfaction rose to the surface like the thick golden cream on the milk-pans. At a piece of news, she lifted her eyebrows and said: "Um-hum." When a remark of Nat's amused her, she wrinkled her nose. She smiled from beginning to end. Ase thought with pain and pity of his own mother, starved for just such nourishment from Benjamin, driven mad, perhaps, for lack of it. Yet her fever had been devouring. Ben had been saving his body and soul when he begged his brother to keep from her his whereabouts, lest she 'hound' him. Nothing would have satisfied Amelia but complete possession of her son, to all intents and purposes returning him to the dark slyness of her womb.

When 'Melie and Willis trudged in from school in the November afternoon, Nellie called them to the sitting-room to hear with her a second reading. Today's letter from Nat was filled with news. He and Arent were leaving Alaska at last. They were taking the next steamer south, ready to invest their gold in a stable business.

They had spent three years in the field. The first year had been a hard one. There was no alternative for Nat but to freeze like other men in the winter, fight mosquitoes and gnats in the summer, tramp or mush great distances, to break his back with pick-axe, to crouch, aching, over the cold streams, panning his gold. By the end of the year he began to use their modest hoard of dust and nuggets for other tactics. He bought claims outright of sick, starving or discouraged men, bought shares from others, who, undiscouraged in the face of a promising vein, needed an immediate subsidy with which to continue. He re-sold the worthless claims to newly arrived 'tenderfeet' at far higher prices than he had paid, often, Ase knew, with misrepresentations. Nat had once written that a few nuggets 'planted' under a boulder returned higher dividends than the best bank stock. He re-sold the promising claims to the big syndicates, retaining shares for himself and Arent. One of these had recently proved to contain a rich lode. Instead of lamenting that he had not kept and worked it entirely for himself, he pointed out that he did not expect all the luck in the world, only a generous portion of it, and a year or two of hard labour might as easily have been spent on sterile ground.

He had found that the poor or dubious claims were more readily sold, and at better prices, if he erected the roughest sort of shack for shelter, with a cot, chair, crude stove and table, for by the time the tenderfeet reached the interior they were likely to be frightened by the vastness of the country, and a tar-paper roof over a few boards gave the illusion of a home. It was this that had given Nat his present idea. He wrote now and Ase read:

"We're coming out with better than thirty thousand. Shares in some of the claims will continue to pay off. Most fellows here push their luck too far, stay too long and lose everything. The North-West is booming. There's money pouring in from gold and timber and ship-building and fishing. I'm going to have a look at Seattle and Portland and some of the smaller places and go into real estate and contracting. The land itself is still dirt cheap, it's houses and stores and office buildings that are wanted, and a little later it'll be roads and bridges and more railway-lines. Not such quick money as one big lucky strike in the gold, but safe and sure, and I'll expand as fast as possible. Buy and build and sell, buy and build and sell. Take the real big jobs on a cost-plus basis, and I'm just the guy to see there'll be more plus than cost.

"Now Ma, paper money's scarcer than gold around here, but I got hold of a hundred dollar note, and here it is, and I want you to blow it. There'll be more later where that came from. Let me know how Pa's face looks when he sees it. He never said anything, but I always sort of figured he thought I was a tramp, thought maybe I'd end up like Uncle Ben, well, he'll see. That reminds me, I've told you I just kept missing Uncle Ben up here, and yesterday I heard he'd gone back to the States, stony broke, working his passage back. He did pretty well at one time, they say, then lost down to his last nickel at cards, couldn't leave them alone.

"Now, Ma, I'll be too busy to write much for a while, it'll just be a line or two, but don't ever worry about

"Your loving Nat."

Nellie smoothed the greenback in her lap.

"I guess now, Ase, you can stop worrying about him," she said. "He's going to get everything he ever wanted."

But the danger, Ase knew, had never been that Nat might not succeed, but that he would.

'Melie's eyes glittered. At eighteen, she was a handsome girl except for the too-small black eyes and the too-thin

252

mouth. An occasional beau appeared, to squire her to a hay-ride or a dance, but the same one seldom came twice. Her snapped orders were not appealing.

She said: "Pa, when I finish the Academy this year, I want to go to the university for a Home Economics course."

He smiled.

"You may go. But you won't learn more than your mother could teach you."

"Yes I will. On a different scale. Nat's going to need me. I'm going to run his big house for him."

Nellie laughed.

"First I've heard of Nat's big house. Better wait till he has one."

"He'll have it. I want to be ready."

'Melie looked at Willis speculatively.

"You'd better get ready, too. Better begin taking all the business courses. You waste too much time reading."

Willis said: "Get ready for what?"

The girl frowned.

"To work into Nat's big business, silly."

"He won't want me."

"It's a sure thing you'll never amount to a thing by yourself."

"I don't expect to amount to anything. I want to be let alone."

"We'll see about that. Nat and I'll know what's good for you."

Nellie said: "That's right, Willis. You can't go wrong sticking with Nat and 'Melie."

The boy shrugged his shoulders. He was still pale and slight. His eyes were red-rimmed from reading late by lamplight. Nellie protested, but Ase would not forbid this solace of books. The boys' adventure books had been replaced by Scott and Dickens and Thackeray, past Willis's years, Ase thought, reading them himself with pleasure. The Peytonville library was standardized and meagre. Ase picked up eagerly each new volume that Willis brought home, but for all the warmth the Dickens gave him, he was still unsatisfied. Surely there must be other books that told of larger worlds, books more like his Shakespeare and his Bible, to carry a man's mind and spirit soaring, to stab him with questions, and having drawn blood, to staunch with answerings. It was the great thinkers for whose words he longed, unknowing what he longed for.

It occurred to him to speak now to Willis, to stand with him against the others. If encouraged, the boy might have the makings of a scholar, a man of dignity and depth. Nellie and 'Melie bustled together to the kitchen, and when Ase turned from his thoughts to attempt to speak, Willis had slipped away.

He sat alone until he was late for his chores. He was depressed. Willis needed something from him, had perhaps always needed something, that he was unable to give or the boy to take. Yet there was still time. College was the next step, probably Willis would find there the direction for his life. His depression deepened. It was not for Nat. His concern for the taint on his eldest son was too old a thing to disturb him now unduly. As he had consoled himself so often, he hoped again that the 'success' towards which Nat was forging would of itself soften him. He had read that various industrialists, whose millions had been cut from the bodies of little men, were giving vast sums for noble purposes. Probably a certain type of man must first satiate his—he recalled the phrase—o'er-vaulting ambition, before he was free to give himself to a common humanity. It was not Willis or Nat who held him here, unable to plod on to the milking of his cows.

It was Benjamin. Nat's casual news brought back painfully a similar picture once painted by the gypsy queen, of Ben going away laughing in his ragged coat. That was how long ago, more than twenty years? Ben was then still young, so that the laughter ameliorated the rags. In his middle age, had he laughed again, embarking on the passage that must be worked for? And was he grey and worn, or was the hair yet tawny, the green eyes yet bright with cat-fire? The old longing, the life-long loneliness, swept Ase, and as he sank under its sweetness and its weight, it came to him for the first time to wonder if Benjamin needed him, if his brother yearned for him, too.

34

It seemed to Ase that Nat's plans went forward over the years as though he worked steadily at a difficult jig-saw puzzle. Nat's confidence in the Pacific North-West was justified. He poured his earnings back into his various businesses and projects. He found himself occasionally over-extended, strapped for cash, stretching his credit, but it was at these times as if a piece in the puzzle refused to fit for the moment only. He found its proper place shortly, and the design took shape, having been definitive from the beginning.

He and Arent lived as bachelors. He sent for 'Melie before she had quite completed her course in home economics.

"I'll always handle the budget," he wrote, "and if Ma hasn't taught you to cook by now, you're hopeless. Anyway, it won't be long before the big house and plenty of servants. You might as well get in practice."

The big house became a reality. It was not big enough, Nat wrote, and in a few years there would be a larger one, the finest mansion in the North-West. 'Melie was hostess as well as housekeeper, as the time had come when Nat was ready to entertain, to establish a social position in keeping with his financial one.

Nellie commented to Ase: "Don't see why he bothers about Society if he isn't going to get married."

Yet she read with satisfaction the newspaper cuttings that reported on the affairs of 'the rising young tycoon, Nat Linden'. She fretted that he stayed so long away. At last he returned to the farm for a brief visit, with 'Melie and Arent in tow. Nellie rejoiced, exhausting herself and big Elsa with cooking for Nat's gourmand delight.

Ase found himself again shocked. Nat and 'Melie had a hard, depthless glitter. They were grossly over-dressed. Nat, not quite thirty, was florid. After each of Nellie's abundant meals he patted tenderly the paunch he was too young to have developed. He boasted so flagrantly of his success that it seemed to Ase that Nat must be as loathsome in his own territory as here. Then it struck him that his son comported himself far otherwise, no doubt, where the opinions of men were to him important. Ase was aware of a subtle insolence in Nat's bragging before him.

Arent had not changed in the nearly ten years of absence, had neither hardened nor softened. He was still so much a nonentity that Ase, even during the few days of the visit, often forgot that Arent was in or about the house. Arent was dressed expensively, but with a drab modesty that made Ase once again unhappily certain that Nat kept his satellite inconspicuous for his own reasons.

Ase was most disturbed by the response of Willis to this visitation of the apparent mighty. The boy was attending the Normal School, studying to become a teacher.

Willis had a wry wit, and for all his aloofness, Ase remembered, the boy had said to him: "I'm not any good, Pa. Maybe I can teach kids that are smarter than I am. Just telling them nobody knows anything, and to go on from there."

But now Willis followed Nat as a moth to a candle. The truth appeared. Nat had had business in the central part of the country, and had, apart from his commerce, returned to the Linden farm for the main purpose of taking Willis away with him.

Nat expounded his plan. It was to take Willis back with him, to send him to the new university near-by, to take his degrees towards a professorship, to meet and mingle with men of prominence.

Nat said: "Seems to me Will is cut out for geology. I can make him the greatet geologist in the West."

Ase said: "I think he should stay here."

His protest sounded small and narrow even to his own ears.

Nat said impatiently: "Now, Pa, you had fits, in your funny sort of quiet way, when I wouldn't finish college. Here Willis has a chance to get somewhere, be somebody, and all you can say is: 'I don't think he should go.' There's no future for him here. I'm trying to help him and you're trying to hold him back."

Nat's proposition was valid on the surface. Ase searched his mind for an answer and could find none. Only an obscure instinct warned him. There was something behind Nat's apparent altruism. Ase could not put his finger on it. He recalled with relief his own idea that success might soften Nat. Perhaps this was the first sign of it. He turned to Willis, and as he did so, Nat spoke.

"Will, you're a great guy. Pa doesn't seem to think so. It's up to you, fellow. You want to stick around here, teaching in a country school, or following a plough, or you want to go with me? I believe in you, boy; by God, I need you with me."

Willis looked at his father. His face was transfused with light.

He said: "Nat really wants me."

Ase wanted to cry out: "I want you, I believe in you, too, but something here is wrong," and could not say it.

He said: "Well, son?"

Willis said: "I want to go with Nat."

So, it was done, his offspring were gone, strangers all. Eric drove them to the Peytonville station of an afternoon. The carriage had no sooner disappeared over the bridge than Nellie shrieked. The garden tomatoes were over-ripe and must be canned at once. Ase trudged to the log cabin to inform big Elsa of Nellie's need for her.

For all the kitchen bustle, the Linden house seemed empty.

Ase sat at twilight with Eric Svenson on the south steps of the log cabin. Eric puffed on a clay pipe. Ase whittled out the rough shape of an ornament for a mirror frame he was making for little Elsa, her mother's namesake. The child leaned against him, her long fair hair flowing over his sleeve.

She stretched out her hand to the rosette he was carving.

"I can see the shape now. It's going to be a hollyhock."

He had been following, as for Nellie's cake tree, a design he had seen in his encyclopaedia.

He said: "It wasn't, but I can make it a hollyhock if you'd like it."

"Oh, please."

The realistic flower would not satisfy him, he knew, but he would do his best for her. The little girl had the appreciation of his small gifts that Doll had had. At first he had thought she was Doll come back to him. The fair hair and blue eyes had snared him in her babyhood, and her reaching out her arms to him from her cradle. She was dear to him now, and always would be, but as time passed he recognized the disparity in the two child natures. Elsa was passive where Doll had been volatile. Elsa's imagination went with his so far, then stopped short behind the increasingly plain, sweet face. No, she was her good mother all over again, and no Dolly. Theirs was a friendship past the gap in years, a solid thing, he was sure, but there was no glory in it. He began widening the swirls of the rosette, to make a hollyhock.

Eric said: "Willis was pretty good help. I hated to see him leave us. We'll be short-handed."

Ase did not answer.

"The peach orchard has to be pruned this autumn, Mr. Linden. Maybe it can wait until the crops are in, but I think it's going to make us nice money if we take care of it properly."

From the south of the log cabin the peach orchard was remotely visible on its hill above Pip Lake. Eric had been as enthusiastic as he in its planting and nurturing, the trees ready now for full bearing, after two small crops.

Eric had said: "It will make us money, if we take care of it," and Eric had no stake in the orchard, none at all.

Ase laid down his carving. Eric had given more than he had received. True, they were raising the stock on equal shares, the lambs, the pigs, the calves, even the colts, but Eric was still the hired hand, owning neither land or home. Well, he was a tenant, too. He had forgotten for too long a time that he himself owned neither land nor home.

Eric said: "I want to fix up the cabin. Elsa and I hoped we'd have more children after little Elsa, but I guess, at our age, we were lucky to have a child at all. We've saved money, Mr. Linden, and I'd like to make additions to the cabin, if it's all right with you. We need another bedroom and a bigger kitchen and Elsa wants a back porch. I can do the work."

"I'll provide the materials, Eric. I can't let you spend your own money."

"Mr. Linden, would you consider selling us the cabin, even with only an acre or two of land?"

"I'm sorry, I can't."

"I know how you must feel about it, the original house and all."

"It isn't that, Eric. I don't own it myself."

Eric's alarm was clear.

Ase repeated: "I don't own my own house or any of the land. My brother has allowed me the use of it."

"I'm sorry. I never knew. Where is your brother, Mr. Linden?"

"I don't know."

Eric twisted his crippled hands together. It was a constant habit, as though he might so restore the crushed bones and tendons.

Ase said: "If you want to buy somewhere, Eric, I won't hold you here."

Eric said slowly: "No, I've put myself into this land. I couldn't leave it. It would be like leaving my two Elsas. The use of it's good enough. It's home, Mr. Linden."

They stared together over the rich farm, the rolling hills, the lush crops and orchards.

Ase felt relief from a weight he had not acknowledged. He had dreaded Eric's leaving for land of his own.

He said: "I should have told you when you first came, but——"

"But I was a down-and-outer. Having the cabin, and a job, and Elsa, it was more than I'd hoped for. The other doesn't matter. I guess you feel the same way."

"Yes."

"And it's home to you, anyway, too."

To this Ase could not answer, nor would he. His home was otherwhere, unknown, unfound.

"Hard to see why your brother would leave it. It's beautiful land, Mr. Linden. I guess you have to love it."

"I expect any land is beautiful if you love it."

"Or if you love it, maybe that makes it beautiful."

The two men smiled across the golden head of the child in understanding. Eric could not fill the place of Tim McCarthy, or Mink Fisher, or the gypsies, as young Elsa could not fill the place of Doll, but Ase took comfort from his presence. Eric's content warmed him like a hearth fire. Night fell and the summer stars came into bloom like that of orchards. Big Elsa returned to the cabin, laughing.

"Working with Mrs. Linden is as good as going to the circus," she said. "She has supper ready for you now, Mr. Linden. We finished the canning."

He put his knife and carving in his pocket, young Elsa stood on tiptoe to be kissed good-night, and he trudged down the road to his lighted house. It was filled with the acid sweetness of the tomatoes. The multiple jars stood upside down on the kitchen table, to be checked for leakage. Supper was laid on the dining-table, strangely large now for the two of them.

Nellie said: "Glad I had something to do when the kids left. I wouldn't want Nat sweating himself out on the farm, Lord knows, but I feel awful empty every time he comes and goes."

He laid his cheek against hers. She was so bustling, so self-sufficient, it was difficult to realize that she, too, ached for a lost loved one. For the moment he forgave Nat his sins, for the love of his mother. Nellie spoke sharply.

"Sorry supper's so late, but you wouldn't have noticed. Off with that Eric, gabbing away, gabbing away. You and your cronies."

He was amused, he was enchanted by her jealousy of his male companionship, now that he understood it.

"Now, Nellie, you know I'd rather have been with you, but you had to can tomatoes. You told me to get my big feet out, remember?"

He put his arms around her in his tenderness. She pushed him away.

"For Heaven's sake," she said. "Not tonight. I'm too tired."

★ 35 ★

NELLIE laid down the letter and pushed her spectacles back on the top of her head. Ase smiled. The effect was as though she wore a humorous little crown. He tried to remember when her hair had turned in colour to a shining silver. It must have come imperceptibly, for he had not been truly aware of a difference until this moment. Her unlined, unwrinkled face was as plump as ever, her cheeks as pink, her eyes as blue. He watched her fatuously.

She said: "Don't you want to know the news? Come on back to earth. What were you thinking about?"

"About you."

"What about me?"

"You're so pretty, Nellie."

"Stuff and nonsense. Listen, now. 'Melie wants to come home to be married to that man Crockett. Nat and Arent and Willis want to come, too. Nat's giving 'Melie the wedding."

"Why, that's fine."

"High time, too. I was sure 'Melie was going to be an old maid. Seemed to be born for it, so bossy. Past thirty, too. Bet she's got a ring in the poor fellow's nose already."

Yes, he thought, 'Melie's husband would gee and haw as she cracked her whip.

He said: "It's been a long time since we've had the children all together."

Nellie said: "Ase, I've got to have new curtains and rugs for the wedding. Nat offers money, 'Melie says, but I don't want to take it. Can you drive me to Trent tomorrow?"

Out of his wealth Nat had showered gifts on his mother. He had had a rural telephone installed for her, paying for two miles of line. He had given her a furnace. In his own modest prosperity Ase had planned to surprise Nellie with these himself. He had been too slow in getting around to them. When Nat's gifts were expensive, Nat mentioned the cost. If Nellie's letters of thanks were slow in reaching him, he wrote impatiently: "Didn't you get the watch? I paid two hundred for it," and "What did Pa say about that five-hundred-dollar sealskin coat? What did they say at the Grange when you showed up in it?"

Ase was embarrassed by Nat's avidity for praise and public acknowledgement. Nellie co-operated, and repeated prices everywhere with naïve pride and pleasure. Nat had asked what his father wanted for himself. Only an interesting book now and then, he replied. Nat had placed a standing order with a Western book-shop, and such a succession of strange books arrived—*A Girl of the Limberlost, Pollyanna*—that Ase wrote hastily to stop them, saying only his thanks, and that he had all the books he needed, ashamed of himself for the untruth. He needed ten thousand books, but not of this ilk. He heard of a great library in the City of New York, and now that he could afford to indulge himself, had written there, asking for recommendations of interesting books, describing himself as a farmer nearing sixty. He had received a catalogue of farm manuals.

The October sunlight had a strange quality he noticed now, as it played over one of the door-knobs. It lay thinly for a moment, moved on to rest on Nellie's enormous potted fern on a tall stand, and slid down the fronds like a trickle of leaf-stained golden water, passed across the carpet and was gone. So, it was late afternoon and time for his chores. He was conscious of the stillness. It was good, in a way, but he was glad the children were returning once more. He had missed them.

Nellie said: "If you'll please answer me, Ase. Can you take me to Trent tomorrow to get things or not? Shouldn't think you'd want Nat to do every blessed thing about the wedding."

"Why, yes," he said. "We can leave as early as you say."

For three weeks the correspondence was heavy between Nellie and Nat and 'Melie. Nat had his way at last, for a church wedding in Peytonville, with a reception afterwards at the Linden house. Both Elsas helped Nellie with a prodigious amount of baking and cleaning and planning. The whole business seemed to Ase like some primitive ritual, the nudent sacrifice of the bride, a tribal thing, and he was amused. 'Melie was no longer young, and he was certain that it was the groom who was being delivered up to her purposes, and Nat's. Well, he was anxious to see them all again, the offspring he had begotten.

Two cars drove up the road and stopped. Ase stared at the strangers walking up the front path. He would have known 'Melie and Willis. He would have passed without recognition the big suave man who was Nat and the shifty-eyed thin one who was Arent. He went down the front steps to meet them. Nat laid an arm patronisingly across his father's shoulders.

"Crock," he said, "meet my old man."

Crockett shook hands indifferently. 'Melie hugged her father.

Nat shouted: "Get on out here, Ma! Ma!"

They crowded into the living-room. Nellie came running, wiping her hands on her apron.

"You would catch me in the biscuit dough."

Nat lifted her from her feet and swung her. She shrieked and pummelled him. The others pushed in for their share of embracing. Even Arent grinned and rumpled her hair.

She said: "There now, that's over. And this is 'Melie's Crockett, eh, poor fellow."

Nat whooped.

"Take a better look at him, Ma. I turned Sis loose on him because he can take care of himself."

Crockett said: "Besides a little item of my knowing too much, Nat. I'm safer inside the family than out."

His tone was light, but his eyes, Ase noticed, were as cold as Nat's. He was almost another Nat, nearly as bulky, almost as smoothly over-tailored as confident, yet Ase sensed a weakness in the face that was not in Nat's. 'Melie was as assured as ever. In her full maturity she so resembled old Amelia that Ase was startled. It was her fashionable clothes that had made her for a moment alien. Willis laid a hand on his father's arm.

"Hey, Pa," he said. "Mighty good to see you. Been 'way too long."

Ase looked hungrily into the face of this, his youngest, the one who had so nearly missed coming close to him, as a needed shower of rain sometimes skirts one field. Willis's eyes were sad, like those of a good dog who has been betrayed.

"Welcome home, Will. You and I'll have to get out of all this and have a talk some day."

He thought perhaps it was not even yet too late for understanding. Willis moved away abruptly.

Nellie said: "Now 'Melie, you take these hoodlums and pick out their rooms. Your Pa and I use the front downstairs bedroom, so there's the downstairs back, and the four upstairs, and if they don't go around, somebody can sleep at the tenant house. You and Crockett should have got married

263

before you came, unless you're ready to double up right now."

Nat said: "Why, Ma, I'm ashamed of you," and roared.

Nellie said innocently: "I hear tell it's been done," and Nat whooped again.

She and Nat had always spoken much the same language, he had been her white-haired boy, and the one quality in him that Ase could approve was his adoration for his mother, a clean thing in the centre of something soiled.

Nat said: "Now, Ma, if you think I'm going to bed down with the hired help, you're mistaken. I want that back downstairs bedroom myself. Never got to sleep there when I was a kid, nobody allowed there but company, and Pa's McCarthy and that old Indian. Think I've spent enough on the house to be company this time."

'Melie herded the family upstairs with their luggage. Nat sat down and lit a cigar.

He said: "You've got things looking pretty good, Ma, for an old farm-house. Listen now, these carpets are too old-fashioned. I want you to take 'em up, have the floors finished and polished, they're hard maple, aren't they, Pa? I'm going to send you some Oriental rugs. Nothing's too good for Nat Linden's Ma. Look."

He drew out his wallet, making a casual show of the notes of large denomination, and brought out a coloured plate of a rug.

"How's that? Pretty fancy? Four hundred dollars and the small ones to go with it a hundred each. Like it, Ma? Here, Pa, how's it look to you?"

Ase studied the pattern and the colours. They were like his south west field in autumn, except that the red sumac, the tawny pasture grass, the green pines, the deep blue of twilight, were in their reality more beautiful. He did not answer.

Nellie said: "Let's see the picture again. I don't know, Nat, I like the carpets. Got this one new for you to come. They're so nice and warm underfoot in winter."

Nat frowned, irritated.

"Now, Ma, that coal furnace I gave you keeps the house hot as hell and I know it. I want you to fix things up, live in style."

Nellie said: "Style's all right for you, that big house you say you have, all kinds of help, but Pa and I like it here just the way we have it."

The rest of the family came trooping downstairs. Crockett was fascinated by the huge zinc bathtub encased in match-wood, by the windmill that pumped the water for the house.

Nat said: "Will, you'd better go around with him. A city guy can get into all sorts of trouble on a farm. Can't have our groom falling in the well."

He was the benevolent brother, watching after them all.

Nellie said: "Nat, I always thought you'd marry young and have a big family. You used to like the girls."

Nat laughed complacently.

"Still do, Ma. Girls. Don't take much to the brood-hens. Maybe some day I'll buy me something handsome for my house."

Nellie said: "'Melie, where are you and Crock going to live when you go back?"

"Why, in Nat's house, just the same as before. He likes to have Crock and me handy. Seems to think I do a pretty good job of running the place."

Nat said: "She certainly does. I have a lot of, well, business and political company, Ma, sometimes late at night, and believe me, 'Melie keeps a whip-hand over that Jap help, gets 'em out to serve the drinks, and the food, oh, man! Not as good as yours, Ma, but mighty fancy."

Ase cleared his throat.

"Political company, you say, son?"

"That's right."

Nat puffed on his cigar.

Ase was stirred. It had always seemed to him that there could be no nobler work, after that, perhaps, of the physician, the teacher, the judge and the minister, than for a man to serve his state, his country, in the legislative halls. He thought that he might have misjudged Nat after all.

He said: "I'd be proud to hear that you're running for your State Legislature, Nat. Maybe even for the United States Congress."

Nat guffawed. He started to flick his cigar ash.

Nellie said sharply: "Now you just wait a minute, young

man. If you've got to stink up my clean house, you don't have to drop that mess on my new carpet."

She brought a kitchen saucer and thumped it down on the table beside him. He patted her arm.

"Ma, if a fellow was dying, you'd be afraid he'd dirty the bed."

Ase recalled Nellie's horror over Tim McCarthy and Mink Fisher. Nat had then this sensitivity, this understanding; surely he had been mistaken in his eldest son.

He said eagerly: "Perhaps you can't discuss it yet."

Nat blew a cloud of smoke.

"Pa, I wouldn't be caught dead in the State Legislature or Congress, either. In another couple of years I'll have our whole legislature right in my pocket, cheap, too."

"I don't understand."

"You wouldn't. You've lived all your life like a stick-in-the-mud—no offence, but you're just an old-fashioned farmer. Politics aren't what you think they are."

Ase was suddenly angry.

"What are they, then, if they don't serve the people?"

"Now, Pa, the people get served. They get roads and bridges and court-houses and railways. Schools, too, and you ought to like that, my God, the stew you made when I wouldn't finish college. Smartest thing I ever did was when I got out."

Nat was angry, too. He leaned forward and waved his cigar.

"And it's Nat Linden—Nathaniel—Grandmother had fits about calling me Nathaniel—hell, I've got to the top as Nat Linden—Nat Linden, a poor farm-boy, he's building all that stuff. And getting his, believe me——"

He took out his monogrammed handkerchief and mopped his face. He stubbed out his cigar on Nellie's saucer. He sat back in his chair.

"Now I don't say but that some time maybe I'd enjoy being Governor. Not so much in it, you know, but still, 'Governor'. Maybe about the time I buy me my blonde."

Ase felt sick at heart.

He said: "I hate to hear that your state legislators can be bought. I don't see why anyone would want to put them in his pocket, as you say. But the Congress has honest men."

266

"Some of 'em, sure. Lot of them the same little cheap guys. Live on a dog's wages, why, they have to make something on the side."

Ase stood up, a lean old man towering over his son.

He said: "I don't believe you."

He left the house in search of Willis. He found him at the barns, stroking the nose of a new-born calf in the stall with its mother.

"Will?"

"Hello, Pa."

"Will, Nat's been telling me things I don't like. Something's wrong. How does he make so much money out of his building?"

Willis said: "You know Nat, Pa. It's more than the building. He has lots of irons in the fire."

"Is he making all this money honestly?"

"Why don't you ask him?"

"I can talk better to you."

"I'm just a little cog in Nat's machine, Pa. It isn't up to me to do any talking, even to you."

"Will, I wish you'd get out. You don't belong with the rest of them."

"That's what I used to think. I can't quit now."

"Why not?"

"It's just too late, that's all."

"You're still a young man, son."

"You get old fast when you work with Nat. Don't worry, Pa. I make a good living. I'd never have amounted to much, anyway."

Perhaps not, Ase thought. Yet something in Willis had been waylaid and destroyed. He had taken the easy road instead of the hard one, but it was the easy road that had proved dark and tortuous.

Ase put off his return to the house. He made his chores last as long as possible. 'Melie and young Elsa were putting Nellie's lavish supper on the table. Nat was demanding another brand of preserves with a jovial perversity, his henchmen were laughing at his wit. Ase washed up and slipped into his seat. The family ate hugely, they were like a school of voracious fish feeding under the sea of chatter.

They talked of the barbecues of the West, of the Pioneer Picnics near Peytonville, of Nellie's freezers of Sunday ice-cream in the summers of their childhood, and ended back in Nat's establishment, describing the Japanese servants and the fabulous parties. Nat slapped his great paunch and said he could not hold as much more as a caraway seed. Nellie brought out her cake tree, long unused. Nat chose first among the cup-cakes like flowers on their wooden thorns, torn between the white frosting dotted with red cinnamon drops and the chocolate sprinkled with silver pellets, the fresh coconut and the raisin-thick spice, and took one of each.

'Melie laid a chocolate cup-cake on Crockett's plate. He pushed it aside and reached for a coconut. He did not, then, allow the ring in his nose to chafe him. Ase was aware of an oddly settled relationship between the pair. They were scarcely bride-and-groom-to-be, but more a long-married couple with a mutual acceptance and no love at all. Their intimacy was obviously of long standing. It must have been almost passionless, an affair, rather than a marriage, of convenience. Nat's tight little family empire ran smoothly.

Ase was anxious for the talk to turn away from trivial matters. His sons and their companion were at least men of the world and would know more of tides and currents than his papers gave him.

He asked: "How does the West feel about the re-election of President Wilson?"

Nat clipped the end from a cigar.

"Biggest fool thing the country's ever done. What does a damn professor know about government?"

Ase persisted: "What do they think out there about the possibility of war?"

"Anything's possible under the guy. He's too full of ideas. No common sense."

Nellie said: "Stepping on toes, Nat. Your Pa was the only man in the township to vote for him."

Nat held his cigar half-way to his mouth.

"For God's sake, Pa, what's the matter with you? You must have known you could have saved yourself the trip to Peytonville. One lone vote."

He said stubbornly: "But it was mine."

268

He must speak now, Ase thought, he must speak of the necessity for a man to make his choice of issues and of values, to respect the privilege of the vote itself, lone voice or no. He tried to think of the words that would express his meaning.

Nat said easily: "Forget all this political stuff at your age, Pa. Time you were sitting back and taking things easy. That goes for you, too, Ma. Let the hired man's wife or that pretty girl of his do your cooking." He winked at her. "That is, after I leave."

He yawned.

"Been a long day. Crock, you and Arent put the cars up the side drive."

Nellie said: "I thought you were going to come by train."

"Did. Had the cars sent on ahead to Trent by freight."

"I don't see why you need two."

"One for my gang and one for me and you, Ma."

He stood and stretched.

"Bed, everybody."

They went like obedient children.

Ase sat alone after the flock had broken up and gone away like roosting birds. 'Melie, he thought, for all her hardness, deserved better than this Crockett. He was aware of a corruption in the man somehow more reptilian than Nat's. He dismissed the concept, but remained disturbed. It would be of no use to discuss it with Nellie. Their daughter was being married elegantly and at last, to a man of Nat's choice. She would, he knew, be as horrified by his suggestion of evil expanding in the family as he found himself by the fact.

The November evening turned dull. He touched a match to the fire laid in the stove. Nellie would scold him for making a mess the last thing at night, but he needed the warmth and the primitive light of the flames. He seemed to stand alone on a desolate shore while the tide went out. He was stranded there, no ship to bear him to sea, no horse to bear him inland. The wind keened high overhead and then was gone, passing trackless towards the uncharted stars.

Ase stood lost and appalled at the wedding reception. Nat had had so many engraved invitations sent out that Nellie had commented: "He must have just used the tax list." Nat had hired a caterer from Trent to provide the feast, complete with champagne. The good friends, the neighbours, the relatives, were filing by the tables of gifts. In their esteem and affection for Ase and Nellie, the Grange had dipped into its treasury and sent a table service of plated silver in its own red imitation leather box. All over the township the women had set to and made their gifts for the Linden girl, a lace-trimmed pin-cushion, three kitchen dish-towels, a cross-stitched hand-towel, a set of calico potholders, a match-holder with two sandpaper cats, one large, one small, and the caption: "Don't scratch me, scratch Mother," a gingham apron, an organdie party apron, a silk sewing-bag, a pair of crochet-edged pillow-slips. Miss Minnie the milliner had hand-painted one of her famous cakeplates in full-blown magenta roses, neglecting her trade to finish it in time. The banker and his wife, Mr. and Mrs. Peyton of the General Store, the hotel-keeper, the Academy principal and his wife, had sent such store-bought presents as cut glass jelly-dishes and sets of tea-cups. Aunt Jess was too feeble to attend any of the ceremonies. She had sent a note: "For the little girl I helped bring into the world," and with it a rare old gold and garnet brooch, her one treasure, Ase knew. Nellie's family, the Wilsons, had agreed that it was proper for 'Melie to have their dozen heirloom hand-woven linen sheets. These last two gifts stood out proudly, the only ones remotely able to face the array from Nat's business and political associates in the West.

The Governor of Nat's state had sent a mammoth silver service tray. There were a gold-lined silver punch-bowl, pitchers, goblet and two sets of sterling table silver that together would make place settings for a hundred people. There were imported linens, ornate clocks and complete dinner services of Limoges and Wedgwood. Ase discovered the cheap plate from the Grange between the two sterling services. Nat stood near-by, faintly flushed, telling Miss

Minnie the source of each Western gift. Ase waited until Nat turned away from her.

He said: "Nat, how did these things happen to be sent here, when they'll have to be shipped back West again?"

Nat rocked on his heels complacently.

"At my request."

"But they shame the folks."

"That's exactly the idea."

"Why, they'd about forgotten you and 'Melie."

"I haven't forgotten them. And they won't forget me again. Remember when I out-grew my suit and had to go on wearing it to the Academy anyway, and got laughed at? And you peddled wood one winter? Let 'em look at Nat Linden now. And I've just started."

So Nat had built his life on a boy's bitterness. No, Ase thought, this was only an excuse to build as he would have done, anyway.

He noticed the Widow Bedford standing in front of the display of silver. Her knotted hands held her shabby black purse against her stomach. She had dressed up her old felt hat with a tail feather from her red rooster and the feather, working loose, dipped towards her shoulder. He pushed his way to her.

She said: "My, it's elegant, Ase. If we'd of known, been better not to of tried to give to 'Melie. She'll think cheap of us."

"Which is your present? I didn't notice."

She turned with a flash of brightness and pointed to another table.

"Pin-cushion."

He took it in his big hand. Its fat surface was covered with an assortment of pins, plain and colour-beaded, arranged in a geometric design.

He said: "This is fine. Only trouble, 'Melie'll hate to use the pins and break up the pattern. Isn't this real lace around the edge?"

She touched it tenderly.

"From my first baby's christening dress. Satin's from my wedding petticoat. Hated to cut into it, but I said to myself: 'Don't you be selfish, Lulu Bedford. Get it over with and

271

you can make pin-cushions other times. weddings and Christmas and the like.' I do love a pretty pin-cushion."

He was desperate. He gathered his courage.

He said: "All that fancy silver and china doesn't mean a thing. It came from men Nat does business with. Like paying a drummer's commission. It's presents like this one 'Melie really needed."

She looked up at him.

"Now that's so. She'll likely put all that other away and never use it. Know I would. Guess we've given her a good start on housekeeping, amongst us. That embroidered set from the Sewing Circle, I helped on that, it's nice, but not too nice to use."

She took the pin-cushion from him and replaced it on the table.

"Excuse me. Never could get over the idea a man'll always get dirt on anything white."

She looked with satisfaction over the cross-stitched towels, the pot-holders, the pillow-slips.

"Another thing, too, Ase, these'll remind 'Melie of home. My, she must get lonesome way out there."

He said: "Maybe we seem way out here to people way out there."

She chuckled and left him, to hunt out the president of the Ladies' Sewing Circle. Ase went slowly past the gifts from the home friends, memorizing as far as possible who had made or given this or that. He spoke awkwardly and admiringly of stitching, of crochet, of pansy-painted velvet plaque.

He clung like a drowning man to the Widow Bedford's words, repeating: "It's what 'Melie needed for housekeeping. It will remind her of home."

He reached Miss Minnie. In a moment of panic he forgot the nature of her gift. It had probably been a hat. Perhaps a fichu or a jabot, he had heard such terms. He remembered talk of 'Melie's 'going-away' costume.

He said cautiously: "'Melie was pleased with her going-away present from you."

"Mr. Linden, you haven't got the faintest idea what I gave 'Melie."

So, he had lost his hold on the floating log, the straw.

It would be politic to say, 'Whatever it was, I heard 'Melie speak specially of it.'

He looked at her helplessly. She patted her stiff grey curls and arched her eyebrows.

"Just what I always say, a man doesn't ever notice. Never mind, I understand you dreadful creatures, so I'll tell you. It was one of my hand-painted cake-plates, the nicest I've ever done, if I must say so myself."

He recalled at once the magenta roses and his life-raft. He swallowed.

"It's what 'Melie needed for housekeeping. It will remind her of home."

"Why, Mr. Linden, you do notice. Come to think of it, I remember when you bought the bonnet for Mrs. Linden, gracious, how long ago? You wouldn't have anything but that blue bonnet and I said to myself then, 'Now Mr. Linden appreciates the artistic'."

She lowered her voice.

"You're the only one I can ask: please tell me, did you think the roses had too many petals? I did suffer so, wondering if they were too full. I get going on rose petals and I can't stop."

He was rescued in his time of need by Nellie.

"Come on, everybody. Nat's present's just been delivered. The photographer's here, too. Nat wants pictures of everybody outside."

Nat's 'just delivered' gift to the bride and groom was a red Cadillac car. It had been waiting in the carriage-shed for two days.

The farm-house was still in confusion two days after the reception. 'Melie's wedding gifts were strewn everywhere, half wrapped for shipping or mailing on to the West. The furniture was disarranged. The flowers dropped in baskets and vases, not quite dead enough to be thrown away. In the woodshed Ase helped Willis and Crockett with the re-crating of the bulkier gifts. Nat strolled into the shed.

He said: "Ma and 'Melie and I have things all worked out. Arent and Will and I will drive back in the new car. I've got business on the way. 'Melie and Crock will wait a couple of weeks and then come out by train. Pa, you and Ma are coming with them."

Ase laid down his hammer.

"The whole trip's on me. Won't cost you a cent, Pa. Winter coming on, you ought to get away for a few months. Time you crossed the country and saw the world."

Ase thought of the many times he had imagined himself crossing the country and seeing the world, the panorama of the whole United States unfolding before his hungry eyes. He might even find Benjamin, where Nat's search and wide connections had failed to find him. Then he knew that he could not go as Nat's guest. He had prospered. He could well afford to pay his own and Nellie's way. He knew again that it was not Nat's world he longed to see or could bear to see. He could not go at all.

He said: "Thank you, son, not this year. Some other time your mother and I will set out on a trip and drop in and surprise you."

Nat said: "Pa, you old stick-in-the-mud. You've never been beyond Trent in your life. Don't you have a scrap of curiosity in you? Don't you want to see farther than your own fields and fences?"

Why, Ase thought, his feet had itched all his life to walk on stranger roads. His heart had awakened him, pounding in the night, from dreams of meeting stranger people, red, white, yellow, black and brown. In the dreams he sat with them beside their various hearth fires, sharing with them the alien foods of the encyclopaedia, mysteriously communicating freely in alien tongues. He was half blind in his mind's eye from peering across the continent, and into the suns of foreign lands, and beyond them, beyond the Coral Sea and the Caribbean, to Europe and Iceland, Cape Horn and the newly discovered North Pole, past Africa and India, the Great Wall of China and forbidden Nepal and the steppes of Russia, into the Alps, the Andes and the Himalayas, and high above these, up into inter-stellar spaces, so dazzling that he might be unable to face it if he found it, the home he yearned for, the true and final home that was not, and never had been nor could be, the old Linden farm near Peytonville.

Nat said: "Listen now, Ma wants to go."

"What were you saying?"

"Pa, I don't see how she puts up with you. I was saying, Ma's got her heart set on this trip."

"Oh."

Ase picked up the hammer and drove another nail in a crate. He thought warily that he must speak with Nellie alone, to make certain of this.

He said: "If she really wants to go, no reason why she can't go without me."

He was surprised when Nat pounded him on the back.

"Pa, that makes sense. Ma wants to see the world and you don't. One of the Elsas can take care of you. You never know what you're eating, anyway. God, Ma will knock 'em dead out West. We'll stop in Chicago and rig her out. Sort of old-timey stuff, bonnets and flounces. She'll have the Governor eating out of her hand."

Ase could only privately agree with him. Nellie would be an asset, with her wit and charm. Nat had always been ashamed of his father. Yet was it conceivable that Nat was using his mother, as he used the others?

He said: "If it's all right with your mother, I think all of you had better leave at the same time."

Nat puffed on his cigar.

"Guess that's a good idea. Sure. Two weeks in the Cadillac, six days on the train. 'Melie'll get there ahead of me to have things running."

Willis looked up from his work on the packing of 'Melie's crates.

He said: "Nat, I think I'll stay behind with Pa for a while. He'll be pretty lonesome."

Nat said coldly: "Well. We can get along without you fine, just fine."

Ase sensed the hostility.

He said: "I'll be all right alone."

Willis repeated stubbornly: "I'll stay here a while."

Nat said: "Just a while? Planning to quit? You haven't forgotten that business in Compton?"

"No, I haven't forgotten."

Nat shrugged his shoulders.

"Your own funeral, Will, if you have ideas, for a change."
Willis said: "I know."

It was true, Ase found, Nellie was exhilarated at the prospect of the trip West. Nat wanted to drive her to Trent for her necessary shopping. Ase insisted on taking her himself in the buggy and paying for the new clothes and luggage. She rejected firmly a fur-trimmed broadcloth suit that was most becoming, because of the price. Ase made an excuse to leave her and slipped back to the shop to buy it. The family was delighted with her wardrobe. Nat gave a grudging approval.

"Good enough to start out with, Ma. I'll fix you up right later."

She said tartly: "Now I've no intention of letting you rig me out like a Christmas tree. Seems to me we've already overdone things."

Nat laughed.

"You'll change your mind when you see the clothes at Townsend's."

The two sections of the family got on their way in a confusion of equipment. The Cadillac left, heavy-loaded. Eric drove one of the cars to the freight station, Willis the other. Ase drove Nellie in the light buggy. She clutched his arm in a sudden panic.

"Ase, I don't want to go. I can't leave you."

He reined in and held her close. She cried against his shoulder.

He said: "Now, Nat and 'Melie want to show you off. Just have a good time and tell me all about it when you come home. I'll get along all right."

She sniffled and blew her nose and sat up.

"I know. I'd have to have gone some time. And, Lord knows, Elsa's a better cook than your mother was, and you put up with that. Now, Ase, your winter underwear's in the bottom drawer of the cherry-dresser. You get it out the very first day of hard cold."

It was more painful than he had expected, to see the train puff away, to wave after her. Perhaps he should have gone too, if only to have spared himself this needless loss of her. He drove home with Willis and Eric. The house was naked, only the kitchen cosy. Nellie had left so much cooked food that Elsa was not to come until the next morning.

Willis said: "Pa, you don't know how peaceful this is, in the kitchen. Let's eat here and not bother with setting the dining-room table."

Together they set out a portion of the prepared dishes. Ase made coffee. Willis brought butter and cream from the pantry. They ate in a comfortable silence. Willis stacked the dishes in the sink. They lingered in the kitchen, where the wood range glowed red.

Willis said: "Pa."

"Yes, son."

"Did you wonder why I stayed behind?"

"Well, yes."

"Pa, you were right. I've got to get away from Nat. It's worse than you imagined. It's more than Nat's being crooked."

Ase shoved a stick of wood into the stove.

He said: "You'd better tell me."

Willis leaned forward.

"Pa, Arent and Crock do the dirty work. Nat keeps his own hands clean, as far as anyone's been able to prove."

"I suppose Nat makes deals, as they say, to get the contracts for those roads and bridges and building he talked about. He probably pays money to men in the legislature to pass bills for the appropriations."

"That's the least of it. Most of the time he builds with inferior materials. Some of his buildings are fire-traps, ways that don't show on the surface. One of his bridges has already fallen in. A car full of people just made it across. He got the blame shifted to a sub-contractor. The fellow's in jail right now. One state senator had been fighting Nat. He had some proof——"

"Go on, son."

"They called it suicide. Maybe it was, maybe it was."

"If it wasn't?"

"If it wasn't, it was Crock. Nat would keep Arent out of a thing like that."

277

"Will, what is your part in this?"

"Well, Pa, I'm a front for Nat on some of his new projects. Mining, oil. Remember, he was going to make me a famous geologist? That's what I am, all right. You just bet I am, Nat planned it that way. I got my Master's degree and my Doctor's degree, and Nat said I didn't need to go any further, he'd set me up in a laboratory of my own. I'd always thought I'd like research instead of teaching. Research, sure—— Analyses, sure—— God."

Ase said: "But Nat told me you were doing this."

"I'm doing it. For Nat. He has me set up in this famous geological laboratory, and I'm not supposed to have any connection with him, and he sends in 'samples', samples of ore, samples of soil where oil might be promising, and I run the tests and make the reports, and then Nat sells this land all through the West where there aren't any minerals or oil at all, and all the little fellows that buy his land are stuck with it, ruined."

Ase said: "But aren't your reports correct?"

"They are, but what Nat does is to bring in samples to my laboratory that don't have anything to do with the land he's selling, the companies he sells stock in. Somehow, he keeps just within the law."

"You'll have to leave him and go into some other laboratory or company, Will."

"I signed a contract with him. I can't work at my profession for anyone else. He paid for my education, remember. I signed before I knew."

Willis turned his face to his father in the dusk.

"Pa, you tried to keep me from going. When you did, did you know about Nat?"

Ase felt the sweat on his forehead.

"Because if you did, you should have told me."

Willis, the shy, the mild, was suddenly his accuser. What could he say now, and what was the truth of his knowledge of Nat, after all? The ruthless greed he had always recognized. Other men were cursed by it and it did not lead them into devious ways. The gypsy boy that Nat had pushed into the bog—but he may only have jostled him in a boy's rough play, quite without malice. Nat's own letters from Alaska—

the desperate men who bought with their savings the worthless claims, where a few gold nuggets under a boulder paid high dividends—but sometimes a worthless claim had suddenly proved out, and every man who had gone into the fevered Yukon had known he was gambling.

"Will, can you be sure about these things?"

The fire in the wood-range burned low. The kitchen was in darkness, no lamp lighted.

"The bribes, the rotten crookedness, yes. The big things, no. I couldn't prove them. Nat's too smart to let them be proved. I just know that Nat is bad, Pa. All bad. Did you? Did you always know he was bad?"

"I was afraid for him, son, but I didn't know. We don't know now, do we?"

"Maybe you think it's only that I'm jealous of Nat. Maybe I am. I used to be. Ma and Grandma made such a fuss over him and you had Dolly. I didn't seem to belong."

The man was explained, and the boy he had been. Ase grieved for him. He gathered his thoughts to tell his son of his own youth, outcast. Willis stood and spoke briskly.

"No, Pa, it isn't jealousy. It's just all too rank for my stomach. I'll figure out something to do. I'm not going back if I can help it, but it may take a miracle."

"Will, think about the farm. It's doing well. I've always hoped one of you boys would stay."

"Thanks, no. I'm on Nat's side there. No use slaving away on land you don't own. Good-night, Pa."

"Good-night, Willis."

Ase went to his bed, strange without Nellie, and lay long awake.

⋆ 37 ⋆

It was as though Willis's confidences had never been. Ase prodded his own timidity, to speak, to try to reach his son again, and Willis evaded him. He seemed to have regretted his revelations. He lingered on at the farm, withdrawn and brooding. Eric sensed some impasse, did his best to interest Willis as a scientist in the problem of the orchards. New diseases were attacking the fruit. The apple orchard was past its prime, true, but a sickness was on it that was not of age. Eric suggested experiments with sprays.

Willis said: "That's out of my line," and would not be allured.

Big Elsa mothered him and young Elsa was kind, even tender. Their company seemed to solace him and he spent long hours at the cabin. Ase had a sudden hope of the sweet-faced girl, born to be wife and help-mate and mother. He was disappointed when she came to him with the news that she was shortly to marry a Jan Rabaski. Willis was unconcerned. Elsa brought her Jan to Ase in shy pride.

"He's sensitive about his English," she said, "but he's learning fast."

Ase was drawn at once to the young Pole. He was as plain as Elsa, as honest, and as dark as she was fair. He had fought in his country's army and later with the French, had been invalided out, his lungs affected by gas, and now, in early 1917, had migrated to America. He was anxious to explain his position, lest it seem equivocal. He tapped his deep chest.

"I get this cured," he said earnestly. "I go back to fight Boche some more. Maybe you have American army fight then. I join."

Willis too found him interesting. Jan came of farm stock, small land-owners, prosperous enough so that he had planned to become a scientist. The war had ended that, and now his parents were dead and their land ravished. His hope lay in America, and though, his own dreams over, he must make his living as a hired farm hand, it was good that his children would be Americans, they would go on where he had left off. He was 'lucky man', he said, to have found his Elsa, and, a stranger here, so soon. He was working for the Grimstedt sons.

"Hard boss," he said, showing his white teeth, "me hard, too."

He turned to Elsa.

"Me hard? I hard?"

"Almost right, Jan. We would say 'I am hard, too'."

He repeated after her, an adult and serious scholar: "I-am-hard-too," stressing the consonants.

When they left, Ase said to Willis: "I'm uneasy about Elsa and her young man."

"I don't see why."

"The work at Grimstedt's is too much for an invalid."

"He's not an invalid. He's keeping up with it, isn't he? He's ready to fight again, if his gassed lungs get better, isn't he?"

Willis stalked away. Ase had noticed his disappearances and did not know to what obscure refuge he went. He recalled his own retreats, to Tim McCarthy, to Mink Fisher, to the gypsies, to his flute. He had not played his flute in years. He had no desire to play it now.

The weeks passed, Willis sullen, Jan Rabaski and young Elsa shy and rosy with their love. Jan swore his fits of coughing were lessening. Jan and Elsa were married in the cabin, a simple ceremony that seemed to Ase more valid than the marriage of 'Melie and Crockett. A lone peach tree had blossomed early, and Elsa wore a wreath of peach blossoms in her fair hair. Since Jan and Elsa could only return to the Grimstedt tenant house, Ase gave them for wedding present a cheque. Willis approached his father. Having abandoned Nat, he was without money, had used all his small pocket cash.

He said humbly: "Pa, can you do something for me? Get something for the kids, as if it came from me? I'll pay you back some day."

'Melie had discarded the set of plated table silver given her by the Grange. Better to have it used than to collect dust in the attic. Ase and Willis took it to the bride.

Willis said: "For when you have your own place, Elsa."

She said: "I will use it here. I would use satin and gold if I had it, to make a home for Jan."

The Grimstedt tenant house was shocking. It reminded Ase of the hovels Nat had reported erecting in Alaska, no more than four tilting walls and a roof. Elsa had scrubbed it inch by inch, and hung white curtains, and Jan was making rough furniture.

Ase said: "I wish I had room for you at my place."

He thought of the space of the Linden house, empty and hollow once Willis had gone away again. It would be pleasant to have the young couple living there. He could afford to pay another hand. In the same instant he knew that Nellie would have none of it. She would drive them off like a mother bird who will accept no fledglings but her own.

Elsa said: "Maybe some day we can come to you."

Willis was increasingly restless. Ase wondered if he were waiting for Nellie's return, not to leave his father entirely alone. He could not question him. The wall between was as high as ever.

On a day in April, 1917, Ase's county paper gave the news that the United States had entered the war. Willis read the headlines over his shoulder. He paced the room and turned abruptly.

"Well, Pa," he said, "here's my miracle."

Ase read again, as though to change the fact.

Willis said: "Mind me driving to Trent?"

"Are you sure you don't want to think it over?"

"I'm sure. Any objections? You wanted me to get away from Nat. This is it."

Ase had volunteered in his time for the Spanish-American War, had been rejected, as family men were not needed and he was over-age. He had offered himself for the simplest of reasons. It was a man's duty to fight for his country. He thought that many men must have many reasons. Willis's was not ignoble. He was risking his life to save his soul.

"No, son. No objections."

"I'll be ready by the time you've hitched up. I haven't got a thing I want or need. It's all Nat's, he paid for it from my overcoat to my tooth-brush. You can send it back to him. He has plenty of flunkeys my size."

They drove to the recruiting office in Trent in silence. Willis waited in line. Ase found the new library and browsed through it futilely, not knowing what to ask for. He drove back to wait for Willis. His was almost the only horse and carriage on the streets. Nat had wanted to give him a Ford car, but he preferred the leisurely pace of wagon and buggy, the clop-clop of the horses' hoofs, the sweet smell of harness leather and of living hide. He did not see how a man would have time to watch the land, time to think, behind the wheel of a car. Willis came down the steps.

"I'm in, Pa," he said. "They're sending me on to camp tonight."

His chin was lifted. His pale eyes held the look, half unbelief, of a long-penned dog turned loose from chain and kennel.

Ase had been home an hour when the telephone jangled its two rings. Nat's voice came harsh from across the country.

"Pa? Get Will on the 'phone."

"He's gone, Nat. He enlisted."

"Christ, the damn fool! I knew he'd try it. I should have called the minute the news broke. Sure it's too late to stop him?"

"It's too late, Nat."

"God damn! Wait a minute, here's Ma."

His heart beat fast, hearing her, a bird singing over the humming wires.

"Nellie——"

"I'm coming right home, Ase. Somebody'll wire you about my train."

"Nellie——"

"What did you say?"

"Nothing. I'll be waiting."

Eric and Elsa had to laugh at him over the days. He wandered in a daze like a bridegroom, they told him. He smiled, unoffended. Elsa scrubbed the Linden house from top to bottom, beat carpets and hung clean curtains.

"I'll only cook enough for the first meal," she said. "Mrs. Linden will want to get to the kitchen herself. I know her."

It was true. Nellie returned like a small whirlwind. Within twenty minutes she was out of Nat's satins and into gingham dress and apron. There was little fault to be found with Elsa's work, but with immense satisfaction she found mealy-bugs on one of her dining-room begonias.

She said: "I don't know why I stayed so long. Nat's hard to get away from. I won't be talked into it again."

She bustled about, examining cupboards and supplies,

rearranging furniture. Ase followed her from room to room. Once she turned so suddenly that she tripped over his feet, on her heels behind her.

She said: "You don't have to dog me that close," but she allowed him to hold her.

She was fretted about Willis, yet her concern was spotted with Nat's anger.

"Nat said Will would never have been drafted, he could have kept him out. He said he never thought Will would turn out a traitor to him. Said he'd seen it coming, though."

In his joy at her return, he would not take issue with her. Later would be time enough to talk with her, if he could manage the words and she would listen, of the nature of loyalty. She had never yet listened when he fumbled at abstract discussion. Tim McCarthy would have been his man to probe with him this matter. He would bring it up with Eric, perhaps, although Eric's thinking moved along more concrete lines.

He made a futile attempt with Nellie on one of the rare afternoons when she sat quietly rocking in the living-room. His approach was unfortunate and she snapped him short.

"I don't want to hear another word," she said. "You're going to say something against Nat, and I won't have it. You've always had it in for him and you just don't realize what a big man he's turned out to be."

She quoted Nat constantly. He would not be hurt, seeing her pleasure.

Eric's Elsa died in December of pneumonia. Eric was stricken, became suddenly an old man, crippled now not only of hands, but of mind and spirit. He had waited so long for his love, and it was taken from him untimely. Ase shared his grief.

He had not dared suggest to Nellie that young Elsa and her Jan Rabaski move to the Linden farm, to live in the many-roomed Linden home. Now she was the first to suggest that they move to the cabin, Jan to replace Eric as hired hand, young Elsa to replace her mother in casual help for Nellie.

The young couple moved into the old log cabin. Jan had

offered himself to the American Army and had been rejected, his lungs still hard-tissued from their gassing. Young Elsa was already happily pregnant. Nellie took a maternal interest in them, found young Elsa of her own mind as to the importance of using enough butter in various dishes. The Linden and Rabaski families lived together in content.

In July of 1918 the rural telephone rang. There was a death message, by wire, and since the telegram could not be delivered and death messages were supposed to be delivered in person, would the Lindens accept it?

Ase said, knowing the message: "Please read the telegram."

He listened to the reading of the telegram from the War Department.

He said: "Thank you."

Nellie was at his side.

She said: "Who's calling? Was it Nat?"

"No. It's Willis. He was killed at Château Thierry."

Even as he comforted Nellie, he felt an unreasonable exaltation.

'He got away,' he thought. 'Willis got away.'

★ 38 ★

NAT's exhibition at the time of 'Melie's wedding had satisfied him. Twice he returned briefly and without ostentation, only then because of business in a not too distant city. He preferred to have his mother visit him each year. Ase insisted on paying her fare, allowing Nat to do as he chose about decking her out in made-to-order ruffles of an earlier era. He refused stubbornly to go West with her. The trip would have to be in his own way and time, and that had never seemed to come.

'Melie came home alone several times in the years after her marriage.

Nat, Arent and 'Melie arrived for a quiet celebration of

Ase's and Nellie's fiftieth wedding anniversary in February. It was more and more apparent that Crockett was less 'Melie's consort than the chief of Nat's cohorts. He had stayed behind to take care of business. Nellie had not been feeling well and had written Nat that she would wring his neck if he tried to make another show of the anniversary. Nat had agreed, but, on appearing, suggested that the marriage ceremony be repeated.

He said: "You know, Ma, this is going to be in my newspapers, and it would sound mighty cute."

Nellie said: "The very idea, I won't have it, rigging up an old woman in her wedding duds. As if we were going to bed and start all over again."

Nat roared with laughter.

He said: "Okay, Ma, any way you want it. I'll bet for Pa that the spirit's willing but the flesh is weak."

For himself, Ase thought, another fifty years with Nellie would be little enough. Yet the afternoon on a windy hill, when sky and earth had reeled around them, should be put away in camphor, like her wedding dress. It too had best be left undisturbed.

Aunt Jess was dead and gone, along with Miss Minnie, storekeeper Peyton and Dr. Holder. Only a score of friends and relatives joined the Linden family for the anniversary celebration. Nat's gift to his mother was a diamond brooch which 'Melie had selected with an eye to her own later use.

Nat took his father and mother aside that evening. In his middle age he was florid and thickened. The perfection of his grooming and tailoring gave a smooth covering to his coarseness. He swelled out his chest, as he had long had a habit of doing, before speaking. He clipped a cigar and lit it. Nellie pushed an ash-tray nearer him.

He said: "Now, Pa, I've had enough of this nonsense about you and Ma sticking it out on this damn farm. I know, you've done mighty well, made a lot more money than most farmers. You've got Will's insurance money. You're both still fairly tough, too. But any day one of you'll be having a stroke, or breaking a leg from trying to do too much at your age. You've got to expect to find yourselves failing."

Ase frowned. More than ten years ago Nat had harped on their age, when he and Nellie had been in the fullness of their strength. It was as though Nat wanted them to be old, feeble and incompetent.

He said: "Nat, your mother and I have talked this over. We're satisfied here."

Nat flicked his cigar ash with his little finger.

"Listen to me, Pa. You're so stubborn. There's something else you probably won't understand, but take my word for it. We're going to have one hell of a depression any time now. I'm all set for it. I've been selling most of my stocks on the high market and putting it where it's foolproof. Never mind where or how. When it's over with, I'll own about half my state."

He puffed comfortably.

"Now listen. When the depression hits, your crops aren't going to bring what it cost to raise them. You wouldn't like that, would you?"

Ase said mildly: "It's happened before. A farmer never goes hungry."

Nat sat up impatiently.

"My God, Pa, all you've ever been interested in, your whole life, was just getting by, 'making a living', you call it. On land you don't even own."

The familiar expression irritated Ase. Over the years Nat and Nellie had worn it thin.

Nat went on: "Of course, you haven't noticed how close the Trent industries are coming. The newest plant's taken over the land around Lancey Lake, not four miles away."

Nellie said: "We used to have the Pioneer Picnics there."

"That's just it, Ma. You used to have Pioneer Picnics. Now you've got progress."

He leaned forward. His jaw tightened, his voice deepened. Ase had a glimpse of the power that Nat must turn on at will, like a water tap.

"What we'll do here is plan for a factory, with workmen's shacks built around it. Rent the shacks at a fairly high rate, but not so high that you get an expensive turn-over in labour. Give the dumb bozos free seeds for gardens, tie 'em up. Most of the labour around here these days is foreigners, they'll damn near work for nothing once they've got their own vegetable garden. That's business psychology, Pa."

Ase said: "We were all foreigners here once. I don't know much about psychology."

"Naturally not. I don't expect you to follow me all the way. Now, this is just as important. The minute the depression begins, everybody'll be in a panic, I'll step in and buy up the farms between you and Lancey Lake for a song. When the up-swing begins again, there'll be a big Linden industrial development here. You'll be taken care of, Pa. You'll be in clover."

Ase watched Nat's cigar smoke drift through the room. It seemed to him as ephemeral as Nat's sense of values.

He said: "People can put up factories and workmen's shacks anywhere. The land all around here is too good for anything but farming."

Nat stubbed out the butt of his cigar and spat.

Nellie said: "All right, Nat, how do you go about putting up a factory on somebody else's property?"

Nat rose from his chair.

He shouted: "Who's paid the taxes all these years? Pa has! The law takes care of that! I've been talking with men at the court-house. One word from your stupid husband, Mrs. Linden, and it's all arranged."

Ase stood, tall and angry, towering over his son.

"This is my brother's land. You cannot use it for your dishonest schemes."

Nat's eyes narrowed.

"Ma, anybody in the family ever been crazy besides Grandmother Linden?"

"Nobody but your Pa."

She saw his stricken face.

"Ase, you never know when I'm teasing. We'll stay right here and run the farm as long as we're able."

She laid her hand on his arm.

She said: "Nat, I'm not going West with you. I know, I promised, but your Pa needs me. Go finish your packing. You always wait to the last minute so somebody else will get nervous and do it for you."

Nat's shadows rose as he rose.

He said to his brother and sister: "Let's get going."

He turned to his father. He spoke quietly.

"Don't think I'm through with this for a minute."

Nellie saw them off tearfully. Ase felt responsible and guilty. Having supported him against Nat, now she snapped at him.

"A fine thing, to call your own son dishonest. He only wants to do the best thing for us."

He said: "You should have gone with him."

He was surprised at his own tartness. It occurred to him that the increasing patience of age was as great a myth as the unalloyed joy of youth. The longer he lived, the less tolerance he had for the patently evil. And Nat—— He put his arms around Nellie. Her plumpness was gone. Her fragility startled him. Her passion having spent itself, he had not held her tight for several years, for she had seldom ever permitted him to hold her unless she desired him. She was so thin, so small.

He said: "I'm sorry. Maybe you're right, maybe Nat wants to do the best thing for us."

She cried a while against his lean old breast, then pushed him away with her lifelong gesture, her little hands rejecting a monolith. She pulled his handkerchief from his pocket and wiped her eyes and blew her nose. She sniffed the air. She darted to door and windows and threw them wide.

"That awful stink," she said.

It was Nat's expensive cigar smoke to which she referred, but he too welcomed the clean inrush of cold air, wiping out for the moment a greater stench, his own along with it, for he had compromised once again.

Nellie sniffled and said: "Ase, take me to see my folks. I just can't get along without some family."

Her mother and father were long since dead, but two of her brothers, with their wives and families, still lived prosperously on the old Wilson farmstead two miles east along the road. He hitched up the remaining horse, how many generations removed from its ancestor, old Dan, he could not recall, and drove her in the light buggy to her kin. He decided that he must buy a motor-car, after all. Nellie was sociable, she needed to meet everywhere people in whom she had no concern, for whom she felt no affection at all. This had always puzzled him, but he accepted it as part of her.

On his return he went like a homing pigeon to the cabin, to the Rabaskis. Young Elsa, he could only think of her so, and her Jan had been prolific. There were six children from the ten years of their union, four boys and two girls. His close friend among these was the six-year-old, young Jan.

The boy ran to Ase as he knocked on the door of the cabin.

"I saw you coming," he said, and reached up to take his hand. "I felt it in my stomach. Do you feel it in your stomach?"

"Yes, Jan.'

The child's phrase was as accurate as the Biblical yearning of the bowels, he thought, for the warmth that surged through them when they met. They went together into the cabin. Eric lifted his head from his chimney corner. He was not as old as Ase, but the life had gone out of him with his Elsa, and he hugged the hearth like an ancient.

Young Elsa called from the kitchen: "Coffee and cake in a minute, Mr. Linden. Glad to see you."

The three elder children were at school. The two toddlers waved their toys cheerily at him. Eric's sadness was only a faint shadow on this sunny threshold. The aroma from the kitchen was delicious, a mixture of foreign seasonings and spices, for young Elsa had added to her mother's Swedish dishes the Polish ones her husband had described to her. Young Jan led Ase to a deep chair opposite Eric by the hearth and settled himself in his lap.

He said: "I know you had to pay attention to your company. You came home as soon as you could, didn't you?"

Ase said: "Yes, as soon as I could."

It was true. Because of this boy, as grave and frail as his Dolly had been, as adoring of him, because of the miraculous community between them, the old cabin was more nearly home than his own. It was here he found meat for the teeth of his spirit.

39

THE Seth Thomas clock whirred and struck three of the afternoon. The notes hovered like birds in the comfortable warmth of the living-room. The thin sunlight streamed through the bay window and turned the pale green of Nellie's house fern to silver. The fronds of the fern on its high stand touched the floor. Ase thought it was almost like having a young willow tree inside the house. A cricket, excited perhaps by the striking of the clock, began chirping from somewhere under the fern. It had escaped Nellie for weeks, but sooner or later she would take it unaware and flip it out into the snow. Ase took her word for it that crickets were as bad as moths for eating woollen clothing, but a hole in a jacket elbow seemed to him a small price for the cheerful piping in the long winter stillness.

The dog at his feet, sleeping in a patch of sunlight on the carpet, roused and lifted his head. Nellie in the kitchen heard the sound from the road and came hurrying. She pushed aside the lace curtains at the front window and peered out. A strange Ford passed, its wheel-chains clanking on the frozen snow.

She said: "Pshaw now, I hoped it was going to stop."

Ase said, teasing her: "No matter who was in it?"

"Near about. Haven't laid eyes on a living soul for three days. Seems as if the kids had been gone three months."

They had been for him three days of beauty and peace, the snow as white as swan's feathers, the sky pale blue, the air sharp and clean, the house cosy and silent, except for the cricket, the clock, and Nellie's casual chatter. Much of the time he paid no attention to the words, only listened with delight to the sound of her voice, as he often listened to the brook purling under the ice.

She said: "I thought maybe it was Joe Wilson and his wife, going home. They'd have stopped in."

She returned to the kitchen and came back with a plate of ginger cookies hot from the oven. He did not see how he might manage even one, for she had made him finish the chocolate cake at noon dinner. He made a pretence of pleasure and of hunger, taking three of the cookies. He ate one, and while she was hunting for the cricket under the sweeping fern fronds, he fed the other two surreptitiously to the also overfed but greedy dog. It seemed that she could never get out of the habit of cooking for a large family. The doughnut and cookie crocks were always full, varieties of cakes and pies accumulated in the pantry, a few wedges cut out of each. Whatever friend or neighbour did stop for a visit went away loaded with baskets of pastries, of baked beans, of salt-rising bread. When callers had been too long absent, he had known her to look with disgust at an untouched plate of jam tarts, sweep them into the swill-pail for the hogs, turn to and make a fresh batch of the identical tarts.

He wondered whether this was truly habit, or the expression of her longing that her children would suddenly appear, to surround the dining-table, to eat and praise her bounty, saying: "Some more, Ma," returning to her the sense of being loved, useful and no longer lonely.

She was all he needed of companionship, except for the inexplicable ache in his heart that he was never done with. Now young Jan was easing it. He was forced to recognize that he alone had never completed her life. There must always be the lover and the beloved, and he had been the lover. Himself still yearning for Tim McCarthy, for Doll, for Mink Fisher, for his brother Benjamin, none, he thought, could know the nature of another's need. Yet Nellie's seemed so plainly for her children, even for any passer-by to serve her gay gregariousness.

He said: "Maybe Nat's right about our not staying here. Do you want to leave the farm and move to town?"

She was sitting in the Boston rocker. She touched her foot to the floor and set the chair in motion. She rocked and did not answer.

He said: "Ben will turn up before we get too old. Then we'll sell the farm and buy a little house in town for the three of us."

"Ben had better hurry. You're seventy-one. How long do you expect to live?"

He smiled.

"I hadn't thought much about it. I suppose for ever."

"If you figure on being immortal, you'll have to do it without me. Living one life's almost killed me."

He wondered if he could explain his sense of timelessness. He did not think of it as another life, nor yet quite an immortality of the same one. It was only, he felt, that individual lives could no more be separated from life itself than drops of water from the mass of ocean. He was willing to give to life the name of 'God', since men knew no other large enough with which to speak of the ineffable, the Word made Life. He supposed men were not yet fit or ready to be entrusted, desperately as they needed it, with the secret of the Word. No, he could not explain.

He said: "Well, Nellie, if you won't go with me, I won't go either."

She looked at him over her spectacles.

"I know you've always thought crazy, Ase, but talk sense when you talk to me,"

He had never talked anything but sense to her, he thought. That was the trouble, the sense was insufficient.

"Has it been such a bad life for you, Nellie?"

The cricket chirped from under the far side of the fern and she decided on a frond and lifted it. The cricket turned bright eyes on her and waved its feelers. She pounced. She held it triumphantly between two fingers.

"Got you, you little devil. Here, Ase, kill the thing or throw it outdoors."

He took it from her, careful not to crush it. He went through the kitchen to the woodshed. He released the cricket at the back of the pile of stove wood.

He said to it and to himself: "You talked too much. Keep quiet the rest of the winter so she won't find you again."

He closed the door behind him. He did have crazy thoughts, he supposed, and it was surely not sensible to talk to a cricket, even in his mind.

He reported to Nellie: "I took care of him."

"Good. I can't stand any kind of bugs in the house."

He thought she had forgotten both of his questions.

She said: "Ase, I don't know. It's been kind of a mixed-up life. You'll never know what I went through with your

293

mother. And we worked so hard and then found the place wasn't ever ours. And Ben didn't play fair."

"Does it still hurt you, Nellie? Ben going away?"

She went to the kitchen and brought a pitcher of water for her fern.

"Should have watered it yesterday," she said.

She replaced the pitcher on its shelf and returned with her mending-basket.

"Yes, if you want the truth, I've always missed him."

She began darning one of his socks.

She said: "I must say, Nat's made up for almost everything. Can't see why you won't ever visit him with me. Why, Ase, people fall all over him out there, you never saw anything like it. You've hurt Nat's feelings."

She re-threaded her darning-needle.

He studied her. Her soft curly hair was snow-white, with a silver overtone. The wrinkles around her mouth and eyes were laugh wrinkles. She was still pink and white and it seemed to him that she had never been more beautiful.

She said: "Stop gawking at me."

"You're so pretty."

She used an expletive that shocked him.

She darned steadily. At last she finished and laid down her mending.

She said: "About leaving. Maybe so. You can't sell, as long as you're so stubborn about getting Ben declared dead and gone. Do you suppose you could let the farm? Think you could get enough, with what we've saved, to rent a nice place in town?"

He was frightened that she might be serious. Yet if she was unhappy here, chose actually to leave, he would do as she wished.

He said: "I'll see the Rabaskis. I couldn't trust everybody."

She nodded.

"I know. Most folks'd ruin the land. Why don't you go over right now?"

"You'll go with me?"

"No, thanks. I have to make a dried-apple pie for supper."

He groaned inwardly. She would eat one small piece and

294

would bully him to finish the rest. He had given up trying to dissuade her from this extravagant cooking and baking. It was too deep a satisfaction for her.

"How much rent had I better ask?"

"Oh, just let them name a figure, if they're interested. Then we can make up our minds."

If he was obliged to leave the farm, he could leave it in no hands except the Rabaskis'. Jan was in the cabin, and Eric and young Elsa. The babies were sleeping. Young Jan had gone to play with the cats in the barn.

Ase said: "I've come on business."

Eric roused from his lethargy.

He said: "You've got another tenant?"

Jan caught the old man's anxiety.

"Haven't I suited you, Mr. Linden?"

"No, no. I mean, yes, it's the other way round."

He was shocked to see their fear leap, like a flame ready to devour their house. Their insecurity was greater than his own. There was perhaps for them not ever any haven. Young Elsa dried her hands on her apron and drew a chair close to the men by the hearth. Her blue eyes were wide. He wanted to speak quickly, and to the point, to ease them.

"It's this. My wife is restless. She's very lonely with the family gone. My son thinks we're too old, he thinks we should leave the farm and move to town. She hasn't made up her mind, but we wondered if you would consider renting the farm?"

Jan and young Elsa looked at each other, then smiled.

She said: "Oh, Mr. Linden, you did scare us."

Jan said: "My lungs almost good now, but I thought sometimes, when I have to cough, maybe you want stronger man."

"Jan, I couldn't ask for a better man."

He should have said it years ago.

Eric was watching him shrewdly. Jan drew a long breath and reached for his pipe.

"So, is good then. I thank you. Now, the business. I say my side."

He puffed on his pipe.

"If I rent farm, I have to hire other hand, just like you

hire me. Is so much cash there. So, then I pay rent, is so much cash there. Maybe it cost more than crops pay. Excuse me, I think in the out loud, is surprise idea."

Elsa cried out: "Oh, Jan! We'd certainly break even. If it would help Mr. Linden——"

Her eyes were clouded with tears. Jan rose and bowed gravely, first to her and then to Ase. His dark face paled.

"Mr. Linden, I die of the shame. I am stranger, and you take me in. You give me the life, you give me the bread for wife and childs, you give me the roof for head, you give me the friend for heart. I turn like wolf, give you the ungrateful. You must forgive. Is only, all my life before, is cat eat dog, I think selfish, I have fear. I am poor soldier after the all."

He bent to lay a fresh log on the hearth fire.

"My Elsa is the right," he said: "We do fine, rent your farm. The rent, is what you say, what you need."

Eric spoke from his corner.

"Mr. Linden, it isn't what you want at all, leaving the farm, is it?"

His old friend's eyes were twinkling. He could only be honest.

He said: "No, Eric, it isn't what I want at all."

"Then you go right home and tell Mrs. Linden nobody could afford to rent the farm. Just tell her off."

Ase wanted to say, as he had longed to say to Dr. Holder in the danger of Dolly's birth: "But Nellie is different."

He said, instead: "Jan, I don't think you would lose out by renting. But it must be as Mrs. Linden wants."

Eric said: "No man who loves the land he works on wants to be a tenant. I've told Jan and Elsa about your brother. I've had the idea that some day, when you and I and your brother are gone, they may be able to buy the farm. Your Nat and Arent, they won't want it."

Ase had not carried his confused thoughts on death down so practical a road. Death had shown him various of its veiled faces. One had been a snow-swept stranger, riding away into the night with Dolly. One had been a rescuer in armour, reaching down to save Willis from his abyss. The death that had taken Mink, and Tim, and the Old One, had neither stolen nor saved. They had slipped easily into other elements where they were at home, in bog, in earth, in summer wind. For himself, he would not know until the moment came. But of course, the land would remain, to be disposed of.

Eric said: "All Nat will want will be to turn it into cash. You know that."

Yes, he knew. He knew as well that the value of the land as a farm would not satisfy Nat. Once he himself was gone, nothing would stop Nat's factory settlement schemes. The Rabaskis could only move on then as tenants elsewhere. It seemed to him that he should prepare them now. Yet meantime no other land-owner would give them such advantageous terms, so good a house, so generous a share of the breeding stock. He could not bring himself to speak of Nat's greed.

Jan said comfortably: "Things work out okay. I know one thing, Mr. Linden, we going have two fine farmers pretty soon, my Carl and my Louey. Nine and eight years, they milk good already, love help plant seed, everything. Hans, I don't know, he got that mechanic Swede in him from his grandpa here."

Eric chuckled. He seemed like his old self today.

Jan said: "Young Jan, now, maybe you know what do with him some day. I think sometimes maybe is going be crazy." He winked at Elsa. "From the mama side. Or awful smart, from papa side. Mr. Linden, you know that boy better I do, don't he seem kind of like old man? He ask goddammest questions, things I never think of."

Ase said: "He's smart, Jan. He asks me questions, too, I can't answer."

Many of them, he thought, were ones he himself had asked of an unanswering void.

Jan said: "Anyway, is good Rabaski kids, all. Carl, Louey, Hans, learn good in school. Mr. Linden, don't you think I turn out pretty good American? Got citizen paper, don't I learn talk American like anybody?"

Ase put his hand to his mouth to cover his smile. Elsa burst into laughter. Jan turned to her, his eyebrows lifted.

She ran to him and held his dark head against her breast.

"You talk wonderfully."

"Don't laugh like crazy, then. You understand okay when all I can say was: 'Love you, Elsa.' So what?"

"So—oh, Jan."

Eric and Ase stared into the fire, each with his memories of love. The cabin door slammed open and young Jan ran in.

"Mr. Linden! I just saw your tracks in the snow."

The boy climbed into his bony lap, as always, as though he merely claimed his own.

"How long have you been here?"

"A little while. I was talking business with your mother and father."

"Do you have to go back right away?"

"No."

The boy spoke passionately.

"Then tell me. Tell me some more. Tell me when Dolly was six years old. Tell me when you were six years old, like me."

Young Jan was not at the moment the wise old man, he was all child, delighting in tales, some of them oft told.

"Tell me!"

Elsa lifted a finger.

"Don't let him wear you out, Mr. Linden. I'll make coffee, for when you're through."

Ase began, to the intent child: "I told you about Dolly and the little pig. The one she dressed in the doll's clothes."

"Tell it again."

He repeated the story. Eric joined Elsa in the kitchen. Big Jan left the cabin to see to the lambs. Ase was alone with the boy. He had never told him of Mink Fisher. He told him now.

He said: "When I was six years old, I had an Indian for a friend."

"A real Indian?"

"A real one."

He had told some of his tales of Mink Fisher to Dolly, but there was a difference here, he was telling them now to a man-child, and so he told of the hunts, the trapping, the camping. He told young Jan, as he had told his Doll, of the mythical trek across the Milky Way.

Young Jan said: "But you couldn't really walk across it, could you?" and it was the question Doll had asked, and Ase was shaken, and said: "No, only in your mind."

"Tell me more about Mink Fisher."

"Well, Jan, I was in trouble, and my brother was in trouble. Mink Fisher found my brother and brought me word from him."

He found himself telling the story of so long ago, of Mink's long search for Benjamin, of Mink's return with news, of Mink's death. He became aware that the boy was trembling. So, Ase thought in misery, he had been stupid again. Having found his tongue, his words, he had alarmed the child.

The boy said passionately: "He was your friend. He came all that way because he was your friend."

Ase thought, this was not to be believed, this young understanding.

He said: "Yes. And he was my father, too. Not my real father, but the one who taught me."

Elsa called from the kitchen: "Coffee ready, Mr. Linden."

He said: "No, I must go."

Young Jan clutched his legs.

He said: "Please don't leave me. You're my friend. You're my father."

Elsa called out: "Now, Jan, let Mr. Linden go."

Ase trudged back to his house. Nellie had supper ready and waiting, including the pie he must finish.

He said: "The Rabaskis don't think they can afford to rent the farm."

She said placidly: "That's all right. I decided I couldn't bear to have another woman's bread in my pantry, not even Elsa's."

He realized that she had made her decision long before she had sent him on his errand. He felt that a crisis had been safely passed.

40

THE late April day was balmy. Spring had come early this year, and the bees were frantic with the bounty of the apple blossoms. The strong scent of Nellie's lilacs absorbed the cooler perfume of the fruit bloom. The tulips bordering the front path opened their gaudy cups, but the bees had little time for their meagre honey.

Nellie sat on the edge of the bed to rest before Ase finished helping her to dress. Since her stroke, she had been impatient with any touch but his. Even Elsa annoyed her. Nellie had recovered, but one hand was almost useless. Ase adjusted her lace collar. She lifted her chin for him to fasten the collar with Nat's diamond brooch. His big gnarled fingers took out a hairpin and tucked back one of her wayward curls. He put an arm around her and helped her to her feet. She clung to him as she balanced. It was strangely sweet to him. She had never clutched him so, so turned to him, calling eagerly: "Ase! Ase!", if he left her for a moment in the hot days and nights of their youth. It was as though the need of him, that she had not felt in her passion, filled her completely, now that all passion was gone.

He asked anxiously: "You're sure the drive won't be too much for you?"

"Feel the best I have in a long time. I want to see those new buildings in Peytonville."

He chose a coat from her cupboard, warmer than she might need, since an April day could blow hot or cold at a moment's notice. He took down a hat-box from a shelf.

"Ase, don't make me wear a hat."

She had always worn one as seldom as possible, perhaps for vanity in her hair. The only ones he could remember her wearing had been actually not hats at all, but the hood attached to the red cape of their early time together, and later the blue quilted bonnet he had given her. From both of these her curls had stood out charmingly around her face, as she must have known. He opened a dresser drawer and selected a pale blue gossamer wool scarf from the large assortment. He wondered why people gave old ladies almost nothing but scarves and handkerchiefs. Nellie liked toilet water and candy and sherry wine. He arranged the scarf over her head and tied the ends loosely under her chin. He pulled out a few silver curls around her ears.

"Now it hides my brooch," she complained.

"If the day stays warm, you can take it off when we get into town."

"Shall I come to the front door or the side door?"

He said sternly: "You sit right here until I drive the car around and come back for you."

"You forgot my handkerchief."

He picked one of her best ones and sprinkled it with her favourite cologne.

"Put some on me, too. Here, give me the bottle."

She took it in her good hand and doused herself liberally. He reached for it and she gave the bottle a quick slap upwards, so that his sleeve was drenched with 'an indefinable fragrance', according to the label. He tried to mop it off.

He said furiously: "Now how can I go into the bank smelling like a confounded woman!"

She laughed like an imp.

"Ase, you should see your face."

How many years had it been that he had been falling into her traps? Sixty years, and he was still her fool, her willing and delighted fool. And for sixty years she had been saying: "You should see your face."

He said, not entirely appeased: "If you don't care what people say about your husband, it's perfectly all right."

He leaned down and kissed her forehead. "Never mind, anything you do is all right. It always has been."

She said, suddenly sobered: "I know. Oh, Ase, you've been a good husband."

He marvelled that it was necessary for him to reach the age of eighty for her to say what she had never said before. Then he knew that he could not have borne it earlier, as he could not have borne this new dependence of hers in her illness. If these things had been present with his young passion for her, he would have exploded, would have perished from too much joy, and so have been unable to nurse her now in her quite different need.

He said: "Don't move until I come."

301

Yet when he drove the motor-car to the side of the house she was waiting. She stood there, holding to the door, so proudly that he could not scold her.

She said: "I couldn't wait. I'm not used to it. I've never been an old woman before."

He lifted her in his arms and deposited her in the front seat of the car. He set out for Peytonville, driving slowly and carefully. He had bought his first car ten years ago, when she had made the decision not to leave the farm. It had proved wise and helpful, for he could deliver her to Peytonville quickly, compared with the time of horse and buggy. She had been able to visit her friends as often as she wished and had been more contented. This was his second motor-car, but he was never done with the marvel of such transportation.

Neither had he ever got over a certain uneasiness as the car started. It reminded him of the long-ago horse Prince, who gave the same leap forward and was never to be counted on not to bolt at once. His own absent-mindedness was something of a menace. He could not safely sit hunched and abstracted with slack reins, leaving the road to horse or team. The ditches were a constant peril, especially when Nellie was not there to remind him sharply. His slow speed was his protection. His long legs were angled and cramped under the wheel, his bony elbows made acute angles, so that pedestrians often smiled as he drove by. Nellie said it was the first time an over-sized daddy-long-legs had been seen driving a motor-car. It had seemed to him that it would have been easier to learn to fly an aeroplane. If a man was going to leave his feet, the back of his horse, or the earth-hugging wheels of buggy and of wagon, a plane somehow seemed more logical an advance than the horseless carriage, which was exactly that and no more.

Nellie said: "Now you're coming to the highway. Remember, the car won't turn itself and there'll be other cars going like the devil."

He had indeed not noticed that they were leaving the Linden country road. He came to a full stop and watched to his left while Nellie watched to the right. The traffic was heavy. Trent had become an enormous industrial city. Peytonville had acquired several prosperous minor industries with an expanded population and now called itself 'Peyton City'. The younger residents and the newcomers were outraged when the old-timers persisted in speaking of 'Peytonville'.

Nellie said: "All clear this way."

He accelerated and the car leaped like Prince into the middle of the highway. He turned left towards what he and Nellie still referred to as the village. He remembered the day so many years ago when he had imagined himself following Ben to the West. He recalled that even then he had wanted to ride the eagle. The aeroplane was man's tame eagle. It was more, it was man's desire for wings, no longer to be earth-bound. He thought of the story of Icarus in the encyclopaedia. It had stirred him deeply, for he felt himself in accord with this man's craving. He had acquired a new encyclopaedia, being unsatisfied by the old, and here he had read in rapture of the Wright brothers, who had adapted the principles of bird flight to human flight. Mechanical and clumsy though it had proved to be, their principle seemed to him important, but why, he could not tell.

Nellie said: "Now go real slow, Ase. Are those the grain elevators?"

"The two tallest are. The other is the new office building."

"Look, Ase, you didn't tell me they've fixed over the Peyton House. Like a city hotel, isn't it?"

The car crept along the altered streets. Main Street had been widened. There were street lights and four traffic signals. Among the new buildings an old shop here and there stood as always, narrow and shabby. The notion store was fighting a losing battle against a bright-fronted five-and-ten. Doc Brown the druggist had made concessions, enlarging his show windows and carrying a line of goods in which he had little interest. His soda counter was almost the same, and folk still came from miles around for his home-made ice-cream. He had taken over the small circulating library, its contents the modern equivalent of 'The Duchess', so that Ase no longer troubled to study the titles. The town had no other library.

Some years before, he had discovered the public library in Trent. He went once a month for a book or two, being a slow reader. When Nellie did not hurry him, he browsed among the open stacks, looking into books whose titles seemed the keys he had so long searched for. Too often a title was misleading. Some of the books that provided the richest fare were hidden under unrevealing names, like a rare soul behind a drab face. He had begun to find his way past the magic gates, down a long corridor and into the world he had dreamed of. Yet it was almost too late, as for a man who, dying of starvation, cannot now digest the banquet that earlier would have saved him.

Nellie said: "Nothing much changed through here."

The streets outside the business district were lined with elms and maples. No one of the white-painted houses was newer than fifty years. They varied from the neat little box of the Lilley sisters, through modest homes unobtrusively Victorian, to an occasional small mansion a hundred and fifty years of age, or more, columned and serene. The yards were green with new grasses. Many of the housewives were working the flowers and shrubs in their perennial beds and borders. Nellie waved to those of her acquaintance. Ase stopped the car often for a particular friend to speak with her, to ask details of her health, to urge her to come in for a visit. It was her first trip since her illness, she explained, and she had best not get out. She held her little court along the way with gusto.

Ase drove into the outskirts where mediocre bungalows were closely clustered, and on to the section of bleak flats where shacks had been thrown up for the industrial workers. Nellie wrinkled her nose in distaste. Ase circled by the new factories and returned to Main Street. He had Doc Brown send out a chocolate soda to her while he did his own business at the bank. He had a sizeable deposit to make from the sale of early spring lambs.

At the turn of the highway towards home, he asked: "Shall we go on to Trent?"

"What do you want there? Just some more books? Another time, Ase, I'm sort of giving out."

He looked at her anxiously. Her exhilaration had passed. Her face was pale and pinched. There were blue circles under her eyes.

"I'm afraid I've let you overdo it today, Nellie."

He drove faster, concentrating on the rutted country road the last few miles. He drew in by the side of the house. He opened her car door and held out his arms to lift her down.

"Ase, I feel so faint——"

Her head in the blue gossamer scarf jerked backward. Her eyes closed, opened, then rolled, unseeing. She collapsed on the seat. He carried her, a limp rag doll, into the house and to their bed. He felt for her pulse, but could not tell whether the beat was hers or from his own heart. He stumbled to the wall telephone. He could not remember the name of the young doctor in the village. He rang.

He said to the operator: "Please send the doctor right away to the Linden farm."

The precise voice said: "I beg your pardon. Number, please."

He had forgotten the enlarged telephone exchange, and that the elderly maiden lady operators who knew everyone, with whom messages of any sort could be left, had long since been replaced by younger, more efficient women.

He said desperately: "I want the new doctor in Peytonville."

"I will give you Information."

The doctor was out when the call reached his office. Ase could only ask that he be located and sent as soon as possible. He was asked for explicit directions.

"But everyone knows where it is."

"Sorry, sir, Dr. Manley would not know. Four miles out of town on the Trent highway—a right turn on to a country road—four miles—the first and only house on the left—— Thank you, sir. You are positive this is an emergency? The doctor is very busy——"

It seemed to Ase that it had taken no longer than this for Tim McCarthy to hitch up, to drive horse and buggy to Peytonville, that by now Dr. Holder would have been reining in sharply, hurrying with his black bag. He went to Nellie. He must see her again before he called across the road to Elsa. He leaned over the bed. Nellie's eyes stared at the ceiling. He understood that they would never close of themselves again. He dropped on the bed beside her body. She had gone away without him. He had not been there to brush back her curls, to stroke her forehead, to hold her hand. He lay a long time, touching now and then her small mouth, her throat, her breast, he knew he could not touch her again when she was cold, for that would not be Nellie. He was aroused towards evening by the sound of a car in the drive. He heard voices. He went to the door. Elsa brought in the doctor.

"Mr. Linden, why didn't you call me? I didn't dream she was sick again."

The doctor said: "Where is the patient?"

Ase stared at him.

He wanted to say: "I don't know."

Where was his little Nellie Wilson indeed? His sense of the oneness, the timelessness, of God, of Man, of Life, had failed him. Nellie did not seem to fit into the pattern. Her mischievous vitality had no place in his theories or his philosophy. She would reject the outer cosmic spaces, as she had rejected all thought of immortality of body or of spirit, the one life, she had said jestingly, having almost killed her. Yet surely she was not lost entirely. Something of her would for ever breathe with the lilacs, would give delight to other lovers on other windy spring-time hills. Elsa poked the doctor with her elbow.

"He's very much upset," she whispered. "I've never seen a man so crazy about his wife. Come with me."

The doctor returned.

"Mr. Linden, your wife has been dead for hours. You are a farmer, certainly you must know death when you see it."

Yes, Ase thought, he knew death when he saw it. He did not answer. The doctor took out pad and pencil.

Elsa said: "I'll give you any information you need, Doctor."

The afternoon alone with Nellie had been a rare blessing. He would prefer to go now to the Linden cemetery and dig her grave with his own hands. He would like to carry her there, just as she was, in his arms, as he had carried Mink Fisher to his more secret burial-place. He would smooth the earth over her and plant in silence living flowers from her garden, peonies and tulips. Instead, there were unctuous strangers to be admitted, ceremonies to be gone through with, Nat and the others to be sent for.

He had been prepared for the loss of Nellie when Doll was born. He had looked then into the face of death, which, once seen closely, may never again so shock and terrify. Death had sat by his hearth-side, waiting for Tim McCarthy, for his mother, for Mink Fisher. Death, not he, had carried into his house the frozen body of his Doll. He had long ago drunk too deeply of his cup of anguish to be befuddled by it now.

He said: "Sit down, Doctor. I'll answer your questions. Her name was Nellie Wilson Linden. Her age was seventy-nine——"

★ 41 ★

ASE stood under the yellowing poplars waiting for the rural mail carrier. He thought of the early days when he must drive to Peytonville on Saturday for mail and newspapers. It had been the most satisfying day of the week, for there were always at least the two weekly papers in his box. Visiting the post office had been pleasant, too, and the trading of Nellie's eggs and butter, always more lively when she went with him. The rural free delivery later had been a great convenience, of course. Now so often the carrier passed by, calling out cheerily: "Nothing for Linden today!" and then the disappointment was severe. Since Nellie's death in the spring, the children wrote him only occasionally.

The carrier was running late. Ase eased himself to the ground and stretched out his long legs. The day was warm, for October, but under the shade of the poplar trees he became conscious of the chill of the earth. He got stiffly to his feet again and moved closer to the road to stand in the sunshine. He looked out over his fields and orchards. The farm crops had been abundant this year, almost every one had been harvested profitably, but the orchards were another matter. In his lifetime he had made three plantings of the short-lived peach trees. The last planting, set out by Jan Rabaski and his sons, would produce perhaps ten more years, then be done for. The apple orchard was nearly sixty years old. The trees were gnarled, the apples small and unmarketable, except for making cider. He should have replaced it years ago, but with an unreasonable tenacity, which he now acknowledged to himself, he had thought of it as Ben's orchard, to be preserved in its original state against his brother's homecoming. He had been a stubborn man, he thought, about the wrong things.

He listened to the familiar farm sounds. The breeding bull was bellowing from his enclosure, the cows and heifers were answering from their pasture. Big Jan and Carl and Louey were anxious to enlarge the herd, for a sizeable dairy would be most profitable. The sheep required much attention at lambing time, but they paid well. Nellie had taken care of her money-making flocks of chickens and turkeys until her first stroke a year or more ago, when he had cut them down to the modest numbers that Elsa could handle, along with her help in the Linden house.

The Rabaskis had thrived with him. They were cheerfully using their savings to send Carl and Louey to the Agricultural College. This had meant a car for the boys' use as well, so that they might live at home and work mornings, evenings and week-ends at the farming that would soon, they promised, be entirely scientific. In another year Hans would be ready for the mechanical courses. He was inclined to think that he would stay on the farm, too. The acreage was large enough to warrant the use of his talent for machinery. A big dairy herd would require electrical milkers, an electric pump, and so on. The power machines, the cultivators, reapers, binders, balers, sprayers, the silo with electric hoist that Ase had as yet not been talked into by the Rabaskis, would take a full-time mechanic.

There would be no money left, Rabaski said, for college for young Jan. At sixteen, the boy was frail, and a dreamer. He loved the farm as passionately as the rest of them, kept up his end of the chores, but was of little help otherwise, and never would be. He worked at odd hydraulic experiments in the running brook, or sat beside it and wrote poetry. Nat was right in one respect, Ase thought. He himself was of no help here, either.

He heard the mail carrier's car and moved hopefully to the mail-box. The carrier stopped.

"Plenty of mail today, Mr. Linden."

It was towards the end of the week, and there were half a dozen assorted papers and magazines, and two letters.

Ase recognized Nat's engraved stationery as the carrier remarked: "Know this will please you, hearing from the West."

Ase lifted his hand in thanks as the mail car drove on. He walked slowly up the front walk and into the house. The constant dull throbbing in his heart always became more acute when he entered the house and Nellie was not there. Sometimes, when absorbed, he forgot that she was dead. He found himself looking for her, in kitchen, pantry or cellar. Then a cold blast rocked him back on his heels as he remembered.

He sat down in the Boston rocker in the front room. He laid the periodicals on the round table and opened Nat's letter. Nellie would have rejoiced in its thickness. He himself had always a vague dread when he heard from Nat. He put on his spectacles and read.

Dear Pa:

I think you will agree that we have been patient with you long enough. You are an old man and you cannot continue trying to oversee the running of the farm. We went through all this after Ma died. I hoped you'd have come to your senses in these six months.

For your protection as well as ours, I am going ahead with the plans I outlined to you. My lawyers are now making the preliminary arrangements. They have drawn up papers to have Uncle Ben declared legally dead, having advertised for his whereabouts, with no response. This should have been done years ago.

You will be given title to the property. You will then convey your title outright to the Linden Development Corporation, which is made up of Arent, 'Melie, Crockett and me. This will save us a sizeable inheritance tax, as the place has become more valuable than you realize, because of its proximity to Trent. As I told you in the spring, after Ma's funeral, your suggestion that the Rabaskis be allowed to buy the land as mere farm lands, 'when the time came', as you put it, could not be more ridiculous. All they could offer was a modest down payment and a mortgage, where there will be a small fortune in my ball-bearing factory, with the surrounding settlement of workers' cottages on a rental basis. Such rentals are infinitely more profitable than outright sales. And now is the moment for such a project. Whether or not we are drawn into this new European war, in case you have read anything about it, the war will be a great money maker, even more so, I must say, if we are fools enough to become involved.

You said that you 'owed' a great deal to the Rabaskis. You owe them nothing. They are foreign transients. You have always been too generous with them. They will do just as well on some other farm.

Don't think for a minute that I am not considering your welfare. We should prefer that you make your home with us, but if you still insist on refusing, we shall arrange for a comfortable boarding-home in Peyton. This will probably suit you best, as you seem never to have cared to venture beyond your township. I shall of course provide you with a generous income.

I am extremely busy, as I plan to run for Governor next year, but I have taken the time to write you at such length in the hope that you will understand the situation and will feel satisfied with what I am doing. I have expressed myself as simply as possible, but if there is anything you do not understand, ask me questions. Your mind was definitely wandering when we came for Ma's funeral. Dear Ma, I'll never get over missing her. Sometimes I worry about you, remembering that Grandmother Linden was crazy.

I will have everything settled in a month or so. Give the Rabaskis notice, and plan to leave the farm yourself by the end of November.

Your loving son,
Nat.

Ase dropped the letter on the table as though to rid himself of something obscene. He pulled out his handkerchief and wiped his fingers. The anger that filled him was a long-dammed flood. He began pacing the floor, stooped and trembling. His rage was so great that he felt that if he had Nat there before him, he would be strong enough to shake him until the teeth chattered in the hard, complacent face. He was obliged to sit down again. He mopped his forehead.

Nat's evil had come home to him to roost. He understood the letter entirely too well. He was sickened by the implied insults. 'In case he had read anything about this new European war——' This was the first day in months that he had not turned first to the foreign news in his papers. He felt surely, but humbly, too, conscious of his ignorance, that horror was abroad on the earth, and had asked himself what any one man might do to stop it. He could not be alone, or simple-minded, in considering war too primitive an attempt to resolve the differences among men's varying greeds, among their differences of mind and philosophy.

He reached for one of his newspapers. He must try to answer Nat, if Nat could ever be answered. He opened the newspaper on his knees. The second letter in his mail dropped from between the pages. He smiled. It was addressed in pencil in an illiterate hand and was stamped from the west coast. This would be Joe again, his hired man of years before, telling as usual a fabulous tale of hard luck which would seem to call for a regiment of troops and a thousand dollars to rescue Joe from his troubles, and ending with a postscript asking for the 'loan' of a five or ten.

Ase opened the letter.

Dear Sir,
    A gentulman in my house, Mr. Benjamin Linden, has ask me to write you to tell you he is very sick. He says will you please come. He says you are his brother.
                                    Yours very truly,
                                        Mrs. Athalia Brown.

★ 42 ★

The road that had been so long twisted seemed to him to run plain and straight before him. He even felt no great need of hurry. Benjamin would wait for him. There would of course be time for thinking on the way, but some things had best be decided now. He who had lived a formless life would make plans at last. He could not gather all the loose and tangled threads together to make a pattern, for the last one lay, as it had always lain, in his brother's hands. The farm. In his need, Ben might already have disposed of it, the Rabaskis might well, at this moment, be shelterless.

In the years that he and Nellie had had the rural telephone, 'Nat's 'phone', Nellie called it, her life-saver for communication, he had seldom used it. Only towards noon it occurred to him that he need not drive to Peytonville to send a telegram. He rang, with the sense that it was too easy for so important a matter, and dictated the message to Athalia Brown: "Am coming." Hanging up the receiver, he wondered why he had not addressed the wire to Ben himself, knew then that his first words to him must be in person. He heard sounds from the kitchen. That would be Elsa, come to prepare his dinner. He was not ready for her, neither for appetite nor giving her his news.

"Mr. Linden?"

It was young Jan, calling from the doorway. The familiar warmth came over him. It was this boy to whom he wished to speak.

"Mr. Linden, Mother sent me with your dinner on a tray. She sends her apologies, Greta seems to be coming down with the measles and she didn't want to leave her. Is it all right?"

Ase said: "Come in, Jan. It's all right. Are you hungry?"

"We had our dinner early."

"Then sit down, Jan. I want to talk with you. I have had news from my brother. He has sent for me."

"I'm glad, Mr. Linden. You never gave him up, did you?"

"No."

"I think when you feel about someone as you do about him, you would know when he died. A radio wave would be interrupted, some sort of static would tell you communication was broken."

"Even if the communication had always been one-way?"

"I think so. Of course, when it's two-way, the static must be terrible. It would be like lightning."

"I hope it never happens to you, Jan."

"It will happen when I have to lose you."

The boy spoke simply, having made his declaration of love

in his childhood, so that it was natural now to reaffirm it so.

He added: "You mustn't let it happen any sooner than you have to."

"I'm an old man, Jan."

"Has it seemed long?"

"Why, no, Jan. It hasn't seemed any time at all."

"You'd never be any different yourself, Mr. Linden, but would you do things differently if you had the chance again?"

"Very differently."

"I've always thought you wanted something you never had. It would help to know in time, wouldn't it?"

"Yes. Jan, have you decided what you want?"

"Not actually. I have to know more, to be sure."

The boy leaned towards him. He was pale. His mind and spirit burned with an almost visible white flame. It seemed to Ase that this accounted for his physical frailty. His tall, fine-boned body had an insufficient margin of strength, as though it could not support at once itself and that consuming candle-power.

"It has to be something in science. But abstract science, I'd want to be a physicist, not an engineer. I won't know whether I have a good enough mind for the kind of thing I mean until I go farther and learn more. Father can't manage college for me, on the heels of Carl and Louey and Hans—we had to get them through, for the sake of the farm. I'm going to begin working my way. I can't understand why I'm not tougher, there's nothing wrong with me. If I give out, I'll have to go as far as I can with just reading. The trouble is, I don't know the right books, even books on abstract thinking. But I can find out."

Ase said: "I never knew the right books, either. In time. When I began to find them, I couldn't quite understand. I suppose a mind has to be used."

"It's a catalytic process."

"You see," he said, "I don't even know what that means."

The tall fair boy smiled, too.

"What you wanted to be was a philosopher," he said. "You are one. It's all been locked up inside you. I'll explain catalysis some day, when I'm sure I know what it is myself."

"Now who is the old man? You were born old, Jan."

The understanding flashed between them.

Jan said shyly: "And the poetry keeps messing me up. Nobody knows about it but you. I don't even know whether it's poetry or only me, trying to put in words what I see and feel."

"Perhaps it's all the same thing."

"Perhaps. But what I mean, could anybody be a physicist and a poet, too? I have to *know* more, one way or the other, or even both ways."

Ase was certain now. Jan would set his goal in sight. Whatever he became, scientist or poet, physician or professor, he would bring to his life's work an integrity, a purity, a dedication, that were the marks, Ase recognized belatedly, of great souls.

He said: "I probably don't need to say this to you, Jan, but it's taken me eighty years to know it. There is good and there is evil, and every man has to throw his weight on one side or the other."

He paused, embarrassed, astonished to find himself articulate at last.

Jan said: "I've never thought of that."

"That's what is dangerous. We don't always recognize the moments when we have to choose."

"But a good man would never choose the evil."

"No. He compromises, Jan. Or he does nothing. Sometimes he only says nothing. He could have put up a small barrier, but he leaves the way clear for the evil to move in."

The boy nodded.

"I see what you mean. It's a battle, and you can't be passive. I think that would have been my tendency. I'll watch out for the moments."

This much was done, then.

Ase said: "My brother is very ill. I must take the train tomorrow, if I can take care of some business today."

"What can I do to help you?"

"If you'll drive me to Peytonville now, before the bank closes. I'm not a reliable driver even when I have nothing on my mind."

"Mr. Linden, we've let your dinner get cold. Mother'll never trust me again."

"Never mind. I'll have something later."

They drove with little talk. Their silences together were as companionable as their speech. The bank was open. Judge Simmons's lawyer son was in his father's old office. Ase sent Jan to buy his ticket, and then to wait for him.

Simmons listened carefully, without interruption, tapping his pencil in his father's habit.

"I see. Yes, Mr. Linden, your wishes can be carried out very simply. The only possible dispute might come over whether a portion of the livestock could be considered as part of the farm property, instead of your own, since your brother allowed you only usage. It would certainly amount to too small a matter for Nat to quibble over. Your provision for him is generous, in any case, especially since, as you say, and as I know, he could buy and sell all of Peyton City and never miss the money. You must be very proud of him."

Simmons began to jot down notes.

"The sum of five thousand dollars outright to Nathaniel Linden—it would be customary to say, 'my son, Nathaniel Linden'——"

"Just the name will do."

"Said sum representing payment of debt to Nathaniel Linden for education of Willis Linden, deceased——"

The five thousand dollars were from Willis's war insurance policy, which he had made out to his father. Ase and Nellie had never touched it, having in fact no need to. It was blood money, Ase thought, he would prefer to have disposed of it otherwise, but let it return to Nat, perhaps to shame him. It would at least be a sop thrown to his greed, deterring him from fighting for all possible.

"'To Jan Rabaski, senior, and/or his heirs and assigns, all livestock on the Benjamin Linden farm, all farm machinery and equipment'—(it might be a good idea, Mr. Linden, to say 'bred' as to the stock, and 'acquired' as to equipment) 'since usage'—(I'll check the date)—'allowed me, Asahel Linden, of such stock and equipment by owner, Benjamin Linden.' Mr. Linden, this part of your arrangements would be much simpler if you wait until after you have seen your brother. You will know then whether he has already made some disposition of the farm."

Ase had himself wondered if he were being precipitous. There were answers to be had from Ben that would resolve so many puzzles. It was strange, he felt no hurry in reaching his brother, but he felt a compulsion for himself.

He said: "I want to do what I can, now."

"Very well. Now we come to the provision for Jan Rabaski, junior, not mentioned in your will. It is your intention to establish a trust fund for him at once? To relinquish your total cash holdings towards that purpose?"

"That is my intention."

"But, Mr. Linden, if you do this, you have nothing left for yourself but the five thousand devised, on your death, to Nat. You are of tough pioneer stock, sir, like my father, you may live to be a hundred. Assuming that for one thing, and for another, that the Linden farm may have passed to other hands, you must retain enough to live on. You must protect yourself."

Ase said: "I am protecting myself for the first time in my life."

"Just as you say, but it seems a risk. So, for this young Rabaski, the trust fund, he is to have the income to use as he chooses, until he is of legal age, twenty-one, when he is to have the principal, to use again as he sees fit, for study, travel, I believe that is what you mentioned? Are you sure of this?"

"I am sure. I must ask you another question. Could it be claimed that I was of unsound mind in doing these things?"

Simmons laughed.

"Not in this township. Mr. Linden, you don't know how we respect you."

Ase said: "Can we finish the business today? I must leave tomorrow, to go to my brother."

"Certainly. I'll have my stenographer type up your will, and we can have it witnessed here. We'd better go to the bank, to finish the matter of the trust fund for this exceptional, you say, young man. Then you can go West in peace."

Ase drove back to the farm with his only true though unbegotten son, their kinship not of the blood but of the spirit. The physical continuity of the generations bore little or no relation, he thought, to that kinship of mind that flashed its inexplicable recognition, one beacon signalling another across the darkness.

★ 43 ★

THE towns flashed by the train window, the farms and open fields flashed by. If it were not for an occasional rocking on the rails, for acceleration now, deceleration then, Ase thought that it was like sitting in a magic vacuum, watching the earth roll by. An east-bound train roared past on the next track, and then his own west-bound one seemed indeed stationary. The other was gone with a final swish like the crack of a bull whip. The landscape resumed its swift-moving panorama. Ase had the double seats to himself, and he stretched out his long legs comfortably. This was an astonishing way to cross the continent, in speed and luxury. He had always thought of the crossing in terms, if not actually of the covered wagons, at least of plodding struggle. True, Benjamin had gone West by railway those sixty years ago, but Ase recalled the ancient, dingy, sooty trains out of Peytonville, jerking and faltering, as though the effort to reach the West would be too much for them, as it had once been for many of the oxen, the men and women and children.

The train altered its rhythm over a bridge, and there was a wide river beneath. Ase stared at the swirling waters, muddy with the waste of top soil. He had never seen a river, no body of water larger than Pip Lake, and the brook that ran gently under the weeping willows except in time of flood. Even in flood the brook had been a puny thing, compared with this slow, powerful stream like a winding serpent. The river vanished, and he saw an expanse of forest, quite different from his own small woods. Without slowing, the train passed through the main street of a village. The gates were lowered, a bell was ringing, and ragged children waved at the side of an old watchman. Ase waved back to them.

It seemed the train would shear off the shabby house-fronts. The broken porches, the bare yards with a few dusty zinnias and dahlias reached almost to the railway-tracks. He was astonished by such poverty. The farms beyond the town were poor and eroded, the buildings were shanties, the stock was haggard. Somehow he had expected the land to be richer the farther west it went. Then great dairy farms appeared, with enormous silos and sleek cows with udders that must hold gallons for each milking. There were long narrow truck farms, with the autumn vegetables laid out in green and orange rows as handsome as Nellie's flower garden. The train slowed but did not stop, and there were grimy suburbs and tall office and factory buildings visible across a waste of billboards and dump-heaps, and he understood that the prosperous dairy and truck farms fed some large city. The train clacked across a switch, passed rows of freight cars, then left all trace of the city behind, and there were farms again.

The sun dropped towards its setting. He looked through the opposite windows at the western glow, the orange of the squash and pumpkins of the past miles. A man sitting across the aisle caught his eye and spoke.

"Days getting shorter. Soon be dark."

Ase nodded.

"Yes."

It gave him a warm feeling to be spoken to by a stranger. He cleared his throat, trying to think of a further item of conversation.

"They don't seem to have had much frost on the crops out here yet," he said.

"I wouldn't know about that. Crops to me are just something that ends up on the table, mighty high-priced, too, in the city. I expect you're a farmer."

Ase inclined his head gravely.

"Yes, sir. All my life."

The stranger did not reply. Something more in the way of courtesy seemed to be called for. Ase noticed the man's small leather case on the seat beside him.

He said: "I suppose you are a drummer, sir."

The man threw back his head and laughed.

"I haven't heard that word since I was a kid. They call us travelling salesmen now. We don't drum up trade any more, you know. It's a favour when we sell you something you don't want."

A call came through: "First call for dinner." The stranger left.

Ase remembered that Nellie had told him of eating on the diners on her trips to and from the West, but Elsa had packed a shoe-box full of food for him. If the train would ever stop at some small place where he might hand over the box to such children as he had seen at the railway crossing, his conscience would be clear, but the train went swiftly through such places, and he was unwilling to waste the food, not for its value in money, but because it stood for too many hours of men's labour. He ignored the waiter's half question at his side: "Diner, two cars to the rear," and opened Elsa's box. There were fried chicken and hard-boiled eggs, bread-and-butter and ham sandwiches, pickles and apple-tarts, all planned to be eaten neatly out of hand. He spread the enclosed napkin over his knees and ate most of the food absently.

The lights came on in the train. The world outside was shadow, dark masses moving by, rising and falling with the terrain, as though in the process of creation. Here and there distant windows shone like eyes in the night. Once the train passed so close to a small house that Ase looked in and met the eyes of the family sitting at the supper-table. He saw them stare with a never-fading wonder at the long brightly lighted box on churning wheels that passed so swiftly each night with its cargo of strangers, hurtling to their unknown destinations. He wanted to stop and go into their house and say: "I at least am not a stranger."

The porter asked: "Do you wish your berth made up now, sir?"

Ase looked up into a kind brown face. He was relieved. He said: "I've never travelled before."

"I'd suggest, sir, you're such a tall gentleman, if you'll undress in the men's room, I'll make your berth ready."

"I can't walk back in my night-shirt, can I?"

The porter chuckled and Ase smiled with him.

"You can slip on your overcoat, sir, if you don't have a robe."

He had a fine silk robe that Nat had sent him, that he had never worn. The porter led the way with his bag to the dressing-room. It was difficult to undress and wash against the motion of the train. He felt like a crane making its way through mud. When he came out with his bag some time later, he was lost. Most of the aisle was curtained off and he could not tell one berth from another. A woman in a kimono and hair-curlers brushed past him and disappeared into one of the cubicles. The porter hurried to him, speaking in a muted voice, not quite a whisper.

"Here you are, sir. See, you're No. 9, if you get up in the night. I've left the upper berth closed to give you more head room. Here's your reading-light, it goes on and off, so, and here's your ventilator. You don't open the window when there's air-conditioning."

Ase lowered his own voice to match, understanding that others in this odd intimacy might be already sleeping.

"Do people really lie down and sleep in these little places?"

Of late years, Nellie had taken a compartment on her trips, but apart from the difference in cost, he had not wanted to be isolated from others on his first journey.

"Yes, sir. You'll find the berth real comfortable. Here's the bell to call me. You be sure and ring it if you need anything. Even if you just get anxious."

"I'm anxious now."

They smiled together in the dim light of the precipitous long box. It was easy to speak with this dark, quiet man.

"I'll put your shade up, sir, so you can see out. The moon comes up right soon. It's nice to lie and watch the moonlight while the land rides by. It's us who's riding, but it seems the other way."

"I noticed that, but I thought it was because it was new to me."

"No, sir. You could ride the train a hundred years and you'd always think it was the earth moving and not you."

Ase said: "I expect we're all moving all the time, all together, only we don't know where or which way."

It seemed natural to be murmuring such things back and forth with a brown man out of the encyclopaedia. He had known it would be this way, once he truly travelled.

He whispered: "Thank you for your courtesies."

He held out his hand to his new friend. The porter grasped it with what seemed to Ase almost a hunger.

"Good-night, sir. Sleep well."

Ase said: "Good-night to you, too, sir."

He stretched out his legs as far as they would go in the berth. There was still not room enough. There were four soft pillows at his head and he piled these high, so that by resting his shoulders against them, he found the extra inches for his length. He reached up and switched off the small light. For a moment he could see nothing at all out of the window, then again the obscure landscape rose and fell, rose and fell, in its prehistoric convulsions. The moon had not yet risen, although he sensed a vague lightening of the sky. He was moving west, the moon would rise behind the train, he would probably not see it directly. The berth was indeed comfortable.

He became aware of a brightness outside the small thick window. The full moon was quieting the earth's upheaval, was smoothing the fields, the pastures, the now dark farm-houses, the small towns through which the train was passing with sad sweet whistle blowing. He saw the moon itself. The railway-tracks must have taken a turn, so to bring the moon into view. The steady pound of the train was soothing. He fell deep asleep.

. . . . .

He had supposed that a change of trains at the big city meant only a change of tired engines. He was confused to find that he must leave the train that had been his home and go inside the huge station, and then, two hours later, search out a new strange train through a maze of gates. His bag had been taken away from him and loaded with many others on a hand-truck, and it seemed impossible that he should ever find it again. He was swept along with the crowd hurrying from the train. He heard running footsteps behind him. His brown friend spoke to him.

"I'll get you settled, sir, so you'll have no trouble. Just let me have your ticket."

He was grateful for the strong hand on his elbow, guiding him through the confusion. The ramps, the entrances and exits, were endless. He could have wandered helplessly for hours, he thought, unable to stop any one of the rushing humans for directions and for information. They came out under a vast vaulted rotunda where people milled back and forth like a disturbed ants' nest. A loud-speaker was announcing trains almost unintelligibly. He caught sight of the baggage-truck ahead. His friend whistled and the truck attendant turned and waited. The two consulted, his friend pointed back to Ase, showed his ticket, and the other, a brown man, too, nodded. The friend returned.

"That man there, sir, will come for you when your train is called. All you do is follow him."

"Then I won't be anxious any more."

The jest was warm and secret between them.

"Now if you'll just sit right here, sir. If you leave for anything, come straight back to this seat. Here's your ticket, and you'll have two hours exactly to wait. It won't seem long, watching people the way I've noticed you watch them."

"I don't know how to thank you, sir. Excuse me, I forgot, I should have given you a tip, on the train."

He fumbled in his purse. The brown man held up his hand in negation.

"Thank you, no, sir. I couldn't take anything. It's been fine, meeting you. I've got to get back."

Ase shook hands with a sense of loss. His friend began to run, threading his way across the crowds like a brave chip fighting its way up-stream against a strong current. Ase saw him swallowed up at last, returning to his unfinished work and the mystery of his life. Ase sat down and stared around him.

The milling hordes were faceless. In among the distracted ants, restless masses boiled aimlessly, like maggots. Here and there a solitary figure stood inert a moment, perhaps lost, as he himself would have been without his friend, then moved and was absorbed by the human swarming. The light from the high dirty windows had no vitality. There was no colour here, only shades of grey, a green coat or a red hat vanished as soon as seen, as in a whirling spectrum. The vaulted space was filled with a roaring cacophony of sound. Ase tried to separate its components.

Underground there was the puffing and chugging of the trains. The joined murmur of voices in the station rose to the ceiling, was trapped and could not escape, echoed downwards to meet another swell, again hopelessly rising. Under the mass-voice and above the incoming trains and the outgoing, he identified an odd muffled sibilance, and this was the shuffling of feet on the marble flooring, back and forth, around and around, sluff, sluff, sluff. Against the muted greys the black iron gates, entrances eventually to the trains, opened and now closed, like the gates to Hell. The loud-speaker boomed out over the coagulation of sound. The words came clearer this time.

"Track seventeen. Track seventeen. All aboard for the Dixie Special, going South, going South. Louisville, Memphis——"

The other place names ran together, so that Ase was glad he was not obliged to recognize his destination among them.

"Track seventeen."

The loud-speaker was like the voice of God, calling to faceless men to prepare for nameless places. A section of the rotating ant-like human beings resolved itself into a definitive line, rushing blindly towards track seventeen. Ase took out his handkerchief and mopped his face. This, he thought, was a sort of Purgatory. All here were caught, if not quite between Heaven and Hell, at least between going and coming, in the eternal lost and homeless sojourn on the earth.

He became aware that a shabby woman had sat down next to him, with a nursling and two older children. Her luggage consisted of several pasteboard cartons. He wondered where she was going, and why. The woman had a worn face, sad and sweet. His horror left him as he saw her give the breast to her babe. He forgot the grey shuffling mob. It was only necessary to acknowledge the individual, courageous human, to leave the terror of the mass.

The friend of his friend stood before him, saying: "Your train is called, sir."

He had not realized that his two hours had passed.

He said: "Thank you."

The red-cap said: "Follow me through gate two, sir, I'll have your bag on board."

Ase hurried along behind him. His ticket was checked at the gate, he found himself in the new train, the brown man was pushing his bag under the seat. Ase hesitated. This also kind man was not truly his friend, as the other had been. He offered him a five-dollar note and was satisfied that he had done the proper thing when the friend of his friend thanked him, bowing from the waist.

He settled himself for the remaining days of his trip. He felt now at home among the complications. He gave himself to a rapt study of the country. He had known from his reading that it was different in different places, but he could not believe his eyes before the infinite variety. The plains with their miles of wheat and corn astonished him. His fields, his and Ben's, would be lost in their least corner. The prairies seemed somehow frightening. There was no place where a man might stand upright above his fields to view them, he would be dwarfed among the crops of his own raising. Yet when he saw the mountains, he thought a man must feel the smallest here, whether living on the peaks or in the valleys.

The conception of the Continental Divide stirred him, to know that from this torn and towering plateau all waters flowed one way east into the Atlantic, the others west into the Pacific. He was puzzled as well, for such a phenomenon should properly lie in the very middle of a continent, instead of so far west. Then he remembered from the encyclopaedia that these mountains were younger than the old hills of his home, had been spewed high from the restless earth eras later, and he was dizzy for an instant, picturing the continent tilting, as though the whole earth mass were slowly rotating in and out of the vaster seas. He begrudged his sleep at night, lay wakeful late, watching from his window, rousing with the first light of dawn to drink in all the marvels, having been so long athirst.

All was new, yet all was familiar. All delighted him, yet was alien. In the last hours across the thousands of miles of the beautiful, the fabulous nation, he understood that he had been watching so eagerly in the hope that he might recognize

324

his home. It was not here. Neither had he left it behind him.

The porter on this train was without the tacit understanding of the first one, but was still his friend, a grizzled man who must be almost as old as he. The negro seated himself opposite.

"Train running a little late, Mr. Linden. Anybody meeting you?"

"No."

"Big town, Mr. Linden, know how to find your way, where you're going?"

"I have the address."

Ase took out the pencilled envelope from Mrs. Athalia Brown. The porter looked at it, looked sharply again.

"Mr. Linden, this a rough neighbourhood. Could be there's a mistake. You better take a taxi and have the man wait, till you make sure."

"Thank you, but I'm sure."

The porter left to speak to other passengers. Ase had had his bag packed for hours. He followed the crowd. The bridge train was waiting. Its bell rang with a soft clang like an old-fashioned door-bell. It crossed a waterway as though it spun its own tracks under it as it went, like a spider. It passed over a cantilever bridge and on to its thin track again and tinkled into the smaller terminal. From this, Ase walked out with his bag into a strange, exciting world.

He took a deep satisfied breath after the days of closeness. The air was implicit with the sea. It was a tangible air, strong and moist and sharp as hard cider, so that he seemed to drink rather than to breathe it. It was the winds of the end of one world meeting the winds of another one beginning. If he had been lifted by a pair of mighty fingers and deposited here like a man jumped on a draught-board, he would have known he had reached the end of a land.

He shifted his bag to his other hand and walked on a wide curving way on which he found himself leading towards the west. The time was nearly sunset, but when he came at last to an open vista, and saw the sun, it was not a solid ball, but a series of concentric rings like a spinning top. As he stared, it vanished entirely. The Pacific fog was rolling in. Red beacon lights appeared above the piers. In a moment they too were obscured by a tumbling grey mass that must, he thought, resemble ocean breakers. He heard a sound like the bellowing of a bull, another answered, and another, and these, he knew, could only be the fog-horns. Thin high tootings of tugboats sounded in a panic, like mice under the feet of the bulls.

He was aware of exotic odours, roasting coffee, spicy foreign foods, and, enveloping them all, the pungent, salty fish-and-seaweed-laden fragrance of the sea. And then the fog was over him and around him. Ghost fingers brushed his face. The thin greyness swirled and passed, was followed by endless phalanx on phalanx of insubstantial substance, and he was lost in the fog, standing alone at the outer rim of the world, and could not see his way. Other sounds came to him, trolley bells ringing in a staccato rhythm with the flatness of a cracked tea-cup, car horns crying for mercy in the slowed traffic, feet running, and near-by a harsh dance music. He groped his way towards the music. It came from a penny arcade a few yards away. He felt his way through the open door and set down his bag and looked around. A pock-marked man was picking his teeth behind a counter.

"What you want, Gran'pa?"

Ase said: "I'd appreciate it if you would get me a taxi. I'm a stranger here."

"Yeah? Too bad."

The dingy place was filled with silence.

"Where you want to go to?"

Ase drew out the envelope.

"To this address."

"Yeah? What d'you know. No taxi ain't goin' to take you nowhere tonight."

Ase said: "If you could direct me, I don't mind walking, but it seems hard to see in the fog."

"No? Imagine that. Tell you what I'll do for you, Gran'pa, just for a favour, send one o' my boys with you. Hey, Louie!"

A pale little man shuffled from the rear of the room. He reminded Ase of Willis.

"Louie, this nice old gent'man with his nice bag is lost, and I want you should accomp'ny him to where he's going. Get it?"

Louie said sullenly: "I get it. Come on, Gran'pa."

Ase stopped at the door and drew out the envelope again and pointed.

He said: "You won't be able to read the address when we get outside. Here, see——"

Louie glanced at the inscribed street and number.

"Sure," he said. "I know the place."

Ase followed him out into the fog.

"Is it far?"

"Couple o' blocks."

"You're very kind to do this for me. I hope you'll let me pay you for your trouble."

Ase stumbled at the kerb. He clutched at his guide.

"Do you mind if I hold your arm? I'd feel safer."

The man stiffened under his touch.

Ase said: "I wouldn't want anything to happen now. I've come all the way across the country to find my brother. I haven't seen him for sixty years."

Louie snorted: "Jeez, a guy should live so long."

"I suppose it does seem a long time to a young man. I'm past eighty now."

He realized that his affairs could be of no interest.

He asked courteously: "Have you always lived in the West?"

Louie grunted and seemed to hesitate at an intersection. He set off at a faster pace along a street lined with tall narrow houses. Even through the fog they showed poverty-stricken and shabby. Louie stopped and pointed up a flight of steps. A pale light illumined a sign: "Rooms 50 cents a night."

"There you are."

He shook off Ase's arm and turned away abruptly. Ase fumbled for his wallet.

"Wait, please, Louie, let me give you something with my thanks."

Louie snarled. "Put that thing away, Gran'pa, before I change my mind. Get your ——ing brother and get the hell out of here fast."

The man began to run as though in mortal peril. Ase started up the steps, understanding now how great had been his own. Louie's swift padding vanished in the fog-ridden night. The steps were steep and broken and he groped his way to the front door. Through a dirty etched glass panel he saw a corridor lit by a small hanging electric bulb. He found a door-bell at the side and pulled it. The sound clanged far back in what seemed an empty house. A woman came from the rear, wiping her hands on a soiled apron. She opened the door a crack.

"Full up tonight," she said, and slammed the door.

Ase beat on the panel. The woman continued down the corridor, then turned and walked back quickly, opening the door wider. She looked him up and down, saw his good over-coat and old, decent bag.

"Say, what's your name?"

"Asahel Linden. You wrote me. I came to my brother Benjamin."

"Come in."

She shut and bolted the door behind him.

"Figured that's who you might be when I took a good look. About gave you up. This way."

Ase followed her mechanically up dimly lighted stairs, up one flight, two, three, and four. She took a key from her apron pocket and opened a door. She felt for a wall switch and a hanging bulb came on, wan under a fluted paper shade. An old man lay on a sagging bed against the far wall.

Ase set down his bag.

The woman said: "He owes me for two weeks, but mind now, I'm not the kind to let a man starve. I've fed him, what I had to spare."

She eyed him sharply.

"He said you'd pay."

She brushed back her grey, straggling hair.

"I hate to bring up the pay, but you don't know what I go through, old men dying on me, still owing, and then others not wanting the room if they hear about it. I've got my living to make, not like a rich gentleman like you. You will pay, won't you?"

"Yes, I'll pay. Thank you."

She sighed.

"Sorry I don't have no room for you tonight. Maybe down the street a ways, if you'd care to give me something on account before you go."

"I'll stay here."

The woman hesitated.

Ase said: "I won't slip away. Here."

He drew out his wallet and gave her some notes. The woman sniffled.

"Thank you, sir. I knew you was a gentleman. Please don't think me hard——"

She went down the stairs. Ase closed the door. He went to the side of the bed. How could this shrunken thing be Benjamin? This man was so old, so very old, so peaked of features, unshaven and unshorn, so small and desolate. Benjamin had been tall and lithe and strong, with bright cat's eyes and tawny hair, and laughing, always laughing. Ase wondered if there had been some mistake and this was not Benjamin after all.

The gaunt face turned to him. The unshaded light was pitiless on the sick eyes.

A voice croaked: "Asahel?"

"Benjamin——"

He took the withered hand.

"I was afraid—you wouldn't come in time."

"Have you had a doctor?"

"No use. I'm finished."

The eyelids closed. They were parchment-thin.

"The light hurts."

Ase turned it out. He sat on a straight chair close beside the bed. The hand groped for him and he held it.

"Asahel, I've always missed you."

"I never knew. I've never been done missing you."

"I have to tell you things, Ase. You tell first. I'm so tired."

"What do you want to know, Ben?"

"Your family. You've done well?"

Ben's voice was now almost familiar.

He said: "No, Ben. I failed."

"Tell me."

He could tell it in the dark, one old face not having to see the other.

He began: "One child was good. Her name was Dolly. She died when she was six."

Ben said: "I remember. You wrote me. Mother killed her."

Ase withdrew his hand, because it was trembling.

"No, Ben, I never wrote you that."

"You didn't need to. I knew. I knew Mother better than you did."

"Was she always mad?"

"Always."

He could ask it, the unaskable, knowing the answer, he could say it, the unsayable.

"She was evil, Ben, wasn't she?"

"Always evil. Go on, Ase."

"There was another child, the youngest, a boy, Willis. He would have been good if I had helped him. No, he was good, after all. He died in the war in 1918."

"Go on."

"The oldest is Nathaniel. We call him Nat. He followed you to Alaska. He tried to find you."

"I know. I dodged him. What's wrong with him?"

Ben spoke with the ancient authority of their youth together.

"It's this. He's evil, too. I might have stopped him."

"How? When?"

Ase thought back in time. But of course, when Nat was only six, and had despised Tim McCarthy's gift of a silver dollar because it was not enough. He remembered with the old anguish the matter of the gypsy boy in the bog, he remembered the revelations of Willis, all of it swept over him, and as though his brother were his confessor, he told it all. There was a long silence.

Ben said: "There were two others."

"Yes. Arent and 'Melie."

"Tell me."

Ase told. Of Arent's passive following of Nat, of 'Melie, so like Amelia, not quite so evil, and certainly not mad at all.

Ben said: "Nellie?"

Ase said: "She died in the spring. Did you love her, Ben?"

The skeleton on the dirty bed chuckled.

"No more than a hundred others."

Ase was obliged to say: "She never got over loving you, Ben."

"Nellie didn't love anybody, Ase."

He said: "It doesn't matter now. She was a good wife. I loved her."

The silence came again.

"Anybody else?"

"Yes. A boy of sixteen."

"Tell me."

He told of Jan Rabaski. He told his plans for him.

"Good. He makes up for the others. You've done right, Ase. You've done well."

The longed-for praise was sweet.

"That's all. What about you?"

"Never mind. I'm too tired, Ase."

"Why didn't you ever come home, Ben? Why didn't you ever write us?"

"I was ashamed. It was wrong to be, wasn't it?"

"Yes, it was wrong."

"I guess—I was always looking—for something that wasn't there. I thought I had to—find it first."

The voice from the ancient bones was a whisper.

"Lift me up. It's hard to breathe."

Ase fumbled in the darkness to help his brother.

"The light, Ase."

He turned it on. The shock was fresh. Ben was gone under the glare, and in his place he saw again the stranger.

"Under the pillow, Ase. Hurry."

He groped, not knowing for what he was to search.

"The deed, Ase. The farm."

The folded paper was grimy, dark and stained with age.

"See. It's made over to you."

Ase put on his spectacles. The notarized date was of many years before. The farm had been his own almost since his mother's death.

He said: "I don't understand."

"I gambled it away, Ase, the minute I got it. A pal staked me and I won it back. It frightened me. So I had it conveyed to you. Before I could do the same thing over again."

Ase closed the paper.

"I should have sent you the deed then. Ase, I liked to have it in my pocket. I liked to show it. I might have lice in my rags, but I was a man of property. I was weak, wasn't I?"

"No, you were strong."

"Only for an instant. But I couldn't let you be put off the farm. You knew that, didn't you?"

"Yes, I knew."

So, he had been right about Ben, always. His decades of fidelity had not here been wasted.

Ben said: "Did it make much difference, Ase, not knowing the farm was yours?"

He could answer truly, as he had once answered Tim McCarthy, as he had answered his wife and children: "It didn't make any difference at all."

"Put the paper in your pocket. I have nothing else."

The paper was precious. Its simplicity made possible the last step in his plans. He need do only as Ben had done. He would convey the deed at once to Jan and Elsa Rabaski, would put it in the mail, and not all Nat's tentacles could take it from them. The Linden land was safe.

"Where are you, Ase?"

"Right here, Ben."

"Take me back home, Ase. Promise."

"I promise."

The breathing seemed easier.

"Ase?"

"Yes, Ben."

"The woman fed me."

"The woman?"

"Athalia Brown."

"I'll pay her."

"I knew her forty years ago. Wild—— Pretty——"

The sound was a chuckle. It was faint, as though it came from far away, and in the instant it was gone, and there was not even the breathing. For the last time Ben had gone away laughing in his ragged coat.

Ase pulled a battered rocking-chair to the one window, then switched off the light. Sounds were muffled by the fog. The cable cars, the boat whistles, the foghorns, were far away. The greyness swept past the dusty window, not quite tangible, not quite visible. He sat all night like a disembodied spirit, keeping an appointed vigil. Towards morning, the fog lifted. Sunlight touched the roof-tops. Sparrows stirred. In the distance he saw a glimmer of unfamiliar light and colour. He knew that he was seeing a fragment of the bay, the beginning of the sea. The Pacific had halted Benjamin as he had once prayed.

He stood up stiffly. He felt as emptied of life as the body on the bed. He had come to the end of a long road. He was without pain, now that Ben had left him past any finding. Nothing was different, his brother was no more lost to him than he had ever been. It came to him with a sharp knowledge that in his loneliness he was not alone.

He thought: 'Every man has lost his brother.'

⋆ 44 ⋆

Not the wings beat, but the motors. The plane was a great bird with two hearts, palpable and pulsating. It ran across the runway like a plover, like a plover lifted suddenly into the air. Ase was conscious of the straining climb. Space was a heavy thing, it pushed the weight of the universe on the metallic bird to hold it down, the twin hearts throbbed against it. More than ever Ase felt that men were not held to earth, and by it, but were crushed there by an imponderable vastness. The tallest trees could grow no taller, not that their roots chained them or the force of gravity but because their strength was unequal to the greater pressure. The earth had thrust up its mountains as high as possible and the mountains were collapsing not from below but from above as though the kind firm hand of a master pressed on a dog and a great voice said quietly, 'Down.'

The plane levelled off. The twin hearts had won their battle, the motored bird was in its element and there was now no sense of motion at all. Ase had imagined that, even enclosed in the belly of the mechanical bird, he would be conscious of flight. He wanted to feel the effort, the winds.

of the world streaming past his face. The sense of height was compensation. He saw the earth plainly as a battered planet. The skin was cracked and wrinkled, gashed with canyons, torn and split by rivers. Mountains were jumbles of sterile stone. Cities were already ruins, as though he saw them a thousand years in the future, or in the past. Only the farms and fields were beautiful. Green and red and gold and violet squares and rectangles spoke of man's sole kindness to the earth. Ase wished he had celestial seeds to scatter, to drift down on the brown fresh-ploughed acres, there to grow some rare unearthly crop. He would tell young Jan of this fancy, and they would smile together.

It had occurred to him to telephone the farm this morning. He had talked with them, one by one. They pleased him with something deeper than their gratitude. They would cherish the land and not despoil it. Young Jan was grave before his trust. This, too, would never be betrayed.

The boy said at last: "We miss you. We are waiting for you. We are your family now."

He was welcome. He had given away the very roof over his head, and, for the first time in his life, he was wanted under it. He was warmed, who had so long been cold.

The boy had said: "You'll need to rest," and he had answered: "I've had a taste of travel, Jan. Perhaps I'll just keep on going."

He folded his bony hands over the box that held his brother's ashes. He should have made his flight, he thought, the other way round. There was no need for hurry now, returning whence he had come. Had he flown west, they would have had long days to talk together. And of what more would they have spoken? It had all been said. For a lifetime they had carried the words and the love within them, had shared all they ever could have shared, a continent apart.

He, too, he recognized, had sought to find the unfindable. He had lost and sought a brother, and it was in the faces of all men he should have peered. He had been homeless, and knew that for such men as he there was no home, only an endless journey. He had sought to know the unknowable. He and his whole race, great, slow, groping, God-touched children, would have to wait a long time, he supposed, for that, learning one lesson a millennium, sometimes forgetting it and having to begin all over. He himself, he thought humbly, had learned far too little. He had done much harm. He had known good from evil, and he had sat miserable and mute when the fight was called for. He had carried his standards into battle perhaps not quite too late. He could not know whether his good had been greater than his evil. No man could balance the delicate scales, for he himself weighted one end and could not reach across to weight the other. An invisible hand would add or subtract. An unheard voice would speak the answer.

Ase was recalled to the immediacy of the plane. A flock of south-bound geese slanted past him. The plane had suddenly lifted its nose. It climbed so steeply that the earth ball seemed visibly to roll towards the east. The sky was torn by the plane, the clouds were tattered, they fell away in streamers, massed again in a billowing sea and hid the world below.

A group of strangers, boxed together, was rocketing towards the sun, the stars. Most of them were frightened. Ase felt a surge of joy. It was of the purity of his boyhood, when with Mink Fisher he had imagined himself walking barefoot across the Milky Way. The consciousness of flight was so powerful that he lifted his hands from his safety belt and held them stretched before him, like an angel on the wing.

A stewardess balanced herself against the acute angle and leaned over him.

"Are you all right, sir?"

"Of course," he said, astonished.

"We climb for another half an hour, then level off. After that, the flight is normal."

She turned across the aisle to speak to a white-faced woman.

But this, he thought, was normal. Some hunger, some obscure instinct, was assuaged by this swift reaching into space. His excitement mounted with the plane. He longed to have the half-hour last for half a millennium, to keep on and on, higher and higher, farther and farther, to the core of the cosmos. He recalled his years of watching after the bird migrations.

Perhaps, he thought, this was what afflicted men. The battered planet he had seen under him could not last for ever. Something in man was surely eternal, if only his awareness of eternity. Perhaps, he thought, perhaps—— man might be migratory, too. In his blood and bones there might stir the same blind avian impulse towards unknown places. Since man could not soar alone, he had evolved these miraculous instruments of flight, making ready for an ultimate home, aeons and aeons hence.

Ase felt a constriction of his heart. There was a spasm that was more of pressure than of pain. The pressure increased. He could endure only a little more of it. He would not cry out, to alarm his fellow passengers. He clenched his hands. He looked from his window. The land was reeling away from him. The fields were indistinguishable. He wished he might recognize a winter wheat field. After all, the earth was pain to leave. To know it was to love it. Perhaps those distant migrants of his imagining would feel a nameless nostalgia, would think wordlessly, as he thought now: 'Dear earth, place once of my abiding.'

The pressure was a flood. He was not afraid.

It had been so brief a sojourn, not even a full century. He had been a guest in a mansion and he was not ungrateful. He was at once exhausted and refreshed. His stay was ended. Now he must gather up the shabby impedimenta of his mind and body and be on his way again.